CW01455464

The public have been bombarded with scientist about the perils of climate ch and many shelves worth of books pai... phe. But like the lad who cried wolf these warnings seem to be having less of an effect, and for the same reason as did our endangered juvenile. Dr. Lawrence offers a different approach by putting the very real dangers into believable human contexts. The science is sound but so also are the human responses. In this sequel to *Climate Dragon*, *Cloud Dragon* addresses the spread of tropical diseases to temperate areas and the vulnerability of an electrical grid overtaxed by increasing demand but vulnerable to disruption by climate dissidents armed with little more than off-the-shelf rifles. As a medical doctor, Lawrence fully recognizes a new disease when only a few have the requisite expertise. And Americans take for granted that the electricity will always be available and interruptions with be few and short-lasting. This book shows just how. Sandy Lawrence has written an exceptional climate trilogy.

—John [Sebastian] Ernissee, B.A., PhD, Curator of Geology,
Consulting Editor for *Rocks and Minerals Magazine*

Lawrence confidently delivers a depiction of the medical response to a puzzling disease, lectures on the vulnerability of the power grid, and the plans of disgruntled patriots in a story shaped by climate change. The subtle impact of changes to weather patterns, disease vectors, and grid reliability accurately portray some of the real consequences of our inadequate response to multiple existential crises.

—Clare Fogelsong, Climate Program Manager City of Bellingham,
Member American Society of Adaptation Professionals

A thought-provoking story in the modern world. From new diseases to cyber-attacks on power infrastructure, to a weirding climate, the author's expertise shines through the characters' adventures.

—Sheila Kluck, PE, PG, P.Eng, Geological Engineer

Additional Praise for Cloud Dragon

An entertaining tale, woven around the possibilities and risks identified by the fascinating science and technologies that surround us. Countering the currently disturbing political climate (especially with respect to the literal climate) requires a moderate level of science literacy and this book is an effective way to get there. The world we humans occupy and have modified is complicated. If you are wondering how we got here, *Cloud Dragon* will give you some clues on how to put some of the puzzle pieces together.

—Claus Stober, PhD, Mining and Mineral Processing

S.W. Lawrence, MD, delves into pressing global themes of climate change, social responsibility, and the importance of diversity, equity, and inclusion. The narrative unfolds across multiple interconnected stories that portray characters grappling with both personal and collective crises. The prologue frames climate change as an adversarial "dragon" that humanity must confront . . . The book juxtaposes individual struggles with larger societal themes, fostering a narrative that invites readers to acknowledge the significant impact of their choices on both their immediate communities and the planet. Throughout, the readers witness a complex blend of healthcare challenges, environmental issues, and human resilience, ultimately advocating for informed action in the face of escalating global issues.

—Dan Welch, AIA, MArch, CPHC, LEED AP

This amazing, deeply researched novel shows, through the stories of Abbey and Jake and their entwined friends and students, how climate change is affecting daily life at many levels, from weather hazards to infectious disease. Their positions as teachers in medicine and engineering provide an opportunity to explain, at a granular level, some of the complex energy systems including fracking, geothermal and solar energy, and electrical grids that are involved. Of course, there are others who have different ideas about how to handle the problem.

—Linda Crabbe, MA. MD

Sandy Lawrence has written an exceptional climate book series. He leads with a thrilling story, and we follow. It's fast moving, vast, and wise. It has the power to explain climate change, awaken our curiosity, and offer clear solutions. It is big. It is honest. Heroes and villains mirror today's real world. Recommending him is easy. He demonstrates how much we have to live for.

—Henry Duren, NORAD: Top Secret Clearance Special classification ICAN/COSAN networks, [Nuclear Deployment Systems], Joint Chiefs Alerting Network, JCAN [Chief of Staff Alerting Network], COSAN [Presidential Protocol enable Secure Weapon Systems Authorization]

Embark on a thrilling journey in *Cloud Dragon*, the final installment of S.W. Lawrence's trilogy. Following the success of *Climate Dragon*, this sequel continues to weave accurate climate science into a captivating narrative. While specific plot details of *Cloud Dragon* are forthcoming, readers can anticipate Lawrence's signature blend of suspense, scientific insight, and compelling storytelling. Prepare to be enthralled as the saga unfolds, offering both entertainment and enlightenment on the pressing issues of our time.

—Lorinda Boyer, author of *Straight Enough*

CLOUD DRAGON

CLOUD DRAGON
CONSPIRACY, CONTAGION, AND CATASTROPHE

S.W. Lawrence, MD

Sidekick Press
Bellingham, Washington

Copyright © 2025 by S.W. Lawrence

All rights reserved. No part of this publication may be reproduced, distributed, or transmitted in any form or by any means, including photocopying, recording, digital scanning, or other electronic or mechanical methods, without the prior written permission of the publisher, except in the case of brief quotations embodied in critical reviews and certain other noncommercial uses permitted by copyright law. For permission requests, please address Sidekick Press.

Publisher's Note: This is a work of fiction. Names, characters, places, and incidents are products of the author's imagination. Locales and public names are sometimes used for atmospheric purposes. Any resemblance to actual people, living or dead, or to businesses, companies, events, institutions, or locales is completely coincidental.

Published 2025
Printed in the United States of America
ISBN: 978-1-958808-43-6
LCCN: 2025908940

Sidekick Press
2950 Newmarket Street, Suite 101-329
Bellingham, Washington 98226
sidekickpress.com

Cloud Dragon: Conspiracy, Contagion, and Catastrophe

Cover design by Bob Paltrow

Half-title image: Artist unknown
Dragon design by anonymous artist, circa 1900. Offered for sale by Abbott and Holder in late June 2020.

Quotes Used by Permission

"Each bud that opens embraces becoming as if it has never happened before." Quote used by permission of Shellen Lubin, Facebook post.

"I didn't have the guts to become an artist; I had the ignorance." Quote used by permission of Jack Sorenson, September 17, 2024.

Scripture quotations are from The ESV® Bible (The Holy Bible, English Standard Version®), © 2001 by Crossway, a publishing ministry of Good News Publishers. Used by permission. All rights reserved.

Diversity, Equity, and Inclusion
for All Critters
Great and Small

It is not the critic who counts; not the man who points out how the strong man stumbles, or where the doer of deeds could have done them better. The credit belongs to the man who is actually in the arena, whose face is marred by dust and sweat and blood; who strives valiantly; who errs, who comes short again and again, because there is no effort without error and shortcoming; but who does actually strive to do the deeds; who knows great enthusiasms, the great devotions; who spends himself in a worthy cause; who at the best knows in the end the triumph of high achievement, and who at the worst, if he fails, at least fails while daring greatly, so that his place shall never be with those cold and timid souls who neither know victory nor defeat.

—Theodore Roosevelt

CONTENTS

The Final Journey

If you know the enemy and know yourself, you need not fear the result of a hundred battles. If you know yourself but not the enemy, for every victory gained you will also suffer a defeat. If you know neither the enemy nor yourself, you will succumb in every battle. —Sun Tzu

Ancient Chinese cosmologists characterized four types of dragons: the Celestial Dragon known as *Tianlong*, who guards the heavenly dwellings of the gods, the Dragon of Hidden Treasure or *Fucanglong*, who defends the kingdom's wealth, the Earth Dragon or *Dilong*, who rules the waterways, and the Spiritual Dragon or *Shenlong*, who holds sway over the rains and winds.

Mine will be a tale as sharp as a dragon's talons, as blustery as the beats of a dragon's wings, as fiery as a dragon's exhalations. It is finally time to call out our players—hardy warriors one and all—for this climactic action, the last measure of this three-act play. We recognize now that our global dragon is the threat facing the planet, which like a spinning coin can only fall one of two ways. Either we slay the climate dragon or the dragon chars and parches and scorches us with spiraling heat and melting ice.

We are not the only creatures on Earth. It has always been true that we owe our very existence to an entire web of life, but now we have turned existence topsy-turvy, such that the survival of all the critters, plants, fungi, and microorganisms depend on our wise choices in the next several decades. For most people alive today, it will be clear how this great struggle will turn out before the end of their existence, for better or for worse, joyfully or regretfully, sustainably or untenably.

The Frostian fork in the road could not be laid out more clearly. Choose wisely, choose well—or choose failure for all.

Latch On, Latch Off

Each bud that opens embraces becoming as if it has never happened before. —Shellen Lubin

A bbey London struggled, releasing a heartfelt sigh. "Come on now, if I'm going to blatantly open my blouse and offer you this beauteous, bountiful breast, you'd better be gentle with me. It's only fair."

Jake Harper looked at the woman seated on the couch across from him, the woman with hair of weathered copper and freckles dusting either side of her nose of nearly the same hue, and thought her bosom was indeed beautiful. And bountiful. So, he said it out loud, calmly but in all seriousness, with a little smile at the corners of his mouth.

Abbey looked up from struggling to get baby Hope to latch on and frowned at him momentarily. "She bites sometimes, you know. And it hurts, it does, even though she doesn't really have teeth yet. But when she closes her eyes in concentration and suckles hard, it actually feels good, sometimes all the way down to my . . . toes," she finished with almost a whisper, looking down at her infant, who was no longer a newborn, and well past her first month.

He could see the dusty dark under her eyes and knew how tired Abbey was, because he was almost as exhausted. His blondish hair was even more tousled than usual, and he'd showered but not shaved after his late afternoon run the day before, since this day was a Saturday, the second such occasion in April. But Hopie was still waking up every couple of hours all night long. Life balanced out though, as the tulips were just coming into full blossom, and the day was sunny, just a few cumulus clouds lazily floating by on their backs, not even paddling. And it was a weekend, and fortunately they had no guests at Dragonfly Inn today, the two-story, well-maintained craftsman bungalow that Abbey's parents had converted into an Inn.

The weather stood in stark contrast to what had happened ten days before. The rains had been torrential, almost tropical, which was an apt description since the culprit was Hurricane Jace, winding from Category 3 on the Saffir–Simpson scale while in the Caribbean down to Category 1 as it hit the New Jersey coast, supercharged by the additional moisture content of the warming atmosphere from the weirding climate. The Potomac River rose but with no significant flooding of the capital. New York City, on the other hand, took the brunt of the blow, with videos of water cascading down stairs leading to the subways, high water in the Brooklyn industrial area of Gowanus, and city buses with "cross sea" waves on the floor inside, sloshing not from the wind but rather the starts, stops, and turns taken by the driver.

Abbey's uneventful delivery early in March capped what had been a rather more bloodcurdling than uncomplicated first-time pregnancy. Abbey, a doctor specializing in infectious diseases, at the beginning of January had been exposed by contaminated needlestick to the virus of Crimean-Congo hemorrhagic fever, never previously seen in the Western Hemisphere. Fortunately, the several antibody cocktails she'd received were credited with possibly having warded off infection, though she'd been protectively quarantined in George Washington University Medical Center for more than a week, and monitored for several months thereafter. The potential for infection during pregnancy had been so grave she was initially under the care of a perinatologist in the hospital, then her group's obstetrician post-discharge, and ultimately by a young certified nurse-midwife when Abbey finally went into labor.

But it could be said in their circumstance that all's well that ends well, as the delivery was accomplished by Charly—short for Charlene—in the hospital where Abbey had finished her specialty training just the year before, and Jake had concurrently joined the faculty in the university's engineering department.

She looked down at their daughter, her face softening. "When she looks up at me and starts to smile, I gotta be careful she doesn't slip off my nipple." Abbey tossed her head back and rolled her neck, feeling it between her shoulder blades, as Hopie was just beginning to get heavy to pick up and cart around. Now the little imp was starting to slow down, pausing between sucks, breathing contentedly, then pulling off to yawn.

"Let me," said Jake, as he stood up to come over to pick up his daughter, first arranging a spit-up cloth on his left shoulder, then resting her sleepy head against his, alternately patting her back and rubbing it until suddenly she brought up a big burp. "Would you listen to that? She gets this belch from me, you know." He kept up his pat-and-rub routine until she let out another lesser illustration.

"Why don't you check her diaper and change as needed, then put her down for a nap," said Abbey. "In the crib in the nursery, not the bassinet next to our bed. If she falls asleep, then I should lie down, 'cause she's gettin' me up so many times I lose track. You'll be awake, because I know you need to work on a seminar. And I'm on call for my partner Dan all Sunday, so I need to pump some more breast milk." She sighed. "Just not . . . right now."

"You know how delighted Anne was to become a grandmother for the first time," Jake reminded her, "and Colby was great the way he helped out opening up that storeroom for the nursery. It's just too bad we ran out of time to finish painting it, life just got too busy." He stopped. "I really like your dad, you know, I feel like I got to know them both a lot better. That fancy baby carriage was an outstanding gift." He shifted Hope down to his left arm, ready to head to the nursery.

"And I'm glad Dad had enough seniority in the State Department," Abbey said, as she put her nursing bra and blouse back together. "Not to mention vacation time saved up by both of them, so they were able to insist on a full two-week furlough before returning to Abu Dhabi." She gazed at the two of them, father and daughter, savoring and saving the picture in her mind. "So, get that kid into the nursery, love. And don't forget to put her on her back to sleep, because of SIDS risk," she said, starting to yawn herself.

I know it's important, but she must have told me that half a dozen times.

Abby continued. "And Rachel and Brian are going to drop off dinner again, I'll bet with some of his trademark loaves of bread. Good thing your friend's quite the baker."

***

When he heard the soft knock at the front door, Jake walked swiftly but quietly from his office in back of the Inn down the hallway to the entrance set next to the boot room on the right.

Opening the door, he motioned for them to be quiet. "Hey, guys, they're both asleep, so come on into the kitchen."

Both Brian and Rachel were carrying baskets. She was wearing a broad-brimmed hat to corral in her dark chocolate curls, a light jacket, no jewelry, no makeup. She gave Jake a quick hug, then tiptoed into the first door on her right, and put her basket on the small kitchen table, the food covered with a monogrammed dish towel.

Brian, only slightly the taller of the two, shook Jake's hand firmly. Bri had on his usual jeans with a wide belt set off with a brass dragon belt buckle. His ponytail was longer than Rachel's hair, his sweatshirt not ex-actly slovenly but clearly not new. Brown eyes, darker hair, Brian was one year behind Jake but a graduate student in mechanical engineering instead of the electrical flavor. He was going to finish up in June. He was not planning a teaching career but was rather already being recruited by several firms in the area. Opening his hamper, he pulled out two loaves of sour-dough and placed them on the kitchen island.

Jake gave a low whistle of admiration for their offerings as he looked inside Rachel's basket. "This is so great for the two of you to do this, guys, but we've been home for a month and you know I have a few culinary skills, right?" They sat down, Rachel and Brian at the table, Jake on a stool at the island immediately adjacent.

"How're they doin'?" Rachel whispered, as she leaned toward Jake.

"Hope is fine but we're both tired. Not like back when Abbey was in the hospital, more like just new parents trying to get used to—everything," he said, shrugging his shoulders.

Brian harrumphed, saying, "Yeah, but Jake, you're back to teaching full-time, Abbey's sliding into more hours besides just weekends, and now Dragonfly Inn is starting to accept some paying guests again? Are you crazy or what?"

Jake shook his head more firmly. *The show must go on.* "It's not as bad as it sounds. We're mainly just accepting reservations from people who've been here before, a few of whom change their mind when they find out they might hear a baby crying during the night. And we have diaper service for at least the first three months, courtesy of Colby and Anne. And some of the lectures I'm giving are just updated from what I gave back when I was a teaching assistant." He stood up to start slicing some of the bread Brian had brought, setting out plates and putting the toaster to work.

"I will confess," Jake continued, "that Abbey has taken on another responsibility after achieving such a high profile from her work with the friggin' Crimean-Congo trainwreck. The Center for Disease Control is asking her to consult and coordinate with their center for something like Emerging and Zoonotic Infectious Diseases. That's right in her bailiwick, because as you know she has this irresistible attraction to any infection transmitted by mosquitoes or ticks. She tells me this center is part of the international outreach by the CDC to surveille and identify new pathogens, whether naturally sourced, from laboratory accident, or from biowarfare work by bad actors. Kind of like that old movie, *Contagion*, with Dustin Hoffman and . . . um, and Rene Russo."

"What was that, back in the 1990s?" Rachel asked.

"Yeah, that was it," Brian agreed, after a moment's thought.

The two of them knew where the butter and jellies were in the fridge and pitched in to help.

"I'll get the coffee going," Jake said, setting out mugs and plates on the two sides of the table adjacent to the wall and on the island for himself. "And I know you guys heard we're going to be interviewing a possible nanny in a couple of days. Her name's Mina, she's a friend of Charly's, she's from Vermont, and she's had some formal training."

Brian buttered up some toast for the three of them.

Rachel raised an eyebrow. "Would she stay in one of the rooms upstairs?" But Jake shook his head, adding his favorite apple jelly to his toast and taking a big bite.

"No," he said, "she'd be a live-out, not live-in nanny. I'd heard one of our neighbors on the other side of the block had put up a sign about a room for rent, so I walked around to talk to the Petersons last month. Nice folks, they share a back alley with us, so a nanny could come from their backyard gate through our gate, then a straight shot into the house."

He saw Rachel and Brian were devouring their toast as well, though both had opted for grape jelly.

Brian stretched his arms up with a groan probably from a bike workout, then asked, "What kind of hours and what kind of pay are you offering a person like this?"

"We're thinking of her starting at seven or eight in the morning," Jake said. "Monday to Friday, finishing up when one of us gets home. And I do a fair amount of work on my computer here in the back office, but I could let her take care of the kid if I need to keep working here, to maintain her hours and my productivity. Mina's references sound great so far, but we need to call a few more people before we finally meet her in person." He tapped his fingers on the table, a habit from the old days.

"We're checking to see what typical pay scales are for Virginia," Jake said, continuing, "and Clarendon in particular. With a variable schedule, pay should be on the order of seventeen or eighteen bucks an hour from what we've found out so far. It's not physically challenging, and it's only one kid, but obviously this may entail some negotiation.

"One more bit of news, guys," Jake said. "Apparently the Nuclear Regulatory Commission got word of the help I was in locating that Stenger guy last year, you remember, the one who carried out a successful cyberattack against the Peach Bottom nuclear plant."

"Have you heard how long those two reactors are going to be out of commission?" Brian asked, but Jake shook his head.

"I don't know," he replied, "but I suspect it will be many, many months. My help was almost negligible, if you ask me. Just an email and follow up to a conversation I had with one of our guests at the Inn, where we had talked about FERC, the Federal Energy Regulatory Commission. The long and the short of it is that since most of my research deals with the electric grid, I've been asked to consult about susceptibility of the grid to attack, either electronically or by physical disruption. It means of course, that I'll be doing a ton of extra reading. I might even incorporate some of this into my classes. Nothing classified of course, although they tell me I will need to apply for some sort of low-level security clearance."

He shook his head again.

"That sounds downright fascinating, Jake," Rachel said, smiling.

Brian stood up, polished off his last bite, washed his hands at the sink, and said, "Well, buddy, Rach and I have some shopping to do at the food co-op, and after that it's shaping up to be a great day to get some biking in, at least an easy twenty-five miles or so."

Rachel followed suit, remembered to grab both baskets, gave Jake another quick hug, and said, "Take care of that kiddo. And remember Bri and I get to be honorary uncle and aunt. Or maybe godfather and godmother."

Brian couldn't resist, as usual. "I've seen those movies, and I really think I could be a godfather."

Ignoring that, aside from rolling his eyes, Jake said to Rachel, "Either way sounds good to me." He walked out the front door with them.

For a moment all three stood still and admired the tulips, then the two of them were off on their quest.

Shootin' the Breeze

Fast is fine, but accuracy is everything. —*Wyatt Earp*

Always drink your whiskey with your gun hand, to show your friendly intentions.
—*A plainsman*

Matt looked over at Buck to chastise him in all good humor. "Come on, you know ya gotta set up the beer cans, stop bitching about it." He held some authority here, having been the only one of the three with a record of actual military service, on the ground in Kabul in May of 2011 when Osama bin Laden was taken out in Pakistan. Not that he had anything to do with the operation; he served protection for the US embassy in Afghanistan, never left the city. Rangy and muscular, with black hair and a perpetual five-o'clock shadow, he stood there, hard olive eyes focused on Buck, who, grumbling, refused to look up at him.

Matt rarely took his trucker cap off, though he'd turn it around when he bellied up to the Pearl Handle Bar in Lockhart in southern Texas. He was the only one who wore cowboy boots, even when he engaged in local delivery for Longhorn Propane. His jeans were held up by an old leather belt with a rodeo buckle, which he had won back in high school years before.

Squinting, Buck looked around at the sky and spit out some tobacco juice. "Hell, Matt, why do I have to be first every time?"

But it was his brother Elliot who replied. "Because you drink more beer than the two of us put together, you're the youngest asshole here, and I'm the one ya call to get bailed out of jail on Saturday nights, remember?" Taller and stockier than his brother, he was generally willing to follow Matt's lead. He had eyes the color of a barber's strop, and old leather hiking boots of the same worn color. His work as an electrician took him to Austin, only thirty miles away from the small town of Lockhart, not considered much of a commute around these parts. "And if you were smart enough to not keep all those empty bottles and cans in your truck, then maybe that sheriff's deputy would be more likely to let you go with a warning."

"He's right, Buck," Matt said, "but since you got 'em, get out there and set 'em up." The two older men, best friends since high school, looked at Buck. He was a shorter guy with brown hair and mustache, long sideburns, oil-stained work boots and permanently stained fingernails from his work as a mechanic at one of the local Exxon stations. They knew he was deathly afraid of rattlesnakes and coral snakes and especially scorpions, but they didn't ride him about that. He was the one most likely to blow his top and get kicked out of a bar, but also the only one with a current girlfriend. She didn't like him chewing tobacco, but she apparently appreciated his excitable nature, and was willing to overlook him missing a couple of front teeth from getting into brawls.

Buck gritted his remaining teeth, stomped back to his pickup, opened the side door, pushed the front seat forward, and started hauling bottles and cans out, pitching them to the ground. The Texas sky was cloudless, a true cerulean blue, and the prairie seemed to stretch forever in all directions, except right in front of them where there sat a small hill, half a dozen miles outside of town, that they used as their firing range. This was Texas, and they all owned weapons of various calibers, and they weren't hunting anything unless Buck caught sight of a snake. He filled his canvas bag and stomped out toward the hill, then set up their targets on all the usual outcrops and stumps, holding back several bottles for the final aerial show. Matt and Elliot got their guns out, both semiautomatic pistols.

They stayed quiet when Buck got back. As far as Matt could tell, he seemed to have blown off some steam, almost smiling in anticipation of hurling some lead. Buck pulled out his gun belt and classic Colt Single Action Army revolver from his front seat and joined them.

"Buck, you get to go first this time," Matt said, "since you pulled the hard duty here. When we get done, I got something to talk over with you two outlaws."

All three put construction earplugs or wads of cotton in their ears and always wore antireflective shooting glasses. Only Elliot used earmuffs as well. Long ago Matt and Elliot had come to understand Buck fancied himself a gunslinger, so they waited patiently as he buckled up his gun belt with the holster hanging low on the left, with the cord tied around the inside of his thigh just above his knee. Buck stepped up to a couple of mesquite bushes that served as their firing line about twenty-five feet away from their targets of mayhem, spread his feet shoulder-width apart, and crouched subtly, with his left hand next to the holstered revolver.

All three comprehended that the greatest risk with quickdraw was firing off the weapon before it cleared the holster, so the key idea was keeping the index finger outside the trigger guard until the weapon began to rotate up toward level. Matt could tell Buck had not been drinking, and he knew the young man never did until the bars opened up at four in the afternoon, unless he was home watching sports. *He may be a wild man, but he's conscientious around firearms, I gotta give him that.*

Buck waited, immobile aside from his breathing, then drew quickly and smoothly and fired three shots in as many seconds. One bottle shattered and a can went flying. He holstered his revolver, turned slightly to the right, and drew again. This time one can went spinning as the concussions reverberated away like distant thunder.

The boy deserves some support. "That's good shootin' there, Buck. One-handed and level with your belt. I couldn't come close to that." He turned to Elliot and told him to give it a try. There were still a couple dozen targets out there.

Elliot positioned himself in a standard shooter's stance, wiped his dirty-blond hair back from his eyes, then raised his pistol with an eye-level, two-handed grip. He shot a bit slower than his brother, and sent flying three out of six. He shrugged and stepped back to reload.

Matt moved up to the same position and used the same technique but took out four straight targets—one was from a ricochet off a nearby boulder.

They continued for another half hour or so, even trying unsuccessfully to hit a few bottles thrown up in the air, until all of the glass was busted up and the cans had at least one hole apiece. They didn't wear cowboy hats and none of them had a horse, though they knew how to hold a saddle. Even so, they were Texans and proud of it. The guns were now reloaded, on safety, holstered, and ready for cleaning later.

They sat down for a while after they were done, ears open to the wind whistling by, with a few dust devils in the distance to the northwest.

Matt rolled himself a cigarette and lit it, while Elliot pulled out a pack and held a match to one of his own. Target practice was thirsty work, so they popped open cans of Lone Star before wiping their damp hands on dusty jeans.

Elliot directed his gaze at Matt. "You said you had something to talk to us about. Now's as good a time as any."

Matt was the one slowly surveying the sky this time. He lifted his cap and swiped at his sweaty, balding crown. "Boys, you know I ain't happy about the way this country is headed. None of us is. But we've been talking about it for a long time."

Elliot spoke up. "But not doing shit about it."

Matt smiled. "And I think the three of us are finally ready. Are you with me on this?" He looked each of them in the eye and liked what he saw.

Buck just grinned. "Hell, yes."

THREE

Hoofbeats and Zebras

For my part I know nothing with any certainty, but the sight of the stars makes me dream.
—Vincent van Gogh

Doubt is not a pleasant condition, but certainty is absurd. —Voltaire

Abbey looked at the fourth-year in front of her. She was wearing sensible shoes, blue scrubs, and the classic short white coat worn by students not yet out of med school. The young lady had slender eyebrows and nose, a pink streak on the left side of her brunette hair, no rings, and the harried look of a student post-call, up all night but still working. *It takes a while for them to get used to the sleep deprivation*, thought Abbey. *If they ever do.*

She began with: "So, I see—by your name tag—that you are Madelyn Pennyfarthing, which clearly sounds English to me. I'm Abbey London, which is an English name, while your accent sounds more like New York."

"Yes, ma'am, as it so happens, I am from New York."

"Ordinarily I'd ask to speak to your resident, but I know all of them are at report at this hour of the morning, so I wonder what you could tell me about your case." Abbey peered at her intently, wanting to know what the team thought about this patient before she reviewed the chart and completed her own exam.

"Mr. Bennet is a thirty-six-year-old white male carpenter who was admitted last night for recurrent fever. We have him on the floor in an isolation room, because he's still a bit of a mystery. He's experienced two prior episodes of fever lasting approximately three nights, each time with a few days or a week or more with residual lassitude, then a recurrence."

Abbey itched to start asking questions, but knew she was here in part to further the education of these students about proper case presentation.

Interesting, recurrent fever, raising lots of possibilities.

"He first became ill two weeks ago, with a presentation of fever and chills, headache, myalgias, arthralgias, vomiting, and diarrhea. He was alert but weak, with fever at that point of 102 degrees Fahrenheit—"

Without taking her eyes off Madelyn, Abbey corrected her. "About 38.9 degrees Celsius. You gotta get used to this."

"Sorry, yes, almost 39 degrees. White cells were elevated to fourteen thousand, anemic with hemoglobin slightly down at 12.8. His chest X-ray was normal, urine clear. Since he was alert with no neck stiffness—"

"Nuchal rigidity you mean," Abbey corrected again.

"Okay, no nuchal rigidity, so no spinal tap. As a healthy young guy without diabetes or immunodeficiency or acknowledged drug use aside from occasional alcohol and a bit of marijuana, he was sent home from his primary care office with a diagnosis of presumed undifferentiated viral infection and a suggestion to use ibuprofen or other antipyretic for aches and fever. Subsequently his tests for coronavirus, influenza, and HIV all came back negative.

"A week later he returned—to the ER this time—with almost identical symptoms except slightly higher temperature, and they admitted him. His labs were normal aside from a further minor drop in hemoglobin, plus elevation of some liver enzymes, the aminotransferases but not alkaline phosphatase. Though he had a normal alk phos, his bilirubin was up to 1.5, so slightly elevated, but blood tests for hepatitis A and B and C came back negative. This time he had one-plus protein in the urine.

"Reportedly though, he looked more acutely ill, so they proceeded with further evaluation. Abdominal CT was negative except for borderline sple-nomegaly, though no one could actually palpate a spleen beneath his left ribs. Two sets of paired blood cultures were negative for any bacteria. As they were awaiting other blood tests and imaging, his fever melted away, so he was discharged for outpatient follow-up unless he relapsed."

Abbey nodded. "Which, of course, he did."

Madelyn just shook her head. "Since this was such a troublesome case, he came to an academic medical center and got admitted by a fourth-year med student. No irony there. His hemoglobin is down a bit more at 12.1 but he shows a pronounced reticulocytosis, so he's certainly busy making replacement red cells."

Abbey tilted her head, asking, "Did you think to get a haptoglobin to see if there might be some red cell breakdown, hemolysis taking place right in the bloodstream?"

Madelyn lifted her chin. "Still pending."

Abbey ranged more widely over some possibilities. "No travel history, no pet or animal exposure, no recent vaccinations, no unusual family history of fevers? No enlarged lymph nodes on exam or CT?"

Madelyn shook her head to each question.

"You said he's a carpenter. Do you know where he's been working?" This time Madelyn just looked mystified.

"No tick exposure either I assume. Okay, Madelyn, I'm sure you have other patients to go take care of. I'll review the chart and complete my exam. When I'm done, I'll write a brief note with recommendations, and my longer dictation should be back by this evening. At this point I'm betting on a subacute infectious process, not autoimmune or neoplastic disease. And my partner and I appreciate the request for an infectious disease consultation."

After Abbey finished the note, she headed straight home, because she didn't have her gear for breast pumping and felt engorged, though not yet painfully so.

She mused about Mr. Bennet, who had been working over by the airport for the last couple of months, helping frame out an outbuilding. And his history was so classic and so much like another case of airport malaria she'd seen during her two years of infectious disease fellowship that it was a slim but realistic possibility. In med school she was taught "When you hear hoofbeats, think of horses, not zebras." But this might actually be time to consider a zoo animal. Washington, DC, had so many foreign visitors coming in from far-flung countries, perhaps in the cargo compartment of an airliner an infected female *Anopheles* mosquito had hitched a ride. She shook her head. Unlikely but not impossible. Malaria has dual hosts, mosquitoes and humans in this case. By now she was outside and headed to her car.

She reviewed the five species of *Plasmodium* that infect humans with malaria, the most common and most serious infection being *Plasmodium falciparum*. Except that's not a cyclical or recurrent infection, so it would have to be one of the other four. Regardless, the sporozoite stage of this protozoan infection makes its way into the salivary gland of the mosquito, which injects its salivary enzymes into the human host to assist in sucking up a blood meal. The sporozoites along for the ride travel through the bloodstream to infect human liver cells, which in turn release the merozoite stage—this time to infect red blood cells, chomping down on the hemoglobin.

That's the way they make their living.

Abbey continued to cogitate. *If this turns out to be malaria, we won't know the country of origin. But the CDC offers malaria-drug-resistance testing for all cases free of charge. At any rate, I'll have specific drug recommendations for this young healthy male who has uncomplicated malaria if he has it at all. Probably the drug combination of artemether and lumefantrine.*

***

Later she would be glad she'd recommended thick and thin smears of blood to rule out malaria, because instead they ruled it in. The studies showed the signet-ring stage of trophozoites, fortunately inside less than five percent of the red cells in his bloodstream. This young guy would do fine, and she'd garnered another feather in her cap.

Her partner Dan would be impressed she'd lassoed another zebra.

FOUR

And Nanny Makes Four

Sweater, n. Garment worn by child when its mother is feeling chilly. —*Ambrose Bierce*

A torn jacket is soon mended, but hard words bruise the heart of a child.
—*Henry Wadsworth Longfellow*

A bbey and Jake were not waiting in the kitchen for a knock on the door, since they knew an arrival was reliably heralded by the sound of tires on the gravel driveway. Better than a guard dog really. It was a Saturday, because so many good things happen on a weekend, but more pragmatically, it was harder during the week to sync everyone's schedules. So today was the day they finally got to meet their best candidate for a new *au pair*.

Or nanny, whichever she preferred to be called.

Abbey was in sweatpants and a T-shirt over a nursing bra, topped off with a well-worn robe featuring sunflowers large and small. She'd brushed her hair out and was free of makeup, not that she ever wore much. Both had had some oatmeal for breakfast, with orange juice and turkey sausage.

Jake knew Abbey had slept better because Hope slept better, which clearly made the whole world look rosier.

So, this morning Abbey's face was unlined, and she was more relaxed, more rested, more like when her folks had been here to help out right after the delivery.

Thinking back, her parents had followed clearly delineated roles in their assistance. Colby had long walks and talks with Jake, whom he seemed to prefer to call Jacob. Jake knew he was a formal guy in his professional work, but they didn't talk about that much, aside from entertaining stories about the Middle East. The two of them had talked about Emmanuelle though, whose role in the federal government, somewhere in the intelligence community, was known to Colby even though she and he had never met and never talked except for one salient phone call when Emmanuelle contacted him, seeking endorsement of the reliability of this young couple, whom she had met during a stay at the Inn.

When Jake told the story of the discussion he had had with Abbey about Colby's role in the foreign service, he simply chuckled at her discomfort and would confirm only that he wore a couple of different hats in the embassy. But he volunteered nothing more. *Perhaps someday*, thought Jake.

Colby was quite the woodworker, which explained the shop area set up in the garage around the loop of driveway in front of the house. They had pitched in together to set up the nursery in the old spare room downstairs, mainly mastering the assembly of the crib with only a couple of references to the instructions. It was Anne, though, who was generous enough to suggest getting another infant car seat for whatever car belonged to whichever nanny got chosen to care for their granddaughter.

Anne, in whom Jake could see Abbey more and more, was the perfect grandmother, calming and playing with her granddaughter, sitting on the rocker in the parlor across from the kitchen, singing lullabies to her. She gave her daughter loads of tips on breast pumping, changing diapers, and every other issue under the sun. When weather permitted, the two of them had taken Hope for frequent spins in the baby carriage around the neighborhood.

"Are you seriously going to wear those jeans?" asked Abbey, with no hint of humor. "She could be arriving any time now," she added, raising her eyebrows at him.

"These are so comfortable, and my other jeans, the ones without the holes, are in the wash. Hey, wait a minute, are we going to be asking this nanny to wash clothes? And maybe dishes?" he asked, with a hopeful look blatantly obvious on his face.

"Jake, come on. We want a reliable young lady who will completely focus on taking care of our child. Clearly, you're just trying to get out of your responsibilities around here."

To his credit, he tried to look a bit crestfallen, rocking his head back and forth with an innocent gaze directed at the floor. He tapped his fingers on the table, a sure sign that he was mulling things over. Then he almost jumped up, and said, "Okay, tires on gravel. Let's go greet her on the porch." *Discussion over about my jeans, and she never even got to my sweatshirt, which I need to get into the wash.*

They stood side by side on the porch, not holding hands, but clearly a united front. They looked at the old VW Beetle just shutting down near the garage. It had clearly seen better days, but the engine sounded good and there was no visible rust. The young woman who got out waved at them enthusiastically and said, "Good morning, good morning." She was dressed in corduroy pants and jacket, with a pink blouse and laced-up leather boots. Jake would have called her buxom if he were allowed to say such a thing out loud, but she was also carrying a bit of a belly.

Jake figured Abbey must have immediately noticed two rings on each of her hands, as well as a pierced nose with a smallish golden loop.

As she got closer, Jake could see she had short, straight blond hair, dusky gray eyes, and no freckles, but a beauty mark near the left corner of her mouth.

She strode right up to the porch and climbed the three steps.

Presents herself well, thought Jake.

"Welcome to Dragonfly Inn," Abbey said, reaching out to shake her hand.

Mina took her hand in both of hers and looked her straight in the eye. "This place is so wonderful. I love the porch swing. I saw the pictures on your website, but they must have been taken at a different time of the year."

By this time, she had taken a firm hold of Jake's hand and looked him right in the eye as well. "I know what all the guest rooms look like, and the parlor and dining room, and I'm just dying to see all of it."

"Well, come on in," Jake said. "We'll sit in the parlor and talk. Just be aware Hope is asleep, so we can't give you the full walk-through until she wakes up, which should be soon."

Abbey offered tea, which Mina accepted as the two of them found a comfortable place to sit.

Jake put some water on to boil and joined them. He chuckled as he walked in and said, "First, you've gotta tell us how you got the name Wilhelmina."

"Well, everybody asks me that, in school or anyplace I'm just starting out. It is my legal name, came from one of my mother's favorite great-aunts from Germany. So, with the alternatives of Willie or Hell, I decided by about kindergarten age I was gonna be a Mina. All I can say is my mom got over it pretty quickly. So, Mina Felicity Butler," she summarized, as she bowed her head with hands out wide and palms up.

"Tell us a bit more about your family," Abbey suggested.

"My mom works in the Community College of Vermont, in Middlebury, where I was born and grew up. She works in the Center for Online Learning, and she was the one to suggest continuing independent study combined with work. Before I left, I'd taken a couple of classes in person during Covid, trying out anthropology, meteorology, and geology, but more and more felt I wanted to teach kids."

Clearly a positive sign, Jake realized.

"My father operates a plant nursery in town, my older brother Craig is a journalist with the *Addison Independent* newspaper. My younger sister Heidi is a sophomore in high school. All three of us have done a lot of sports, mine were swimming and lacrosse and yoga."

Jake observed, "So only one younger sibling, but young enough you probably got to help provide care for her."

She looked at him and said "Yes" emphatically.

"Your references all checked out," Abbey commented, "a couple of staff people at the community college, also from the US Nanny Institute, and of course your parents and our midwife Charlene. I understand you and Charly went to the same high school together."

Mina beamed. "She's a year and a half older, but we hit it off, both of us were on the swim team. And of course, she was the one who let me know that you were looking for someone to care for your daughter, but not to live in your house . . . I mean Inn."

Abbey tilted her head left, then raised the other eyebrow. "You've completed some coursework at both schools, but don't yet have either a degree from the community college or the certificate from the . . . nanny school. Explain, please."

Mina crossed her hands in her lap. "Both schools offer a lot, *a lot* of virtual classes. I wanted to try someplace besides Vermont, and it was about time to move out anyway, much as I love my family. To do that, I needed employment. I figured working five days a week with nights and weekends off would give me a lot of time to study online. But also a chance to explore new places, where I might wanna settle down and teach later on."

Abbey nodded, but succumbed to curiosity. "What is that ring on your right middle finger, may I ask?"

Mina rotated the ring forward with her left hand. "It's an opal, my birthstone, I was born in October."

"Very pretty. But tell us a bit more about what you're studying."

"Okay, let me tell you about each school. At the community college I'm currently signed up for two classes, Introduction to Early Childhood Education and Literature for Kids, basically age-appropriate selections obviously. The nanny school offers certification after completion of a number of classes, like newborn care, nutrition, positive discipline, sleep training, and baby sign language. These are all on-demand, online classes, each with a multiple-choice exam after completion."

"Baby sign language, sounds interesting, do you—" Jake tried to ask.

"Well, I haven't taken that class yet," Mina said, "but I'm looking forward to it, for sure. Enrolling in two schools for classes, I figure it'll take me eighteen months or so to finish up both. I'm a quick study."

"That's good," Jake said. "What degrees will you end up with again?"

"An AA from the community college and an official transcript and certificate from the Nanny Institute."

Abbey heard a soft cry from the baby and moved to stand up. "Are you certified in CPR by any chance?"

Mina just shook her head.

"I think Hope's ready to get up now," Abbey said. "Why don't you come with me, we'll check her diaper, and if she needs a change. I'll let you show me how you do with cloth diapers. Then we'll go over the section of the refrigerator dedicated to breast milk, and how to heat it up and such."

Mina jumped to her feet in a lively manner.

Jake thought to himself, *This would be a great time to check my email,* and followed behind, ending up in his office, but still half-listening to their conversation, lots of *oohs* and *aahs* and "What a gorgeous baby" sorts of comments. *What mother would ever argue about that?*

He heard the nursery door open and he slept his computer monitor and came out to rejoin them. *Funny how electrical substations just seem to blend into the background in an urban environment.*

When they had all regrouped in the parlor, Jake sensed the positive mood in the room and led off with a description of their proposal. "The room for rent just around the other side of this block would be with the Petersons, a kindly older couple who have had an empty nest for some time apparently. For some years they have been renting a spare bedroom on the first floor to one college student after another, but the last one just graduated. They told me they're looking for a quiet, responsible, single person on a month-to-month basis." Jake could see Mina was listening intently.

"They told me it's furnished with a bed, dresser, and a desk, and is situated close to the kitchen, kind of like our arrangement here. I don't know what they're asking, but Mrs. Peterson said first, last, and a security deposit, that's all we know."

He pulled a piece of paper out of his shirt pocket and handed it to her. "That's the contact information, but you might want to call first and then walk over and talk to them today. It's the middle of April, but certainly a prorated charge for the first month is easy to calculate."

Mina looked back and forth from him to Abbey and just couldn't stop grinning. "Sounds like we could make a deal. But my parents said to be businesslike about it and be sure to look over the contract before signing."

Wise young woman, Jake thought. "Online we found a typical contract for a nanny in Virginia. Our particulars include a standard hourly rate of seventeen-fifty, with time and a half for anything over forty hours a week, which we suspect would happen only rarely. Incidental expenses for the baby on your part or mileage would need to be detailed and reimbursed with the next semimonthly paycheck. There's a lot more detail in the contract, benefits and such, so may I suggest you take it home overnight and bring it back tomorrow. If it looks good, we'll sign two copies and give you one at that point."

Abbey added, "I understand you're staying with Charly temporarily, so you might want to review the document with her and maybe even call up your parents as well for discussion."

"How soon would I start?" Mina asked.

"It'd be great if you could come as soon as Monday morning." Jake could hear the hopeful tone in Abbey's voice, but Mina was already bobbing her head up and down. "I'll be sure to be off that morning to get you all oriented."

Jake said, "We'll be having you use one of our car seats for her, but we don't anticipate any particular reason for you to leave the Inn for the first few months regardless."

Mina nodded then said, "Abbey, why don't you show me where you store the pumped milk in the fridge and how you set that up. After that I'm gonna go visit the Petersons. Maybe Charly and I can go someplace for a celebratory dinner later."

***

"You can tell how excited she is," Abbey said, leaning against the doorway to his office just before sundown. "I think she's a good fit. Of course, I wish she'd had about four younger siblings and more experience with toddlers."

"She is awfully young, but I guess *au pairs* usually are. One thing for sure, she's going to learn all about withholding of payroll taxes when we hand her a first paycheck."

"She already knows about bottle feeding, sleeping positions, and she understands why we're going to have a video setup in the nursery."

Leaning back in his comfortable chair, Jake said, "Certainly no camera in the parlor or anyplace else a guest would see and feel uncomfortable about. Only you and I would have the passcode to access the video feed when we're at work or out someplace. I'm gonna have to discipline myself against spending too much time watching her sleep when I'm at work."

Abbey walked around Jake to rub his shoulders for a moment. "And Jacob, she plays the guitar and wants to know if she could bring it over here, maybe store it in the boot room. She asked permission to sing songs to Hope, can you believe it?" She slowed, then bent down to nuzzle first his ear, then his neck.

"Guitar, sounds good, just as long as it's not hard rock or . . . anything." He reached up his arms to fold around her head, then turned to kiss her. "We should have pointed out the small desk in the parlor, she could set up to study there or in the kitchen when Hope's asleep. I'm sure it'd be okay for her to interact with guests, who usually go out during the day, but she should not feel obligated. If she needs to study then I'm fine with her doing that."

Abbey looked reflective, then said, "Time will tell."

"I always get to be the optimistic one," Jake responded, "but I gotta agree with you there."

FIVE

Oath Breakers

If there is a hole in your story or your fence, something you rather did not get out, will.
—A plainsman

A new oath holds pretty well; but . . . when it is become old, and frayed out, and damaged by
a dozen annual retryings of its remains, it ceases to be serviceable; any little strain will snap it.
—Mark Twain

It was starting out as a slow afternoon at the Pearl Handle Bar, the popular place in Lockhart where the neon sign out front was a big revolver, duplicated on its business cards. The town had not more than fifteen thousand hardy souls, but had been featured in dozens of films, like *Secondhand Lions* and *What's Eating Gilbert Grape*. Buck favored the saloon both for its cheap beer and because he could brag to the women behind the bar that his gun matched their sign. He and Matt were waiting for Elliot, who had let them know their package had finally come in, delivered to a personal mailbox or PMB he'd set up in Austin with fake IDs.

Caroline sidled up to their table, "I hate to interrupt deep thinkers such as you guys. But any of you fellas interested in another beer?" She looked at each of them in turn, batting her fake eyelashes at Matt, who ignored the woman just looking for a bigger tip down the line.

"I may just nurse this one until closing time, sweetheart," he said, smiling up at her.

She put a hand on one hip. "It's friggin' five-thirty in the afternoon, Matt. I know you're thirstier than that. How about a sandwich then?"

"Okay, Caroline, ya got yourself a sale. Gimme one of them Reuben sandwiches on rye, why don't you."

"Buck, what about you? Thirsty or hungry?"

He shrugged his shoulders. "Not yet, honey. I'll let you know." He watched as she walked back to the kitchen, and Matt knew his taste ran toward blowsy blondes with wide hips.

Matt also knew Elliot had done some electrical work off the books for a pawn shop in Austin in exchange for two forms of fake ID with a forged notary public stamp and signature. It was sophisticated enough that the clerk at the UPS store had set up the PMB with no questions asked, and so he paid up front all in cash for three months.

Elliot took off his work ID the day he set the box up, parked around the block so his vehicle wouldn't be visible, used a fake address from a house he picked out at random when driving around in Austin, told the guy he didn't use email, and gave the clerk nothing but the number of a burner phone he'd picked up at the same pawn shop.

Then it came down to a waiting game. Elliot called every Monday until they told him a parcel had come in. He waited a few days so as to not seem too eager, then went to the UPS place on a busy day wearing the same clothes he'd had on the first time, a nondescript shirt from Goodwill, his regular jeans, a baseball cap pulled down low, and a surgical mask like he was a guy worried about Covid.

Which worked like a charm.

Now he sauntered into the bar and walked over to their usual table in the back room, waggling his eyebrows at his brother and Matt. "Got to say, boys, it went very sweet," he said, pulling up a heavy wooden chair and leaning back. "Not—a hitch."

Matt regarded him for a couple of seconds. "Did ya get rid of the phone like I told you?"

"Right in the Colorado River in the center of Austin," he said, lifting his chin. "Even wiped it down for fingerprints. And before ya ask, Matt, yeah, I did sign for the package, I did use the fake name, and I did clean off that fancy electric pen they give you."

Matt raised his eyebrow. "Did the guy see you doing that?" But Elliot shook his head.

"Don't forget the cameras in the UPS office, brother," Buck said, hitching up one shoulder.

"Even with most of your face covered up," Matt said, "if the Alcohol and Firearms people ever come around to review that video, they'll know your skin color, height, and general build."

"I ain't worried about them damn folks, there's no way in hell they could ID me from video and they got no reason to suspect me as long as the seller from the Oklahoma gun show covered up his tracks."

Matt grumbled, "Fur what we paid for these three cans, over a thousand goddamn bucks apiece, he sure as hell owes us to do this right."

"Nothing cheap about this whole operation, if you ask me," Buck said. "We had to work some overtime to pay for these, the mailbox, and everything else so far."

Matt leaned forward and whispered harshly, "What we're planning has been done before, in a coupla places, but never smack dab in the middle of a big city. We're going to try and keep it low budget, but you gotta have the right equipment for the job, right? And now we've scored almost everything we need."

They were all quiet for a moment, then Buck said, "Tell us about the firecrackers again, what's that for?" They all leaned forward subconsciously, trying to keep quiet.

But then Caroline showed up with Matt's sandwich, with a paper napkin and plastic fork and knife. "Okay, you two. Elliot, you're the smart Thorne brother, whaddya want?"

Elliot said, "Just a beer, Caroline, an' a burger with fries."

"Want cheese on that?"

"No."

"And you, Wyatt Earp, what would you like to try tonight?"

Buck glowered at her for a moment. "Burger and fries, same as my brother."

She flipped her order pad shut and ambled off to the kitchen without another word. Matt grinned to himself as he watched the other two follow her progress, knowing they thought she looked better from that point of view, with which he kind of agreed.

Matt scowled and continued, "We're gonna be using .308 caliber cartridges, bullet and case together are 2.8 inches long. These suckers are rimless, bottlenecked, and centerfire. Reliable, pack a serious punch but they are hellaciously loud. They got a muzzle velocity over 2600 feet a second."

Elliot said, "You know my rifle is bolt-action, so I may be a tad slower than you fellas. And I understand the muzzle velocity is necessarily slowed down by the sound suppression."

"Don't matter," said Matt, "accuracy is what counts. But these cans you picked up today weigh in at 17.5 ounces, titanium alloy, so over a pound. Nine inches long and 1.5 inches in diameter—"

Buck interrupted, "That's exactly what I tell my girlfriend."

Matt almost slammed his fist on the table. "Goddammit, Buck, keep your head in the game here. I'm trying to tell you a couple of things. These noise suppressors are going to throw off the balance of your rifle, so we're gonna have to do some significant practice at about a hundred yards or two hundred, and I don't want to do it at the Lone Star Gun Range. Would advise against just going in there and screwing these cans on our rifles in public. That could generate talk." There was silence for a couple of seconds as they pondered that.

Matt calmed himself down. "Elliot, I know you've got the equipment in your garage to get our guns ready, starting with a gun vise to hold it level. The thing to understand is if you make a mistake mounting your suppressor, you won't get a second chance. And we've got the right Geissele alignment rod to make sure we don't bungle the job. We all got threaded muzzles, which most guys use to hide the flash, whereas we only need to tamp down the noise, not the light. We're gonna clean off the threads with a nylon bristle brush." He paused for another sip of beer and a bite of sandwich.

"Or maybe a wire brush."

Elliot said, "I've got a tap and die I can use to chase the threads and make sure they're clean. And we gotta inspect the bearing shoulder the suppressor seats against."

Matt nodded. "If we need washers to get the right spacing, we gotta use the ones from the manufacturer that come with the kit. The Geissele rod goes into the barrel to guarantee alignment. The washers make sure it gets seated securely. We'll come help you get this all done. It ain't rocket science but it's gotta be done right."

Matt took another bite of his sandwich.

"So, why do we need firecrackers?" Buck asked. "Stop acting mysterious and all and explain, dammit."

Matt finished chewing and swallowed. "With the cans in place, the noise the gunshot makes is about what they call 115 decibels loud. That's still powerful, but almost exactly the same as a firecracker."

"So . . . what?" Buck exclaimed.

Elliot said, "I think Matt's sayin' we blow up some firecrackers to help cover up the racket."

"How the hell's that gonna work?" grumbled Buck.

Matt stared him down. "We get some firecrackers in a cardboard box and set up a long fuse, or even a timer, or maybe a remote detonator. All our watches synchronized, just like a military operation. We drop off that box about a block away from where we need to set up near the target."

Elliot slowly smiled. "I think I'm beginning to understand what you're saying." Both he and Matt looked over at Buck.

Caroline came back with two plates and a bottle of beer on a tray. She put the plates and utensils in front of the Thorne brothers and the beer next to Elliot. "Enjoy, you hooligans. Let me know if you need anything else."

Buck had almost a pleading look in his eyes. "All I can think is your firecrackers are going to add to the hullabaloo. I mean, what the hell?"

"What happens a couple of months from now, Buck?" asked Matt.

Buck knit his brows and said, "I still don't get . . ." He leaned back and slowly grinned.

Elliot laughed. "Finally, lunkhead . . . the Fourth of July. What kind of patriot are you anyway?"

They all chuckled and dug into their food.

SIX

Caprine Capers

Don't depend too much on anyone in this world because even your own shadow leaves you when you are in darkness. —Taqî al-Dîn Ahmad Ibn Taymiyyah,

The blood of a goat will shatter a diamond. —Aristotle

Jared kissed the warm, exposed cheek of his wife, who was sleeping on her side as usual, then whispered, "I'm going to head out to the barn, but maybe you could think about what to fix the kids for breakfast." *She's as fragrant as rising bread under a kitchen towel.*

She mumbled an okay.

Their JC Lazy Acres farm in Brandy Station, Virginia, was set smack dab in the middle of horse and wine country and featured not horses but rather goats accompanied by a few chickens and ducks. The dogs were a pair of enthusiastic Jack Russell terriers that greeted all visitors. They were delighted to offer their fealty to Jared when he exited the back of the house, jumping vertically like beach volleyball players on defense. He took a deep breath, loving the smell of the growing hay and appreciating the delicately rosy dawn. He swung his shoulders around one at a time as he walked, a habit from his college swimming days. His boots kicked up small clouds of dust with a solid crunch, and he knew the morning coolness could not last.

Part of the farmhouse was clearly old, with stone walls, small windows, and a chimney at both gable ends. But the rest was just as obviously of younger vintage and painted a mustard yellow, an architected, wood-framed addition with tall windows, a front door facing south, and midnight-blue solar arrays on the roof.

The pasture on one side of the long, curved driveway was fenced for goats and extended around to the back of the house, divided into multiple paddocks for rotation of grazing and separation of the different breeds. All the sections fanned out from the barn, three to a side, as the structure had originally held horses, was larger than the original house, and featured the same weathered and mossy stone. The mansard roof at the gable end had an extension for the hayloft lift with a winch, operated by an old-school triple compound pulley, and a similar but simpler double pulley arrangement for each of the metal gates leading to the sections of pasture, also operated from inside and by hand.

The weathervane up top of the barn featured a dragon, while a dinosaur was painted on the backside of the barn, which the kids identified as a *Dilophosaurus* from the double crests on its head. When Jared Cooper and Jacey Carrington bought the farm, they had limited information about the history of prior families, but they decided these touches just added to its charm and idiosyncrasy and would definitely stay.

And the kids had slowly adapted to love the area, after initially exhibiting great resistance to the idea of leaving the Big Apple and all their friends.

There was a separate, smaller mustard-yellow one-story structure for the chickens and ducks, with a third-of-an-acre pond shaded on several sides by trees, including several black willows.

The three breeds of goats were rotated every other Sunday into an alternate paddock, usually with an empty space separating the three small herds, which helped to maintain caprine domesticity, not to mention avoidance of haphazard crossbreeding.

The Boer goats were meat goats, sold live on the hoof.

The cashmere goats were shorn several times a year for their fine, soft wool, prized by spinners. The first year they brought someone in to do the shearing, but now they both worked alongside the fella and were slowly getting the hang of it.

The Nubian goats were dairy, a breed that fortunately tolerated the hot summers. These were specialized for production of home-pasteurized goat milk, which Jared and Jacey sold at the farmer's market, or off the farm directly with a sign at the road. There was some discussion about branching out into cheeses, but he was less excited about the extra work than Jacey seemed to be.

Jared had cashed out of finance in New York City a couple of years after he hit thirty, having made his money mainly in cryptocurrency, getting in early and getting out before another big crash. Jacey was part of a local three-attorney practice in family law, though she too had initially resisted the move to the country. Both were tall, as were their kids, Tobias ten and Joyce seven.

Jared had black hair and a goatee, while Jacey had blond hair cut short and a pixie nose.

They told their friends back in the city they were living the dream, except that Jared was troubled this morning. One of the Boer does had miscarried during the night, six weeks early and stillborn, quite unusual in their limited experience. He had gloved up and buried the twin fetuses and afterbirths before going back to the house to tell Jacey and the kids. After breakfast he put in a call to their veterinarian, Benjamin Harris.

"Dr. Harris—Benjamin—we lost a pair of premature twin goats sometime during the night, I have no idea what happened."

"Jared, sorry to hear that, which of the goats was it, and what was her history?"

"Molly is a Boer doe, four years old, and twinned successfully the last two years without problems."

Benjamin was at his computer, pulling up records. "She's up to date on her vaccinations, including clostridia," he said, pausing for a moment, then continuing. "Anything unusual about the placenta and membranes? Any smell, discoloration?"

Jared realized the vet knew he and Jacey only had a couple of years' experience with animal husbandry. "Nothing different from what I've seen before, except the babies were really small compared to full-term. I didn't want our children to see this, so I buried everything way out back when they were still eating breakfast."

"Okay, okay. At this point I'd just recommend you keep her separate from the other goats. She'll show signs of distress, calling for her lost kids, but that resolves over a couple of days. Keep an eye out for fever, poor feeding, listlessness, any other signs she's not thriving. As long as she recovers and the rest stay healthy, no testing necessary and no reason to bring her in. But keep a close watch on her."

Benjamin arched his back, stretching his free arm over his head.

"Gonna be hot today. Looks like we're in for a blazing summer, bet you've already heard that. Everybody knows Virginia has broken five or six high-temperature records already this month. And the mosquitoes are going to be a bear what with this wacky weather. Give me a call if anything else comes up."

"Thanks, Benjamin, I'll stay in touch." *Just hope I don't need to call him back.*

SEVEN

Grid Guidance

A good friend will know how you take your coffee. —Anonymous

The United States remains in a heightened threat environment. Lone offenders and small groups motivated by a range of ideological beliefs and personal grievances continue to pose a persistent and lethal threat to the Homeland.
—National Terrorism Advisory System Bulletin, issued May 24, 2023

Jake knew his friend Brian liked a dollop of oat milk in his coffee. Anticipating his likely arrival, he often put some extra French roast into his magical machine when he had to think hard about something. He also knew Brian kept his cream equivalent in the small refrigerator in his office just for this reason.

"I swear sometimes you must smell when I'm brewing up some java," Jake said, as Brian walked in through the office door as if invited. *Course he knows I'm always here on Tuesdays at one o'clock.*

"Nah," said Brian, "I could hear you gettin' something going all the way from the grad student office down the hall, Jake, plus I know you usually need some caffeine about this time in the afternoon." He walked over to the fridge and pulled out his small carton of milk. "So, what are you mulling over now?" He sat down and put up his boots on a second chair.

"There are so many things that can go wrong with our grids, it's not like we needed another headache. I had a very small role in identifying Stenger after he pulled off that cyberattack on the Peach Bottom reactors last year . . . you know that whole story. But fortunately, my name was kept out of it and bottom line is I prefer to remain anonymous."

"Rachel and I have been very careful, and only a couple other faculty in this department know anything about it. I know it sounds hackneyed, but your secret's safe with us. It was so random you had anything to do with it anyway, like winning a lottery."

Jake shook his head. "I read the bulletins from the Homeland Security folks that come out every six months or so, the last one just this week. They are warning about the enhanced risk of domestic violence by rightwing 'lone wolf' actors, and argue that what with all the inflammatory Republican rhetoric about the weaponization of federal departments and book banning and LGBTQ+ folks . . . maybe individuals rather than organized groups will be responsible for more of these attacks."[1]

Brian crossed one ankle over the other and set down his coffee mug. "So, where do you come down on all this, Jake?"

"These are crimes inspired by extremist ideologies obviously, and the warning sign should have been that attack back in 2013, that one I told you about, remember?"

Brian tilted his head up. "Near San Jose as I recall," he said, rubbing his nose, "somebody shot up an electrical substation."

"PG&E, you know, Pacific Gas & Electric, had—and still has—the Metcalf transmission substation in Coyote, in California.[2] The sniper or snipers fired on seventeen transformers, resulting in more than fifteen million dollars' worth of damage in just a few minutes. The odd thing was it didn't meet the FBI definition of terrorism, because it wasn't that hard to carry out, there wasn't any message afterward, and the perpetrators or idiots weren't even very good shots, ironically." Jake tapped his fingers on the side of his mug.

"They never caught anybody, right?" Brian asked, after a pause.

"We'd have heard about the story if they had. But the problem is, or was, the publicity about it. And the radicalization of the population. Since then, there have been a thousand reports of actual attacks on electrical infrastructure."

Brian took his legs off the chair. "You're kidding, right, really a thousand?" But Jake was already shaking his head.

"Brian, yeah, truly a thousand in barely a decade and a half. A guy named Michael Jensen—who works at the National Consortium for the Study of Terrorism or some such at the University of Maryland—says seventy percent of people carrying out terroristic attacks in this country are either individuals or part of 'isolated cliques,' just three to four people. They hang out in the dark parts of the internet where they can exchange ideas day and night. And as far as domestic extremists go, ninety-five percent are rightwing. Think here of the Proud Boys, other white supremacists, anti-government groups, and especially anti-immigrant groups. Jensen went on to say, 'These individuals might be lone actors, but they're not lonely actors.'" Jake took another sip of coffee.

"Seriously bad shit," Brian said.

Jake opened up a document on his computer. "I'm pulling together a lecture on risks to grid components from this sort of sociopathy."

Brian drained his mug and got up to put it in the sink.

"Here's another person, Susan Corke, intelligence project director at the Southern Poverty Law Center, who said when a shooter or someone takes violent action, while they may act on their own, she doesn't really think of them as solo actors. Yeah, then here's her other quote, 'People do not 'self-radicalize'—they exist within social and political structures that perpetuate these ideas, often through deliberate disinformation and active recruitment from groups espousing hateful ideologies.'"

They were both quiet for a moment.

"What's been done so far to harden the substations?" Brian asked.

"What PG&E figured out is to put up higher fencing that's opaque enough that targets cannot be visualized, put some of their video monitors facing outward and monitored around the clock, add lighting that can't be knocked out easily, and set up masonry or concrete walls protecting the most critical equipment. Designing in redundancy of the broader system is pretty obvious, so a damaged substation, whether transmission or local distribution type, can be bypassed temporarily without loss of service."

"You know, Jake, you might think of some sort of off-campus project for your seminar students to practice making an assessment of electrical infrastructure."

"Damn, Bri, you might be onto something—sounds like a great idea. I'll mull that over for a bit."

"Rachel said to tell you it was our turn to have you two and the babykin over for dinner at our place, maybe sometime this weekend?"

Jake smiled. "I'll have my people get ahold of your people and we'll see what we can work out."

EIGHT

Carriage House

The ornament of a house is the friends who frequent it. —Ralph Waldo Emerson

Friendship is always a sweet responsibility, never an opportunity. —Kahlil Gibran

When came the knock at the door of the second-floor apartment over the garage, Brian yelled out, "Come on in, guys, you're right on time." When he saw what they were carrying, he added, "Which is pretty impressive considering all the gear required to move one small baby around." Brian was wearing a black T-shirt with a picture of a glass of water, and a checklist of an optimist who says the glass is half full, a pessimist who says the glass is half empty, and an engineer who says the glass is biphasically replete with air and water.

For obvious reasons, everybody typically ignored his engineering humor. Jake and Abbey had actually arrived with a pretty efficient kit and caboodle. The baby carrier separated from the rest of the car seat and a diaper bag with all the fixings, and they were pretty much good to go.

Rachel came forward to hug Abbey and the baby simultaneously. "Look at the sweater on this kid, with a baby dragon. I love it. And the little matching hat." She tickled under the infant's chin.

"Hope may be a little cranky," Jake said. "She had her first vaccines this morning at the two-month visit. The same family practice doc who took care of her in the hospital."

"Actually, Jake," Abbey said, "remember, her first vaccine was for hepatitis B the day she was born, but today was the start of the early series of vaccines at two, four, and six months. So this little tyke got injections for rotavirus, diphtheria, pertussis—which is whooping cough—really the whole nine yards. She has several little round Band-Aids on both thighs, so just hold her gently. Don't worry though, kids are tough."

"That seems like a lot of shots all at one time for a baby only two months of age—" Brian started to say.

Abbey was not exactly appropriately patient. "Brian, we give shots at two months of age because these diseases can all occur in the first year of life. Therefore I gladly held my baby in my lap while they turned her thighs into pin cushions, and she cried . . . a lot . . . and then I breastfed her and I will be confident that her chances of survival in the first year—and life-long—have just been significantly improved."

Jake thought, *Hopie may not be happy tonight but she'll have no memory of this. With any luck.*

"We're gonna be sympathetic for all three of you guys, that's all I wanna say," Rachel said.

Hope was handed off to her while Jake and Abbey took off their rain gear. There was only a bit of light rain trailing off after three days of absolutely drenching downpour, product of a tropical storm that had started in the Caribbean the week before. It had warmed up a bit the last day, so the humidity was wicked.

"Heard there was some flooding in the capital," said Brian.

"Yeah," said Jake, "about a dozen roads closed, flight delays at Ronald Reagan airport, the usual. Becoming all too frequent, in fact."

Rachel cooed with the baby as she sat down on the couch with her.

Jake noticed how tender she was with the infant, opening the top two snaps on the onesie. "Brian, we brought a salad, some spring red cabbage with all the ingredients. Also have some dressing and croutons, but haven't added them yet. What have you got going?" he asked, as he placed the salad in the middle of the table set for four.

"On the stove is a special treat called Brunswick Stew. Virginians claim this as their very own invention, but apparently North Carolineans and Georgians debate that point. The only part of the story the three states agree on is that the original meat used was smoked squirrel."

Rachel glanced up from the baby. "I'm here to reassure you no squirrels were sacrificed in the preparation of this dish."

"She's right," Brian said, "instead I used chicken, smoked chicken, plus some salt pork. Also chunks of tomatoes, beans, and corn. And some okra, to adhere to the history of this concoction, as well as a liberal amount of barbecue sauce. If you believe the history, this was invented in 1828 by a Black chef named Jimmy Matthews, who was hired to cook for a squirrel-hunting party in Brunswick. Virginians used to call it Brunswick ambrosia."

"Well, the aroma is heavenly," Abbey said.

"I've not made it before, but the recipe says it has a distinctly smoky taste, which I'm looking forward to trying out," he responded, as he looked over at her smile.

"Oh, also a side dish of broccoli with melted cheese," Brian added, looking back. "Altogether, must be at least a dozen food groups in this. Let me go ahead and cut up some bread to dunk in the ambrosia," he finished up, as he pulled out a cutting board.

"And what kind of bread is this?" Jake asked.

"It's called honey buttermilk bread. Set it up this morning so it'd have time to rise. Helps me use two very common ingredients in almost everybody's kitchen."

Nodding, Jake said, "Assuming most of you might want to try some wine, I brought along some cabernet."

"Just three glasses," called out Abbey.

Brian couldn't resist. "Abbey, do you seriously think you should drink that much wine?"

She sighed, "I wish, but I know you're kidding, I'm just suggesting you only get out three glasses for those of you who get to imbibe. I never drink that much anyway." Hope began to whimper a little, even rooting on the edge of the onesie. The two women looked at each other, probably communicating without words.

Rachel handed off the infant. "Now, now, little one. Please don't cry, momma's got ya now."

Abbey draped a blanket over her left shoulder, then undid three buttons on her blouse and opened the nursing bra. Jake appreciated that Brian was studiously not looking in their direction, but Rachel apparently was fascinated by the whole process.

"Okay, kiddo," Abbey said calmly, the baby now mostly covered by the blanket, "here you go, that's the way," and the infant got down to business. Noisily.

She's been so fussy today she'll probably sleep soundly when she finished, thought Jake.

The other three lined up in the kitchen and ladled out bowls of the stew, returning to the table to fill up smaller dishes with salad. A platter of bread was set on the table, with butter nestled next to it.

Rachel made an observation. "Looks like Hope gets to eat first but Abbey last. Oh, well," she joked, raising her eyebrows.

"It's not like we're gonna wait," Jake laughed. "Hang on a second, why don't I butter up a piece of bread for you, Abbey, I know you're hungry," he said, and she happily agreed.

"Women multitask better than men," Rachel offered up, and nobody demurred. "Jake, you'd be interested in this. Bri and I were talking about an article I pulled up this morning from a year or two ago.[3] You know my interest in Chinese shipping, we've talked before about the fact China has built some icebreakers, several nuclear-powered, even though they have no shoreline north of about the forty-third parallel. It turns out the Chinese have also spent a couple of decades building up their coast guard."

"That sounds related to their interest in icebreakers and the Arctic, does it not?" Jake said.

"Which is exactly what I said this morning," Brian commented.

"But these upgraded coast guard boats are fitted out with seventy-six-millimeter cannons and anti-ship missiles, and are longer than US Navy destroyers. This article says the Defense Department reports eighty-five of China's coast guard vessels carry anti-ship cruise missiles.

"They also have helicopter pads, crushing water cannons, and guns about the same caliber as what you see on our M1 Abrams tanks. Instead of the battleship-gray color, the hulls are painted bright white, with, get this, 'China Coast Guard'—written in English—on the sides.[4]

"Great propaganda value when and if there is a collision or active naval battle. Not just the Chinese, but the world would see us as an aggressor against mere coast guard vessels."

"Sadly," Rachel said, "this armament upgrade upends a two-hundred-year tradition where the world's coast guards helped out all ships in distress, regardless of the flag a vessel might be carrying. Respected by all." Her grimace was obvious.

Brian asked as an aside, "So, how's the stew?"

Jake lifted his spoon. "Most excellent my friend, has the smoky barbecue taste you promised. Well done." He dipped his first slice of bread in the broth and tasted it. "Sweet bread, mixes well with the stew." He could see from their expressions Rachel and Brian were pleased.

Rachel resumed. "Japan plans to upgrade its coast guard and incorporate it into the Ministry of Defense. In similar fashion Taiwan is hardening its coast guard and crafting defense plans for breaking any future blockades. After a near collision between one of China's large cutters and a smaller Philippine patrol boat, we've promised to give them six new and upgraded patrol vessels."

"How many Coast Guard boats do we have?" Abbey asked.

"Some 260 in multiple categories, like national security cutters, high endurance cutters, medium endurance cutters—"

Abbey almost raised her hand. "And a cutter is what exactly?'

"A cutter is any vessel sixty-five feet in length or greater. Lots of other types, construction tenders, buoy tenders, harbor tugs, and more. I had an uncle who was in the Coast Guard and he loved it. Grew up in Michigan and spent a lot of time on the lake."

Abbey asked which lake and was told Lake Michigan of course.

"The same article quoted a guy named John Bradford, a retired US Navy commander and senior fellow in the Maritime Security Program in Singapore. He says a lot of countries in the area are starting to use their coast guards to 'assert sovereignty.' Also asks, when a coast guard vessel gets missiles on it, how is it different from a navy vessel except for the color of the paint on the hull?"

"Good point. Clearly this remains a focus of your international studies. Tell me again what you plan to do with this degree," Jake said.

"Personally, I think it would be a good fit for a congressional staff position. I certainly wanna stay in Washington, and I love policy. Might combine that with some teaching. But there's something else that grabbed my interest. There is a research unit in the State Department that no one has ever heard of called the Bureau of Intelligence and Research, or BNR, which is sort of an American diplomats' in-house intelligence agency. This was before our time, but in 1961 these guys warned that South Vietnam's battle against the North and the Viet Cong insurgency was blundering badly, and would ultimately flounder because the Viet Cong had the support of villagers in the South. This was even before the Geneva Accords of 1964. And then in 2002, the CIA, the Defense Intelligence Agency, and the rest of the intelligence community concluded Saddam Hussein was still trying to build nuclear weapons and was cooperating with Osama bin Laden, when we all know now both claims were cynical pretexts and complete bullpucky. With my special interest in coast guards, I figured they might be interested in what I have to say. So I submitted an application, though I haven't heard anything back yet. We'll just have to wait and see."

"Okay, Jake, Hope's finished," said Abbey as she stood up. "Now, how about if you take over so I can get a bit of what you say is an excellent repast." She handed off to Jake first the blanket, then the child. He put the blanket over his shoulder and cradled Hope in his left arm.

Jake murmured to Hope, "Hush little baby, don't you cry." He patted her back as he walked out of the room. When he got to the bathroom, he muttered to himself, *Coulda warned me about the full diaper.* But he removed the diaper carefully and dipped it into the toilet bowl several times, wrung it out, and set it aside to go into a repurposed plastic bag. He cleaned up the little munchkin, put on a dry diaper and plastic diaper cover as she wiggled on the floor, and snapped the bottom of the onesie. Finally, he washed his hands thoroughly, remembering someone had said kids go through some six thousand diapers by about two and a half years of age. *Well, one down. Nobody gets a medal for doing this.*

"I hear what you're saying about coast guards, Rachel, but I'm concerned about something more prosaic: mosquitoes," Abbey said meanwhile. She filled up her big bowl with the stew and decided to worry about the salad later. "*Aedes* mosquitoes, to be more specific, with the expansion to the Americas of *A. aegypti* from Africa and *A. albopictus* from Asia. Both of these darlings are expanding their range worldwide, and have definitely reached this part of the Northeast. What I worry about is the diseases they may carry, viruses like dengue and zika virus. If they weren't so dangerous, you might think they were beautiful. Adult *Aedes* mosquitoes have a narrow body, and alternating light and dark bands on the legs. It's been said they look like they're dressed up in Lycra tights for gymnastics." She spooned in more of the stew.

"Any other novel infections keep you up at night?" Brian asked.

"Hmm, interesting you should ask. In 2016, Uganda's Ministry of Health began testing for a subset of diseases that can cause hemorrhagic fevers, using rapid assays for Marburg virus, Ebola virus, Rift Valley fever, and Crimean-Congo hemorrhagic fever. But that would be ludicrous for us, because aside from the last one on the list, North America has never reported a case."

Rachel asked, "Honey, that CCHF virus was the one you were exposed to, doesn't that just give you the shivers anytime you run into one of these patients?"

Abbey shook her head. "Actually, no, for two reasons. First, I'm not pregnant now, so CCHF would likely be a lot less serious. Second, the public health community has done a lot of outreach with the drug-using population around here, and the prevalence of infection has plummeted almost to zero. But we plan to stay vigilant."

"Are you still being tested for that?" Rachel asked.

"Not like before, with PCR. But once we calculate the antibodies in the cocktail that I received in the hospital have all been metabolized, having perhaps accomplished their protective job, I will get testing several times a year, to see if possibly I experienced asymptomatic infection and have my own antibodies or T lymphocytes that have been elicited by actual infection . . . the implications would be twofold.

"First, it would mean the passive antibody cocktail I received actually protected me from disease, from symptoms. And second, I would likely have persisting immunity to CCHF." Another spoonful. "This is wonderful stuff, Brian. Let me try the bread, too.

"Oh, and let's talk about how wonderful Mina has turned out to be. Hope definitely recognizes her as one of her caretakers now. And she has proven adept at feeding her my pumped breast milk, or a bit of applesauce. She sings to her, and plays guitar, it's all very touching."

"Mina also seems very comfortable interacting with our guests," Jake said. If they're downstairs finishing off breakfast, or just sitting in the parlor, Mina is happy to bring along the kiddo to listen to the conversation.

"People love babies, but she wouldn't let them hold Hope even if they asked, which they don't . . . perhaps because they sense a nanny should be more protective than even a parent. And if Hope is sleeping, then to study, Mina sometimes uses the desk in the parlor or the table in the kitchen, wherever she is less likely to intrude on guests. You're not going to believe this," he said, laughing, "she started her class in baby sign language, and practices on our daughter."

Brian started to speak up but Jake headed him off, saying he had not learned any of it, but it looked pretty intuitive, just saying something like "Want a bite?" and miming a motion at the same time, like pointing a finger at her own mouth.

"Cute," Abbey said, "but I don't want my daughter growing up to be a mime." She turned to face Brian. "Speaking of which, what're you gonna do when you grow up? And tell me again what mechanical engineering is exactly, I'm a little hazy on the details."

Brian leaned back in his chair. "It's one of the oldest and broadest of the engineering branches, overlapping only a bit with electrical engineering. People usually trace this back to the start of the Industrial Revolution in Europe in the eighteenth century, but really it goes back several thousand years. The six classical simple machines were known in the ancient Near East: the wedge, inclined plane, wheel, and so on.

"Modern mechanical engineering combines principles of physics and mathematics with materials science. Core areas include such things as classical mechanics, thermodynamics, and structural analysis. We use tools like computer-aided design or CAD, and computer-aided manufacturing or CAM, to analyze and design industrial equipment, heating and cooling systems, aircraft, watercraft, robotics. Even medical devices, you'll be glad to hear. Conversely, weapons systems, which I have no interest in personally."

"But Brian, what I'd like to hear more about is what you yourself plan on doing," Abbey said.

He nodded. "I've been applying to companies in the greater DC area and already have some tentative feelers. Scanogen is a startup company working on a nucleic acid detection platform. The Richmond Group USA works on mechanical, electrical, and piping projects. The one Rachel thinks I should seriously consider is with the US Architect of the Capitol. Their emphasis is on various complicated engineering projects, most importantly the mechanical infrastructure systems in the power plant and utility distribution system.

"Get this, it's responsible for providing steam and chilled water from the central power plant to the Government Printing Office, Union Station, Library of Congress, and the Capitol Campus, which comprises House and Senate Office Buildings, the Capitol Building, the Capitol Visitor Center, US Botanic Garden, and the Supreme Court."

"Sounds like you'd be in great company, whaddya you think about it?" Abbey asked.

"I have the usual problem of lack of work experience, not to mention certification as a professional engineer, which doesn't happen immediately upon graduation. For example, the lack of a PE certificate is an immediate roadblock for the capitol architect position, at least for now."

Abbey looked from Rachel to Brian and back. "It seems to me you are both looking for work in the same city. This wouldn't be a coincidence, would it?" Abbey asked, raising and waggling both eyebrows. She looked back at Rachel, whom Jake thought appeared to be starting to blush.

Abbey mused out loud. "You know, this reminds me of one of my favorite movies. Who doesn't love a rom-com. In it a Brit, Sam Claflin, plays English writer Henry, and a Spaniard, Verónica Echegui, plays Mexican writer Maria. They start off with a fiery relationship because of their conflicts about writing. Somehow, they remind me of—"

Brian and Rachel started off at the same moment, "We don't—" and everybody laughed.

"Anyway, what's the name of the movie?" asked Rachel, looking at Brian and clearly trying not to smile.

"*The Book of Love*," Abbey said tenderly, "came out a couple of years ago, 2022 I think." There was a pause. "Perhaps you two should see it together. It is very romantic."

Jake could see the couple was looking at each other intently.

Brian did something he had never done before in his life. In front of everybody, he surprised himself by saying to all, "I do love this woman and I can't imagine us apart."

Rachel stood up and strode straight to Brian, hugging him tightly.

"Ah, Americans do love their happy endings," Abbey whispered, obviously more to herself than the room at large.

NINE

Rifting Behavior

Many are those around the world who are ill or dying without any certainty about the malady afflicting them—typically they lack means or access to expert care and existing diagnostic tests.
—Anonymous

J ared on awakening was about to experience not one but the first of two headaches in a day and a night. And he almost never got headaches. His wife had frequent migraines often linked to her periods, but he was blissfully inexperienced personally with this sort of assault.

His first vexation as he woke from a restless night was the painful recollection that two of the goats on Lazy Acres had miscarried in the last week, both times losing twins. Benjamin, the veterinarian, had come out each time to check on the livestock, but could not be particularly reassuring. Jared kneaded both sides of his forehead in frustration and then rolled out of bed quietly, so as to not wake Jacey.

The first case two weeks ago had been a Boer mother, and these meat goats were normally robustly healthy. The second, though, was a cashmere goat, raised for fiber, and instead of beginning to recover like the Boer, she became seriously ill and could not stand without support, so the vet had transferred her to his hospital the night before. She was on IV support and receiving a combination of empiric antibiotics but unhappily not looking good. Jared had been over to the veterinary hospital yesterday to visit, but Jacey and the kids had stayed home. The household was quiet and morose.

Benjamin Harris collected multiple samples from the hospitalized goat, including its afterbirth, and gathered specimens from the pasteurization equipment as well. He had notified the health department and sent off samples to the state lab. The tests for brucellosis and listeriosis and other diseases common in goats were negative or still pending. He was laudatory about the cleanliness of the equipment they used for processing goat milk, and appreciated the notebook with typed instructions for pasteurization and records of all the milk they sold.

"Elliot," Benjamin had told him, "your milk goats, the Nubians, all appear healthy, but you know you cannot consume or sell any goat milk products until things get sorted." He shook his head. "You can glove carefully and milk them—but discard all the milk underground, away from your pond—otherwise their udders may go dry. And wash your hands really carefully afterward."

"Any risk to the kids, or us?" Jared's voice was a little tight. *We can get through this but I gotta keep everybody safe.*

"We'll know a lot more in a couple of days. Keep me up to date on how the rest of the herd is doing. I'll call you in the morning." They didn't shake hands, but Benjamin clapped him on the back. "Probably a good idea to keep your farm clothes out in the barn, including your boots. Hang in there."

***

Jared felt a little dizzy when he stepped out of the shower that evening, almost slipped on the wet floor, and caught himself with both hands on the edge of the sink. Suddenly he felt a bit nauseated, so he leaned over the sink for a minute until that passed. *Can't brush teeth right now, without upchucking.* He began to shiver as he toweled off, and knew he had to get into bed. He kept one hand on the wall as he walked down the hallway, then called out to Jacey once he made it to the bedroom.

"Jared, what's the matter with you? Let me get this light on," she said, and saw at once something was wrong. He was shivering and pale. Even his lips were blanched.

"I'm . . . I feel like someone shoved me under a bus. I just took a hot shower but now I feel cold and shivery. My whole head is throbbing, and you know I don't get headaches. Really, my muscles ache all over, even my joints . . ."

"It's not flu season, honey. I haven't heard you cough. Is your nose stuffy? You know you get allergies in the spring, but it can't be that anyway. Let me check your temperature." She put the back of her hand on his forehead and knew at once he was warm. "I need an actual thermometer, let me just grab it."

She was back in a minute, her face still drawn. "Okay, I got you some aspirin, but first let me check your temperature." She ran the device over his forehead. "101.5 degrees, Jared. Better take these aspirins." She handed him the glass of water.

When she helped him to sit up to drink, he grimaced as he came off the pillow. "My neck muscles must be stiff, too," he moaned softly.

"Better get me a spit-up pan, just in case. Damn, this came on fast . . ."

"I'm going to call Benjamin to ask him if he thinks this might be related to the goats." She brought the bowl first, and told the kids something was going on with their father and that they should keep it quiet.

When she returned, she said, "Dr. Harris said he doesn't know for sure if this is related to the animals, to try and get some rest, push fluids, and to keep you under observation. If it gets worse though, he said to take you to the university hospital, as a tenable case can be made this is something you picked up from the goats."

Jared nodded weakly, not wanting to lift his head from the pillow again. He just mouthed okay, breathing rapidly and shallowly, and closed his eyes.

They both woke at 2:00 a.m., because the sheets on his side were sodden. Jacey had to change the top and bottom sheets, as they were drenched. Acetaminophen and ibuprofen this time, but when it happened again at 4:00 a.m., she knew she had to take him in. She called Shelly next door, asking if she could please send her older daughter Nancy to come over and sleep on the couch. The kids upstairs slept through everything, that wonderful knack young children have.

In only minutes Nancy arrived, sleepy-eyed and wrapped in a light coat. Jacey had set out some sheets and a blanket and a pillow on the couch.

"Nancy, Jared is sick enough I need to take him to the hospital at George Washington. I don't know when I'll be back. We have each other's phone numbers, but I don't think I'll call you until after sunrise, so just try and get some sleep and be here for the kids when they wake up. Thank you so much for doing this—"

"I just hope he gets better fast. Drive carefully." She hugged Jacey, who squeezed her back tightly, then went out the door to join Jared in the car. He was in pajamas and a robe and wrapped in a comforter.

Now his teeth were chattering and his whole body was shaking uncontrollably with rigors.

Jacey drove as fast as she dared.

TEN

Haboob

Cowboys don't take a bath, they just dust off. —A plainsman

A horse ain't being polite when he comes to a fence and lets you go over first. —A plainsman

Lockhart had been skeleton-dry for weeks, every day the sun hot as a blister, and now the whole region was blanketed in a suffocating layer of dust that had been kicked around by three days of winds faster than a horse could gallop full out. "These are the kinds of winds that you see with tropical storms or hurricanes," said Harrison Sincavage, a forecaster with the weather service.[5] "But rather than have all the rain, everything is dusty and brown, and occasionally on fire."

While there were no wildfires this week, there was a red flag warning and a high wind advisory. And visibility and air-quality warnings to boot. When at first the dust began moving, the sunrises and sunsets were picturesque, but the intense, gritty sandstorm evolved into a "haboob," dropping a bronze filter over creation and turning the indigo sky a dark beige.

Buck came in cursing, pulling the neckerchief down off his mouth and nose. "Damn dust gets into everything—" He stopped to sneeze explosively several times. He stomped his feet and beat off his hat, which didn't help anything or nobody.

"Buck, just shed your coat and boots by the door, I realize you can't help bringing in a load of dust, it's just the season of dust storms," Elliot said.

CLOUD DRAGON · 53

Matt, wearing his baseball cap indoors as usual, heard the resignation in his voice. "We had it worse in Afghanistan, boys, both the heat and the dust. Just keep it out of your nose and weapons as best you can.

"Speaking of which, Buck, I see you brought your long gun carefully wrapped up. Elliot and I were just about getting ready to set up in his garage for assembling the silencers. But sit down a spell and let's talk."

"I made you a sandwich, Buck," Elliot said, "tuna on white bread, the way you like it."

"Mayonnaise, pepper, and celery?"

"Just the way Mom used to make it. But you'd better wash off your face and hands before ya dig in, you are a rare sight right now."

"If you closed your eyes and held still, we might think you wus a dust-blasted prickly pear cactus. Though not a very big one," Matt said. Elliot grinned at his brother, but Matt sounded stone-cold serious.

Buck apparently felt that was beneath him, not worthy of comment, and headed for the bathroom. After finishing his washup, he came back out with the sandwich on a plate and a beer in his hand, sitting down across from both of them.

When there was a dust storm this bad, they usually brought the patio furniture inside for safekeeping, and threw a sheet over the couch and another one over the TV.

Matt scratched his stubble and started off slowly. "Getting the weapons ready is only the first part. We gotta plan and prepare ourselves for this whole expedition. All the little pieces need to fit together. The three pairs of Idaho license plates, for example, were not easy to get. I had a guy I know who could get them for me, basically discarded in that state after ten years, following which the government makes you get a new one.

"The hard part was Elliot going online and getting a good description of the stickers on the rear license plate. You get them when you renew the registration every one or two years, whichever you choose. They're hard to copy, but if you know the colors you can get contact paper that's the same. Whatever you use has to be *real* sticky.

"In Idaho the stickers cycle between red, white, and blue, and it's white this year."

"Goldang, yes, Idaho is white this year and every year, gotta admire those guys," Buck said.

"And that's why I had some contacts up in the Gem State. Here's something you guys probably didn't know, Sarah Palin was born there, not in Alaska."

Elliot leaned forward. "So, where exactly was she born?" he asked.

"Sandpoint, for what that's worth, which is not much. But she had nothing to do with the people that I know," Matt said.

"You wish, Matt," Buck said. "Remember MILF? Mothers I'd like to fuck?"

"All too well, all too well."

"Kind of flamed out though, didn't she?" Elliot said, to general agreement.

"Anyway, we should be getting a package in the mail soon from Idaho, a town called Post Falls."

Buck rubbed his ankle with the other foot. "How are we gonna mount these fake licenses over our Texas plates?"

Matt snorted. "They're gonna send the same number of license plate mounts, the metal or plastic border, which don't identify any specific town.

"Then we attach a coupla hooks on the top, one clip on each side. It's only going to be used when we're headed for our targets on the Fourth. When we reconnoiter a few days ahead of time, we'll have just our existing legal Texas plates. I want the Idaho plates to be easy to clip on and unclip, front and back."

Elliot was shaking his head. "They won't stand up to close scrutiny if we get pulled over by a cop."

Matt scowled at him. "We'll put them on only a few miles before the target, then remove them once we move away the same distance. But that evening as we skedaddle out of town, we'll ditch them a longways down the road. An old license plate along a highway don't raise no suspicion from nobody. Better yet, wait 'til we find some body of water. Even if the cameras mounted around the target pick up the license, it won't do them any good. But they'll sure as hell know what our trucks look like, so we'll keep moving, as much as possible on back roads, always at the speed limit, boys.

"And I'm talking to you, Buck, hotshot."

"You can shove that where the sun don't shine, Matt," said Buck, as he slouched down further in his chair.

Elliot said, "Calm down, brother, why don't we get started on mounting the silencers."

It took them a good chunk of the afternoon. All three had mechanical skills, but Elliot was the one with experience in precision work. He patiently set up the first rifle in the vise, then began the task.

"Okay, guys, here is how this works. The most common way to mount what we call a sound suppressor or a moderator or a silencer or a 'can' on a gun is a direct thread mount. And the most important thing is to get the barrel and this device absolutely centered and parallel."

"Which is what we're gonna do, right?" Buck said.

Elliot nodded. "Yeah, first I'm gonna clean up the run of threads on the end of the barrel, using this metal brush. And here is the tap and die I mentioned for the next step to make sure everything's clean."

Matt was looking at the instructions from the kit. "It doesn't say here anything about whether to insert your special rod in the barrel if you're running the die along the threads."

"Think about it, Matt, the internal diameter of the die is wider than the barrel bore, so that's probably why they don't say anything."

"Yeah, man, makes sense," Buck said.

"I'm also reading that since the National Firearms Act was signed into law in 1934, suppressors have been regulated. But not impossible to own, which is good for us," Matt said. "Course, our whole idea is we sure as hell don't want the ATF to know about us . . . Hey, wait, get a load of this, the official name for these guys is the Bureau of Alcohol, Tobacco, Firearms, and Explosives. Shoulda been the ATFE, seems to me."

"Damn, all this time I thought the first letter stood for general asshol-ery," Buck said, then laughed at his own joke, leaned forward to dribble tobacco juice into a soda can, and wiped his mouth with his dusty sleeve. "And maybe the last letter means enemies. Or extreme."

Elliot kept gently tapping the rubber mallet to move the die down the end of the barrel, about an eighth of a turn or less with each strike. "Okay, when this is done, then we need to know the exact distance the suppressor needs to cover the end of the barrel, no more, no less."

Watching intently, Matt nodded, appreciating the precision which El-liot brought to the task. "Remember, the kit comes with a set of washers of different thicknesses, so we can seat the suppressor tightly against the shoulder. Finger tight, then using a wrench, that's the last step."

Elliot responded, "Using eye protection is gonna be especially im-portant when we start using these. We'd better start some nighttime practice, not with infrared goggles but rather with low light from a fire or a lamp set out there near our targets."

"You boys are going to practice assembling the whole kit in the dark," Matt muttered, "or with blindfolds, just the way I taught my guys in train-ing. Gotta be quiet and quick at the same time. Then adjust to prone and seated shooting positions, with a gun rest up front."

"Okay, this is the Geissele rod, I'll pass it around but don't drop it. It's finely machined and I wanna keep it that way." Elliot handed it to his kid brother first, who rubbed his fingers along it and then passed it on to Matt.

Within minutes Elliot had used his micrometer to determine the span of the threads committed to the suppressor, with the residual requiring washers. "I'm gonna need 3.2 millimeters of washers, Matt, so hand those to me." Once the washers were in place, he inserted the rod, then rotated the suppressor over it, seating it with a wrench for the last fractional turn. Then he pulled out the guide rod, with only a trace of gun oil on it. He set it aside on a clean white cloth, avoiding the adjacent dust.

"I did my rifle first, because it's bolt-action so I can open the firing chamber and get some light in there." He looked down the whole length and whistled. "Ain't that purty. Have a look."

Buck was first. "Damn, Elliot, that looks real clean, I can see rifling in the bore of the barrel and the cutouts in the suppressor. I gotta say it looks just about perfect."

Matt was next. He stood back up and said with a satisfied smile, "We'll get to the acid test of trying these out on our range in daylight, but not until the dust settles down. Don't know when that will be, maybe another couple of days at least. The weather forecast is not looking good. Okay, now let's start on Buck's gun next."

Matt said he had places to go and people to see when Elliot was finishing up on his weapon. But he was surprised by what he heard next.

He saw Buck was leaning forward with his elbows on his knees. "I've been thinking about this for a while, so I gotta say something. I know we can do this, we can pull this off, but if I get caught—I'm not gonna go quietly."

There was silence for a couple of seconds, then Matt spoke up. "Buck, you better think this through better. We are going after hardened targets, not people. We are going to create some serious disruption and send a message. We are not going to shoot anybody, not military, not police, not civilians. Nobody. I kinda understand you might want to resist arrest physically, but not with a weapon." He stared at Buck. "Do you hear me?"

Buck wouldn't look up, so Elliot spoke. "Listen, brother, use your head. I know you're thinking about the people arrested and tried after January 6. I know you're thinking that they all got released by our MAGA man, so that's why you don't want to resist getting arrested, because shit, he'll just let you go anyway. And remember those outlaws were not maimed, not dead."

Buck looked up, his lips thin, his face pale. "I can't go to prison. Just being in jail a coupla days is bad enough. The hell with it."

Matt crossed his arms. "Maybe you're missing an obvious point. Eventually enough Republicans get elected—including in the White House—and everybody's gonna get a full pardon, as long as they didn't hurt nobody.

"Next time we get together I'm gonna talk about how not to give up information to the cops. Which would give enough time for the other two of us to get away. Not to Texas, I've got a better idea. But next time, not now.

"So, Buck, don't start thinking about pulling the pin on a grenade if you get into a tight situation. Okay? Okay?"

Buck said nothing.

ELEVEN

Puzzle Palace

The world is full of obvious things which nobody by any chance ever observes.
—Sir Arthur Conan Doyle

The true mystery of the world is the visible, not the invisible. —Oscar Wilde

The rain had been coming down all night long, rivulets racing down the windows of George Washington Medical Center, puddles pooling in the parking lots, people playing hopscotch trying to keep their shoes dry.

It had been a long shift, with two calls for admission from the ER coming after midnight for Andrew Wyatt, a second-year resident. Just before nine o'clock in the morning, he found a chair in the lecture room on the third floor of the med center moments before the resident report was about to start, and continued scribbling notes. Andrew had black curly hair and a strong Afrikaans accent and had attended the University of Cape Town as an undergraduate, so he knew he sometimes carried a chip on his shoulder. His academic credentials were actually superb, having attended med school at Johns Hopkins.

Stacey Armstrong, the chief resident, was known both for her promptitude and her commanding-heights presence. She wore her hair in a tight bun in back, and carried her stethoscope in the pocket of her long white coat rather than around her neck, a distinct sign of authority, thought Andrew. Rumor had it no one had ever seen her smile.

Gregory Pickering, another second-year resident, had just presented a case of pneumonia, but apparently Stacey questioned his choice of empiric antibiotic for community-acquired infection.

"This is a middle-aged pack-a-day smoker, otherwise previously healthy female with infiltrates in both lungs. You tell me the gramstain on her sputum showed mixed gram-positive cocci and small gram-negative rods. No lymph nodes in the center of the chest. No fluid outside the lungs. What was your thinking at that point?"

"The gram-positive organism would most likely be pneumococcus, and the gram-negative bug *H. influenzae.*"

"So, you are assuming she has COPD? Chronic obstructive lung disease at the age of thirty-eight? Any other possibilities? Did you do an acid-fast smear on the sputum for tuberculosis, considering the possibility of typical or atypical mycobacteria?"

"No, I did not. She had no personal or family history of tuberculosis, no weight loss or night sweats, just an acute presentation."

"Okay, I'll buy that. But why vancomycin and chloramphenicol for antibiotics? Vanco would clearly be indicated if she had staph, or bloodstream infection, but with community acquisition, using more narrowly focused antibiotics would make sense, would it not?"

"Yes, but—"

"And chloramphenicol? Why choose anaerobic coverage? You are probably right that she has the typical organisms seen in COPD. So why use expensive broad-spectrum antibiotics unnecessarily? Did she seem sick enough to justify blood cultures?"

"She did not."

"Might she have interstitial lung disease like sarcoidosis, autoimmune disease like Goodpasture syndrome, or blood vessel disease like multiple pulmonary emboli? The point I'm making is—don't make the mistake of narrowing down your differential diagnosis too early."

Dr. Armstrong paused, looking at him. "We hear the constant refrain that American medicine is extravagant and overpriced, that we spend twice as much per capita on health care as any other industrialized nation. So I would suggest a skin test for TB. And next time simplify with something like amoxicillin coupled with clavulanic acid for initial coverage. And always keep thinking about those other possibilities.

"Next case, please. Andrew, you were also on call last night. What do you have for us?"

Andrew sat up straighter and cleared his throat. "Jared Cooper is a thirty-seven-year-old white male retired from a New York City hedge fund and living in Virginia with his family on a farm. His wife brought him into the ER last night with a five-hour history of diffuse achiness, headache, photophobia, and drenching night sweats, fever to 38.6 degrees Celsius at home, up to 39.4 degrees when he hit the ER. No infectious contacts among his family and friends, no recent travel, no tick or mosquito bites recalled. Only anomaly was that two of his goats suffered miscarriages in the last ten days, and one is apparently close to death at the local veterinary hospital. It almost goes without saying their animals have been suffering from the hot spell we've all been experiencing.

"On exam, Mr. Cooper appeared to be athletically built but acutely ill, prostrate, flushed and sweaty, with neither rash nor petechiae, nor tracks on his upper extremity veins or elsewhere. Minimal conjunctival injection. Throat moderately red, without exudate. Neck was a bit stiff, perhaps marginal nuchal rigidity. No lymph node tenderness or enlargement anywhere—"

"Let me stop you there for a moment," Stacey said. "You actually checked all the superficial lymph nodes? Not just cervical and supraclavicular, but occipital, pre- and postauricular, axillary, epitrochlear, periumbilical, inguinal, popliteal?"

"Yes, ma'am, I did. Nothing remarkable." And feeling a little irked, he continued. "Chest was clear to percussion and auscultation. Heart sounds regular without murmur, click, or rub. Abdomen soft with perhaps diminished bowel sounds and no palpable liver edge or spleen tip. Neurologic exam normal. In particular, extraocular movements and pupillary reactivity normal, though a tad sensitive to light stimulus, more than the usual.

"White cell count elevated at 14.5 with increased lymphocytes and monocytes, not the expected neutrophils if this were a bacterial infection. Hemoglobin and platelets normal. Coagulation parameters normal. Kidney and liver function tests normal.

"Final step was a lumbar puncture. Opening and closing pressures were high end of normal. The spinal fluid appeared clear and colorless, with no xanthochromia. No red cells, but white cells slightly elevated, twelve in number with eleven lymphocytes and one neutrophil."

Stacey looked down and shook her head. "So, definitionally, this is pleocytosis, since a limit of five cells in spinal fluid is regarded as normal. And even a single neutrophil is bothersome."

With a slight frown, Stacey challenged, "Your assessment and plan?

"These cell counts are not that extraordinary, so I would suggest not a meningitis or early meningoencephalitis at this point unless of viral etiology.

"You've not made any case for encephalitis yet; your patient is alert and oriented without any abnormal neurologic signs?"

Feeling chagrined, Andrew slightly shook his head and took a deep breath. "I'm only implying this is so acute a presentation that it might progress in that direction."

Stacey nodded, though she didn't look convinced. "Go on."

"We sent blood and spinal fluid cultures and saved samples for later tests. Because of the possibility of bacterial meningitis with the common pneumococcus or meningococcus, we started him on ceftriaxone as his sole antibiotic, with the plan to withdraw treatment if the spinal fluid gram stains and capsular polysaccharide antigen tests come back negative—and cultures remain negative—for forty-eight hours. I think we'll get our answer from the viral serologies, so I've submitted assays for Eastern encephalitis—"

Armstrong shook her head and crossed her arms. "Most viral meningitides are of lesser consequence, but not all and not always. And most cases are from non-polio enteroviruses like rhinovirus species A–C and enterovirus species A–L, with multiple subtypes. Arboviruses such as

West Nile virus. Mumps and measles viruses, both preventable with MMR vaccine. Influenza viruses can be the culprit in flu season. Herpesviruses, including EBV or Epstein–Barr virus, HSV or herpes simplex viruses, and VZV or varicella-zoster virus. The list is long. Let me throw this out to all of you, what are some other possibilities?"

Andrew, as usual, mentally translated VZV into the causative agent of chickenpox in kids and shingles in adults.

Andrew's friend Phyllis said, "Lymphocytic choriomeningitis virus."

Andrew was pleased to see her receive a nod of approval from Stacey.

"St. Louis, Eastern, and Western encephalitis," said another second-year.

"Okay, now think about this. Why do we even need to know the specific causative agent?" There was a pause as Stacey scanned the small group.

"For purposes of public health . . . epidemiology . . . for surveillance of reportable disease," Andrew said, "or to identify an agent transmissible person-to-person, to communicate risk, if any, to family and other contacts."

"All good points, Andrew," she said, "but there are too many possibilities to not be selective. What can we do to narrow down this list?"

"Seasonality is a factor. We're in May, so past influenza risk," said a third-year resident.

"Pretty much population-wide acceptance of MMR vaccine, though unfortunately resisted by the anti-vaxxers. Should prevent mumps- or measles-associated meningitis," Phyllis said, pushing her blond ponytail off one shoulder.

"What if the patient developed clustered vesicles or larger blisters on his body, especially around the mouth or in the genital area?"

Andrew responded, "Time to think about HSV or VZV and consider initiating treatment with valacyclovir or other anti-herpes therapy."

Stacey paced for several steps back and forth, shaking her head. "Correct, Andrew. What I'm saying is simply we need continued observation to see what other manifestation this guy develops. If his bacterial cultures come back positive, you'll have a diagnosis. If new symptoms and findings crop up, then follow the scent like a bloodhound. If he develops unusual manifestations or gets sicker, consider an infectious disease consult.

"Okay, our time is up. All of you have attending rounds in about five minutes, so gather up your interns and med students and get ready for those more detailed presentations. As you all know, I always like to finish up with an axiom, and today I want to submit one on the public health effects of our changing climate. There are some 375 known infectious diseases in humans, and recently researchers found that more than half, fifty-eight percent, are exacerbated by one or more of the ten types of climate-linked extreme weather. More than half, according to an article from Nature Climate Change.[6] I can get you the reference if you're interested."

Andrew thought to himself, *Means doctors need to stand up in the public square, not just in the hospital and clinics.* As the group dispersed, everyone saw the rain outside was still tropical and torrential. He thought about the mosquitoes greeting folks in the afternoon heat and humidity. Already he'd had to swat at a couple of them this week, and it wasn't even June for a couple of days yet.

Then he set his shoulders and got back to work, heading for rounds with his attending physician.

TWELVE

Unnatural Gas

Let me never fall into the vulgar mistake of dreaming that I am persecuted whenever I am contradicted. —Ralph Waldo Emerson

But then arises the doubt, can the mind of man, which has, as I fully believe been developed from a mind as low as that possessed by the lowest animal, be trusted when it draws such grand conclusions? —Charles Darwin

The atmosphere had been unsettled the last three days, changeable as a chameleon, fleeting wind from any quarter now and again strong enough to bring down small branches and invert the odd brolly or bumbershoot, leaving its owner startled and wet. Intermittent rain kept the first two days sodden, enough to ward off the picklers and tennis players from the courts across the street with all their internecine sarcasm and squabbling.

But today, this day, the dark clouds were as deep as a subsea mountain range, jagged and roiling. Krakens of lightning bolts jumped from peak to peak in the far northeast, but the clap of thunder stomping its feet was still muted by distance, a rumbling deferred by so prolonged an interval that Jake had to count seconds several times following an isolated ribbon of lightning before being confident the storm must be still about four miles away.

This particular Wednesday was unusual in that he didn't have to be at work until the afternoon, so this morning he felt no time pressure to get to the school. Nevertheless, he'd gotten up early as was his usual wont, partly because he was responsible for breakfast for the pair of guests upstairs, partly because he thought he might get a bit of time to catch up on the newspapers to which the Inn subscribed, *The Washington Post* and *The New York Times.*

Abbey had breastfed Hope one last time before getting dressed, then gotten her into her onesie for the morning, a dashing strawberry color, and left her in the carrier, which Jake brought out and set on the far left end of the counter where he could entertain her and wash dishes and prepare food at the same time. He kept an eye on the young tyke but also on the lightning storm rampaging toward them.

He began his prep as he pondered what Abbey had told him about the visitors who arrived yesterday, but then left for a dinner engagement prior to Jake finally making his way home. She had said something about them being fancy dressers.

Karen Hawk was in Mizzenmast, the first room upstairs, and Abbey said she looked to be in her forties, had brown eyes with blond hair probably out of a bottle, hailed by way of Chicago, and was wearing a chestnut-colored pants suit. She was scheduled for some congressional testimony today, representing a natural gas group.

Jake's ears had immediately perked up, as he doggedly pursued every distortion and deception by the oil and gas concerns.

The other player was Agatha Schmidt, in Windlass, the third room upstairs, who Abbey explained had a classic Bostonian accent, looked more to be in her sixties, and arrived later than her cohort. Abbey said the older woman was dressed in a light gray pinstriped power suit, with startling blue eyes, a deeper voice, and elegant hair pulled back in a bun. She also represented natural gas interests and was likewise headed to Congress today to give testimony. They had coordinated their arrival and engaged in quiet palaver for quite a while in the parlor, thick as thieves, before heading out to town.

The middle room, Quarterdeck, had been empty last night. Both Abbey and Jake had fallen asleep before their guests made their way back through the unrelenting storm.

Breakfast this morning had been planned several days ago. Inn policy was to usually serve two hot courses. First up for today was calico scrambled eggs, which started with a quarter cup of two percent milk, dill, and equal amounts of pepper and salt whisked together until blended, then heated in a large saucepan. Bit by bit he added chopped green peppers and tomato and onion, then finished up by mixing in butter and six large eggs. He gently stirred as he continued to talk with Hopie, turning off the heat once no liquid egg remained. He explained to his infant daughter it was called calico because of all the colors in the vegetables, and she burbled in delighted agreement.

Precocious, if not manifesting early signs of genius.

His next recollection was that, since it was almost seven o'clock, Mina should be arriving any moment.

He placed the covered pan in the preheated oven on low heat.

Next up were cornmeal pancakes, another standard at the Inn. He always made up the batter from the instructions right on the box. He was mixing the other components with the cornmeal in a large porcelain bowl when he heard their nanny coming in the back door, happily humming to herself.

Mina sauntered into the kitchen, with a smile and "Hello," going around the island to pick Hope up out of the carrier. "Hello, my darlin'," she said, as Hopie evidently got excited to see her, cooing. Mina did her baby sign for hello, but Jake for the life of him could not see his daughter react any differently, at least not yet.

Time will tell, he thought. *Baby sign language.* He shook his head.

Mina sat with Hopie at the island, talking nonsense to her, while Jake concentrated on setting up two places at the kitchen table, as the dining room was reserved for when they had four or more guests. He decanted the first three puddles of dough into a large skillet on the cooktop, about the same time he heard signs of life from upstairs.

Jake had the next three in the skillet by the time their first guest arrived. "Morning, I'm Jake, and I'll be your cook this morning," he said in a jocular tone.

"And I'm Mina, the nanny, and this little tyke is Hope Aurora Harper, their first child."

"I had a grandmother named Hope, so I've always liked that name," Agatha said, smiling and adding, "She was named Hope since she was the third girl in a row. It must have worked, because after, her two boys arrived one after the other." She poured herself some coffee and added a small bit of cream, but no sugar. "But—Aurora—that's certainly an unusual name," she said, looking at Jake for an explanation.

He proceeded to tell the story of the northern lights that silently flared so memorably in the early morning hours as they headed to the hospital for Hope's birth. "Abbey told me your accent sounded Bostonian, and I have to agree," Jake said, and Agatha said they were in fact correct.

"So, may I ask what's for breakfast?" She turned around at the sound of footsteps on the stairs. "Oh, and good morning, Karen, how are you?" The rain was just starting again outside, a sudden avalanche of sound.

Karen introduced herself. Jake's first impression was that he agreed about blond not being her original color. "You're in Mizzenmast, room one, from what Abbey told me. May I ask how didja sleep?"

"Well, thanks, even with the two-hour time zone difference."

"You two may have gotten in just before the weather changed again. Big lightning storm forecast for today." A crack interrupted his next thought as if in agreement, and the rolling thunder followed much more closely this time. "Oh, as for breakfast, to answer your question, Karen, you can see I'm making some cornmeal pancakes, and in the oven there is a dish we call calico eggs."

"Sounds delightful," Agatha said, and Karen agreed.

"If you two are ready, then have a seat, both of you, and I'll serve you up some of the eggs." He put on an oven mitt and pulled the saucepan out of the oven and set it on the induction cooktop, always a ready hot pad for setting down very warm dishes. He pulled out a large serving spoon, raised his eyebrows in turn to each in question, and ladled out their first portions.

"Smells wonderful," Agatha said, and applied a generous amount of pepper.

Karen voiced agreement and added both salt and pepper to hers.

Jake got out a small platter of slices of cantaloupe from the fridge. "This is almost certainly from Mexico this time of year," he pronounced.

Another crash of thunder, almost simultaneous with the lightning strike, seemingly less than a quarter mile away. Hope started to cry and Mina shushed her, saying, "I think I should take her to the parlor and see if I can calm her down. But first I've got to warm up some of Abbey's breast milk." She got some of this precious nutriment out of the fridge, put it in a small pan of water on a separate site on the cooktop, and pulled out a clean glass bottle and nipple.

They all heard the rain intensifying outside.

Jake thought he might calm the waters a bit. "Abbey and I don't know what we'd do without Mina. She's gotten very adept at taking care of Hope when we're gone or if I'm busy in the office in back. I do a lot of research and lecture prep at home—" But the next strike just down the block deafened and startled them, rattling the windows, and was followed by the sound of a tree shattering and toppling over. "Don't worry, folks . . . fortunately we've got lightning rods up on top."

He had the presence of mind to flip the pancakes before quickly stepping out to the porch to see if he could detect what had happened, but noted nothing obvious. *Better finish their breakfast first, then go have a look.* He came back in time to turn the pancakes one more time, pulled the platter out of the oven as he turned it off, combined the new with the old, and placed them on the table.

"For the pancakes, you have a choice between yogurt or syrup or molasses. If you need anything else I can always whip up some oatmeal, with either raisins or brown sugar—" Another flash lit up the window, not as close or as loud this time. "And we have oat milk or old-fashioned cow's milk to go with a cereal of your choice as an alternative."

"Jake, thanks, but this looks scrumptious and more than enough. I must ask though, how often do you get thunderstorms like this?" Karen said, as she dug into her calico concoction.

He wrinkled his forehead and paused. "I'm always leery of subjective assessments, but it seems to me they're coming more often. I'm afraid I might be biased because of all the climate information I read. Heat-trapping makes the air warmer, which allows it to hold more moisture, and both these factors boost the chance of thunderstorms. I was just working some statistics into a lecture I'm prepping slides for, as my area of expertise is electrical engineering and the grid is clearly vulnerable to damage and outages from lightning. There are something like twenty-five million individual lightning strikes per year in the lower forty-eight states. A major study from 2014 estimated that each additional degree Celsius of warming causes about twelve percent more lightning, which suggests we may be looking at an increase by half by the end of the century."

"That study is over a decade old now, so perhaps we are climbing that curve," interjected Karen.

"Which is why I'm worried I might be biased," he said and nodded, "in telling you subjectively there's been an increase here in Virginia and the District." He got up from his seat at the island. "Looks like you two may be ready for a topping for the pancakes." He stepped to the fridge and got out the requested yogurt for Agatha and syrup for Karen. The thunder was moving farther away, and Jake could hear sounds of Hope contentedly getting started on her bottle.

"I mentioned lightning rods earlier, an estimable invention by Benjamin Franklin in the eighteenth century that protects buildings directly, and indirectly people. I also worry about climate-accentuated drought, which affects vegetation, which in turn heightens the risk of lightning-triggered grass and forest fires. The US Forest Service argues about forty percent of western wildfires start this way. The grid can be either the instigator of fire or the recipient of damage from fire and lightning. Among other measures, I work hard to persuade utilities to accelerate their work undergrounding transmission lines, which would solve a host of problems.

"Incidentally, this rain, if it extends far enough north, may help put out the fires burning in Ontario again this year, and help the smoke particles to rain out. I for one am tired of an orange sky, like some dystopian post-apocalyptic world."

"Especially with a baby in the house," Agatha observed, and he shook his head.

"Either of you want some juice?" he asked, looking at some unfinished pancakes in front of them, but both shook their heads. "So, Abbey mentioned you both have the honor of speaking at congressional hearings this afternoon. What can you tell me about that?"

Agatha took the lead. "I am a congressional liaison for the AGA, the American Gas Association. We represent more than two hundred energy companies that provide natural gas service to 180 million Americans. The AGA was founded in 1918—"

"So, during World War I," Jake said, reminding himself to try to not get too confrontational.

"That's right, during the War. We consider ourselves a resource for local, state, and federal policymakers when it comes to regulating the natural gas industry. We have an abundance of potentially recoverable natural gas, more than a century of supply."

"Potential reserves, not probable and especially not proven," Jake surmised. A short silence ensued. *I'm gonna show them I'm no amateur here.*

"Natural gas is affordable, reliable, safe, and essential to environmental improvement," Agatha continued smoothly.

Jake took a sip of the cup of hot chocolate he sometimes had at breakfast. "Not quite sure how you're suggesting environmental improvement."

Karen said, "If your expertise involves the grid, then you know that American natural gas provides more electrical generation than any other source . . . more than coal, nuclear, or renewables."

"And I am aware that the relative and absolute use of gas generators is increasing, though many environmental types have strong reservations about its use," Jake said.

"Exactly," Agatha said, "yes, cleaner than coal and growing, and you must also recognize that with LNG, or liquefied natural gas, we are supporting the European and Ukrainian effort to confront the Russian invasion."

Jake had heard enough. "I think we need to not discount the carbon cost of burning propane and methane gas, whether delivered by pipeline or by ship. Since the two of you represent the industry, you must be aware that compression of methane to ultra-cold liquid consumes about one-tenth of the original gas. Then the LNG tankers use up another five percent of their cargo for propulsion and refrigeration and overpressure relief during the voyage—"

"Would you have the Ukrainians simply submit to Vladimir Putin then?" Karen asked. Jake imagined he saw a flush just beginning to rise in her cheeks.

He tilted his head and said, "I can only justify its use until the Europeans accomplish what the Germans coined *die Energiewende*, the energy transition, and Ukraine is kept independent and restored as close to its original borders as possible, including Crimea. The Europeans have demonstrated impressive resilience and adaptability. And Volodymir Zelensky is never going to back down. It's a cage fight of Vladimir versus Volodymir."

"So, you accept the pressing strategic necessity of shipping natural gas overseas," Agatha said, in a sharper tone than before.

Or was it resigned? he wondered. "Only in transition will I grant that. But in turn, do you not recognize that when you combine the near three percent leakage of gas in the whole supply chain with the fifteen percent loss in transshipment, then gas is substantially worse than coal in terms of carbon cost?"

Karen sat up even straighter. "Are you forgetting natural gas does not have the heavy-metal contaminants of coal, like arsenic and mercury?" she challenged, as she shrugged and looked over at Agatha.

He resisted snorting. "Gas at a minimum does have benzene as a contaminant, which is biologically dangerous."

Another fraught pause.

"The entity most important here is the Federal Energy Regulatory Commission," Jake said, "which was established by the Natural Gas Act of . . ."

"1938," said Agatha smoothly.

Jake nodded, continuing, "And amended by the Energy Policy Act of 2005. As I'm sure you're aware, only FERC has the authority to approve or deny applications for LNG terminals."

Another hiatus ensued, during which Jake tapped his fingers on the countertop.

"We can all agree, can we not, that industrial and chemical concerns will need hydrogen to manage their emissions; therefore, the production of what we in the industry call 'turquoise hydrogen' helps clean up the climate," Agatha declared.

Now she's trying to sidetrack me. "Turquoise may sound pretty, but I think what you're proposing is methane pyrolysis. Which—of course—uses extraordinarily high heat in the absence of oxygen to break apart hydrocarbons like methane for their hydrogen atoms. Isn't the temperature requirement something like two thousand degrees Fahrenheit? And don't you usually accomplish this with grid electricity, or even burn more methane to get up to that temperature?"

"Jake, that could be cleanly accomplished with nuclear power, or whatever mix of generators the grid relies on now," Karen said.

Jake put up a hand to cut her off, took a deep breath, and let it out slowly. "But clearly, sourcing hydrogen your way consumes almost as much energy as it will be worth," explained Jake, "so it's nothing like 'green hydrogen' from wind or solar or geothermal energy."

Before they responded, he belatedly decided to remember he was, after all, their host. "Listen, I'm sorry, Abbey tells me I get riled up too easily sometimes. So let me calm down and ask you to please tell me where you'll be giving your testimony today."

"I'll be speaking at the House Subcommittee on Energy, Climate, and Grid Security at one o'clock." Agatha said.

"Right up my alley, the grid," Jake murmured.

"And I'll be presenting data to the House Subcommittee on Environment, Manufacturing, and Critical Materials at 2:30 this afternoon," Karen followed up.

"But . . . let me ask, what proposals are you going to address before these subcommittees?"

"LNG Penn in 2023 began the Federal Energy Regulatory Commission's formal application for a 7.2-million-metric-tons export facility on the Delaware River, not far from Philadelphia," Agatha said, "which we would now like to expand further." She turned to look at Karen.

"In 2019, the Freeport LNG export terminal first became operational, with the original shipment of natural gas after its construction of three so-called 'trains' for liquefaction of natural gas. To speak to your objections of the chilling operation consuming ten percent of its own methane, you should know Freeport is the only terminal in the country where that is solely accomplished using electricity," Karen said, clearly looking superior.

"I c-confess I am surprised," Jake stammered, "I did not know that. But I suppose it would depend on the source of power, renewables would be one thing but—"

"As of 2022," Karen continued with polished intonation, "the United States had more LNG export capacity than any other country in the world."

"Jake, we would love to talk more, but really we have some preparation of our own to complete before we head into DC," Agatha said, wiping her mouth with a napkin in genteel fashion before she stood up slowly.

A picture of elegance, thought Jake. *I think I've just been one-upped.* "I'd better get some dishes in the sink, we all have work to do."

Now I know how it feels to be hog-tied, he thought. "Will you be going in on the Metro Orange Line?" Jake asked.

"No, actually we will be picked up in about half an hour," Agatha replied.

Bet that's gonna be a limousine, Jake thought, nodding but not wanting to venture anything out loud. *Expense account stuff.*

"If you didn't bring raincoats, or wanted to borrow an umbrella, we'd be happy to lend you what you need. I understand you'll be here one more night." He stood up. "I really should go check to see what happened down the street."

***

It was worse than he anticipated, just in the next block. Two trees had been felled by the lightning, an eastern redbud leafed out after its spring blossoming and a honey locust. Both had split and blackened trunks. The locust had crashed into its owner's home, taking out a large front window, with broken glass inside and out. The redbud had fallen clear of any structures aside from the mailbox, but it extended most of the way across the street. Jake was relieved to see the Johnson family unscathed, all four of them. The neighbors had gathered in huddled groups, several of them extending reassurances to the parents.

Jake joined the huddle, then waited for a break in the conversation. "Eric, Nancy, I see you guys are alright."

"Quite a shock this morning, that," Eric said, turning to point at the front windows. "Sounded like the whole place was coming down around our ears."

"We're lucky it didn't happen in the middle of the night," Nancy offered. "What it sounded like was the stroke of doom, like in a movie."

Jake knew he had a bit of time this morning. "You know, I've got a small chain saw, it's electric so it's not very loud. We have a couple of guests at the Inn this morning, but I've already fed them breakfast."

Eric was already shaking his head. "Thanks, Jake, but I'm going to call the arborist we've had over here before. Looks like he is going to get some firewood."

"Okay, but let me know if you change your mind."

***

A patrol car rolled up away from the tree, the light bar turned off as they came to a stop. One of the officers talked to the family; the other shepherded the gawkers clear of the downed trees.

Jake contemplated the situation as he walked back home. No power lines down, as this kind of neighborhood had had its lines undergrounded years ago. No injuries. No damage to vehicles. The city would clean up the street, but the owners would be on the hook for the downed trees filling up the front yard. Insurance agent to call. Contractors to bid on the home repairs. Their lives had just gotten very busy.

He looked up but saw no lightning arrestors on the roof. *Course, it was not the house but the taller trees that took the stroke.* Jake sighed and shook his head. Part of the adaptation to climate change. In this case, it would not have helped. But still, the future was feeling very uncertain at the moment.

Mina wanted to know what had happened, and Jake explained the situation.

"How did your discussion with the two ladies go?" asked Mina.

"I've gotta say I felt blindsided, but it was two to one, and I'll see if I can do a bit better tomorrow."

Mina smiled brightly. "There's always another tomorrow."

THIRTEEN

System Operator

History, in general, only informs us what bad government is. —*Thomas Jefferson*

I believe there are more instances of the abridgement of freedom of the people by gradual and silent encroachments by those in power than by violent and sudden usurpations.
—*James Madison*

J ake gazed expectantly at the students entering Tomkins classroom 302 for the first session of the summer semester. On his computer screen at the lectern, he tried to link the faces he saw with their pictures from their freshman year, but some were sophomores and juniors now. Recognition was feasible with most, and with only fifteen students in the seminar, he should be able to swiftly get a sense of each of them individually. Most were casually dressed, but he himself set the standard with jeans and a neat open-necked shirt. Clean and white perhaps, but never touched by an iron.

He saw a few of them were carrying the assigned textbook for the class, a good start. He moved to the center of the room, with an entire wall of whiteboard framing him from the back.

"Okay, folks, I like to get started on time, as you will come to appreciate. I don't particularly care if you arrive a bit late, we all know about the vagaries of scheduling, and distances between classes and such, but just so you know, you might miss some key opening salvos of information.

"To make sure everyone is in the right place, this class is Precepts of Grid Design, 201 in the department curriculum. Our textbook you presumably know by now is *Engineering Fundamentals and Problem Solving*, 8th edition, by Eide and co-authors, last edition 2023. The e-book is less than half the cost, good for six months. You'll notice I'm not listed as an author, I like to think it's because I'm too young to have written a textbook yet, though I do have some aspirations along those lines. As this is the summer semester, this particular class runs for only the first ten weeks, with online tests for both the midterm and the final exam."

He noticed one last person slipping in the door and recognized the young man as Sam Ricketts. He was blond, with a stocky build and a single illegible tattoo on his left forearm.

Jake smiled at him. "Afternoon, Sam, glad you found the room. I had just mentioned that I always start on time."

"Sorry I'm late, Mr. Harper, but—"

"Again, Sam, no need for an apology. And everyone may call me Jake, that's the name my parents gave me and I answer to it. As you can all see, I like to keep things pretty informal, although any assignments need to be completed promptly and in full.

"To continue, as you already probably know, you have access to the web-based virtual computer-aided design or CAD lab, including such core applications as Multisim, COMSOL, and Tanner Tools. All you need to do is log in with your university user ID and passcode.

"There will also be some off-campus and individual assignments as well. This will include a group visit to an electronics firm here in DC, as well as individual forays out to examine parts of the grid. Grid security is a major concern of mine, and I hope to invite someone from the cleanup process at the Peach Bottom nuclear plant to come speak to us."

He began to pace back and forth slowly.

"Will we be able to visit one of the control rooms for the Northeast Independent System Operator?" Veronica asked. She was easy to recognize, as one of only four women in the class. She had dark hair, tied back in a ponytail, no lipstick, and a long-sleeve emerald shirt with a pocket protector.

"For reasons of security, that may or may not be possible." Jake paused. "Let me get back to you on that one. Allow me, though, to give you a simpler assignment, namely to take a pair of binoculars out someplace with a high-voltage transmission line and check out the multiple strands of wiring and their total lack of insulation." He noticed a few eyebrows raised. *Which means some of these students were unaware of this curiosity.*

"Besides being punctual, I also like to make my classes as interactive as possible, now that we're done with the housekeeping announcements." He paused in his pacing for a moment. "So, tell me, what's the largest constructed object in the world?" An arm shot up, but he pointed at the person and said, "Russell, no need to raise your hand, just speak up if you have a comment or question."

"I'd love to make the provocative suggestion of the Great Wall of China, or the US Interstate Highway System, but the title of the class makes it pretty obvious we're here to talk about the grid." He wore a Yankees T-shirt and had curly dark hair, almost shaved on the sides.

"I had a girlfriend once who said I had a fine sense of the obvious," Jake joked, which brought a few chuckles. "Yes, simply stated, the North American set of electric grids is the largest manufactured structure on the planet. Parts of it are easily visible from space, like the reservoirs behind great dams such as the Grand Coulee and the Hoover Dam." He began pacing again. "By the way, do any of you know which of these two dams has the larger hydroelectric capacity?" He looked around, but it was Sam who spoke up this time.

"From game theory, even though the Hoover Dam is much better known, I bet the answer is Grand Coulee."

Jake nodded. "Do you know by how much?" But Sam shook his head. "Grand Coulee in Washington State has about a threefold advantage in terms of nameplate or maximum instantaneous generation capacity. In fact, it is the largest generator in North America."

"What's the second largest then, another dam?" Veronica asked.

"No, actually, the Palo Verde nuclear plant in Arizona ranks second, which of course also makes it the largest nuke that we have.

"With Google Earth, on street-level view you can visit the exteriors of these and many other components. Scaling down to the other end of size, the innards of a microchip are only visible with atomic force microscopy, with a resolution more than a thousand times greater than visible light microscopy." He realized he needed to break up the flow, so grabbed a marker pen to scribble on the whiteboard:

Instantaneous Commodity

"Electricity is our one and only instantaneous commodity. The internet with its flow of information and imagery may seem miraculous, but it is a piker compared to the flow of electrons carefully corralled within tight parameters of voltage or force, hertz or frequency, and amperage or quantity of energy transferred to do useful work. Like the Matrix, the grid is everywhere, even though it's often invisible."

He stopped for a moment.

"We all know how internet communications can be delayed many seconds or more. If you ever copy an email to yourself for archival purposes, you'll recognize that up to half a minute may pass before it arrives. No way to assess how many server computers all the component packets of data might have had to pass through to arrive back at your monitor in reassembled form. The internet of course is absolutely dependent on the grid most of the time, but assuming you're not operating on grid power but rather battery backup, without at the same time interruption of cable connection, this is an example of small-scale resilience against grid dysfunction.

"I've had the experience myself of grid outage with ongoing access to the internet, though sometimes with a momentary glitch—since we have energy storage capacity at home. Have any of you had similar experiences?" Almost everybody raised a hand this time, causing Jake to grin in commiseration.

"Our electric grids cannot lag in voltage, frequency, or output for more than a few milliseconds. The problem we're facing is that our huge networks are antiquated and dilapidated. Parts of the grid date back to the years your grandparents or great-grandparents were born. Some of the individual parts, such as power poles made of creosoted wood, are over a century old. Transformers are in short supply, and may take months to be replaced, especially those allied with large generators such as nuclear power plants. Increasingly the western grids are responsible for part of the accentuated risk of wildfires, wracked by rolling outages, and stressed by cooling load during atmospheric heat waves."

He used the marker pen a second time:

Interconnection Queue

"As bad as these other problems sound, we must face an even greater dilemma.[7] We've all been in one of those long lines at a restaurant or theater, waiting in a queue, right? 'Interconnection' is the term describing high-voltage, long-distance transmission lines waiting to hook up new electric generating projects of all types. And 'queue'—in grid-speak—is a set of proposed projects such as solar, wind, geothermal, and batteries, listed in order of date of initial application. Let's use as our example PJM, the grid operator that manages the largest power grid in the country, connected to some sixty-five million people in thirteen states, stretching from the mid-Atlantic coast to Chicago. Anybody know what those initials stand for?"

Russell got to it first. "I think they stand for Pennsylvania, New Jersey and Maryland, three of the member states."

"Absolutely correct, Russell, good. You can see in the handout the salient quote, from an article by the National Resources Defense Council in May of 2023. 'As of September 2022, there were more than 202 gigawatts of renewable energy resources waiting in the PJM queue to finally get connected to transmission lines, over ninety-five percent of the total.' Compare that to the figure for the totality of clean energy resources operating in the United States in 2021, almost the exact same number at *two hundred gigawatts*. They are in fact waiting for Godot."

"But in the play Godot never actually shows up."

Jake tried to stay upbeat. "Optimist that I am, Sam, I actually have confidence almost all of these projects will eventually get built. These backlogged grid operators, more formally called regional transmission operators—RTOs for short—are one of the biggest barriers to expanding grid capacity with wind and solar and all the rest. Unfortunately, they are literally running out of time to resolve this by the end of the decade. And we can't afford the delays if we're going to hit decarbonization deadlines and stave off the worst impacts of climate degradation."

Jake set down his marker pen on a desk in front. "Data from the Lawrence Berkeley National Lab showed that average interconnection costs came in five times higher for the last project in the loop, because the last one triggers a requirement for construction of high-voltage transmission benefiting all the early arrivals."

"Sounds like musical chairs, I guess," Veronica said. "The last applicant in line gets stuck with all the broader network upgrade costs."

"Why is that pertinent, do you think?"

"They're being asked to pay for upgrading parts of the high-voltage grid way beyond the point where they would be connecting to it."

"Good answer, but an unjustified and intolerable situation. Exactly as stated, all the new generators in the queue, whether renewables or batteries, or for that matter, nuclear, coal, and gas, should share in that large expense. As should the feds and the states involved."

Jake scratched his forehead, then turned to write on the whiteboard:

Grid Threats

"In not all of North America, rather just the United States, there is another broad issue we will be dealing with in this class. The grid is enormous, with over 73,000 generators, close to 160,000 miles of high-voltage power lines, and literally millions of miles of low-voltage lines and distribution transformers. There are more than 335 million Americans alive now, aggregated with small businesses and industries from the perspective of the grid as 145 million customers. These are figures from the Energy Information Administration, or EIA.

"Regrettably, the threat landscape our grids face is daunting." Jake resumed pacing back and forth.

"Our creaky grid is still largely dependent on legacy technologies. Seventy percent of transmission lines are thirty years old and nearing the end of their projected service. Sixty percent of circuit breakers are more than thirty-five years old, though their planned operating life is only twenty years. According to Utility Dive, aging grids are driving fifty-one billion dollars in annual distribution-utility spending. And just as with your grandparents, with aging comes vulnerabilities."

Jake looked at his notes. "Back in 2023 a fellow named Chuck Brooks published an article titled, '3 Alarming Threats to the US Energy Grid—Cyber, Physical and Existential Events.' You may already have seen this in the syllabus, as it is required reading. The federal departments who worry about this sort of thing include Homeland Security, Energy, and Defense, plus a subset of intelligence agencies and the Federal Energy Regulatory Commission or FERC. Remember this last acronym, we will use it a lot.

"Here is the operative quote by Brooks in your handout: 'The threats can be from cybersecurity attacks (by countries, criminal gangs, or hacktivists), from physical attacks by terrorists (domestic or foreign), or simply vandals, or from an Electronic Magnetic Pulse generated from either a geomagnetic coronal eruption, or from a terrorist or rogue state lofting a missile exploded high in the atmosphere.'

"You place your bets and take your chances.

"Grid planning generally deals with new technologies for 'distribution, resilience, storage, and capability; it is also focused on cybersecurity.' Power companies, like many other industries, use supervisory control and data acquisition devices—SCADA networks—which need to be kept up to date and hardened against both physical and kinetic attack. Brooks discussed in his article the successful ransomware attack in 2021 on the Colonial Pipeline, which breached the SCADA networks and halted the supply of petroleum products to the East Coast for days. This attack succeeded because of lack of anticipatory, preventive, and incident response planning. I hope you're getting a sense of how complex these multifarious threats are."

Jake paused to post up:

Firmware

"Firmware, the increasing integration of software and hardware, creates a digital environment that is increasingly internet accessible."

"But accessible means vulnerable, logically," Sam commented.

"You can say that again, Sam. Networked sensors and SCADA devices are growing like neurons establishing connections in the brain. Nation states, criminal organizations, and terrorist hackers are continually testing the points of entry into these systems, the so-called 'cyberattack surface.' The attack on the Peach Bottom nukes last year were carried out by a single sociopathic terrorist who has not even yet gone to trial." *Not planning to mention now or ever my minor role in that event.*

"Brooks also listed the consumer internet of things, or IoT, devices in many homes and businesses. Malefactors could hijack huge numbers of these poorly cyber-protected high-amperage appliances such as refrigerators and air conditioners. Converted into a robotic network or 'botnet,' a black-hat hacker could provoke a distributed denial-of-service attack, phishing, or disruptive power surges to damage the grid." Jake halted, as he saw Sam wanted to make another point.

"How exactly would a hacker be able to produce a power surge using a botnet?" asked Sam.

"The ideal time to strike would be when demand was already at its maximum, such as record-breaking temperatures in the summer when everyone is running air conditioners. With time-of-use, or TOU, tiers of electricity charges, perhaps people are trying to not charge their EV, or run the dishwashers and clothes washers when electricity costs four times as much at four in the afternoon as it does at four in the morning. Furthermore, refrigerators and freezers are quiescent in their duty cycle the majority of the time. But if a hacker with control of tens or hundreds of thousands of appliances in a botnet abruptly piled into the grid, brownouts or blackouts could occur. Utilities could even be blackmailed to avoid such an attack.

"The Global Positioning System or GPS exhibits another point of susceptibility. All the grids of North America are reliant on GPS timing for monitoring and controlling generation, transmission, and distribution activities. The federal agency NIST, or National Institute of Standards and Technology, prioritizes protection of the smart grid. Brooks thus states, 'Smart grid cybersecurity must address both inadvertent compromises of the electric infrastructure, due to user errors, equipment failures, and natural disasters, and deliberate attacks, such as from disgruntled employees, industrial espionage, or terrorists.'

"Finally, let me finish with the bogeyman of kinetic attacks. The Department of Energy states physical attacks rose seventy-seven percent in 2022. White supremacists hit electrical substations in Oregon and Washington. 'Similar attacks happened at two energy substations in North Carolina where residents lost power after gunshot damage.'

"A bulletin from DHS in early 2023 stated that domestic terrorists 'have developed credible, specific plans to attack electricity infrastructure since at least 2020, identifying the electric grid as a particularly attractive target.' Our problem is that substations, especially in rural locations, are tempting, unsupervised, relatively soft targets. Any idea how many of these structures, with all their gray transformers and obvious high-voltage wires, there are in the United States?" *No one is raising their hands*, thought Jake, *so it's a good thing they're taking this class.*

"There are fifty-five thousand substations situated at key points in the grid in this country. That's a lot of critical nodes royally deserving 'protection by design,' I think.

"That reminds me, I'm going to be organizing a project for all of you to investigate this issue later in the course."

"What's the project?" Russell asked.

"I'm going to keep that a surprise for now, with the only hint that it will take you off campus. See you all on Wednesday. By then I will expect you to have read the first two chapters of the textbook, the introductory material on engineering as a profession, and what we are accomplishing right now, education for engineers."

FOURTEEN

Visual Vagaries

There is just as much beauty visible to us in the landscape as we are prepared to appreciate, and not a grain more . . . A man sees only what concerns him. —Henry David Thoreau

If the clinician, as observer, wishes to see things as they really are, he must make a tabula rasa of his mind and proceed without any preconceived notions whatever. —Jean-Martin Charcot, MD

Abbey looked at the curly dark-haired man standing in front of her, a second-year resident she had not previously met. She had let him tell the short version of the story almost without interruption.

"Aside from the initial findings on the spinal tap indicating perhaps early meningitis, this patient has proved baffling and is failing to get better on empiric antibiotics," Andrew Wyatt summed up. It was midmorning, and he had just presented the case to her, as she was his infectious disease consultant. He was on call today, it was time to start resident rounds, the ER doc had just notified him of a first admission, and a nurse from the ICU had just pinged his phone, so Abbey knew he would be anxious to not let all his time get sucked away.

Though his Afrikaans accent is charming, I will say.

"So, to summarize, Andrew, Mr. Cooper is a thirty-seven-year-old white male living on a goat farm in Virginia. This is hospital day number three and his diagnosis is still ambiguous. On admission you thought his neck was equivocally stiff, and the cell counts in the fluid from the spinal tap were modestly elevated. But cultures of blood, urine, and cerebrospinal fluid have remained negative. Viral titers on blood and cerebrospinal fluid have all been noninformative. Imaging of his brain revealed no findings. His temperature continues to fluctuate widely and he's exhibited no response to your treatment, suggesting to your team that there may well be an unidentified viral process. Unless this is not an infection at all, something more along the lines of, say, vasculitis. The goats on the farm that suffered spontaneous abortion—from a presumptive communicable disorder—are perhaps a red herring, so my first suggestion is we may need to cast a wider net." She hesitated a moment, her eyes narrowed.

"You better head down to the ER to work up that admission, assuming you can afford to miss resident rounds. I'll review the chart and examine this patient. My partner and I appreciate the consult," she said, and smiled some encouragement as she turned away.

He nodded, said thanks, and headed out the door like a center half making a move on the soccer pitch.

Seems a bit frustrated and distracted on this day on call. Knows he'll likely be up almost all night. At least overnight call is only every fourth night now, not third like the old days.

***

Abbey knocked on the door and walked into the room, seeing both the patient in the bed and a woman in the chair on the other side, near the window, holding a phone to her ear. Most certainly his wife . . . *she may have useful information.* "Good morning, Jared, I'm Dr. London. I specialize in infectious disease, and Dr. Wyatt and his team have asked me to see you." She shook his hand and also looked directly across the bed inquiringly.

"Shelly, wait, the doctor just came in," she was saying, holding up a hand. "I'll call you back later." She set the phone on the nightstand and stood up. "I'm Jacey Carrington, Dr. London, his wife. Glad to meet you."

Abbey was nodding as she observed the well-dressed woman in a cashmere sweater, a few lines around her eyes, eyelids a bit puffy.

"Likewise, Jacey, I'm actually glad you're here, because I may have a few questions for you, too." Abbey sat down in the chair on the near side of the bed as Jacey sat back down herself. *Seems like a well-matched couple,* Abbey thought, observing them both unobtrusively.

"While I've discussed your case with Dr. Wyatt and reviewed your chart, I would like to start by hearing your version of the story, Jared, from the very beginning, wherever and whenever you think that might be." She opened a small spiral notebook on her lap. Her first impression was that he appeared wan, head lying back on the pillow, pale with black hair and a goatee. Alert and cognizant of his surroundings.

"It all started with a bad week with the goats. One of the Boer goats miscarried and then one of the cashmere goats got so sick that she's currently at the vet hospital."

"Your veterinarian is Benjamin Harris, correct? With your permission, I'd like to call him later, see what else he might be able to add." They both nodded. "Tell me how the goats are doing, and particularly if they had fever at any point," she said, eyeing him carefully.

"The first goat is recovering, with the usual birth canal discharge after delivery. The vet measured their temperatures, which normally range from 101.5 to 103.5 degrees."

Abbey raised her eyebrows. "I did not know that about goats, interesting."

"The second goat, though, has deteriorated, her temperature has been over 104 several times, so actual goat fever. We never knew any of all this before either."

"How long have you been raising goats?"

"Couple of years now, we still have a lot to learn."

"What other animals do you have on the farm?"

"Chickens and ducks . . . but they're all healthy."

"And two dogs, Russell terriers," Jacey added. They both looked at her.

Abbey adjusted her seating, scooting a bit forward at the same time. "Has any member of the family had a tick bite this year? Do your goats get ticks?" she asked, but the two of them looked at each other, and both were shaking their heads slowly.

"How have the mosquitoes been this year?"

"Some weeks ago, Ben, our vet, said something. He mentioned he'd heard the mosquitoes were more active this year. Or maybe more of them . . . I can't remember exactly."

"Do you think his statement might have biased you in that regard? Or have you actually been noticing more of them?"

"I know I've been scratching more mosquito bites this year than the last couple of summers," Jared said, moving restlessly in bed. He grimaced slightly when he lifted his head from the pillow.

Abbey noticed he was squinting. "Is your neck still sore?" Abbey asked casually.

"Not so much, but I still have a headache."

"Throbbing? Does it change with position? Is it one-sided? Is it altering your vision, your hearing, your sense of balance, your ability to taste or smell?" she asked, but he indicated in the negative to all the questions.

"You seem sensitive to bright light—"

"Because they keep shining bright lights in my eyes."

"But I notice you have the shades drawn, even though it's a pretty cloudy day." And no lights on. *Maybe that's why Jacey is reading by the window.*

"There're almost sixty types of mosquitoes in Virginia, including the *Aedes* and *Culex* families. This is important because there are some diseases they can transmit. The tests on your blood and spinal fluid are not all back yet, but the results we have so far have all been negative. So we know that you don't have, for example, any of the common bacteria and viruses that cause meningitis or brain infection."

She looked at her notes for a moment.

"The kinds of infections goats do get don't seem likely here. You've been tested for leptospirosis, which can produce some of your symptoms, but the blood tests show only modest changes in your liver function, and the specific test for lepto was negative, though you may be only early on in whatever this disease course is. And brucellosis can cause abortion in goats, but again, your blood tests don't reveal any evidence for that.

"Some more common infections that you've probably heard of, like E. coli or salmonella, have been ruled out by the stool tests. Another outlier, psittacosis, can induce pregnancy loss in goats, and is dangerous in pregnant women—may I ask you, Jacey, if there is any chance you could be pregnant?" Abbey looked penetratingly at her, but she was shaking her head.

"I had a vasectomy five years ago, so no," Jared said. Abbey already knew that from details in the complete history in the chart. *But it never hurts to check, because . . . baffling blunders happen all the time.*

"Jacey, may I just confirm when your last period was and whether it was regular and typical?" But she just said two weeks ago and normal.

"No recent travel, either of you?"

"How recent?" Jacey asked.

"We usually think of that as about three months, unless you've gone overseas."

"No, nothing like that."

"Any changes in the skin, Jared—rash, itchiness, swelling, sensitivity, yellow color?"

"Just that I feel like a pincushion."

Abbey smiled fleetingly. "Have you noticed any swollen lymph glands in your neck," she asked, stroking along the front and sides of her own neck, "or under your arms, near your navel, in your groin, behind the knee, or any place else?" But he indicated not.

"Do you notice any spots in front of your eyes, blurriness, double vision, pain when you press on your own eye, difficulty focusing? Do you wear glasses or contacts?"

Jared hesitated a moment. "Come to think of it, maybe a little bit of blurriness this morning."

"Is it on one side or both?" Then she pantomimed covering one eye at a time.

He covered his left eye with no particular response, but when he covered his right, he started glancing up and down, left and right, and his face tightened.

"What do you see on that side, Jared," asked Jacey, reaching out a hand to touch his thigh.

"I'm . . . I'm not sure. Maybe kind of a blurry area."

"Is it in the center, or where exactly?" Abbey pressed, but he was still searching.

"Did you tell your medical team this morning?"

"It didn't come up, maybe I didn't really notice earlier."

"If you focus on my nose, can you see my whole face?"

He struggled to focus. "Your left face is . . . kinda distorted."

"Okay, I'll check on that in just a moment. Here are some more questions. Do you have any nasal stuffiness, discharge, pain, nosebleeds? Do you have any sores in the mouth, any bleeding gums, any sore teeth, any difficulty swallowing?"

But Jared was shaking his head and continuing to test his left eye.

"Any cough, wheezing, shortness of breath, phlegm? Does any part of your chest wall hurt, with a deep breath or twisting in bed?

"No? Then how about chest pain with exercise, palpitation, dizziness with standing?"

"I haven't been out of bed except to go to the bathroom, but Jacey or the nurse has to help me, I feel really weak, and my headache gets worse."

"No abdominal pain? No nausea, vomiting, diarrhea, change in stool color?"

"Not really . . . bit of loose stool maybe four or five times first day, less often after that, but I've had very little to eat in terms of solid food."

Abbey looked up from her notetaking. "No burning when you pass urine, no hesitancy, no frequency, no history of stones?" She knew his urine tests had been negative and his kidney function was normal so far. He showed no reaction to these questions, but she started to appreciate that his breathing looked just a fraction deeper.

Abbey stood up, pulling a tongue blade out of her jacket pocket, opening the paper wrapper, and setting it on the bedside table. She also got out her slim case for the otoscope and ophthalmoscope and set these on the table as well.

"Let's have a look at you," she said, holding her hands palm up. "Give me both hands please." She looked for all the subtle signs of bloodstream infection, such as small purple petechiae, splinter hemorrhages under the nails, bluish color suggesting cyanosis or low blood oxygen, soft swelling or clubbing of the skin just proximal to the nailbeds. She palpated for lymph node enlargement on the inside of the elbow, under the arm, the front and back of the neck. She would check around the navel, the groin, and behind the knee later. Everywhere she was scanning his skin, the biggest organ in the human body.

"Open widely," she instructed him quietly, then used the tongue blade to slide over the tongue, held it down to peer at the throat, pulled out his cheeks to examine the molars. *Throat looks a bit red . . . more in the right tonsillar fossa . . . but no whitish patches.*

She examined both ear canals and eardrums with her otoscope, next the nasal cavities with his head leaned way back, then used its light to shine in first one eye, then the other. She repeated this until she was satisfied the left pupil was actually smaller, and he narrowed his eyes and tried to look away when she shined the light on that side. *Pupils are not equal, round and reactive to light now . . . gotta be a new finding.* But having him look up, down, right, and left demonstrated all his extraocular movements were normal.

Time for the money shot. She picked up her other handheld instrument, an ophthalmoscope, and examined the interior structures of the right eye, with no findings. But on the left—on the left was a different tale. The lens was clear, no cataract. The aqueous humor in front of the lens was okay, but the vitreous humor in back of it was just a bit cloudy. In the very back of the eye, the optic disc, the connection to the optic nerve, perhaps was a bit swollen. But when she moved her head to view almost straight in line, she was sure she saw several small, subtle discolored spots with one tiny hemorrhage. *Bingo. Bad news.*

"Okay, I know that's not comfortable, Jared, a bright light right in your macula, your central vision. I'm sorry. Let me listen to your lungs next." Abbey held his left hand with her left and put her right hand behind his back to help him sit up. She tapped, or percussed, his back, and listened with the flat diaphragm of her stethoscope on his back and sides, but all was clear. She had him lie back down, then examined his heart sounds carefully, using, this time, the cupped bell of her scope, listening for any murmur or scraping sound indicating perhaps an infected heart valve, but all was copasetic.

The abdominal exam revealed normal bowel sounds, no focal tenderness, no liver edge or spleen tip to indicate enlargement. There were no nodes around the navel or in the groin.

"Jared, I'm going to do a genital exam, but skip the part looking for a hernia. Since your wife is here, I won't call in a nurse. So spread your knees apart widely," she said, as she put on a pair of nonsterile gloves and pulled the sheet down. "No skin lesions, no expressible discharge, no testicular or epididymal tenderness or mass." *Explaining what you're looking for helps men relax.*

The neurologic exam—including deep tendon reflexes in all extremities—was normal, except when she lifted his head off the pillow, his grimace and resistance to bending his neck showed trace nuchal rigidity, indicating persistent meningeal irritation.

As she finished washing her hands, Abbey turned to face them. "Jared, you represent a bit of a diagnostic quandary. You have fairly hectic fever but no serious or progressive signs of meningitis, and certainly no encephalitis or direct brain involvement, plus your head CT was normal. Your throat's a bit red. Your liver is modestly involved in this process, but you are not jaundiced. But . . . now there are signs of inflammation in the left eye. So far at least, all your spinal fluid, blood, urine, and stool tests have been unrewarding.

"I'm going to have some suggestions for your team. I'm comfortable now in recommending ceftriaxone—your antibacterial antibiotic—be stopped, as this is not looking like a bacterial infection. I'll propose that they send you down to the ophthalmology clinic on the first floor to undergo a slit lamp exam to thoroughly evaluate the interior of your left eye." *Both eyes of course.* "This is late enough today so that will probably not happen until tomorrow. They will also map out your visual field and have that for a basis of comparison in case this progresses. There is the possibility they'll want you to see a retinal specialist as well."

She could see they were holding hands now, tightly enough to make the skin pale. Jared was blinking rapidly, and his wife might be holding back tears until Abbey left the room. *Be strong for your man, Jacey.*

"I'll be talking to your vet, Dr. Harris, as soon as this evening. We need to compare notes.

"Your team has looked at a lot of the usual suspects, but for right now we can say you don't have zika or dengue or coronavirus or HIV. Since my background is in infectious disease, that is what I think of first, but there are other possibilities, including a possible connection to mosquitoes in this area. And your poor goats. I will be following up on that.

"I should mention further evaluations may include a repeat spinal tap in a day or so, partly to assess changes in the pressures, protein and cell counts, but also to collect a specimen for unusual viruses. I wish I could tell you more about how this is going to play out, but we haven't identified the culprit yet.

"I will stay in constant communication with your team, including the ophthalmologists and your veterinarian. I will also check your laboratory and other tests on a daily basis. But I may not be back personally until a couple of days from now."

She could see Jacey failing to hold back her tears.

"You need to be strong for each other," she said, then she went around the bed to hug Jacey.

***

Abbey sat down at the nursing station to write a note and enter the consult electronically. Almost without thought, first she washed her hands all over again, as after all patient contacts.

FIFTEEN

Submergence

The spirit of resistance to government is so valuable on certain occasions, that I wish it to be always kept alive . . . I like a little rebellion now and then. It is like a storm in the atmosphere. —*Thomas Jefferson*

A man is more than just the worst thing he has ever done. —*A plainsman*

The past month and more had been as dry and hot as the pancaked armadillo at the side of the park entrance, ignored by Matt and his sidekicks as they made the turn off State Highway 20. Saguaro cacti scarred with missing limbs stood sentry along the road, transitioning to bluestem prairie grass amidst bedraggled red cedar and green ash trees in Lockhart Park. Day after day the mirages shimmering off the roads had reflected an azure sky unpopulated by the barest hint of mare's tail cirrus. Sunrises and sunsets had shunned the cloudless bowl overhead. Insects and birds had abandoned flight until the relentless sun settled down near the horizon.

Now however, muggy did not begin to describe the altered reality as this new day dawned. The wind picked up, changeable as a weathervane, and swirled up into dust devils. A sturdy collection of charcoal-tinted cumulus clouds jostled each other far off to the northwest. Nearer to view, tentative tendrils of creamy cumulus began to innocently spread overhead. Weekends in the park tended to be busier with folks from Austin and tourists during the summer months, but not today, perhaps because of the gloomy weather forecast.

The three men arrived early to try and beat the possibility of crowds and the heat not long after dawn with their rendezvous—as always—the old historical water tower and storage area built by the Civilian Conservation Corps back in the 1930s. The boys never bothered to even glance at the small sign above the brass plaque near the entrance to the park anymore.

Beware the thorns of the invasive Macartney rose bush
Caldwell County Historical Museum, open Sat + Sun 1pm to 5pm
or may schedule an appointment by calling (512) 398-5879,
315 E. Market St.
Victoria Maranan, public information officer 512-398-3461 ext. 2520

The plan had been to stake out a site for discussion of various and sundry in a quiet place away from curious eyes and ears. Buck, as usual, wouldn't stop complaining about having to pay three bucks apiece to get into the park they'd been coming to since childhood.

"Quit you bellyaching and get with the program," Matt said.

"Wouldn't hurt you none to help carry all this barbecue we picked up anyhow," Elliot said quietly to his brother. It was just a short stretch down the trail to a spot they favored, with outcrops juxtaposed next to a downed log offering multiple options for spreading out their gear and lounging in the shade.

Buck was the first to open his bag of food. "I just wish locals could come here without having to pay for it, damn it all."

"Yeah, but what makes up for your irritation is we have some of the best goldarn barbecued ribs in the whole state, you know that," Matt said. *Always the hothead.* "So, listen up. I've got something I've been meaning to talk to you about for quite some time. You two boys chaw down on those bones while I get started.

"I never told you that when I got promoted to staff sergeant, I became a noncommissioned officer in the Army. You knuckleheads probably don't know that's an E-6 paygrade in the Department of Defense. Meant I was placed in command of a squad of nine or ten soldiers when I was in

Kabul. Among other responsibilities I got additional training in resisting interrogation and torture, which is what brings us all here today."

"I already told you plain I don't plan to go quietly if they catch me," Buck almost choked.

"Buck, calm down a bit and listen to what the man has to say," his brother cautioned.

Matt kept his face expressionless and paused. "Buck, I don't want you to ever forget we are planning to hit a soft civilian target with nobody around to stop us. The people who live around these sites are not military, they are not police, they are just people in the neighborhood who don't need to get hurt. In fact, if we hurt anybody, our whole message goes off the rails."

He wiped his hands over his forehead and eyes. "My whole idea here is if one of us gets trapped, the first thing the authorities are gonna wanna do is get information out of you. So, if any one of us fails to communicate within thirty minutes of our go-time, then the other two should be immediately suspicious something is screwed up." Matt looked at each of them, his brows furrowed. "Your job is to not give up any information for more than twenty-four hours. If each of us can pull that off, the other two diehards have at least a measly chance of getting across the Canadian border."

Elliot looked up. "The obvious problem is you need a passport to cross the border, either Canada or Mexico. How are you planning to get around that?"

"Yeah, Matt, how about that dang problem?" Buck challenged.

"Okay, boys, calm yourselves down. I been thinking on this for a while. We could get fake driver's licenses and passports that match." He scratched his chin. "I know we can't do that in Lockhart. I don't even think that is doable in Austin. But I've got some contacts up in Houston, old military buddies. They may be able to help out. So, let's worry about that later."

"If someone gets caught, the Texas license plate and vehicle registration will give us away no matter what we do," Elliot said, a bit of steel in his voice.

"What if we use some burner phones to report to Lockhart police our trucks got stolen?" Buck said, raising his eyebrows.

Can see the boy feels proud of that one. But it fails. "Remember a fake ID has to have our real photographs. So the asshole who gets caught is just shit outta luck. But the other two have a chance, if they keep moving right along. Might take the cops a while to connect us all together, just enough time for vanishing in the north." They were all quiet for a while.

"It's gonna cost us to get quality ID like what you're talking about," Elliot said. "Not sure it's worth the effort."

"If I get across the border then I hafta ditch the truck, and I goddamn hate that idea," Buck said, already sounding forlorn.

Matt scratched his chin again. "Maybe passports are too pricey and complicated for ole country boys like us. Too many ways to screw that up. Instead of that, I know some patriots in Michigan, which if we are high-tailing it might be a heap more likely than trying to get into Canada."

Buck shook his head. "Still hafta ditch my truck. We'd have to hide out for who knows how long. And might never get back to Texas."

That brought them all up short.

Matt stood up suddenly and began to march back and forth. He turned to face them. "First things first, fellas, let's get back to what we came here to figure out. Leave the rest for later." He looked up and abruptly stopped speaking. "Hell, will ya take a look at that . . . looks like we're finally gonna get some rain."

The clouds had gotten higher than a pile of flapjacks at a Grange Hall breakfast, though still far away. A couple of wrens flew by in one direction, then a yellow-rumped warbler in another, but all were tracking away south and southeast.

"We could use a little rain," Elliot said. Coruscating lightning was followed by the delayed staccato crackling of remote thunder.

Matt sat back down on his boulder. "We'll keep our eyes on that. I wouldn't mind gittin' a little wet after all this time. And our truck is just down the trail a ways. Now, Buck, you of all people should know what it's like to be taking questions from a police officer. But at least you wouldn't be drunk as a skunk for once. So listen up, you two.

"The instructors who taught the class on how to resist humiliation and torture were British, and they really knew their stuff. Trainees had to learn how to resist techniques like hooding, sleep deprivation, time disorientation, prolonged nakedness, sexual humiliation, and takin' away warmth, water and food. A lot of this breaks international law, but in an emergency ya gotta expect almost anything, especially from the FBI or the Homeland Security pukes. Sometimes a couple of them would wake us up in the middle of the night, drop a black hood over our heads, and haul us off for a third degree."

"But you always knew it was not for real, Matt, right?" asked Elliot. "So that made it easier to resist?"

Matt stood up again to take a few strides to the side, "After you'd been through a couple of days of this, and got so tired you could fall asleep standing up, it sure as hell felt serious to me." He ran his palm down from his nose to his neck. *It was tougher than these boys are thinking.* "So the first thing to remember is ya gotta maintain dead silence regardless of what they're doing to you. When you're in the military, you only need to give up three pieces of information—name, rank and serial number, and date of birth. In our case, they're gonna know who you are, so you got nothing to say to nobody. You could try asking for a lawyer, but wish you luck with that. The idea they gave us was to be 'the gray man.' That's right, the gray man. Not too aggressive and not too submissive. You wanna stay mentally alert but let the man think he's on top of you. Exaggerate any injury you got and try to appear in pain, fatigued, and weak. Especially if they rough you up, let them think it's worse than it really is." He paused to look at the clouds, which were blacker now, and could see even at a distance that heavy rain was falling.

"They taught us the initial interrogation may be rough and kinda unprofessional, and it's used to decide whether or not you're worth shipping off to a more experienced team. Bottom line, if you're alive, they want to keep you that way. They might try stress positions while they're using some tactical questioning to decide what to do with you. But your job is to try and elicit the sympathy card even without talking.

"Now, this is important. You got no reason to accept a cigarette when they offer you one, but never turn down a chance to eat or drink something, because you gotta keep up your strength. Whatever ya do, avoid any sign of submissiveness, avoid saying even a simple 'yes,' or 'thanks,' which could be edited on a tape recorder, which you may not even know is happening.

"If they read you your rights, remember this is the government talking and don't believe a word. You're not in a movie, don't reply, do *not* tell them you want an attorney. Don't even lift a hand if they ask you to sign any document. If there is a whole lot going on around the country, don't underestimate your importance as a captive—"

Elliot tilted his head sideways. "Are you saying something might be going on around the whole—"

Shit, I almost let that slip. "Hell no, I'm just saying keep yer thoughts to yerself. I'm just saying don't let them play you against other captives, the idea of what's called the prisoner's dilemma, that you might get off easier if you're the first one to give up information."

Matt glanced up again and tugged at an ear. "Don't show them anything on a map. And think about this—once you get transported to headquarters your chance of escape is just about down the shithole. So if you see a chance before then, take it. Because once you're locked down, you may not see light for a long, long time. Then they can play around putting you in a stress position, what they call a submission position, which places the human body in such a way that a great amount of weight is placed on just one or two muscles. They could force you to stand on the balls of your feet, then squat so your thighs are parallel to the ground, which creates an intense amount of pressure on the legs, leading first to pain and then muscle failure."

Buck finished his ribs and pulled napkins out of the bag to wipe off the barbecue sauce as best he could. Then he gave up and used his jeans to finish up.

"People have a picture of torture involving electric shock, choking, cutting. But they don't want to torture you to death. They want to be able to put you on trial sometime, so a priority for them is to leave no marks on your body. When they see how you respond when you're desperate for food or water or sleep, they can begin to profile you as either cool or emotional, tough or weak.

"The serious higher-level questioning will be in a bland and featureless environment, with no windows, and only a single light on in the ceiling or right at your face. When they take the hood off there is no reason to look around, or at the person sitting across from you with a desk in between, no reason to get or hold eye contact or glare at the cool guy you already know is waiting for you to crack."

Both the brothers had eyes fixed on him now, not fidgeting. "Remember the eyes are the windows into the soul, so think about the four cardinal directions. If you look up to the right you signal them you're trying to recall something. If you look up to the left you are concocting a lie. If they start to get to you, look down to the left, then right, back and forth. If you sense the interrogator is not looking at you, then grant yourself a moment of quiet defiance." He stopped pacing for a moment, his hands still fidgeting.

"If you begin to succumb to the verbal and physical abuse, or if you have a severe injury, if you can't take it anymore, give misinformation, lie about an extraction point, do not give away a time limit, deny there is a team leader—"

Elliot suddenly looked up. "Matt, wait a second, I hear moving water—"

"You two saw what Plum Creek looked like when we drove in, barely a trickle over those little check dams," Buck said, as he stood up and turned around. "Something's happening."

"We drove right by that crick when we got here, weren't nothing going on then," Matt said. "We'd better pack up our stuff and get it into my truck, I've suddenly got a bad feeling about this. Our only way out is the same way we came in." Big raindrops started falling, splashing off the rocks.

"Yeehaw, we may need to run for it, boys, let's go see what's happening," Buck said, as he gathered up everything in his arms and began jogging back to the truck. They all followed suit.

"Make sure all the doors are tight in case we need to cross through water," Matt ordered.

They slammed the doors and gunned it down the road and around the first curve back toward the creek. "There ain't no way out through all these trees except by using the road." Around the second curve they could suddenly see the water. "Hang on, remember we can't stop moving if we get into high water. We've got the high chassis, a sealed engine compartment, and a snorkel as high as the middle of the windshield to keep it firing, so as long as we don't get above the truck's rated wading depth just below our windows we'll be just fine. If it gets higher . . . then we've got to worry about the electronics and the electricals. Or getting washed away, then it's every man for himself . . . Buck, reach behind you and grab that roll of rope in case we need it."

The creek bed was nowhere in sight. All they could see was a wide jumbled sheet of rushing water, reaching up to the bottom of the doors. Matt downshifted to low gear and tried to follow the middle path through the trees, which gave them the best chance of staying on the road.

Up ahead there was a car stopped off to the right side and tilted part way over. They pulled up abreast of it and saw four people in the vehicle, a man in the driver's seat, a woman in the front passenger seat with a small girl in her lap, and an older boy trying to pull himself between the two seats in front. Their right-side windows were not more than a foot above the water.

Matt pulled just a few feet ahead and a bit to the left, trying to feel for the roadbed. "Roll down your windows, ya varmints. Elliot, help tie the rope around the base of your seat, then feed it out the window."

"Here ya go, brother, turn around and run it around your seat—" Buck urged.

Matt looked at him right in the eye. "Buck, this is all on you. When I say, you got to make your way out your window and we'll feed the rope to you. Get down to their front window and tell them maybe to tie it off to the base of the steering column—then you're gonna help them one at a time to move along the rope, then heave them up into Elliot's lap."

Elliot shook his head. "Don't tie off to their car. If it starts to move we'll get dragged away, dammit. Get the kids first, Buck. Get them to me and I'll shove them in the back seat. We sure as fuck don't have a lot of time." Rope secure, Buck went feetfirst out his back window. He grabbed the line and looped it once around his left wrist and held on with both hands. Elliot fed the line to him as Buck's weight in the water pulled it taut. When he got to the other car, the father had already rolled down the window.

He looked frantic. "*Ayúdanos, no podemos nadar*—s-swim."

"Give me your daughter first," Buck said, indicating what to do with his hands, then motioned to the mother to hand him the daughter, who was crying loudly.

"*Callate, niña, mi amor. Callate, callate*," the mother said, her voice high and tight. Buck pulled the daughter out against resistance and held her tightly under his right arm while Matt helped Elliot pull them up to his window. Buck avoided cursing, then heaved the girl up into Elliot's window. Once she was in, Matt picked her up as gently as possible and pivoted to push her in the back seat as fast as he could.

"This girl has a good pair of pipes, I'll say that for her," Matt growled, as Elliot let Buck back down to the other car. The parents were already helping the boy out of the car, and he wasn't crying, but he landed on Buck with a death grip around his neck. They completed the transfer as expeditiously as the first one.

The mother was next, crawling over her husband's lap and helped by him to drop headfirst out of the car. Buck was ready this time and grabbed her under the shoulders facing away from him so she wouldn't choke him like the son had. They made it back, and the mom crawled over the front seat crying to hug her two kids.

The last transfer was a near thing.

The right side of the other car lifted and began to bounce a bit in the current. Buck had to lunge for the man's wrist as he fell out through the window and the car tumbled away. The combined weight of the two men was almost more than Matt and Elliot could haul up against the current. Once Buck reached and grabbed the door frame, Elliot helped the two of them the rest of the way. Matt, cursing like a sailor, fell all the way back into his seat and took the vehicle out of park and back into gear. The windshield wipers were on, but he kicked them up to high.

Matt's truck was higher, heavier, and now loaded with a few hundred more pounds of weight. *"Gracias a dios,"* the man was saying again and again, as he clambered into the back seat with his family.

Buck got in and sprawled on Elliot's lap, shivering from the reaction and the cold water, muttering, "Jesus Christ, I can't believe we pulled that off. Jesus Christ goddamn Almighty and the burro he rode in on . . ."

The water was continuing to climb, but the way forward was straight across the bridge over the creek, down only a bit on the other side, then a sharp left turn toward the highway. The water level never got up past the halfway point of the door, and the snorkel was never at risk of going under. When they nosed out to the highway, for the first time they could better gauge the size of the calamity. The road to the left was lost with at least a hundred yards underwater, just a solitary road sign partly submerged, vibrating with the force of the current. Matt turned right and headed into town, speeding up to a steady pace and gradually pulling clear of the water.

Elliot turned to face the family. "We're going to take you to town, to the police station—"

But the man spoke up quickly. *"No queremos ir a la policía, no policía."*

Matt just shook his head. "These really are wetbacks, Elliot, sounds like they're saying they don't wanna see the police. Probably not border patrol either," Matt said. "Let's drop them off at the YMCA. Or the library."

Elliot did his best to communicate that to them, then turned back to Matt. "They may be undocumented, we don't know. But they had a car, didn't they? They must have a life here. Or somewhere around here." He turned back.

"Family . . . *familia* . . . *aquí*? Friends . . . *amigos aquí*?" But the burst of Spanish in reply was too much for him to fathom.

When they reached the town, they all piled out. The water had hardly infiltrated past the seal of the doors, but an awful lot of wet people had climbed inside. Matt was the only with a shred of dry clothing, but the pouring rain fixed that. The family got out and stood together, the mother holding the daughter in her arms. The father and the son hesitated, then shook the hands of all three of them. "*Gracias a ustedes, todos de ustedes.*"

Elliot pulled a damp wallet out of his back pocket and handed a small wad of bills to the father, who dropped his head but accepted it.

Matt shook his head again. *I know why he's doing this, I kinda understand. But they're not even Americans.*

Buck pulled out a soaked packet of tobacco but unwrapped it anyway and put a chaw in his mouth.

The mother smiled at Buck and then put her daughter down so she could hug him once, tightly. He wouldn't put his arms around her at first but then relented.

Matt pulled away from the curb. "I'm mighty proud of you boys, ya did well back there. But actually I don't want any police attention either, I can understand that."

"But you know what else? Now we know if the authorities get ahold of Buck, even waterboarding won't extract any information out of him."

Nobody had the enthusiasm to laugh. "Let's take you drowned rats home and git you dried out. Then we're gonna have a lot of work to overhaul this truck."

SIXTEEN

Kauai Cooperative

May there always be Tradewinds behind you, Rainbows above you, and Aloha all Around you. —*Kauai blessing*

Live your life while the sun is still shining. / *Oi kau ka lau, e hana I ola honua.*
—*Hawaiian proverb*

Jake—master of useless trivia—had researched every detail, and was prepared to wax eloquent on the history of the ukulele. He mused about the lute family of instruments, and the popularization of the 'uke' in Hawaii by Portuguese immigrants from Madeira, the Azores, and Cape Verde. He knew the instrument typically featured four nylon strings, and came in the four sizes of soprano, concert, tenor, and baritone. He discovered that an ardent early proponent of the music was "King Kalakaua . . . [and as] a patron of the arts, [the King had] incorporated it into performances at royal gatherings." Jake had also scrounged up a string of plastic flowers from some remote costume party. *Not that I like to do dress up*, he thought. Now on the whiteboard he wrote out the first section heading for the students just now arriving:

Economics of Engineering

Sam and Veronica were the first in the door. "Jake, what's with the costume?" Sam asked, looking at the weak excuse of a lei around his neck. Veronica, wearing long, dangly earrings today, just raised her eyebrows at him and looked for a seat near the front without saying a word.

"Just a prop for today's lecture, Sam," Jake said, as Russell and the others began filing in, unloading packs, checking out their phones, and in Russell's case, bragging about intramural tennis.

Jake glanced at the clock on the wall and announced it was time to get started. "Luckily, I see you're all getting used to arriving on time, so quiet down because we have a ton of material to cover today. These are my props. Anybody know what this instrument is?" Several people spoke up simultaneously. "Okay, so does anybody know how to play it?" He looked around. "Don't be shy, there must be someone."

Jennifer raised her hand slowly. "Just don't ask me to show you right now."

"Don't worry, it's probably not even in tune, I just borrowed this from a friend. For background I can tell you the ukulele was brought to the Hawaiian Islands by Portuguese immigrants, and that one of the later Hawaiian kings was a royal patron." He set the instrument down on a desk at the side and took off his plastic flowers. "How many of you have been to Hawaii before?"

"Twice," Mark said, and others raised their hands.

Jake grinned, raising an eyebrow. "Frankly I'm envious, because I've always wanted to go there, dreamed about it when I was growing up in Minnesota, probably because I read Michener's book by the same name . . . so, someday . . . okay, let's get down to business.

"I brought these items along not to make a spectacle of myself, but because we're going to be talking about the island of Kauai today, as a case study of an independent power system necessarily limited to a single island. Remember when I assigned those two chapters of the text, eight and nine, that deal with engineering economics, so here is our chance to do some real tropical exploring.

"First point is that the islands of the Hawaiian archipelago are far enough apart and the ocean so deep that interisland grid connections are not feasible, especially given the depth of the ocean surrounding them. So, everything we've discussed about the major interconnections in North America fail to be applicable here. And this generalization holds pretty much for the majority of isolated power systems in the world typically supplying limited and geographically remote areas.

"Second point is that each island has its own history, culture, latitude, topography, and electrical infrastructure. In the case of Kauai its particular history goes back centuries. King Kamehameha set up the first unified monarchy over almost the entire island chain, extending out from the Big Island to smaller islands such as Maui and Oahu—but he never reached and took control over Kauai, perhaps because it was at the northwest end of the chain, I don't know the whole history."

"Actually, Jake, there is a small island more distant in the northwest, Niihau, close to Kauai, only a couple hundred residents, minimal tourism," Russell explained. "Kauai in fact is the second oldest of the main Hawaiian Islands, after Niihau."[8]

Jake stood looking at him, sticking his tongue in his cheek quizzically. "Got it, thanks for the correction. In more modern history, a for-profit utility—Hawaiian Electric—also went on an acquisition spree that bought up every independent electrical system in the islands, except guess which one."

"Kauai," Sam said, without even raising his hand or looking up from what he was writing. Today he sported a Dodgers sweatshirt.

Jake lifted his chin in response. "The next step in the evolution of power supply was when the state legislature established the goal of net zero energy by 2045. Kauai used to have a 'Wall Street-owned, for-profit utility,' as do some seventy percent of US customers today. That utility, Citizens Utility Company of Connecticut, eventually decided to sell out."

"Connecticut, really?" Russell exclaimed.

"Yes, really. The island and the company itself had taken a real beating from Hurricane Iniki—the most powerful cyclone to strike Hawaii in recorded history.[9] Their secret? A publicly owned grid. Iniki was the only hurricane to directly hit the state during the 1992 Pacific hurricane season, out of the eleven tropical cyclones in the Central Pacific that year. Reaching sustained winds of 145 miles per hour, it achieved Category 4 status on the Saffir–Simpson hurricane scale, but had gusts up to 225 miles per hour as its center struck Kauai, like an arrow hitting the bullseye. Citizens Utility eventually decided to sell out and residents on Kauai arranged financing to take possession and establish an electricity cooperative in 2002, with the pledge to lower electricity rates, which were the state's highest that year.

"Apparently residents to this day feel the local takeover of the utility was one of the signature moments in their history. The conflict intrinsic to an investor-owned utility is that they serve two masters—shareholders and ratepayers—and their interests are never fully aligned. The fledgling board of the Kauai Island Utility Cooperative, or KIUC, made a radical decision in 2008, when they set a goal to embrace the then-speculative and extravagant concept of utility-scale solar power. Any idea why?"

"I'd say Hawaii must have some of the best year-round solar flux of any of the states," Sam said.

"Granted," Jake said, "but with the caveat that some islands are not as ideal, the Hilo side of the Big Island gets over ten feet of showers per year with drenching rain emptying out a great colander in the sky almost every afternoon.

"The economic and ecological catalyst for Kauai was that in 2008 they were generating more than ninety percent of electricity from imported oil—"[10]

"Hawaii doesn't have any oil since it's volcanic, right?" Russell asked.

Veronica said, "The geologic substrate for oil and gas is sedimentary rocks, not igneous."

"Yep, right again. So the board of the new cooperative went to work. The first large-scale solar installation, an array owned by Alexander & Baldwin Solar, was completed in 2012. Next up, a biomass plant designed to burn woodchips was constructed in early 2013, with the so-called Green Energy Team harvesting trees to use as feedstock, eliminating the need to import the woodchips. The company initially targeted invasive *Albizia* trees, but in the same area they replanted a variety of saplings, cultivated to be harvested every four and a half years. In short order, in 2014 another solar project was developed by REC Solar in Anahola on homestead lands, cementing the progress of solar, biomass, and hydroelectric to the point that they provided thirty-five percent of total electricity and often the majority of generation during daylight hours."

Jake was pleased to see his students rapt in their attention, writing or typing notes. "After the successful solar plants in 2012 and 2014, KIUC embarked on its next gamble, solar panels directly charging utility-scale lithium-ion batteries. May seem passé at this point, but radical at the time. With continued rollout of sustainable technologies, by 2022 KIUC was generating sixty percent of its power from renewables, mostly solar but also hydro and biomass. The cooperative now projects to produce one hundred percent sustainable electricity by 2033, a dozen years before the state's mandated deadline."

Veronica raised her hand this time. "Jake, this almost sounds like a perfect experiment, since all the other islands get power from what you characterized as the private, for-profit Hawaiian Electric utility and its subsidiaries. So how much of the state is served by the big kahuna?"

Should get her to stop raising her hand. "Ninety-five percent, so a ratio of nineteen to one, but obviously they operate in similar climates, over similar topography and under the same state administrative policies. In the last decade, Hawaiian Electric, with more robust resources and the capability of a publicly traded company to raise capital much more easily, had upped its renewables rate to only thirty-two percent, basically just half of what the cooperative accomplished."

Big kahuna, I like that, thought Jake. "And the icing on the cake is that the big kahuna's electricity rates are higher today than they were a decade ago, while Kauai's rates have dropped from the highest in the state to the lowest. This is a serious shift away from the volatile and unreliable costs of fossil fuels."

"And releases less carbon pollution into the air," Sam added.

"Yeah, now look at this slide showing what happened between 2010 and 2024 to the mean residential rate per kWh. A kilowatt-hour, remember, is the amount that could run a typical microwave for sixty minutes.

Or hundred-watt incandescent light bulbs, ten of them, for an hour, though we know LEDs are far superior."

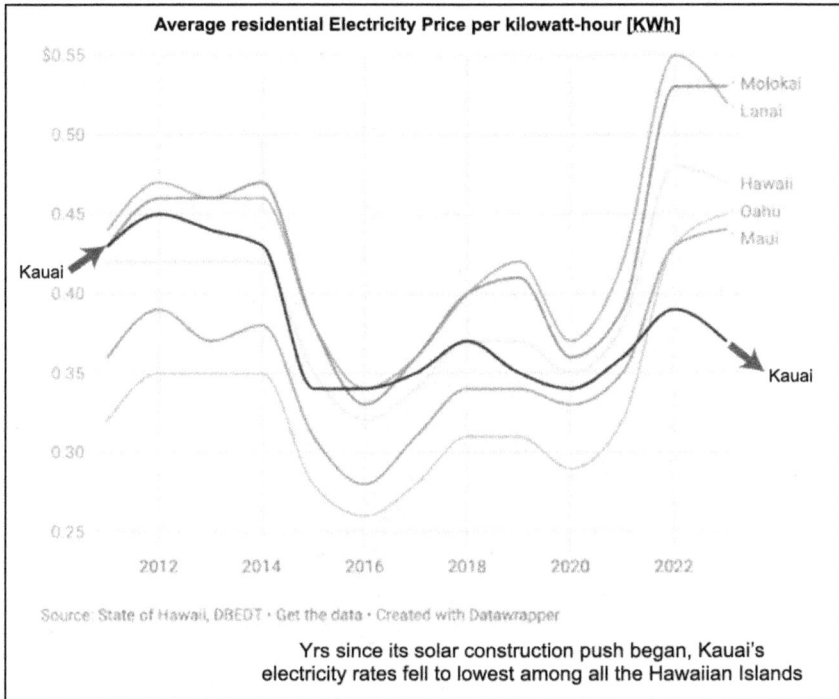

Average residential Electricity Price per kilowatt-hour [KWh]

$0.55 — Molokai, Lanai
0.50
0.45 — Hawaii, Oahu, Maui
Kauai
0.40
0.35 — Kauai
0.30
0.25

2012 2014 2016 2018 2020 2022

Source: State of Hawaii, DBEDT · Get the data · Created with Datawrapper

Yrs since its solar construction push began, Kauai's electricity rates fell to lowest among all the Hawaiian Islands

"There you see it, Kauai at thirty-five cents per kilowatt-hour by August of 2023, compared with a national mean price of 15.9 cents per kWh in the same month."

"Hey, but that's more than double the national mark," Veronica said, sitting up straighter, eyebrows practically meeting in the midline. "So, I guess only impressive . . . in comparison."

"What's been the trend line for the national figure?" Mark asked.

"Marching steadily up," Jake said, looking at Mark and not smiling. He started pacing back and forth again. "Remember the fuel for wind and solar will always be free. Maintenance is less, cost of labor is less. But the upfront costs will be outsized."

He turned to write on the board:

Grid Forming[11]

Beneath that he scribbled:

Grid Following

"I need to address another dilemma, namely rotational inertia. If a grid suffers blackout for any reason, then the solution to standing the grid back up is what we call a 'grid-forming' resource. Historically, in most of the country this would have been a coal burner, a nuke, or hydro generator getting up to a specific number of revolutions per second. This valuable grid service is facilitated by these gigantic rotating masses spinning up to highly specific targets of voltage and frequency. There's a subtle point here. The multitude of induction motors comprising much of the demand in the system are precisely mated to the rotational inertia of the generators producing the power.

"Heavy spinning objects just wanna keep spinning like a child's top, but the match must be extraordinarily precise.

"There are safety cutouts in the generators and similar controls in the operating motors to prevent any significant deviation from the mandated rotational inertia which immediately triggers disconnection of either one—in order to protect the grid. The core insight is that the combined inertia of generators and motors contributes to and augments the stability of the grid. Control rooms maintain that sixty-hertz frequency of current to several decimals of precision." He paused, then returned to pacing.

"Variable renewable sources of energy—even from something as common as passing clouds blocking sunlight from solar panels—could degrade the voltage or frequency or both."

"You're trying to argue that photovoltaic panels don't have any spinning mass—" Mark said.

"Exactly, precisely," Jake said, "and I'm also saying that even though wind turbines use large spinning generators with gearing to produce relatively constant output, the individual spinning turbines may not be synchronized to all the others in the same wind farm."

Jake considered posting another heading but decided against it.

"So, the conventional wisdom was that the new-kids-on-the-block renewables of solar and wind could never be grid-forming resources in the same way a nuclear, or fossil-fueled plant could, that instead solar and wind could only sync passively with an operating grid and slavishly conform to its functioning. The term here is 'grid following' instead of 'grid forming,'" he said, as he pointed to the second posting on the board.

"In the event of an extensive power outage, then the thinking was that keystone generators such as nuclear, peaking methane, and hydropower would first be brought up to restart the grid, then solar and wind would follow along. That this natural sequence was paramount, even irrevocable."

"Was this a reason that doubters of solar energy warned against an overreliance on solar in California?" Veronica asked.

"That there would be no way to restart the grid with solar after an outage? Yeah, that was one of many reasons, including the infamous duck curve of overproduction of solar on sunny afternoons.

"But that assumption about grid blackouts requiring conventional generators to spin the whole system back up turned out to be false.

"This was first shown for solar with modeling, later with actual experimentation with wind farms using grid-forming inverters—which convert DC to AC power—being able to establish stable voltage and frequency and get the rest of the grid to fall in step like good soldiers.

"Then in 2015 the Kauai cooperative signed a contract with Tesla and SolarCity for the first utility-scale combination of solar with batteries. The project was completed in 2017, by which time the two companies had been combined. This was facilitated because, as a cooperative, they had the option of low-cost financing through the US Department of Agriculture's Rural Utilities Service. The specific intent was to store as much solar energy in the batteries as possible, in order to meet the pending evening demand peak with inverter-based resources like solar and batteries, and put off as long as possible the booting up of the fossil fuel generators."

Jake strode to the board to put up another heading beneath the other two:

Synthetic Inertia

He thought for a moment, then scrawled underneath:

Induction Motor Synchronization

"Turns out you can use fancy software and smart inverters to support variable sources with something called 'synthetic inertia' to accomplish grid-forming stabilization. This is essentially a computerized control strategy to make inverter-based resources *act like* a physical inertial device would and automatically compensate in real time for local measured current characteristics."

"So, you're saying the computerized algorithm can create the equivalent of all those spinning generators and motors?" Russell asked.

"Yessiree, Russell. Actually, there are a couple of ways to skin this cat, such as batteries or banks of capacitors. Since North America is universally sixty hertz as far as frequency goes, it means that the current reverses every one-sixtieth of a second. If the supply and demand of the grid get out of balance, the inertia of the grid physically responds, since it constitutes an actual *physical load* pushing back against the force generators must produce to create a flow of electricity. But as I said, all of the generators and all of the induction motors have sensors to trigger or trip offline—if frequency changes by as little as one percent—to avoid suffering damage. These are all large heavy copper and steel devices spinning like tops, and repair can be expensive and cumbersome. One imaginative way to simulate this same phenomenon in a grid overweighted with renewables is a simpler and slightly more costly solution called 'synchronized condensers.' These are basically generators lacking a turbine to generate electricity—nothing but a spinning prime mover—just rotating hunks of copper coiled around a magnet *consuming* a miniscule amount of electricity to stay spinning and synchronized to the grid."

"Sounds a lot like a gyroscope on a missile or airplane, using its mass to signal change in direction but requiring minimal current to rotate," Mark said.

Jake shook his head. "Very smart comparison, very good. The gyroscope resists sudden change in orientation while a synchronized condenser resists change in voltage or frequency . . . I love that comparison." *Mark is one smart guy.*

"Now, if one large generator fails, then cascading failures will spread to other generators unless you can right the ship by—"

Veronica had a question. "What about backup power for protection of these devices?"

"I was just coming to that. You always have to have enough flexibility of what we call operating reserves or contingency reserves or spinning reserves to be able to step in at a moment's notice. Some kinds of generation systems like coal and nuclear and combined cycle gas plants are way too slow to be able to help. The exceptions would be if you had hydro or fossil fuel plants that are committed and operating on the grid—but held somewhere in between their minimum and maximum levels—which allows them flexibility to ramp up or down quickly."

Sam looked at the board and asked, "But you're saying batteries or banks of capacitors could respond even faster?"

"Exactly that," Jake said, then thought for a moment and turned to record on the board:

"Dispatchable" or Flexible Demand

"Everything we've talked about so far is about dispatchable or flexible supply. But what about the demand side of the equation? What kinds of demand are firm or inflexible?" *No immediate takers.*

"In your own life, what do you absolutely depend on for electrical supply?"

"An alarm clock in the morning has to go off at a certain time," Veronica said.

"Or electrical lighting," Jake said, continuing, "a toaster, a coffee maker, a water pump for a shower, my morning computer time. All of these things where I don't want to wait even an extra second. Gotta be Johnny-on-the-spot.

"Firm demand. Inflexible demand. Besides your own home, we have high standards for hospital care, ventilators, other medical devices, stoplights when we're driving. But then we have things in our lives we can schedule for another time besides right this instant. If you have an EV at home, then you can schedule when it will charge. It would be no skin off your nose if your clothes washer or dishwasher were to be scheduled at a low-demand time. This holds for industry as well, with the examples of aluminum smelters or industrial refrigeration warehouses set up with demand response contracts.

"Desalination can run on and off the clock depending on the needs of the grid. Agricultural pumping has long been scheduled preferably at night or when energy costs are low."

"How does demand response work in practice?" Veronica asked.

"When the grid is overloaded with demand, the utility turns them off temporarily, paying for this service with a set fee for this so-called 'ancillary service.' Often the company can rely on its own backup energy storage for a short interval."

Jake thought for a moment, then turned to write:

Geopolitics

"Russia's invasion of Ukraine in 2021 had repercussions around the globe. The high penetration of renewables on Kauai largely protected customers from the suddenly heightened unpredictability of oil prices. Its electric rates had already returned to pre-Ukraine levels by late 2023, whereas rates on jam-packed and populous Oahu were still about fifty percent higher than in January of 2021. Across the nation, however, contrasting the public power sector of cooperative, municipal power systems and federal power providers to for-profit utilities does not show much of a difference, as assessed by David Pomerantz of the Energy and Policy Institute. He stated, "There are leaders and laggards in both sectors, and very, very few actors in either rising to the challenge of rapid and equitable decarbonization."[12]

Looking over at the clock again, Jake said, "Good, we have enough time left to discuss one last Hawaiian issue. Granted, there are a lot of new battery chemistries coming down the pike, but besides lithium-ion batteries and demand-side management, KIUC felt they needed longer-term storage overnight or over several days or more of inclement weather. Fortunately, the west side of the island is mountainous. There were even old plantation-era irrigation ditches that utilized outflow from the mountains. Hawaii's first commercial sugar plantation was created in Koloa, Kauai, in 1835, and sugar rapidly grew to dominate Kauai's economy—and the economy of the whole Hawaiian archipelago—through to the nineteenth and twentieth centuries.[13]

"In modern times, natural and man-made basins were constructed at altitude in the mountains, using abundant solar when accessible to lift the water and top off these impoundments. When called upon, the water plunges down the penstock pipe to convert the pump into a generator. This sort of pumped hydro is by far the most common sort of gravitational storage of energy.

"The cooperative KIUC selected the Arlington-Virginia-based independent power producer Applied Energy Services, or AES, to construct its hydropower infrastructure.[14] AES was founded in 1981 and went public in 1991." Jake looked at his notes. "Okay, here's the quote: The founders of the company 'signaled a commitment to providing its consumers and clients with renewable forms of energy, and their operations across the world have increasingly focused on the construction and provision of solar- and wind-based energy storage systems.'"

"Sounds like the cooperative found the right sort of company for the job," Sam said, nodding his head.

"I'm inclined to agree, Sam."

"But what's the energy trade-off?" Sam asked.

"The figure used in hydropower is seventy-five percent of the pumping energy consumed is returned as electricity on the return trip."

"Therefore, twenty-five percent loss then."

"That's thermodynamics for you." Jake nodded, then continued. "But think about this. With rainfall in the mountains, some of the water arriving from the sky may at least minimize evaporation losses. In fact, in a wet season, it may even exceed losses and produce free energy. But the problem the cooperative is facing now is that an organized group of Native Hawaiian community advocates are concerned about protections for freshwater assets.

"In February of 2023, an environmental law firm filed a suit on their behalf, arguing the state permitting authority had exceeded its jurisdiction and further had failed to solicit an environmental impact statement. The current plan would take water from the already-depleted Waimea River, unless a closed loop water system is set up."

"How would that help?" Mark asked.

"With a reservoir at the bottom of the system to avoid flushing the water to the sea, essentially you'd be pumping the same water up repeatedly. First problem is this would cut off the supply dedicated to Native Hawaiians farming in the mountains. Second problem is that you couldn't scale the system to be as large, so less generating capacity at night." He could tell everybody was cogitating about these trade-offs.

"So, there are community advocates and environmentalists who need to work out their differences. While this project has been hanging fire since 2021, what you have is a power company rooted in and answering to their community, so I suspect this dispute will get worked out eventually.

"Okay, guys and gals, I like to start on time but also finish on time, so read chapter eleven on inferential statistics and decision-making over the weekend. Also, if you haven't gotten to it yet, check out the Amory Lovins article from 1976 from the journal *Foreign Affairs*, all about the initial articulation of what he christened 'the soft energy path.' The title is 'Energy Strategy: The Road Not Taken.'"[15]

"See you all next week."

He added "Aloha" and was answered in turn as they made their way out the door.

SEVENTEEN

Field Cut

It's not what happens to you, but how you react to it that matters. —*Epictetus*

Our greatest glory is not in never falling, but in rising every time we fall. —*Confucius*

Abbey looked at the frankly fatherly veterinarian sitting across the desk from her. Benjamin appeared more unhurried than harried, unlike most health care providers. He wore a bow tie with white and vermilion stripes, the kind of accessory she suspected he wore daily. Unrimmed glasses hung below his neck. The front office assistant had offered her coffee, and Abbey had accepted. *Only one cup a day now that Hope's a bit older.*

When she shook his hand and thanked him for taking this appointment, she made the mistake of calling him Dr. Harris, since she figured he probably had enough years of experience to have honestly earned his gray hair and whiskers.

"Just call me Benjamin, Abbey, we're pretty informal around here."

"First thing I wanna say is, I appreciate your accepting my request to come see you."

"Happy to help out."

"I should also mention that we live in Clarendon, so it was close enough that I thought I would take the time to plumb your brain for some ideas." He smiled.

"How many years have you been in this practice?" she asked.

"Almost forty years. There are three of us now, though I've been here the longest. My younger partners practice almost exclusively small animal veterinary medicine. I grew up outside of Richmond in what was then farming country, so I've always been the large animal vet."

"What can you tell me about the goats on Mr. Cooper's farm?"

"You may already know the goat we hospitalized here died. The other one on their spread survived the first ten days, so there are reasonable grounds for optimism it's going to pull through."

"But both aborted, correct?"

"They did. Jared had already buried the products of conception from the first goat on his farm before he called me. With the second one I collected tissue specimens, including from the placentas, and blood specimens from the recently parturient does. All that material was sent off to the state lab."

"They must still have some of both the blood serum and other tissue?" she asked, knowing the answer was critical. "My initial thought was that the goats might have been an unrelated issue, but now I've come to the contrary conclusion. Jared did tell me . . . incidentally, you know about the HIPAA regulations we deal with in human medicine, but yesterday I told Jared and . . . what's his wife's name again?"

"Jacey, sweet woman," he answered, absentmindedly taking out a small cloth to clean his glasses. "And yes, the lab has not only hung on to blood and tissue specimens, but sent some material on to the CDC."

"So, I told Jared and Jacey I was going to contact you, and really I'm considering you a consultant in this case, so I'm assuming this is no breach of confidentiality as long as we only discuss the infectious disease aspects of his care."

He nodded. "Okay, I agree. Jared also told me he used disposable gloves when he handled the miscarriages. And washed up with soap out in the barn. Fortunately, the rest of the family remains healthy." This time he just scratched his chin.

"You've not seen any other animals with spontaneous abortions or illnesses, or even heard of some elsewhere in this region?"

"No, I have not. I discussed that with other vets in this area. We get together on a monthly basis, much like your meetings at the hospital, I suppose."

"Jared told me something unusual, that you had mentioned mosquito activity seemed higher than normal this year. For a long time, I've been interested in the changing range of mosquitoes and other arthropod vectors, what with the modifications in climate, and I'm concerned this might be the source of Jared's infection." She leaned back a moment.

"So, you suspect a mosquito-borne illness then."

"We have submitted urine, blood, and cerebrospinal fluid for a wider array of infectious diseases than we usually do. Viral studies for varicella zoster, herpes simplex 1 and 2, HIV, Western and Eastern encephalitis. Bacterial infections including the second phase of leptospirosis, plus pneumococcal or meningococcal meningitis. Fungal infections including candidiasis, cryptococcosis, and histoplasmosis. He's had no warm water swimming exposure to think about *Naegleria fowleri*, or any other recent travel to consider any other parasitic infection."

"You're sure about this being meningitis, no component of encephalitis?"

"Imaging with both CT and MR of his head and neck have been negative, including of both orbits with careful attention to the posterior eyes. But by ophthalmologic exam, his left retina has some lesions and he's reporting visual defects corresponding to this location."

"But nothing hinting at a rheumatologic illness, sarcoid, lymphoma, anything else?"

She crinkled her eyebrows. "How do you know about sarcoidosis?"

He laughed. "I'm just throwing out some ideas here. Equine sarcoids are pretty common, about a fifth of their neoplasms and a third of all skin tumors in horses."

She raised her eyebrows and shook her head in appreciation. "Jared was scheduled to be seen in the ophthalmology clinic this morning, but I haven't seen their report yet. Besides the other entities we considered, we thought about cat scratch disease from *Bartonella* species carried by cat fleas, Lyme disease from *Borrelia burgdorferi*, syphilis courtesy of *Treponema pallidum*, and tuberculosis resulting from typical and atypical *Mycobacterium* species."

"Skin testing negative for those?" And she nodded her agreement.

"Benjamin, I'm afraid I need to move along. I'm having lunch with my partner and I'm going to hit him up for some ideas also. After that I'll go to see how Jared is faring. But I can't thank you enough for your feedback here."

"Interested in visiting their farm sometime, Abbey?"

"Thought about that but doubt its utility. You've evaluated them clinically and submitted all the appropriate specimens to the lab. Can you be sure to notify me if you come up with any other ideas? And is it okay if I check with the state lab for updates?"

He stood up to shake her hand. "Abbey, we all want to get to the root of this, for the sake of both the family and their farm animals." He scribbled down the phone number and contact name for the state lab. "Say hello to Jared and Jacey for me, will ya?"

"I will certainly do so, Benjamin. If we can figure out what this is, then maybe there will be a treatment for those goats. And I appreciate your collaboration on all this."

***

Dan and Abbey sat down at their office conference table with their brown bag lunches. He usually had a ham and cheese sandwich, but this time had chosen tuna. They often got together like this at their office midday, sharing stories, discussing issues with their staff. He was unshaven, having been up for a couple of hours in the middle of the night with a patient at another hospital.

"So, you've got a previously healthy guy with signs of meningitis but no clinically apparent brain involvement. Except that now he has a cut in his left temporal visual field from an acute and fairly focal chorioretinitis—are you sure this doesn't look like cytomegalovirus?"

"Not that classic 'spaghetti and meatballs' pattern, no, I've seen a lot of that in HIV patients. But I haven't pulled up the ophthalmology report yet, thought I'd wait until I got to the hospital. It was my understanding that the resident on the case was perhaps planning another lumbar puncture today. We need to collect enough CSF to send further studies, like an acid-fast stain for TB . . . and cultures of course."

"CMV would be almost unheard of in an immunologically normal patient. What other diagnoses are you considering?"

"Since I'm on the wastewater tiger team for the CDC, I keep track of novel infections picked up there. You already know the frequency of genetic evidence for the Crimean-Congo virus has plummeted since the public health folks got out there with the message that this is often a fatal bleeding disorder. But there are a couple of diseases from Africa and Asia that could have arrived with mosquitoes hitching a ride here."

"Part of what makes practicing in DC so fascinating. So—what's your plan?"

"Going to run a couple of ideas by the CDC, like looking for genetic material from novel viruses in wastewater."

"Not gonna work, Abbey, if there is only a patient or two in this area with something new going on. Needle in a haystack. More important would be to solicit information on viruses from outside the US that can attack the retina. Focus on your patient here." *Sounds a little gruff, but that's Dan for you.*

"Now Dan, you know how I obsess about new viruses. I have this article recommended to me by the CDC entitled "Ocular manifestations of emerging viral disease," by Venkatesh et. al., from one of the *Nature* sub-journals—*Eye*. Just look at the abstract. Starts out by saying, 'Emerging infectious diseases (EIDs) are an increasing threat to public health on a global scale. In recent times, the most prominent outbreaks have [comprised] RNA viruses.'"

"How many of these have you ruled out already?"

"Come on Dan, let me finish. Usefully, they list these in four groups, the first being viruses spread by respiratory droplets, COVID-19, and influenza A H1N1."

"Covid and flu, which you have already tested for."

"Second group is direct transfer from person to person, namely Ebola and Marburg." She ran her finger down her notes.

"Your guy has had no perturbation of platelets or coagulation factors."

"And he's not bleeding anywhere. Third group is transmission via arthropods, specifically mosquitoes, including dengue, zika, West Nile, chikungunya, and Crimean-Congo."

"Abbey, I know you screened for Crimean-Congo, not because of your little vacation following a needlestick, but mainly because we know we have the disease right here in our own backyard."

She had to roll her eyes on that one. "I debated about dengue and zika, but went ahead and had our index patient screened for the other four diseases in this group, the full panel. The fourth and last group is zoonotic spread, including from goats, such as Lassa fever, Nipah, Rift Valley fever, and hantaviruses."

"Abbey, I've never heard of Lassa outside of Africa. Nipah is mainly spread from fruit bats, but also through pigs and goats. It often starts with fever and headache, then respiratory symptoms. Main point here is that this is your deadliest possibility, with death in forty to seventy-five percent of cases."

"Dan, he's not that ill and doesn't seem to be getting worse."

"I assume you have him in respiratory and contact isolation."

"His wife has visited him wearing mask and gloves, but we're not allowing his children in. Now our list is down to the last two."

Dan wiped his mouth. "Rift Valley fever is another one with no case reports from the United States or Canada. Hantavirus is spread from wild rats and mice, either from direct contact or their urine, droppings, or saliva. If they have a farm, they likely have rodents."

"So, check them all?" The question hung in the air.

"With the obvious caveat that he may not yet have seroconverted. May not have produced detectable antibodies yet. And we don't have PCR-level tests or enzyme-linked immunosorbent assay for all of these maladies. So, you might get false-negative test results and be no closer to a diagnosis." They were both quiet for a long moment.

She sighed. "I need to go in and review the slit lamp exam findings, check in with his resident, and re-examine the patient." Abbey folded up her paper towel, wiped her chin, and stood up.

Dan scratched under his chin. "While there's a paucity of human treatment options, there may be animal vaccines that would help out your vet. And if the ophthalmologist interprets inflammation in the front or back of the involved eye—that is, anterior or posterior uveitis—they may want to at least treat with anti-inflammatory agents plus topical or injected corticosteroids. Why don't you ask them to collect intraocular fluid for further study if they lean toward something procedural."

"Nothing like a poke in the eye with a sharp stick," said Abbey.

"Not even as complicated as a cataract extraction, so ask them, okay?"

"Roger that."

***

"Andrew, you look post-call again. How are you doing? More importantly, how is our patient doing?"

"Fever is variable. He's sleeping better. Neck is still a bit stiff, but his lumbar puncture this morning had a normal opening pressure, protein was almost down to normal. Cells still show some pleocytosis, twenty lymphocytes two days ago versus eleven today, but no polys, no neutrophils this time." He leaned back in his chair in the tiny conference room on the third floor as Abbey scanned the ophthalmology report.

"How's his vision?" *This is the key question.*

"Perhaps a bit worse. More obvious field cut on the left. He's not happy about it."

"No one would be. Looks like Dr. Eric Vanderschmidt appreciated some cells and flare in the slit lamp exam of the vitreous fluid in front of the retina. And mapped his field cut, looks like about a third of his visual area so far, extending out to his left. The fovea is not involved at this point and therefore his central vision is intact. His diagnosis is simply stated as likely an acute infectious chorioretinitis, most likely viral, but no specific disorder identified. We need more than this, the epidemiology is critical here. No mention of any specific treatment aside from a topical cycloplegic for visual rest on the left. Eye patch, in other words."

"Dr. Vanderschmidt wants to see him again tomorrow for a repeat exam to see if he's progressing. Can you explain the indication for the cycloplegic?"

Wow, he's actually scratching his head.

"It paralyzes the ciliary muscle, so no accommodation for distance is possible. Thus, the lens is not being constantly moved while there is inflammation in the eye. Very disturbing when the other eye is accommodating moment to moment normally. Hence the patch.

"Looking at the lab, seems like platelets and coagulation factors are normal. Obvious inference is that if not at risk for bleeding, could use an anti-inflammatory, something as simple as oral ibuprofen. But Vanderschmidt needs to make the call about topical or injected steroids. I'm going to call him, then see the patient."

"Any other diagnostic work you're going to recommend, Abbey?"

"Results are still pending for a couple of things, but we're going to recommend a few more entities, including chikungunya, Rift Valley and hantavirus. I know his PPD is negative, and his chest X-ray is clear, but I saw you added acid-fast stain and culture for mycobacteria on your spinal tap this morning."

"Yeah, nothing more fun than finding those red snappers on the stain of the spinal fluid."

"Agree of course, Andrew. Okay, I'm going to write down some additional lab recommendations, then call up Vanderschmidt and go see the patient." They both stood up to set about their tasks, though Abbey clearly felt more sprightly. But also a bit engorged. Maybe time to breast pump before leaving the hospital.

***

"Jared, how are you feeling today?" Abbey asked, as she came into the room. *Even with an eye patch, does not look piratical.* Pale, not lifting his head off the pillow.

He roused a bit.

"Has Jacey been here today? Or planning on coming later?"

"Oh, Dr. London, hello. Wasn't sure we'd see you today. No, Jace will be in later, had some parent-teacher conferences for our kids today."

"So how are you feeling then?" Abbey asked again, gazing intently at his face, listening to his voice, noting his breathing was a bit faster than before, but no cough or obvious respiratory distress.

"Your temperature is a bit higher than 101 degrees now, though usually that's not uncommon in the afternoon." He reached slowly over to hit the control to lift the head of the bed.

"I had chills and sweats during the night . . . the nurse gave me something for it."

"Suspect not much appetite then. Remember what people used to say: Feed a cold, starve a fever. Not true anymore, we'd rather get some nutrition into you." She decided to sit in a chair by the bed.

"How's your head feeling? Here, let me check your pulse while we're talking." She held his wrist on the palm side of the thumb. *Radial pulse is regular, but weak.*

"Headache's not better."

"Front of your head, side, back? Steady or throbbing? More one side than the other? Worse if you change position?"

"All over . . . my head." *Seems effortful just trying to talk.* "Haven't been up except to the bathroom with assistance from a nurse—or Jace. Makes it throb more."

"And your vision?"

"Worse on the outside of the left eye, worse than yesterday."

"Any bright lights? Any pain in the eye itself?"

"Just more fuzzy going out to the side."

"So, your central vision is still intact?"

"I don't take the patch off much . . . too irritating."

She nodded. "I'll have you remove it in a moment so I can have a look. The ophthalmologist, Dr. Vanderschmidt, mapped out your visual field in both eyes, and he told me he wants to see you again tomorrow morning to see if there's been any change. If so, he may recommend topical or injected steroids to calm the process down."

He was quiet for a moment.

"He's considering collecting a bit of fluid from the eye itself, which is done with a local anesthetic and is easier than it sounds." His right eye closed and his head rolled back and forth slowly.

"Whatever it takes, I gotta get better."

"We still don't know what this infection is. We've ruled out a lot of possibilities but will need some more blood samples."

"I already feel . . . like a . . . blood donor," Jared got out, taking breaths in between.

She stood up, pulling out a light and a tongue blade. "Okay, open wide," she said, peering at the teeth, which were in excellent shape, under the tongue, back of the throat. Felt for lymph nodes in the neck and above the collar bones near the midline. Helped pull him up to sitting, then listened to the front and back of his chest. Helped him back down again. "I'm going to shine a bright light in your good eye first." She noted normal pupillary reactivity and extraocular movement side to side and up and down. She pulled out her ophthalmoscope and looked at all the quadrants of the retina, finding no defects.

"Jared, pull off the eye patch please. I'm going to come around to the other side of the bed to have a look." He squinted both eyes in response to the sudden light, and both pupils were round, regular, and responsive to the light stimulus. With her ophthalmoscope, the story was a bit different. The optic disc where the ocular nerve entered the retina was clear, but the upper and lower quadrants to the nasal side of the disc showed more of the exudate she had seen two days prior. She judged the scattered hemorrhage had progressed as well.

She pulled back and put away her ophthalmoscope. "Mr. Cooper, from what I can see there is a reasonable chance the ophthalmologist is going to recommend steroids for this eye. The right eye so far is apparently unaffected, but there is no guarantee that whatever condition this is will not ultimately spread."

As he pulled the patch back down, he took a deep sigh. "Is there a possibility this will not get better? That I will go blind in this eye?" He looked at her directly. "I . . . need to know what to tell Jacey."

"Mr. Cooper, I can make you no promises. We are still a few steps away from a firm diagnosis. Raise these same questions with the eye doctor tomorrow morning. Might be a good idea to have your wife accompany you. I'll be keeping watch on all the lab data coming in and working with the whole team."

She cleaned off her stethoscope with an alcohol wipe and replaced it in her pocket. Washed her hands in the sink, thinking she should wash again before pumping breast milk.

"Your temperature curve and cell counts lead us to think you're on the mend. I'm going to arrange for some further special blood tests. I suspect your primary follow-up post-discharge will be with the ophthalmology department."

He turned his face away from her. She could see his cheek and neck muscles tighten, but he remained mute.

The phlebotomist walked in the door and hesitated when he saw Abbey, but she nodded and told him she was just leaving.

EIGHTEEN

NERC for Nerds

Hell is empty and all the devils are here. —William Shakespeare
When you are going through hell, keep going. —Winston Churchill

Jake watched his troops arrive in twos and threes. "Hop to it, folks, lot to cover today." He watched as Sam came in, blond and athletic, wearing a broad smile as he joked with Veronica, who had on her usual jeans. *One of the best American inventions of all time*, thought Jake.

Russell had a tennis hat and, in his pack, a pair of tennis rackets. Mark, of course, had a rugby shirt on, with no grass stains for once. *Maybe a new shirt.* Jake had really begun to know and respect their individual personalities. *Does Veronica have a new tattoo on her arm?* Then Jake remembered she had always worn long-sleeve shirts before. *Better not embarrass her by asking about it.* Everyone filed in and found their usual seats. Jake shook his head and smiled to himself as he wrote out his first heading:

NERC[16]

Then he got serious. "In December of 2023, NERC—the North American Electric Reliability Corporation—put out a sober warning that most regions of the US and Canada would face an escalating risk of inadequate supplies of electricity over the next decade, particularly during extended extremes of temperature, cold snaps, and heat waves. The crux of the problem is major wind and solar and geothermal and certainly nuclear projects were not being installed at sufficient pace. Clearly not enough to keep up with fossil plant retirements and burgeoning demand from data centers, electric vehicles, and crypto mining. John Moura, the director of reliability assessment and performance analysis, said this was 'a real call for action.'"

Jake began to pace as he built up steam. "As you all know well now, NERC is the preeminent grid monitoring organization for almost the whole continent. Moura made clear he is concerned about performance of the grid under conditions of extreme weather events, rising electricity demand, and the shift to sustainable, variable generation facilities not geographically proximate to large urban areas and loads.

"NERC sees demand growing ten percent through 2032, a bit over half a decade. And generation—wait, what would you guess is the projection of growth for generation?" He paused. *Not just a rhetorical question.*

"Five percent," hazarded Mark. Jake just nodded.

"Eight percent," Veronica said.

"As if," responded Jake.

"Four percent," Sam said.

"Game theory again?" Jake asked. "You nailed it, Sam.

"I'm no mathematician, but four percent sounds a lot less than ten percent. Electrification of everything's not gonna happen if supply, transmission, storage, flexiwatts, and negawatts are all inadequate—"

Sam wanted to be reminded of what flexiwatts and negawatts were again. Jake explained flexiwatts were all about demand management, shifting flexible load either earlier in time or deferring to later, and negawatts were all about efficiency measures, such as LED light bulbs.

"NERC stated over eighty-three thousand megawatts of nuclear and fossil fuel generation are slated to shut down as early as 2028, so time's a wastin', folks. Just to pile on, another thirty thousand megawatts are provisionally set to close, but plans aren't final." Jake furrowed his brows, then raised one eyebrow.

"Don't forget, utility managers like to think in terms of megawatts, a million watts, but add on three zeros and you get to gigawatts, which we're all familiar with. Translate all of this to eighty-three and thirty gigawatts— each approximately equal to a single nuclear reactor, as a sort of ballpark figure." Jake turned and scribbled:

Reconductoring

"Failure is certainly not an option, but there are some ways of beefing up grid function. And here reconductoring comes to mind. For example, a company called CTC Global has a novel high-voltage line that can carry significantly higher amperage within the same or even smaller cross-sectional area.[17] The core of these new lines is carbon fiber, which is lighter and stronger than the conventional steel. With greater linear resistance to stretching, there is less sag from overheating experienced due to a combination of high ambient temperature and the resistance to high-amperage transmission. This allows the company to rapidly install higher-functioning replacement lines without the need to replace or modify existing towers, structures, or poles. The company says this 'makes swapping out the old wire for the new wire quick, easy, efficient and affordable.' Not having to go through all the permitting and engineering of widening the ROW—the right of way along the route—saves time and money." He erased his headings from before and put up:

Software Engineering

"I understated the geographic differences in reliability. NERC mainly thinks much of the central and southern parts of the US will face power shortfalls in the next decade. They labeled the Midcontinent Independent System Operator, or MISO—a network of fifteen central states extending from Canada to the Gulf of Mexico—as 'high risk' for failures, with a 4,700 MW shortfall beginning in 2028, the equivalent of nearly five nuclear power plants.[18] Three Canadian provinces are felt to be in this unlucky category as well, preparing to stumble over their own feet.

"Moura argued that reliable power needs to be prioritized, informing flexibility in forcing retirements of gas-fired power plants needed to support voltage, frequency and other critical reliability factors. In the event of a crisis, the Department of Energy could step in with its statutory emergency authority to maintain stability. He also enunciated the importance of thinking of the fossil gas and electric grid systems as one *integrated* whole. Software is just as important, with smart meters being underutilized when they could be providing much more frequent, almost real-time reporting of data, coupled with more sophisticated data evaluation utilizing AI, allowing more responsive and timely management by system operators."

He thought for a moment, then turned to write again:

Hydrogen

"What can you tell me about hydrogen?" began Jake.

Veronica took the bit and ran with it. "First and lightest element in the periodic table, has a single proton and a single electron—and is the most common element in the universe. Usually combines with itself to form diatomic or molecular hydrogen. I think of it as the essential building block for all hydrocarbons. Most hydrogen atoms lack neutrons, but adding a single one creates the isotope deuterium, while adding a second one makes tritium."

"What happens if you smash an atom of deuterium together with one of tritium?"

"Then you're talking about fusion, great-granddaddy of fission. Needs temperatures and pressures similar to the core of the Sun or higher. Lots of countries are working on this, nothing close to commercialization yet."

He had stopped pacing and was facing her alertly. "How would hydrogen work in simple combustion, simply chemically reacting it with oxygen?"

She looked puzzled only for a moment. "Two hydrogen atoms combine with one of oxygen. So—just water and heat."

He scratched his ear. "Cleanest burn in the world, right? No particulates. No or almost no oxides of nitrogen. Nothing but water vapor. What's not to like?"

Mark couldn't resist a dig. "Well, water is a potent greenhouse gas."

Jake looked over his glasses at him with eyebrows raised. "Do we or do we not live on a water planet, Mark? Surface is seventy-one percent salt water, throw in fresh water like the Great Lakes and you're up to seventy-five percent covered by liquid and floating frozen water. How are you going to control how much gets into the atmosphere? From combined evaporation and transpiration from plants?"

Mark and the others couldn't stop chuckling. "Is that going to be on the test?" And now Jake was the one who couldn't resist smiling.

"You wish. So, we agree hydrogen is a beautiful fuel. But where do we get most of it?"

"Mostly from fossil methane," Sam said.

"And the process?"

"The gas is simply combined with water under high heat and pressure," Sam said.

"Right, it goes by the name of steam reforming and is widely used in industrial markets for production of hydrogen and synthesis gas. Usually the transition metal element nickel—supported on alumina—is the catalyst, and temperatures of seven to eight hundred degrees Celsius are needed. Technically, a conventional hydrogen production system is composed of a steam methane reformer, a shift converter, and a hydrogen purification system based on pressure swing adsorption. Quite a mouthful, granted.

"The hydrogen is separated out from the gas mixture that results. Since this comes from some type of petroleum and requires high heat often sourced also from fossil gas, this is all a circus run by the oil and gas industry. Anybody know what color code chemists chose to categorize this?"

"Black? Black . . . methane?" posited Mark.

"Black as the ace of spades, exactly, if derived from petroleum, though just gray if sourced from methane gas. So, black and gray are the worst choices climate-wise."

"Now, what do you think methane would be called if it's produced directly using the Sun?"

"I'm guessing methane sourced from either photovoltaics or directly from sunlight using a catalyst," Matt said.

"Correct on both counts. And the color label?"

"Green methane," said Sam, and Jake nodded.

"But there are now a number of reports of hydrogen sourced directly from underground. For example, in a former coal mining region near the French-German border, scientists in 2023 dropped a probe down a half-a-mile-deep borehole, and were excited to find champagne-sized bubbles indicating a potentially colossal cache of natural hydrogen gas, far superior to methane gas, as it is free of any carbon whatsoever. Their triumphal claim was that they may have discovered one of the largest deposits of hydrogen anywhere in the world. As discussed in a *New York Times* article, this indeed constitutes a holy grail so-called white hydrogen, better even than green hydrogen."[19]

"By what mechanism is this produced?" Veronica thought to ask.

"Apparently, from hot water percolating around iron-rich rock. An example of an iron-rich mineral is olivine, which is a volcanic combination of magnesium, iron, silicon, and oxygen with a greenish color—you'd be correct in guessing the hue of green, not black, olives. The oxygen combines with the iron, and the released hydrogen gas escapes to the surrounding porous rock. And, the respected United States Geological Survey had an article earlier that year that argued"—Jake checked his notes on the lectern—"a previously overlooked, potential geologic source of energy could increase the renewability and lower the carbon footprint of our nation's energy portfolio: natural hydrogen.[20]

"I couldn't have said it better myself. Let me add there are untapped reserves in the US, Australia, Mali, Oman, and parts of Europe." Again, he referred to his notes from the article. "Startups like Gold Hydrogen, based in Australia, and Koloma, based in Denver, are in the early stages of drilling for hydrogen and could be headed to production soon.

"As with petroleum systems allowing extraction of oil and gas, the USGS hypothesizes hydrogen systems are composed of source rock, then porous reservoir rock like limestone or sandstone, and finally a cap stone on top such as slate. The diameter of a molecule of two hydrogen atoms is about equal to that of a single helium atom, so the two gases are likely trapped by similar rock layers." Again, Jake consulted his notes. "Known helium accumulations have been preserved for as long as a hundred million years, so it's reasonable to assume that hydrogen could be trapped for similar time spans."

"Do you think it's possible hydrogen mixed with methane has been vented or flared from gas and oil wells for a long time, and we didn't even know?" Veronica asked.

"Intriguing idea, except I need to dash your hopes. Geoffrey Ellis at the USGS feels the process by which petroleum forms from ancient plankton in petroleum source rocks would consume any available hydrogen." She sat back in her seat and frowned.

"I wouldn't have guessed the primary use of hydrogen at the moment is as rocket fuel, but let's finish up today with other potential uses. Should you use it for desalination of ocean water, or manufacture of cement or steel, then all these processes become much, much more sustainable. But one of the conspicuous end-use devices is simply a classic fuel cell. A really green fuel cell, especially if tasked to cogenerate electricity and process heat. We are all well aware of fuel cells, and I'm sure you've worked with them in the lab.

"But a technology that may be new to you is the free-piston linear generator or FPLG, another unpronounceable acronym.[21] These have actually been around since about 1940, but in the last few decades many research groups have been working in the field, especially after the refinement of rare-earth magnets and power electronics. These devices are long horizontal engines with a stationary mount, as you can see in this slide," as he used his laser pointer.

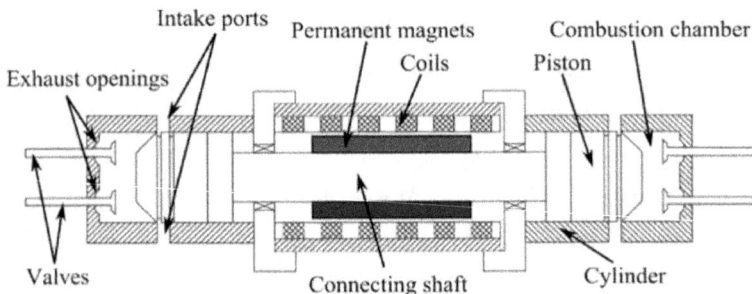

Figure 1: Schematic of an FPLA with two combustion chambers.[22]

"There are a number of engine designs, but this is one with two combustion chambers. They enable direct conversion of mechanical energy into electricity, and benefit from reduced friction losses compared to conventional engines. They also allow variable compression ratios, which enables optimized combustion control. The central piston—comparable to the rotor in a rotating generator—is essentially a large, permanent magnet and is jerked first in one direction, then the other. The exterior cylinder, or 'stator,' has copper coils that interact with the moving magnet to generate a flow of electricity."

Veronica made an observation. "Goes back to the early days of electric motors, just coils of copper moving back and forth in a magnetic field."

Jake nodded and made a final reference to his notes. "The total efficiency of free-piston linear generators can be significantly higher than conventional internal combustion engines and roughly equivalent to fuel cells.

"To sum all this up, fuel cells and linear generators are two technologies that work superbly with hydrogen, producing only heat, electricity, and water vapor."

Matt weighed in. "Seems like both of these techniques might work with electric airplanes, Jake, which I know is one of your major areas of interest."

"You are so right, but our time is up. Next session will be a special surprise. And that's all I'm going to tell you now." The room cleared out quickly.

Jake thought about it for a moment, and then realized it was, after all, time for lunch.

NINETEEN

Pumping for Gold

Prayer is good, but when baked potatoes and milk are needed, prayer will not supply their place. —*Brigham Young*

Whoever said "there's no use crying over spilled milk" obviously never pumped six ounces and accidentally spilled it. —*Anonymous*

A bbey reflexively scrubbed her hands again, though she conscientiously washed her hands before and after every single patient contact. It was second nature to her. *Hospitals are rife with multi-antibiotic-resistant organisms.*

She pulled out her phone and dialed a familiar number, then held the phone to her ear with her shoulder as she began unbuttoning her blouse. "Charly, how are ya?"

Abbey listened to her response as she struggled with the last button.

"Good, good, listen, I'm at the hospital, in an on-call sleep room on three west, number two around the corner from the nursing station. I just finished up a consult, then realized I was feeling too engorged to commit everything to the computer right away. Makes it hard to concentrate . . ."

"Yeah, I love breastfeeding, but it's not always convenient. And it's hard to concentrate when the swelling gets tense. So, I thought if you weren't busy and could come by and visit while I pump, it'd be a chance to catch up . . ."

"Primip in labor at six centimeters? You've got loads of time," she said, gesturing with her free hand. "Come on up . . ."

"Sure, see you soon. Bye." She finished opening the top buttons and then pulled her single-sided manual pump from the carryall and screwed the receiving reservoir onto the base. *Chilly from the cold pack, might make my nipple stand up.* She held it to her left breast first, took a couple of deep calming breaths, then slowly pulled the plunger. After a couple of repetitions, the succulent flow began, first a trickle, then actively spraying out like an early leak in a garden hose under low pressure. Abbey began to tunelessly hum to herself in a low register. *Life isn't always fair. I will always regret only having two weeks at home with Hopie before heading back to the salt mines.*

The first few minutes passed peaceably, then there was a soft knock at the door. "Come on in, lady," she called out.

Charly opened the door and peeped her head around first, then slipped inside. "Well, Abbs, good to see you makin' productive use of your time," she said, with a big grin on her face. "Must be the reason they pay ya those big bucks."

Abbey raised her eyebrows, tilting her head back to look down her nose at Charly. "Hey, you're a certified nurse-midwife and a certified jokester at the same time, and I understand that doesn't pay too badly either. We both know mixing in a little stand-up makes things easier for everybody."

"And how is the young Hope doing?"

Abbey shook her head. "I may have something better than pictures to show you." She pulled out her phone and handed it to Charly. "Find the baby cam app," she said, starting another pull on the plunger, watching the milk surge a bit.

"Is the icon a baby's head?"

"You got it. Put in my first name and then the passcode: Golden#. The livestream from the nursery is the only video camera in the Inn."

"Sure looks like a nursery, but nobody's there," Charly said, the corners of her mouth turning down more than really necessary.

Abbey shrugged. "It just means she's not napping, and Mina must have her out and about, maybe even in the stroller, it's such a nice day. Anywho, she coos and giggles and smiles just like a baby."

Charly tried to look solemn. "Well, I realize you're a first-time momma, but she actually is just a baby."

Abbey rolled her eyes in response. "Mina tells me she's having a whale of a time with her, but also studying hard. Says she's really getting a handle on baby sign language, if you can believe that.

"I think the word Jake would use might be dubious or skeptical or something like that. But Hopie seems to enjoy it. And he's clearly enjoying being a father, not that I ever doubted he would. And I'm glad to know he's back to running regularly. That's his great escape."

Charly was still looking puzzled as she reviewed Abbey's phone. "What are all these commands about?"

"You can do all kinds of tricks with this camera. You can pan, tilt it up and down, zoom. Or check the room temperature, listen to see what noises the baby is making. Even has infrared night vision when it's dark."

"So, you're saying you get this audio and both day and night video all from one device?"

"Yeah, and the system can play white noise or a lullaby to help the baby fall asleep, which slowly decreases in volume at a rate you can control. But you know, there's one feature that I cannot accept," she said, shaking her head. "We refuse to use the audio in parent-to-baby mode."

"Why not?"

"It'd be creepy for my baby to hear our voices but not be able to see us when she looks around. If Hopie needs something when she's alone in the nursery, then one of us has to physically go to her and pick her up and comfort her. Too Orwellian otherwise."

"Gotcha."

Abbey finished up on the left breast and secured that side of the bra. Then she unscrewed the reservoir and poured the contents into a small plastic container, put the lid on tightly and placed it in the carryall next to the cold pack at the side of the bed. She removed a second container to set on the bedside table.

"Round two," said Charly.

"Yep," replied Abbey. She sat back down, opened up the other side of the bra, and set to work. "Is your group still thinking about recruiting another midwife, a CNM?"

Charly took a big sigh. "I promoted the idea so relentlessly that they finally consented to letting me start checking my contacts back from school, and to more actively seek out candidates if I'm not successful." Her eyes were glowing.

"Well, well, congratulations, lady, about time. Now you won't have to be on call so often." Abbey applied the cup and began with a preliminary pull or two, with a quick response. Again, the spray without need for much further stimulation. Abbey took a deep breath and let it out slowly.

Charly's phone rang. "Yes, ma'am, how's my patient? Eight centimeters and about wanting to push? Sounds like it's time for me to show up. Tell her I'll be right down." She hit the end call button and stood up from the chair opposite the bed. "She may be a primip but it's looking like she's gonna be as fast as you were, Abbey."

"Must be nice to have a delivery in the middle of the day for once."

"You'd think so, but hell, sometimes actually I think it's easier to have an uninterrupted delivery in the middle of the night. Right now my office is having to reschedule my afternoon patients or fit them into my partners' schedules. The usual chaos. So, Abbs, gotta go. Say hi to Jake and Mina for me."

"Will do."

"And keep those cards and letters coming," she said, as she sailed out the door, but Abbey just smiled this time.

In a minute she was back to humming, this time an Old English lullaby.

TWENTY

Harmony and Discord

I am an old man and have known a great many troubles, but most of them never happened.
—Mark Twain

It is not work that kills men; it is worry. Worry is rust upon the blade.
—Henry Ward Beecher

A couple of bagels walked through the office door in Brian's left hand. He set them on Jake's desk, then pivoted to pour himself a mug of coffee and finished by retrieving the milk from the small fridge. "Okay, Jake, you have that look of concern on your face, what gives?"

"Print journalists," he said, turning the newspaper around so Brian could see the title. "The paper of record has some great people on their staff, and it's impressive how much they write about climate challenges."

"Spring Allergy Season is Getting Worse," read Brian out loud. "Says here about a quarter of adults in the US have seasonal allergies."[23]

"And Ms. Agrawal, who wrote the article, says the allergy season in North America is starting about twenty days earlier than back in 1990. They used pollen count data from something like sixty stations on the continent to establish the trend line."

Brian scratched his nose. "I don't really have allergies, but on rare occasion I'll use a bit of antihistamine, which seems to help."

"Never had formal testing from an allergist?"

"Nah, nothing to worry about. But I'm reading here that pollen concentrations have risen about twenty percent since 1990. And a guy named An . . . Anderegg, an allergist, says 'warmer temperatures, higher concentrations of carbon dioxide and increased precipitation can all contribute to plants growing bigger and producing more pollen over longer periods of time.' Sorry to hear that. Some folks have this really bad. And Rachel doesn't like me making fun of her when she can't stop sneezing."

Jake tapped his fingers on his desk. "And there's another doctor quoted in the article, by the last name of Marshall, who said he's always treated three separate allergy seasons per year, each lasting about eight weeks. But now the tree pollen in the spring, the grass pollen in spring and summer, and for some people, the ragweed pollen in late summer and early fall now just blend into one long miserable monthslong slog during some of the prettiest months all year to be outside.

"I gotta say Bri, these sesame bagels are better than those pumpernickel specimens you brought in last Tuesday."

"Agreed, buddy, no more pumpernickel. And just so you know, this is the last of the cream cheese in the fridge," Brian said, raising his eyebrows. "What else you got for me to worry about today?"

"I have in my possession a whole file of articles from multiple sources. Here's one from Einhorn at the *Times*, with the title of 'Widest-Ever Global Coral Crisis Will Hit Within Weeks, Scientists Say.'[24] You remember how last week we talked about those extraordinary ocean temperatures over the last year?"

"Yeah, with four factors, let's see if I remember them. Climate change is first. The El Niño winding up by May of 2024. Hmm . . . the loss of atmospheric pollution over the sea lanes due to tightening sulfur-fuel standards for shipping and cruise lines. And wasn't there something involving a . . . volcano?"

"Yep, you got it, a subsea volcano called Hunga Tonga-Hunga something, something in the South Pacific erupted back in 2022, pitching a whole lot of water vapor high up into the atmosphere, high enough to penetrate into the stratosphere, where it hangs out a long time."

Brian took his long legs off the desk and returned his plate to the small sink. "And you keep saying that water vapor is a potent greenhouse gas, just not one we can control."

"Just not one we can control. But all that extra heat in the ocean, including all three basins that host coral reefs, the Pacific, Indian, and Atlantic."

Brian held up a finger. "Wait, isn't that redundant, aren't all reefs coral reefs?"

"Actually, no, you can have oyster reefs, or mixed shelly reefs, or rocky reefs. All of them provide habitat and protect the shore."

"Okay then."

"So, the primary factor causing bleaching is heat, marine heat waves, and it's not just temporary bleaching with expulsion of their symbiotic algae, because if it's hot enough long enough the coral will die. And acidification isn't helping, because the young coral need the right ocean balance between acid and base to create their shells."

"So, how bad has it been?"

"By the criteria of three-basin involvement within twelve months, with a minimum of twelve percent of the reefs heated up enough, this was the fourth global bleaching-level heat stress event, all of them since 1998."

"Okay, this is not okay. Hell, it sounds worse the longer I think about it."

"There are coral scientists who are seeing their life's work being taken away from them. I mean they are seriously losing sleep over this disaster."

"Are you done now, or are you gonna tell me another one?"

"One last one, since we're talking about the ocean today. Journalist this time by the name of Cornwall, this time writing for the American Academy for the Advancement of Science."

"Like the British general who surrendered his army and ended our Revolutionary War?"

"No relation so far as I know. And this is a new one on me." He held up the article for Brian to read the title: "Deadly marine 'cold spells' could become more frequent with climate change, scientists warn."[25]

"Okay, sounds contradictory, but sock it to me." Brian lifted his feet back up on the desk.

"It all started with a large fish kill on the coast of South Africa. Not just small fry, rather giant bat-winged manta rays, bull sharks, and puffer fish. Thousands of them. Usually, these kills are triggered by hot water, low oxygen, or toxic algal blooms, but this dilemma was a sudden cold shock in the middle of the southern summer. Kind of ironic, in that we are usually more worried about marine heat waves happening around the world. The die-off came to the attention of, and I'm reading now, 'Nicolas Lubitz, then a Ph.D. student at James Cook University, who worked with a group of ecologists and oceanographers to piece together what happened and how it fit into broader oceanic trends.' So, they examined the Agulhas Current—which I'd never heard of—which is a fast-moving flow down along the western coast of the Indian Ocean, sweeping down as far as Mozambique then hooking a right turn around South Africa." Jake threw his hands up and shook his head. "But a fast current in the air or in the water sets up eddies that 'reverse like around the boulders in a rapids in a stream.' If this is coupled with easterly winds, the double whammy pulls the surface water away from the coast."

Brian leaned back farther in his chair, saying, "And how is that a bad thing?"

"Because cold water as deep as three kilometers down can be pulled up to replace it. In February of 2021 surface ocean temperatures along the South African beaches roller-coastered down as much as seven degrees Celsius in two days, to as low as ten degrees Celsius.

"Which is about fifty degrees Fahrenheit."

"Humans would get hypothermic in water that temperature and apparently bull sharks cannot survive it or figure out how to move out of the area."

"I guess we are used to swings like that in the atmosphere, but not in the ocean. So, I should assume researchers are calling this climate-driven?"

"Hold your horses, pardna, because the summary in the article is that state-of-the-art general circulation models cannot demonstrate results for this small an area. Instead, there's the usual boilerplate that more work is indicated, including other areas of the globe, to see if this works elsewhere and can be incorporated into a consensus model." Jake shook his head again.

Brian stood up. "Sometimes I think you are too much of a worrywart, Jake. Listen, let's get together for dinner soon. I'll check with Rach and you check with Abbey."

"Can do."

"And we haven't seen Hope in at least a week. I assume you haven't lost her."

"Not me, you know I never lose hope."

They both grinned at the old joke, one that the poor kid would have to put up with forever and ever.

Jake shook his head as Brian walked out the door. *Abbey had to choose that name, but I'm finally getting used to it.*

TWENTY-ONE

Full Metal Jacket

Guilt upon the conscience, like rust upon iron, both defiles and consumes it, gnawing and creeping into it, as that does which at last eats out the very heart and substance of the metal.
—*Robert South*

Those who tread among serpents, and along a tortuous path, must use the cunning of the serpent. —*Thomas Becket*

The sweat ran into their shirts, soaking their backs, and into their bandanas and the brims of their hats, and into their eyes, stinging. It was another hot, windless summer afternoon, quiet as a cemetery at midday. There weren't any insects or birds in the air. The boys were taking a break from long-range target practice, leaning back against the side of Buck's truck, the only shade around. When the sweat dripped off their noses, it dove and evaporated into the sand like smoke. Unbeknownst to the shooters, in some coyote scat off to the side, rainbow scarab dung beetles, each with head and thorax the color of brass, were whittling down the droppings and crafting balls to transport to their larvae.

"Hot as hell today, just like yesterday, dammit," Buck grumbled, wiping his forehead.

"And the day before that, and the one before that, Buck, don't do us much good to keep complaining about it," seconded Elliot.

"Now the newspapers are all calling this a heat dome or some damn thing," Matt drawled. "Hell, they had weather like this in North Africa during World War II—Montgomery up against the Eye-talians and Rommel, the Desert Fox—the armored forces would fry eggs on top of their tanks," Matt said slowly. He took a long drink from his bottle. "Okay, boys, we're shooting at targets somewhere between 100 and 150 yards. We each got a couple of targets out there and each of us is checking through the scopes. When we actually are in location with our targets, we might be even a little closer, or a lot closer, or considerably farther away, depending on the tactical situation. So, how're we doing?"

"I've got about five holes in each target, but nothing like a tight group," Elliot said. He took his kerchief off to wipe his eyes. "And I gotta say without a bandana the sweat would be dripping into my eyes."

"Same here," Buck said, "but probably up in the Northeast I'm thinking it won't be so damned hot."

Matt looked up at the cloudless sky. "Hot enough here the mirage over the prairie feels like shooting over a lake. But really, these are almost ideal conditions. No wind to compensate for. No looking over our shoulders for curious folks or cops coming up to see what's happening. No time pressure, though next time we practice I'm gonna use my stopwatch."

"How much time we gonna get? Ninety seconds, two minutes? In and out fast?" Elliot asked.

"I wish I could tell you that for certain. And I wish I could tell you how many of these targets we gotta hit to make the whole station fail. And I wish I could sneak around on the internet to git more information without worrying about getting tracked. I just think you're going to have a gut feel about all this, in the middle of your excitement, when you think you've done enough damage to quit and skedaddle."

"So . . . it means it might be different for each of us, is what you're saying?" Elliot strung the words out slowly.

After a pause, Matt said, "Yeah." The word hung in the air for a bit, like the smoke from Buck's hand-rolled cig. *I got faith in these two guys.*

Buck coughed, then said, "Explain to us again why we're practicing with one kind of bullet but falling back on using something different, you know, for the operation."

"What we got today is the ammo we bought in bulk, a coupla hundred rounds of 168-grain FMJBT from Armscor. I got these last year when we were out of state, paid in cash, and got the brass casings for long-term storage without tarnishing, especially with the damn-it-all humidity we get around here."

"What does the FM . . . J . . . whatever stand for, Matt?" Elliot asked, his voice gritty.

"FMJ stands for full metal jacket, it's what we usually use for target practice. You take a softer, bullet-shaped core, usually lead, and surround it with the harder jacket—copper, or a metal alloy. Then BT stands for boat tail. You can't see that unless you disassemble a cartridge, but the back end of the for-real bullet narrows like the rear end of a sailboat."

"What's that good for?" Buck asked.

"It raises up a bullet's ballistic coefficient, which is a fancy way of saying it's not as much slowed by air resistance. Gives it a flatter trajectory, higher velocity downrange, and less problem with wind resistance. Great for training because they're cheap and available in bulk."

"Then why ain't we using these when we travel north?"

"Because we wanna do as much damage as we can to the targets. For that we need an armor-piercing penetrator made of hardened steel or tungsten. Or tungsten carbide. This is surrounded with a copper jacket, or copper combined with nickel, which is included to avoid damaging the gun bore. The other reason is the impact velocity of the copper jacket may just for a moment soften the face of the armor and cushion the impact to avoid breaking up the brittle penetrator. Think of this, boys: the penetrator then slides out of the jacket and proceeds forward through the armor, smooth as a greased piglet at a county fair."

"Like when a condom breaks when she's not paying attention, which enhances the whole experience," Buck said, but the other guys were too tired to respond.

Better just not rise to the bait this time, thought Matt.

He suddenly cocked his head. "Didn't I tell you guys about keeping situational awareness? Don't you hear someone coming?" The other two started to pull themselves up to standing, but Matt motioned for them to stay down. He grabbed his Winchester 70 and told the others to do the same.

"I don't really think we need to stash them inside the truck, but let's be a little cautious here."

A single truck, clearly not a police car, was coming down the road toward them, leaving a plume of dust roiling and then slowly drifting to the west. Matt could see two boys in the truck, which meandered for a bit, hesitated, then squeaked to a stop well off to the side. They got out and put on cowboy hats, one of them hitching up his pants.

Matt and the other two had put their weapons on safety and leaned them up against the truck so they could walk out in friendlier fashion. Elliot took a long drag on his water bottle.

The taller of the two boys, the blond one, called out, "Howdy."

Matt responded in turn.

The shorter one, with black hair like Matt's, said, "Looks like you're gettin' in a bit of target practice."

"That we are, boys," drawled Buck, "just finishing up."

Elliot stepped forward to shake their hands. "Hello, I'm Elliot. Think maybe I've seen you two around town."

"We're both in the high school, seniors this year."

Matt nodded. "Getting ready to graduate then."

"Yeah, I'm Jackson," said the taller one, shaking Matt's hand.

"And I'm Andy," the other said, and shook Matt's hand first, then the others'. He turned and looked out at their targets. "Is this some kind of a competition?"

Elliot looked at Andy and said easily, "We come out here from time to time just for a little workout. Not betting any money or anything. So, you boys on the football team? Too damn hot to cart around a letter jacket but I gotta say you look pretty fit."

"Football, yeah," Jackson said.

"What position do you play, son?" Matt asked.

"Quarterback."

"And I'm left tackle," threw in Andy.

"I got to a couple of games this year, you guys had a pretty tough season," Buck said. "What were you, four and seven?"

"Yeah, but third in district with a record of three and three," Andy replied.

Matt looked them both over. "So, what's up for next year, guys?" *Jackson's obviously the leader here.*

"I'm headed for Texas Lutheran," Jackson said.

"That's a private school, right? Pretty expensive?" Matt asked.

Jackson shrugged. "Almost everybody gets financial aid or scholarships, and I got some support from the Lions Club. Plus, I'm gonna stay at home the first year, but I want to live on or off campus after that. I'm going to study kinesiology or athletic training, maybe coach later."

"And you, Andy, what're you gonna do?" Matt asked.

"Last year I took what they call a discovery flight, and that sealed it for me. I've got an uncle with a pilot's license, and I've been up with him. So. I'm going to be attending Texas State Aviation."

Elliot spoke up. "What kind of flying you want to do?"

"I'm looking at commercial instrument or commercial multi-engine classes."

"They fly out of San Marcos Airport, right?" Elliot drank some more water.

Andy nodded. "They say it's a pretty uncrowded airport, which makes it easier to train and learn radio procedures. And I like the idea of flying out over the Gulf of Mexico."

"Maybe you can practice ditching your plane in the water," Buck said, trying to keep a straight face.

Always the jokester, Matt thought.

Andy scratched under his chin.

Matt assumed he wasn't quite sure how to answer this.

"Say, Jackson, didn't you have a sister Stacey, Stacey Pearson? I think I remember her having a couple of younger brothers," Matt said.

"I do, sir, Stacey is my oldest sister, but her last name's Mitchell now. Got a son and a daughter and they live in Austin. She's teaching high school, and her husband's an accountant."

"Sounds like she really settled down. I remember her as a bit of a wild child back in high school, but she was a coupla classes behind me."

"So, you fellas just came here out of curiosity?" Elliot asked.

"Yeah, we heard people sometimes come out here to shoot, and we just thought we'd check it out," Jackson said.

Matt thought he looked relaxed, not squirrely, so he wasn't worried. "We're just finishing up here. Too hot to keep shooting, even our guns need to cool down. Time to gather up our brass and targets and mosey into town, probably settle down for a couple of beers at the Pearl Handle. I realize you fellas are too young to join us, gotta be twenty-one. And I'm just as sure you've found ways to get beer in high school, but we never drink and shoot, that's just for goddamn idiots."

"Yes, sir, we understand," Jackson said. "I think me and Andy will just take it easy and head back to town to pick up some fish cakes and fries."

"Wish you luck in school next year, boys," said Matt, which Elliot and Buck seconded.

After they left with another dust cloud wafting away, Matt stated his assessment. "I don't think these two young boys will spread any information of consequence around town."

"They seem like straight shooters," Elliot said quietly.

"Nothing to worry about at all," Buck said, nodding.

"Still, let's not leave any brass lying around, just to be sure," Matt said, as he turned to trudge back toward their firing positions and out to take down their targets.

TWENTY-TWO

Fire in the Hole

Drill, baby, drill. —Michael Steele, Maryland lieutenant governor

What we've got is the wholesale embrace of fracking domestically, internationally and for export. And this couldn't be further from what we really need to do to address climate change.
—Josh Fox

Figure 2: Drill bit.

A water bottle sat on a small table near the lectern. *Hotter than Hades out there*, thought Jake. As his students came in the door, most glanced up at the slide Jake had projected onto the screen.

"So, what's up with this, Jake?" Mark asked as he sat down.

"I figured some of you must know what this is," Jake replied. *Really, somebody should identify this, or I've misjudged them.*

"Looks like farm equipment to me," Sam said.

"No—that's a drill bit," Veronica said, sounding authoritative.

"I'll bite, lady, how do you know what this is?"

"I grew up in Oklahoma, so got to see a lot of drilling rigs."

"Well, you nailed it," said Jake, as he began his meander back and forth in the front of the room.

"Anybody know how hot it is out there today?" he asked.

"Clearly north of a hundred when it's not even noon yet," Russell said. He was wearing a T-shirt and shorts today, like most of them.

"It's been ten days of this weather, with no break in sight. Four days in a row were heat records for this area, kind of like what happened in July of 2023, except that was global. So, stay hydrated, and in the shade whenever possible.

"Okay, on to business. What you're looking at is a tricore drill bit, designed to produce a cylindrical wellbore hole by rotary drilling. Typically, this is done for oil and gas extraction, but that's not why we're discussing this today. A wellbore diameter can range from three and a half inches all the way up to thirty, while the depth of the hole can range from a couple of hundred up to thirty thousand feet. These bits are expensive, and they wear out, particularly when tackling hard rock like granite. The cuttings from whatever type of bit are usually removed from the wellbore by continuous circulation of drilling mud down and back up again through different channels in the drill string."

Jake checked the notes on his lectern, then quoted, "The first commercially successful rolling cutter drill bit design was disclosed in US patents granted to Howard R. Hughes, Sr., on August 10, 1909, and which led to the creation of what [later] became the Hughes Tool Company."

He stopped to write:

Tricore Drill Bit[26]

"This original bit had two rotating cones; the three cone design, as shown on the slide, came later. The significance of the Hughes Drill Bit was recognized on its hundredth anniversary, 'when it was designated a Historic Mechanical Engineering Landmark by the American Society of Mechanical Engineers.'

"For hard rock drilling, not sedimentary rock which the oil and gas wildcatters tackle, more specialized drill bits have been developed. They are not pictured here, but they have a duplex hybrid design, where the leading portion shatters the hard rock and the subsequent component is a more typical rotating tricore bit, which carries out grinding and extraction of the chips.

"The effectiveness of a drill bit is measured by the rate of penetration—ROP—of a geologic formation, as well as its length of service life. Think of what happens the moment downhole sensors indicate the drill bit is fractured, or the ROP suddenly decelerates. The entire drill string—perhaps several miles long—needs to be brought to the surface section by section and the bit changed out, including the drilling mud which must be recovered for reuse.

"Then factor in the complexities of hydrofracking and its witch's brew of chemicals, the risks of induced microseismicity, leaks of methane, and control of directional drilling and all the rest of this complex business and you can see why this is such a controversial area. And you might be wondering why I bring this all up." He paused for a long beat. "This is supposed to be a class in electrical engineering, not petroleum engineering, so what gives?" Again, he waited.

"Are you talking about exploration for rare earths for electronics or something?" asked Russell, sounding far less than certain.

"No, but that's not a bad guess. What would be the reason for doing this if we take fracking chemicals out of the picture? Anybody?"

"Wait—are you talking about geothermal as generation for the grid?" Veronica asked, arching one eyebrow impressively.

He grinned and nodded his head. "You got it, Veronica. Drill, baby, drill." He scratched under his chin, then put that up as the actual heading:

Drill, Baby, Drill

"Do you know where that phrase originated? You'll like this. It's from a 2008 Republican campaign slogan first trotted out at the Republican National Convention that year. The speaker was Maryland Lieutenant Governor Michael Steele, who was later elected chairman of the Republican National Committee. As you're all probably aware, he later switched allegiance to the progressive end of the political spectrum, and often appears on MSNBC. The slogan of course at that time expressed support for increased drilling for oil and gas. It achieved its greatest prominence when reiterated endlessly by Sarah Palin after she first tried it out during the vice-presidential debate. It was even employed by the last Republican president in response to a voter question during a CNN presidential town-hall in May of 2023.

"You know what I think about the urgency of phasing out fossil fuels, so it should surprise you to hear that I am fully on board with the philosophy of 'drill, baby, drill' when it comes to geothermal. Now, first let me tell you why it's so critical to increase the array of sources of electricity, after excluding fossil fuels. And eventually downsizing the nuclear fleet, my bias." As was his habit, he wrote:

Air Conditioning

"At COP28, sixty nations committed to improve the efficiency of new air conditioners by fifty percent and reduce greenhouse gas emissions related to these cooling devices by seventy percent.[27] But the daunting task is to make sure we don't more than double the demand for electric cooling by 2050, as the UN projects. Some of this can be achieved by using better building design, exterior shading, interior thermal mass, sophisticated insulation, reflective exterior surfaces, urban tree-planting programs, heat pumps and enhanced efficiency fans, air conditioners, and coolers in less-developed countries.

"India is our most daunting example. In 2023 they had three hundred million households, with a population of 1.4 billion people. About nine percent of households have air conditioning, but the government projects that figure will reach close to fifty percent by 2037, and the IEA predicts more than a billion units by 2050. What is now considered a luxury item will have become essential for survival."[28]

Jake halted for a moment, then asked, "Anybody note the ironies here?" It was quiet for a moment.

"Both the generation of electricity for air conditioning and its consumption by these devices, if only because of thermodynamic principles, will increase planetary heating," Sam said, then grimaced.

Jake shook his head in agreement. "Already over a fifth of the world's electricity is used by fans and air conditioners, a proportion expected to bulge further." He pivoted to put up more graffiti, but first turned back to say, "This is one of the reasons for the urban heat island effect."

Halogens

"Refrigerants of sixteen different categories are liquid-to-gaseous, phase-change chemical compounds, most containing halogen elements like chlorine, fluorine, and/or bromine. When first developed in the 1800s, the key beneficial qualities were considered to be a boiling point between minus forty degrees and plus thirty-two degrees Fahrenheit, non-toxicity, nonflammability, stability, pleasant but distinct odor for leak detection—and low cost.[29] It was only later that many of the early categories of refrigerant were found to have a bewildering array of deficiencies.

"It almost goes without saying, refrigerants are used in heat pumps also, but with greater efficiency and lesser electricity demand. The trick is to get governments and companies to roll these out."

Jake scrawled:

Cooling Action vs. Heat-Trapping

"The chemical stability of refrigerants is important for function, but dangerous when released into the atmosphere. The irony is that these vital, cooperative chemicals—whether released during manufacture, storage, transport, injection into or removal from the cooling loops, or leakage—traitorously turn on us to trap heat in the whole vertical atmospheric column and destroy protective ozone high in the stratosphere. An example is the common refrigerant HFC 134a, known by its trademarked name Freon, which exhibits a global warming potential more than a thousand times greater than carbon dioxide. In fact, these CFCs in aggregate trap eighteen percent as much heat as $CO2$. Which is a lot more talked about.

"Pushing the dagger deeper into our backs, in 2021, the International Energy Agency stated a full tenth of global electricity was devoted to cooling, a fraction slated to inexorably rise unless other measures are taken.

Fortunately, tanks of CFCs and HFCs can be destroyed by electric-arc plasma furnaces." *Good riddance to bad rubbish.*

"Even without leaks, refrigeration can fail." Jake looked at his notes again. "The UN has a report stating that twelve percent of food grown globally is lost due to lack of effective refrigeration, often through spoilage at transfer points in the cold-chain transportation system 'from farm to long-haul truck, or cold room to airplane, or anywhere else in the relay race to get a refrigerated product to its final destination, in time and intact, whether that's a hospital, laboratory, restaurant, or your front porch. Any unexpected weather or overpacked freight can be fraught with consequences.'"

Jake thought for a moment, then wrote:

Hot Enough for Ya?

He checked his notes again. "Yeah, 2023 was more than 'just one more year in the ongoing collapse of the world's climate system,' as Bill McKibben put it in a review article in *The New Yorker* in the last month of that year.[30] I suspect you've all heard the story about the monitoring buoy in the Florida Keys that hit 101.1 degrees Fahrenheit in July that year, hot tub temperature, right? What with thermometer measurements for the past couple of centuries, extended by proxy temperature records going back much further, we can say that July third was the hottest day in the last 125 thousand years, and the month of July was the hottest month human civilization has ever known."

"Taylor Swift had to postpone a Rio concert when the temperature topped 106 degrees . . . one of the people at another concert in Brazil died from the heat," Mark said.

Jake checked his documents again. "And the US reported insured losses from storms and other hazards exceeded fifty billion dollars in one year for the first time. So, I guess popular culture, the financial sector, and about eighty-five percent of the general population of Americans are now cognizant of and worried about the rampaging climate." He scribed again:

And the Winner Is?

"Both McKibben and David Wallace-Wells in a *New York Times* piece from the same month had good news to report more than balancing out the bad. In spite of foot-dragging by governments and intransigence by fossil fuel companies, 'global sales of internal-combustion engine vehicles,' pausing for emphasis, 'peaked in 2017.'

"Investment in renewable energy has consistently outpaced fossil fuel infrastructure for several years in a row. In fact, in 2022 about eighty-three percent of new global energy capacity was in sustainable energy, beaten though—by what is so often not recognized—by energy efficiency as the unheralded champion of all in providing end-use energy services.

"As Wallace-Wells phrased it, the 'question isn't about whether there will be a transition, but how fast, global and thorough it will be.'[31] But he also reported that the Global Carbon Project argues the carbon budget for 1.5 degrees will be exhausted in some five years of current emissions, for 1.7 degrees not long after 2050, and for two degrees, as soon as 2080."

Jake scratched his nose almost unconsciously.

"Bill Gates suggested during COP28 that keeping warming to two degrees isn't that likely, but he went on to say, 'Fortunately, if you stay below 3 degrees Celsius, a lot of the ill effects that people have heard about don't happen unless you are really irresponsible and let it get up to the higher range.'[32] I think this statement itself is unscientific and irresponsible. As Wallace-Wells retorted, in the range between 1.5 and two degrees, more than 150 million people would succumb prematurely from pollution produced by the combustion of fossil fuels. It would likely ring the death knell on reefs and the fisheries they support.[33] In that temperature range a sufficient amount of the ice sheets would be committed to irreversible melting, such that over centuries the world's coastlines would be dramatically redrawn."

Gotta say these guys are looking pretty somber.

"Gates is flat-out wrong, we don't wanna get anywhere near three degrees Celsius. That's when wildfires would burn twice as much land as now. Hey, how much of Canada burned in 2023? Anybody have that figure?" His voice dipped into a rasp, and even though he waited, he only saw heads shaking.

"The answer is Canada burned—coast to coast—6,500 fires that scorched so much land that 45.7 million acres charred, more than two and a half times more than any prior year, as reported by Kate Yoder in *Grist*.[34] And for you Americans, a figure over forty-five million is larger than the combined area of our twenty-five smallest states.

"To round out my litany in opposition to acceptance of three degrees, the Amazon would be converted from rainforest to savannah. Which still could burn. Heat waves with potential lethality would become common-place for billions of people, including in the US. But enough of this disaster talk, I just wanted to set the stage to get us all motivated to fix these problems."

Time to perk them up. He turned to write:

Enhanced Geothermal

"After the last couple of decades of slow growth, the judgment on ge-othermal by most energy experts was that it was unreasonable to ever expect it to generate a lot of electricity. That it was too expensive. That too many dry holes were drilled. That existing geothermal reservoirs were being depleted by excessive withdrawals. That it was geographically lim-ited mainly to the West Coast. That it was and forever would be a niche player in the energy space. That it had never generated more than 0.4 per-cent of American power even though the US in 2020 was the world leader in cumulative installed capacity."

Jake shook his fist with each criticism, then checked his notes again.

"There were several counterarguments, starting with the fact that we have vast conventional geothermal resources in the western part of the contiguous forty-eight states, also in Hawaii and Alaska. Several of them, including Cali-fornia, already have a significant role for this energy source. The company Statista takes the stance that . . ." Jake checked his notes again. "Several US energy policy decisions over the years, including the Geothermal Steam Act of 1970, the Energy Policy Act of 2005, and the Advanced Geothermal

Research and Development Act of 2007, have sought to expand [conventional] geothermal energy use in the United States."[35] He looked up. "I added that 'conventional' in there to make a point.

"Which is: geothermal has the potential to explode its reach and capacity because of all the advances in fracking and directional drilling constantly being updated by all the oil and gas concerns. So, another miscellany of ironies. Geothermal should end up stealing the thunder from gas-fired generation by being able to shift-change between baseload production and dispatchable electricity at will. And geothermal as an industry is going to permanently borrow a lot of roughnecks and other skilled staff from the petroleum companies. It's just my profound hope the petrostate won't be able to appropriate and take over the geothermal sector. Perhaps a story for another time."

He shook his head, knowing they all knew his strong bias against these fossil giants—which didn't even know they were dinosaurs heading for extinction, but still roamed dangerously and widely enough to ruin everything.

"There have been a series of breakthroughs in enhanced geothermal, and it is the studied opinion of the Department of Energy and folks at Princeton that in the coming decades, somewhere between ten and twenty percent of our electricity could be based on these discoveries.[36] Think of that—this could solve the problem for a full one-fifth of our electricity, plus lots of commercial and district heating.

"Historically, hot springs around the world have been used for thousands of years, especially in sites such as Japan and Iceland. It was not until 1904 that Piero Ginori Conti, an Italian aristocrat, took control of his family's boric acid extraction field. Boric acid is a molecule made up of boron, the fifth element, with attached oxygen and hydrogen, which naturally occurs in nature as the mineral sassolite. It has been used as an insecticide—safe enough to use against ants entering your home—also as an antiseptic, a flame retardant, a neutron absorber for control of nuclear accidents, and precursor to many boron compounds.

"But Conti looked at the hot springs associated with this field and a light bulb went off over his head. Or rather, he tinkered around as inventors do and designed a boiler from this heat, which produced steam which rotated a turbine which spun a generator and—you know what came next—his four-kilowatt system powered not one but five light bulbs. Start small, right?" He held up his hands palm to palm only inches apart.

"By the 1920s, this new, next big thing began to spread around the world. The first geothermal system outside Italy was in the Geysers in Northern California, initially quite meager in output, but demonstrating a Western Hemispheric proof of concept. This led to . . ." He deciphered his scribbled notes again. "Which in 1955 led to Pacific Gas & Electric Company completing a contract for purchase of power from a developer in the Geysers. In 1960 the first unit came online with what would eventually morph into the largest geothermal installation in the world, as described by a recent article in Canary Media.[37]

"Anybody know what happened in the 1970s that gave this sector a boost?" A brief pause ensued.

"The oil shock of 1973, I think," Veronica ventured.

"That's right, in response to the Yom Kippur War in 1973, then a second time after the revolution in Iran in 1979. Both of these negative supply shocks led to big increases in energy prices, particularly gas and diesel, though also radiating out from methane gas withholding by OPEC. But it was the first one that prompted the crafting of several pieces of federal legislation supporting geothermal plants, which led over the next decade to development of more than half our present geothermal capacity.

"Sadly, by the 1980s, interest in renewable energy waned with the fall of energy prices."

Jake asked what key ingredients allowed access to surface heat, and Mark told him simply underground hot water.

Musing for a moment, Jake turned to write:

Permeability + Porosity

"You left out permeability and porosity, Mark, all the little spaces that allow fluids to move around. Which is more important really, because heat is a given literally everywhere a few thousand feet down, a resource just begging to be tapped, and fracking has shown you can add almost any kind of fluid if you can only create and prop those spaces open. That's right, all you need is elbow room for a working fluid, usually a brine from admixed salts, though freshwater works, too.

"Thomas wrote . . ." Jake ran his finger over his notes, then said scientists in New Mexico working on nuclear weapons conceived of a side project which evolved into the grandly named Los Alamos Hot Dry Rock Program, because they figured out that "the vast thermal reservoir represented by [hot dry rock] at accessible depths in the Earth's crust was an energy supply that could and should become extremely important in the world's energy future."

"This was all a volunteer enterprise until the 1973 oil shock, and then recognition and funding from the feds fell on them like manna from heaven. With arduous effort and ungodly amounts of spending—this being a federal project, remember—they finally created what they named the Fenton Hills system, which generated between four to ten megawatts of power. Crassly, by 1995, shortsighted officials in the Department of Energy killed the project and plugged the boreholes. And that should have been that.

"Except, the next lap of the relay was swum by George Mitchell, an iconoclastic oil guy who stubbornly kept experimenting with hydrofracking chemicals and techniques in an effort to keep his company from going under water. It was not until 1997 that he proved it could work, earning him the moniker 'father of fracking.'

"A parade of admiring oil companies followed suit, combining fracking with a suite of directional drilling techniques. A true renaissance of fossil fuel production followed, for better and for worse. For better, national self-sufficiency and later the support of Ukraine in its war with Russia; for worse, in terms of climate deterioration and for people living near all this oil-soaked infrastructure.

"The next character was a fellow named Tim Latimer, who transferred from the oil and gas industry after an epiphany at his first geothermal conference, which led two years later to his launch of Fervo Energy in 2017, using only off-the-shelf techniques to accelerate the development of enhanced systems. In 2023 Fervo completed its first full-scale commercial pilot system, Project Red, in northern Nevada, which generated 3.5 megawatts of clean power for thirty days, a standard mark geothermal projects must hit to be considered worthy. At the federal level, support in 2021 with the Bipartisan Infrastructure Law and in 2022 with the Inflation Reduction Act boosted interest and funding for searching for more technologies to tap into underground heat.

"All of this sounds exciting to me, but I'm not handing out cigars just yet. The scholars from Third Way project say that the global market 'addressable' by US firms is a 1.5 trillion-dollar opportunity, associated with a hundred thousand new jobs.[38] The last great roadblock is permitting, as in so many energy projects. Financing costs can chew up almost a third of geothermal projects' high cost of capital, in contrast to wind and solar work, with their costs only two to seven percent. Apparently, most of these wells will be sited on public lands, where environmental reviews—including addressing local and corporate opposition—can take up to a decade to resolve.

"I'm going to give Thomas the last word here: 'By contrast, oil and gas companies, which are granted a categorical exclusion from these lengthy reviews, can permit new wells in just a few years' time.'

"So, a number of companies are entering this competitive arena, but we need to move deeper, faster, and further. So we're already drillin' baby, time to put our shoulders to the wheel and get this done.

"From the syllabus you already know to finish another chapter and turn in a completed outline of your individual projects. See you all next time."

As they all started to get up, Jake said, "Remember, taking heat out of the Earth will mean adding a lot less to the atmosphere and ocean, so yeah, the watchword is drill, baby, drill."

TWENTY-THREE

Fire in the Hearth

Friendship is the source of the greatest pleasures, and without friends even the most agreeable pursuits become tedious. —Thomas Aquinas

Love is blind; friendship closes its eyes. —Friedrich Nietzsche

Sweltering and smoky and sultry didn't make for a good mix. Jake and Abbey were both sweating by the time they got home, pulling their T-shirts away from their chests, leaning forward to ease contact with the bucket seats. Shorts and sandals all around. Unseasonably warm for early June. They parked over by the garage, so Jake could plug in. Even Hope was a bit cranky and flushed as Abbey, her hair in a ponytail, extricated her from the infant seat in back. Jake carried in their cardboard box of food. The trees were precipitously, extravagantly leafed out near the garage and home, so they immediately felt less sunblasted and oppressed after leaving behind the wide-open shopping center parking lot, where they had hunted down some Asian takeout and other groceries.

The atmospheric conditions had deteriorated over days, but they were finally getting a break just in time for the weekend. The regional air-quality monitor showed the dominant pollutant—particulates—had finally dropped back down into the green, while carbon monoxide and sulfur dioxide were not now part of the problem.

Therefore, no need for air conditioning, not really; fine to acclimate to the heat and just keep the windows down on the ride home. The policy at the Inn was to open select upstairs and downstairs windows at night when air quality was good and depending on which rooms had guests, and close them by early morning if the heat forecast so dictated. But finally, to use the heat pumps for cooling when the smoke insinuated like a wraith into their lives and their infant's lungs.

"Did you say you're still following what's going on in Quebec with the fires?" asked Abbey.

"It's at least as bad as last year. And it's not just Quebec, but Manitoba, too. Scientists call it pyrogeography, the areas of heightened fire activity, especially when recurrent. Some of these are zombie fires that smoldered under the snow all winter long, then resurrected like mythical fire-breathing dragons in the spring."

"Major bummer. Okay, now set that box down on the counter, and at least put away the stuff that needs to be in the fridge and freezer. Leave out the boxes of Thai and Lao dishes on the counter and maybe put out some soup bowls and plates and silverware. But let's plan to eat on the dining room table." She pushed some stray hair off her forehead. "I'm going to feed this little tyke before she chews a hole in my shirt."

"Brian and Rachel should be showing up in twenty minutes or so. I think we timed it pretty well. And I know our only set of guests planned to be out until after dinnertime."

"They seem cordial. What were their names again? Leslie and . . . ?" she asked, and switched Hope to her other arm.

"Ed. She's the adult dentist and he's the one for kids," finished Jake, retrieving the boxes of food.

"Got it. So, Hopie, are you ready for a bit of Mommie? Oh yes, you are, you most certainly are." Abbey nuzzled the top of her head as she walked with her into the parlor.

"While you get that done, I'm gonna make some of that new coffee substitute, what's the name? Okay . . . here it is," he said, lifting the pink-and-green bag of Northern Wonder to read the label once again. "They call this coffee-free coffee, a dark roast espresso blended with caffeine.[39] I guess we'll see, won't we." He set it down on the counter and then reached in for the real coffee. *Always smart to have a backstop.*

"I know what you should do, Jake. Why don't you go ahead and brew up both the fake coffee and the real thing, put them in separate containers, and run a blind tasting for Brian and Rachel. You know how much he loves his coffee, really both of them do." Abbey was getting Hopie tucked in on her left side first.

Feisty eater, thought Jake proudly. "Obviously I know that, he drinks half of my coffee at work. What a mooch." He began putting out multiple cups and saucers for the dining room table, the usual silverware, but only paper towels for napkins, since friends were different from guests. He turned on the ceiling fan, just to get some air moving.

On the kitchen island he left a stack of plates, a couple of serving spoons, and the boxes of Asian delicacies. It took him only a minute to get the first pot of coffee going. Then he walked to the window over the sink, peering intently at the air over the circle of the gravel drive and the street beyond. "I'm so happy to not see that damn haze today, and to have normal daylight this afternoon. I can't stand that orange color in my sunlight any more than in my—"

"Careful there, honey, you know we don't like to talk politics when there might be guests around."

"But there aren't any guests here," Jake said, holding both hands palm up where Abbey could see him through the doorway into the parlor.

"I want you to practice, so you won't make any more impolite comments like you did last week when those people were here. Remember, I have a lot more years' experience in running an inn."

He raised his eyebrows. "Don't try and pull rank on me, lady." *We keep having this same conversation. And she's only six months older than I am.* The silence slowly ballooned.

When he had the second coffee going, he heard the knock at the door, and then it opened, and in walked Brian and Rachel right on schedule.

"Hey guys," Brian said, as he sauntered into the kitchen, while Rachel poked her head into the study and apparently decided that Abbey feeding Hope looked a lot more captivating.

"Brian, what's up?" Jake said conversationally, setting down the first full pot of coffee in a white container and pulling out another one with a yellow-green . . . maybe chartreuse sort of color.

"Jake, old boy, looks like you've got enough food to feed a high school basketball team." He started opening a couple of the boxes.

"Just the coach's starters, not the subs who may have an appetite but not a reliable jump shot. Anyway, why don't you let the womenfolk know that dinner's ready to be served."

"I heard that," Rachel called out. "I'll be right in, I'm starved, but apparently so is little Hopie here."

The infant by now was on Abbey's other side. "Don't wait for me, Rachel," she said. "Go for it."

The coffee maker signaled it was done, sounding a bit asthmatic at the end, like an old guy struggling to get back in shape. Jake took the pot and poured it all in the second container.

Brian's eyes narrowed. "Why do you have two coffee carafes?"

Jake explained it was for a blind tasting.

"Two different blends of coffee?" asked Brian, looking justifiably suspicious.

"Nah, one isn't real coffee, it's a new product called Northern Wonder."[40]

"What I wonder is why they didn't call it Northern Lights, which would've been catchier." *Name may be already taken*, he thought.

"I've got the bag, Brian. I'm reading it's made from local nontropical ingredients, listed as lupin . . . whatever that is . . . chickpea, malted barley, chicory, black currant. And of course, caffeine is mixed in. Then citric acid to regulate the acidity, not sure why that's necessary."

"Hand that to me," Brian said, reading with pursed lips, the serious face that Jake knew so well. "No fat, no carbs, no sugars, no protein, no salt. Well, as long as it has caffeine, I'm willing to give it a try. Doesn't sound like it could hurt us much anyway."

"Get those out on the table," Jake said, pointing to the dining room and adding, "You'll see each place has two coffee cups. Then come back to load up a plate."

Rachel, meanwhile, had started with a spring roll, of course.

Kind of appropriate to the season, muttered Jake.

Next she chose a bowl of tom yum soup and some stir-fried cashew nuts with tofu. She dropped it off on the table, then went back to grab a small plate and a couple of spring rolls for Abbey, who could eat them with one hand or a fork.

Brian first poured the mystery coffees into his own two cups, but as he lifted the first one, Jake spoke up. "Now don't tell us your pick until everyone's had a chance to try 'em."

Brian tasted a bit of each, but just raised his eyebrows without making a face or a comment. He came back to plate up chicken yellow curry with coconut rice and the green papaya salad, then halted to read the sticker on the box: *Khao Niew Nooh Ping*. "What the heck is this?" He lifted up the container to show Jake.

"The lady said it was marinated, grilled pork with sticky rice and hot sauce."

"How hot?"

"We always order two out of five, I thought you knew that. If you want it hotter, there's some sauce in the fridge."

Rachel took a look at the description, then read out loud, "This not-quite coffee company paid for a life-cycle analysis of the environmental impacts of their own product, which directly makes the review suspect. Nevertheless, they claim their 'beanless coffee requires approximately a twentieth of the water, generates less than a quarter of the carbon emissions, and uses about a third of the land area associated with real coffee agriculture.'"

Should I riff on this? thought Jake. "Yeah, the evolving climate system should at least shift where coffee can be grown. I've read that the most suitable land for this critical product, featuring consistent and moderate rainfall and temperatures, is in the tropical highlands, you know, places like Guatemala or Indonesia or Ethiopia."[41]

"I actually think coffee originated in Ethiopia, then was brought to Europe by traders. They figured out how to grow it under the shade of taller trees," Rachel said, as she put the finishing touch on her selections of food.

As she headed to the dining room, she paused as Jake said, "Some folks estimate the most suitable land for coffee could be cut in half by midcentury. Not to mention hotter temperatures make the plants vulnerable to drought, pests, and fires."

She shook her head, then sneezed and rubbed her nose.

He followed her in. "In fact, coffee is one of the top six agricultural causes of deforestation."

"Why exactly?" she asked, as she turned to look at him. She put her plate down, then took a used tissue out of the pocket in her shorts and blew her nose.

"Because farmers cut down a lot of trees for planting coffee, also for fuel wood for drying and processing the beans. Sadly, those scientists now recognize a climate signal in the proliferation of coffee borer beetles and fungal infections."

Abbey walked in with the kid, just long enough to show off her sleepy head nestled into her shoulder. Jake stroked Hopie's head as Abbey whispered, "I'm gonna put her down in the nursery, not the bedroom."

With a small smile, Jake whispered back, "Remember, 'back to sleep,' honey." *Hah, this time I got her instead of the other way around.* Abbey seemed to pretend not hear him and was back in the kitchen in only a minute, making her own food choices. Jake went ahead and poured both coffee drinks for himself and Abbey.

"Maybe these coffee selections will help you out, Rachel," Brian said. He saw her slightly puffy eyes. "I know you haven't found the perfect antihistamine yet, and you don't like using your steroid inhaler."

Jake pitched in, his usual bull-in-a-china-shop routine. "Abbey's already heard this, but you two should know that allergy season is starting now about twenty days earlier than back in 1970. And there are really three stepped allergy seasons, historically each lasting about eight weeks. The first is tree pollens, with conifers releasing prodigious amounts, even coating the windshields of cars parked outside. Then the grass and flower season. Unfortunately for us in this area, ragweed is last and sometimes worst."

Rachel just shook her head. "You know how I hate ragweed season. But I'm going to try the soup and the cashews and tofu. Maybe the hot sauces will help clear out my sinuses."

"Even though your nose is a combat casualty, Rachel," said Brian, "go ahead and try the two coffees. Partly because I value your opinion on this sort of thing, but also because it might help clear out those pipes."

She dutifully took a sip of each, but then shrugged her shoulders. "They taste about the same to me, but then I can't really smell very much, almost like when I had Covid a couple of years ago." She looked around the table. "But don't worry, this isn't that. I know because my nose is really itchy."

"And you sneeze even at night when we're both trying to sleep. Not that I'm complaining."

Jake knew what a sympathetic guy Brian was, with a heart of gold. A risk-taker and a wild man, but always there for his friends. "Okay, Abbey, our turn." He took a bit of each coffee cup, while Abbey did the same. "And just to finish up what I was saying about allergy season, it really is just one long season nowadays, courtesy of the marauding climate dragon."

"Jake, I'm biased, because I saw you brewing these concoctions up," Abbey said, "but I'd say the one from the green carafe is definitely the Northern whatever-it-is."

"Wonder, Northern Wonder. Now the question is, would you keep drinking it?" He raised an eyebrow fractionally, as usual unable to take his eyes off her.

"Sure, I'll finish this cup. I might even be happy to brew up the rest of the bag, but mainly because I hate the idea of food waste. But I'm not ready to switch."

"Even with all the advantages of less water, less destruction of tropical forests and everything?"

"Jake, I know you're fanatic about all things environmental, but I draw the line at coffee. I'm not gonna give this up." He noticed she'd chosen the chair almost right under the fan.

And we've had this conversation more than once. "I figure most Americans would say the same thing." He turned toward Brian. "Okay Bri, what's your take on these?"

"I've got your back, Jake. Push come to shove, I'd be willing to switch, but I'm not ready yet. And yeah, I can tell this is the real coffee," he said, holding up the cup in his right hand.

"Wait, Brian, I didn't see you pour, which is the one you like?"

"This one," he said, pointing at the green container.

Jake leaned back in his chair and laughed out loud. "Abbey and I set you up." He chuckled again. "I told you she can be pretty sly. The real coffee is in the white one."

Brian leaned forward, tasted both again. "They're both pretty good."

Jake grinned. "Bamboozled. Got ya, Bri." Abbey grinned, too.

"My mouth was affected by the hot sauce."

"Back and fill, Brian You know we're not going to let you forget this, right?" Abbey said.

"You're ganging up on my guy," said Rachel, but to Jake it sounded like she was suppressing a giggle.

Then they all heard the front door open. *Ah, my friend gets a reprieve.* Jake called out for them to come say hello, and the upstairs visitors presented themselves at the doorway of the dining room.

"Ed and Leslie, these are our friends Rachel and Brian," Jake said, pointing at each in turn, "and we are gorging on some Thai and Laotian food."

Ed had a well-lined face and a rumpled suit coat. "Nice to meet you both," he said, nodding his head. "As it so happened, we also went Asian tonight, a Korean place."

"How was the food?" Rachel asked.

"Sumptuous, very good," Leslie responded. She looked quite relaxed, and perhaps a bit flushed from the sake at the restaurant.

Jake didn't want to bring up his own story about one time unwittingly drinking too much rice wine. Instead, he said, "I was in Guatemala for a couple of years in the Peace Corps. They had some pretty hot food there, but it was a great experience."

"Where were you and when were you there?" Ed asked.

"I worked near San Lucas Tolimán, in a small village called Panabaj. And I started right after my undergraduate years, just before arriving at GW for graduate work."

"We've been through San Lucas Tolimán, but I don't remember seeing Panabaj."

"How many years ago?"

"Starting about twenty years ago we joined a group of dentists who had set up annual clinics in several Central American countries. We go down in rotation, about every third year."

"I think I heard about those clinics, but never got to visit when you were on location, it must have been. You folks told me you had some sort of reunion tonight, is that what brought you to the Inn here?"

"That's right," Leslie said. She was wearing jeans and a two-pocket blouse and Jake thought she looked somehow quite comfortable in her own skin. "You heard we're both dentists, and there is a group of us that have bonded around an annual trip providing dental care in Guatemala or El Salvador or Honduras each spring. We often bring along a couple of students from the dental school at Howard University, to gain some experience in that kind of locale."

"What kind of dentistry do you two practice, and do you work in the same office?" Rachel asked.

"Leslie is an adult dentist in general practice, while I do pediatric dentistry in a separate office. We live in Maryland, in Rockville, about a half-hour commute to the dental school, depending on traffic."

"So, you teach there?" Abbey asked.

Each of them for two half days a month was her answer.

"Listen, since we have your attention, would you like to try out a new type of coffee we've been tasting tonight for the first time?" Brian asked.

Bet he's just trying to regain some face, thought Jake.

"You bet, let's try it," Leslie said. And Ed nodded as well.

Abbey got up to grab a couple of cups for them. As soon as she returned to the table, she heard Hope begin to cry. "Actually, this is good. I don't want her to take a long nap now, or she'll not go down easily tonight."

Leslie and Ed had taken seats at the table by the time Abbey returned with Hope.

"What a darling child," Leslie said, smiling as she spoke.

"How old?" Ed asked.

"Just over six months."

"And you're still breastfeeding?

"Mainly at night now. Pretty difficult to pump at work, but still doing that occasionally."

"Can you feel the first teeth coming in? Usually the lower two medial incisors. There may be just a nubbin there."

Abbey ran her finger inside Hope's mouth. "Maybe, not sure."

"First teeth come in about six months, sometimes later. And you know that even if there are no teeth yet, some supplemental fluoride should be started at a half year of age. Except for the fact that Arlington County has a water fluoridation program, so not necessary here. But it wouldn't hurt to use a fluoride-containing toothpaste, and once she has her first tooth, then start brushing twice a day with a small amount of it on a baby toothbrush. Make it playful, they usually get used to it pretty quickly."

"Wow," Jake said, "how useful is that, having a pediatric dentist in the family. Thanks."

"I kinda like having him around as well," Leslie quipped. "This Northern Wonder brew is not bad, but something only a dedicated environmentalist would commit to. Or maybe a monk.

"I will also say from personal experience that breastfeeding gets really interesting once they have a couple of teeth and they learn how you react when they bite down.

"Okay, Ed, why don't we get ourselves upstairs now, let these people enjoy their dinner in peace and quiet while we set the mini-split heat pump to colling mode in our bedroom."

"Yes, dear, always the safest answer. As for the rest of you, it would be really embarrassing if you neglected to brush and floss tonight."

They took their leave and the squad returned to sampling the delicacies. Brian whispered theatrically, "Neither one of them finished their ersatz coffee."

"I think we've achieved a consensus here. Perhaps we can try it again in the morning," Jake said.

He and Abbey looked at each other, then he said, "Perhaps it will age well overnight, like a soup or a stew." He tapped on the table.

"I'm willing if you're willing, Jake, but we'd better not serve it to them," Abbey suggested.

"I'm always willing, honey, you know that." And he winked at her, even knowing that Brian and Rachel would see him doing it.

Abbey just smiled her secret smile, but Jake also saw the flicker of one lowered eyebrow.

TWENTY-FOUR

Beavertown

Some kinds of animals burrow in the ground; others do not. Some animals are nocturnal, as the owl and the bat; others use the hours of daylight. There are tame animals and wild animals. Man and the mule are always tame; the leopard and the wolf are invariably wild, and others, as the elephant, are easily tamed. —Aristotle

People's hearts are like wild animals. They attach their selves to those that love and train them. —Ali ibn Abi Talib

Jake was concerned about the possibility of perplexity, even though he didn't think anyone in the class held philosophical reservations about eating animal flesh.

But somehow—bringing an animal skin to class might not find approval.

His concern turned out to be unfounded. Russell and Mark and the rest filed in and gathered around the desk, making admiring comments about the beaver skin, a deep cinnamon brown with black highlights.

"Folks, a minor correction here," Jake said. "This finished product you're all fondling is a pelt, not a skin. There're two kinds of hair follicles in a live beaver, but the long guard hairs are removed during preparation, leaving behind the luxurious inner hairs. It was stretched on a round rack, hence the final shape. It's been calculated that a postage-stamp-sized area of their skin has something like 126 thousand hairs, about the equivalent of a whole human scalp."[42]

"Where'd ya get this?" Veronica asked, rubbing the pelt against her cheek, then draping it over one shoulder of a frilly and parchment-colored blouse.

"Vermont, in a consignment shop, when Abbey and I and our daughter took a three-day weekend."

"More importantly," asked Sam, "why did you bring this moth-eaten rug here?"

Jake just shook his head. *Always the provocateur.*

"Okay, everybody, time to grab a seat while I justify this. Let me lay some groundwork first. Beavers are rodents in the order Rodentia, the largest ones on the North American continent."

Russell started to raise his hand but apparently remembered they were just supposed to speak up. "Your statement implies there may be larger rodents elsewhere in the world."

"Indeed—the capybara of South America," Jake bit off quickly, then reconsidered adding more.

"But the reason I studied engineering was to get a handle on the morphing climate, and I figured helping reform and reengineer the electric grids had to be a pivotal component.

"We all realize there are multitudinous components to this problem and its solution, but lately I've also been reading and thinking about beaver restoration for mitigation of climate impacts. Mitigation of course is proactive, while its cohort adaptation is reactive.

"The beavers or 'castorids' to consider are *Castor canadensis* in North America, *Castor fiber* in Europe. These are pure herbivores, chomping down on at least forty-two species of trees, thirty-six genera of other green plants, and four woody vines.[43] Not to mention 'cecotrophy,' a trait shared with rabbits of eating their own fecal matter, to really polish off digestion the second time around. Contrary to popular lore, they are not eaters of fish. North America now has an estimated fifteen million beavers, but once held far more, which were decidedly more widely distributed."

"But I've always wondered how much their dams block migrating fish," Russell asked.

"Russell, I'm glad you brought that up, because I was worried about it as well. It turns out concrete megadams—even with fish ladders—are much more of a problem for fish migration. Salmon fry headed downstream are able to wiggle through a wood and mud dam fairly easily, just following the flow of leaks that beavers are constantly patching up. Turns out the beaver tail has a number of sensors that give them a host of information about moving water, and they always eagerly respond. Even so, adult salmon traversing up a stream may be able to wiggle through a dam when necessary or jump entirely over the top." He paused, looking to see if Russell was satisfied.

"I have personal history here, because I grew up in Minnesota. At summer camp we would head up through the Boundary Waters Canoe Area Wilderness and over the previously unprotected border into Canada. From there we explored Quetico Provincial Park and Voyageurs National Park. Traveling by three-person canoes, we ran the best white water I've ever experienced, including on the Granite and Weikwabinonaw Rivers."

"Just try saying that three times fast," Mark threw in, but Jake just chuckled.

"Who were the Indigenous peoples in those areas?" Veronica queried.

"If memory serves, the Blood Indians in Canada and Anishinaabe Indians like the Chippewa and Ojibwe in my state. I'm no ethnographer or anthropologist, but kind of everybody growing up in northern Minnesota picks this sort of stuff up. It's taught in the schools, but also just by osmosis from all the place names." He stopped for a moment.

"But the crux of the story is that we canoed through countless meandering waterways knitting together gorgeous beaver country, featuring impressively sized lodges. I wish I had known then to look for the caches of food stored for the winter, the stumps of trees gnawed to points, the careful design of seemingly chaotic but competent beaver dams, complete with mud-and-stick patches of leaks.

"Historically there were an estimated fifteen to 250 million beaver ponds in our country, which submerged 234,000 square miles, an area equivalent to more than the combination of Nevada and Arizona. Think about this for a moment. Studies show beaver dams and ponds slow the flow of water, and sediment and pollutants settle out better in slack water. This allows more moisture to penetrate the soil and raise the groundwater level, which is now dropping in many areas of the country, such as the Ogallala aquifer, the ancient, even fossil groundwater deep under eight states in the American West. Instead of diminishing velocity of flow, one should 'speak of slowing, spreading, sinking, storing and sharing,' as enunciated by Ben Goldfarb in his beaver book.[44] "Streams that have been eroded to bedrock can be built up by what is called 'aggradation,' which means addition or deposit of sediment in slowed current."

Sam shifted in his seat. "So, with the evolving climate, are beavers moving north into Canada?"

"Absolutely," Jake replied, "Fifty years ago there were no beavers in the Arctic. Why? Because there were no woody shrubs and trees to provide food and dam material. But then, beginning in the 1980s, the migration of woody plants into the Arctic drew in the beaver. As a guy named Jon Waterman described it, 'by 2019, more than 11,000 beaver ponds were counted in northwestern Alaska.'[45]

"Of nontrivial importance, areas of wetland and swamp greatly support enhanced biodiversity, from trumpeter swans nesting on top of lodges, to butterflies and dragonflies and damselflies, to mink and otter and muskrat, who often take over abandoned lodges. And weaving or braided, technically called 'anabranching' streams offer society another protection—from increased storminess and flooding."

Jake turned to write:

Human Dam Protection

"There are over ninety thousand dams in the US, many of them some of the largest structures in the world. Civil and structural engineers rate fifteen thousand of these at highest risk for failure by inundation beyond design limits. In 1976, the last major American dam failure was Idaho's Teton Dam, which killed eleven people and thousands of cattle.[46] Braided streams and beaver dams upstream can and should alleviate stresses on dams during hectic rain events. Thus paradoxically, they help deal with both flooding and drought.

"Remember we previously talked about how dams can release methane from anaerobic decomposition of branches and other vegetative material. Detractors argue that beaver habitat also release methane, but that has been quantitated at about one percent of what human dams produce."

"Why were beaver pelts so valuable anyway?" Mark asked, sitting up from a slouch.

"Hmm, fashion mainly, pelts made great hats of many different styles."

Jake squinted in concentration, pushing his glasses farther up his nose, then turned to write:

Wildfire Control

"Beaver products were popular in China and Europe, not to mention the east coasts of Canada and the US. But more pertinent now to this discussion is the issue of wildfires. Countries hard hit by these infernos include Australia, Canada, and America, but also now for the first time Sweden and other areas in Europe. Fortunately, studies show that areas of marsh and swamp and impounded ponds dramatically avert the risk of wildfire, often creating a natural firebreak as conflagration destroys uphill areas on either one or both sides. I don't have any data on this, but I suspect power lines set along beaver habitat would be less likely to either precipitate or suffer destruction from fires." He smiled to himself for a moment.

"So, where does Alice in Wonderland come into the picture?" Jake looked around but saw only incomprehension. "Does the phrase 'mad as a hatter' come to mind?"

"Ah," said Veronica, "the tea party. Hatters back in the day used mercury as I recall, to finish the pelts. They absorbed and inhaled the heavy metal, right?"

"You got it, the expression 'mad as a hatter' was commonly known to the Victorians, if not the root cause.

"I gotta tell you a story about how beavers are being reintroduced to the wild. As far as I can tell, nobody who writes a book about beavers can resist spinning this tale. Idaho was once a rich beaver habitat, but they were almost rendered extinct in the fur trade. It's pretty rugged country for driving around a truck full of beaver cages as a remedy of repopulation. So, biologists first tried putting a pair of equally balanced cages on either side of a horse or mule. But the beavers were unenthusiastic and their mounts were reportedly 'spooky and quarrelsome.' Therefore, somebody came up with the idea of parachuting them in. They performed experiments with an adult male beaver dropped in various experimental contraptions that would spontaneously disassemble when striking the ground. Made of metal instead of wood, for obvious reasons."

He stopped to scrawl:

Castorid Paratroopers

"Can anybody imagine what they named him?"

"Crash test beaver?" Sam offered.

Jake pointed at Veronica with a question in his eyes, but the response of 'Banzai' did not satisfy.

"Justin?" suggested Mark.

"No, guys, but close. They called him 'Geronimo.' The problem was Geronimo didn't like being volunteered for hazardous duty. He reached the point of passive, non-resistive civil disobedience. Nonetheless, over the course of 1948, seventy-eight beavers were loaded onto aircraft and transported up into a series of high montane valleys. The big guy was pushed out of the plane simultaneously with three young female companions. The three youngsters immediately started exploring their new territory, but the repeatedly traumatized male took considerable cajoling to exit his contraption and get started on building 'castorid' habitat. The plane flew several passes over the valley but couldn't confirm that he had exited the drop box. Fortunately, the follow-up next year showed abundant signs of beaver works there and elsewhere, rated as an overwhelming success.

"Problem solved? In more remote areas unambiguously. But near roads, towns, and agricultural areas, a more disputatious interaction. The first beavers in an area might be a real attraction for locals and tourists alike, but once streets and fields became flooded, researchers realized they had surpassed the cultural carrying capacity of an area unless some limits could be set. Some trees had to be protected. Some ponds had to be ratcheted down a tolerable amount." He paused for a sip of water.

"Human transportation is extremely dependent on bridges and culverts under roads and railroad tracks. An example of what can go wrong occurred in 1973, when Hurricane Irene blew through the Northeast and took out over two thousand road segments and obstructed more than a thousand culverts.[47]

"But sadly, castorids can also be the culprit where culverts are concerned. A roadway would be a perfectly acceptable dam as far as they are concerned, except for the flow though these large concrete, plastic, or corrugated metal pipes. Which they happily go to work to block, like putting a cork in a bottle." Pausing, he decided to put up another heading:

Pond Levelers

"So, to the rescue came people who knew how to install a nifty device called a 'pond leveler.' First the culvert is fenced in on the upstream end, with galvanized metal fencing. A gap is left for an underwater thick plastic pipe extending perhaps thirty or forty feet farther into the pond. A circle of fencing—with a roof like the cage for monkeys in a zoo—protects the more proximal pipe end. These rodents may go a little crazy for a while trying to stop the very obvious turbulent flow through the culvert, until they eventually become resigned to a lower pond level."

"Who builds these cheat devices?" Sam asked.

"County and highway departments for the most part, but also private landowners. Usually, this work is contracted out to small companies in the area who carry out both the initial installation and annual maintenance. It saves a lot of money and the sacrifice of beavers, so everybody wins."

"What about giardia?"

"Good question, Veronica. My partner Abbey could explain at great length since she teaches and consults about infectious disease, as you know. Indeed, *Giardia lamblia* is a parasite commonly carried by these critters. Additionally, *Echinococcus*, which serves as a marker of fecal contamination in waterways. For prevention, all you can do is practice good hygiene with handwashing and the filtering of water if camping.

"As a final point, with the climate of the future already assaulting us, tundra of the far North is being converted to taiga, where small trees are added in as the tundra warms and melts. And yes, the beavers are moving in without help from us. Given the severe fires we have seen in places like Siberia, these castorids may offer some serious mitigation. And we humans need all the help we can get.

"Should I ask you all if I have made an adequate case for discussing beavers in an engineering class? Whaddya think?"

There was a pause. "Well," said Mark, "it makes sense in terms of mitigation, I guess."

"I'm looking for an even more basic answer . . ."

Jake took longer to make his final points. "Beavers were important hydraulic engineers here long before our species came to this hemisphere."

A few heads were nodding.

"So, beavers are engineers, too?" asked Veronica.

This time it was Jake who nodded. "Beavers are engineers who must become important again, for their sake and ours.

"And—as for all of you engineering students, may Geronimo be your inspiration to think outside the box," he said, then smirked a little.

Ignoring all the groans, he completed his comments with, "Finish that next chapter, chapter thirteen, entitled 'Mechanics: Strength of Materials.' See you all next week." He began shutting down his computer.

Several of them softly caressed the pelt thoughtfully on the way out.

TWENTY-FIVE

A Leg to Stand On

Do not be afraid; our fate
Cannot be taken from us; it is a gift.
—Dante Alighieri

It matters not how strait the gate,
How charged with punishments the scroll,
I am the master of my fate:
I am the captain of my soul.
—William Ernest Henley

Juliette Chén was known to all as Julie of course. She and her tall, beautiful, blond partner Emma Robinson had been experiencing an idyllic weekend away from school until this evening Em—everybody called her Em—developed a painful limp. The day at Sandy Point State Park beach had been hot but gorgeous, perfect for getting into the ocean on the west side of Chesapeake Bay Bridge.

It started so innocently, with a telltale abrasion from soccer over the front of her left ankle the day before they left Georgetown University. It was just a spontaneous pickup coed soccer game, so no shin guards or anything. But as a crack soccer star from high school, she couldn't resist a sliding tackle that blocked a goal.

Being diabetic, Emma had carefully cleansed the wound and applied combination bacitracin and polymyxin B antibiotics, a four-inch gauze pad, and a tangerine-tinted adhesive wrap over the superficial abrasion, which of course got soaked the next day when they bodysurfed the ocean waves. She washed it off again when they got back to their room and re-applied a dressing, but it began to pain her, and her limp was worse by the time they arrived for dinner in a cozy restaurant near one of the Historic Inns of Annapolis.

"Hate to say it, Juliette, my adored one, but this really stings, this ankle thing. And I'm feeling kinda punk."

Julie saw Em grimace, push back from the table, and reach down to put her hand over the bandage. Her face was suddenly a pale and flushed patchwork quilt. Her nostrils flared as she took a shaky breath. They had fallen hard for each other sophomore year together, and now they were juniors and rooming together.

My lovely lady is not a complainer. "Then let's get this seen right away, Em. We need to get you upstairs and check your blood sugar."

"I didn't want to ruin this weekend—"

"Bullshit, lady, you know better. Let me help you over to the stairs, then I'll settle the bill here and at the front desk. Get your things packed, then lie down, that should help you feel better. I'm thinking we want to get you back to DC, less than thirty minutes if I drive fast, but not just the school infirmary."

"Whaddya . . . mean, Julie . . ." Emma said, then closed her eyes for a long moment.

"I mean we can't mess around here, and the best place to go is the GW Medical Center. In case this gets serious."

"My belly doesn't feel great—I'm really thirsty. I need to get something . . . in my stomach."

"Okay, look, don't go upstairs. Just stay here, drink some water, see if you can get some of this food down. I'll pay the tab, throw everything into our suitcases, and bring the car around front. Then I'll help you out after we check your blood sugar." Julie stood up, put her hand to Emma's forehead. "You're not burning up, but you feel a little warm. Let's get cracking."

***

Emergency rooms are always busy on Saturday night, and this was no exception. When Julie helped Emma out of the car at the front entrance, the triage nurse could see immediately a wheelchair was called for, and brought her back to one of the critical care stabilization bays after initial evaluation. Julie was sent to park the car and finish up the paperwork at the front desk.

Kate Whitlock was an experienced nurse. Once she helped Emma out of her clothes and into a gown, she started recording her vital signs as they talked. "Okay now, Emma, tell me what's going on."

"I've . . . been an insulin-dependent diabetic for about four years. Usually well controlled with injections twice a day. But I got this scrape on my left ankle playing soccer yesterday morning, and now it feels a lot worse . . . I almost can't bear weight on this side. I think it might have gotten infected, maybe by swimming in the ocean this morning."

Kate checked her temperature with a digital thermometer, then wrapped a blood pressure cuff around her arm. An oximeter placed on her fingertip showed a pulse of 114, which was fast, and oxygen saturation of 94 percent, just below normal.

"What were your blood sugars today?"

"Normal this morning, about 100, but when I started to not feel well at dinner I got up to 228, then on the way here it was higher, something over three hundred . . . I can't even remember exactly. So—I injected an extra ten units of regular insulin in the car, about half an hour ago . . . I feel really weak and dizzy. And kinda short of breath."

"Emma, first a quick fingerstick, then I'm going to start an IV," Kate said, as she vigorously rubbed an alcohol pad over the side of her index finger. The drop of blood was placed in the glucometer. "I'm gonna grab an IV setup and let the resident know you're here. Be right back."

Admitting medical resident Charles Baker was an experienced second-year, juggling multiple patients on this shift and overseeing medical students and interns. With his movie-star stubble and blue eyes, he was a favorite of many of the nurses, both male and female. He came in with the electronic chart just as Kate was setting up for an IV start with an eighteen-gauge needle. "So, Emma Robinson, nice to meet you, I'm Dr. Baker, sounds like you need some help here. Tell me the story again about this wound on your ankle." One by one Kate placed three electrodes across Emma's chest under the gown.

"How about a nasal cannula for oxygen at two liters a minute, Kate," Dr. Baker said.

As Emma struggled through the events of the day again, Kate and Dr. Baker cut off the dressing on the anteromedial aspect of the ankle, exposing the wound situated right over the long saphenous vein but not penetrating it.

Right about then Julie made it to the exam room escorted by a nurse and quickly introduced herself as Emma's friend and partner.

"Honey, why don't you sit yourself down in that chair here in the corner," Kate said, after a quick appraising glance at her.

Juliette could tell the nurse and doctor were concerned about the wound, taking several samples from it. They kept glancing up at the monitor with the readouts on pulse and the cardiac monitoring strip.

"Kate, let's start with a liter of normal saline to be run in over the first hour. Emma, how long ago did you say you gave yourself the ten units?"

But it was Julie who answered. "It was at 7:30, I kept track, so almost forty minutes ago."

"Good, that helps. Kate, let's go with another ten units of regular insulin IV push now, followed by an infusion of 5.5 units of regular an hour to start. Then I'm going to need a complete blood count with differential, metabolic panel, hemoglobin A1C, serum ketones, a pair of blood cultures drawn from separate sites. And a couple of extra clot tubes for other tests later. UA as soon as she can give us a urine sample.

"Emma, are you right-handed?"

Again, it was Julie who answered quickly. "Yes, right-handed."

Scarily, she's not completely alert.

"Emma, I'm going to put an arterial line in your left wrist. This hurts more than a blood draw, so I'm going to inject some local anesthetic into the skin and down to the outside of the artery first. We need this to monitor the pressure and pH of your blood, because right now you have ketoacidosis, diabetic ketoacidosis, and we have to get that under control quickly. What triggered this was most certainly your leg infection. Once we get these several infusions started then we're going to admit you to the hospital. I see in the records that your next of kin are your parents in Massachusetts. While you are twenty-one, we may need their assistance with decision-making here. Kate, get us a room in the fifth floor ICU."

I know her parents don't approve of me, thought Julie. *This . . . could get complicated.*

Dr. Baker put firm pressure over the radial and ulnar arteries on the palmar side of the left wrist to conduct an Allen test of the circulation. He tried to have Emma make a strong fist several times, but she wasn't able to really cooperate. When the whole hand finally paled, he released the radial artery and saw blood immediately enter the hand and pink up on both sides. Then he repeated the test with release of the ulnar artery, with an identical result. Now confident that the hand would remain viable even if the radial artery clotted or was damaged, he performed the sterile prep with chlorhexidine, injected lidocaine subdermally and down toward the radial artery, then used a twenty-gauge intracath to enter diagonally toward the elbow. When bright red blood suddenly spurted back into the syringe, he externally compressed the artery higher on the forearm, removed the inner needle—leaving the catheter in place—and screwed on a three-way stopcock in practiced fashion.

Julie was feeling a bit queasy but didn't want to say anything, so she just leaned forward and stared at the floor, trying to slow her breathing.

Kate attached to the stopcock an IV line leading to the transducer, and up on the monitor the upper systolic and lower diastolic blood pressures started displaying in sinusoidal fashion. She removed the now unnecessary blood pressure cuff, and collected a sample of arterial blood to be sent off for blood gas determination of pH, oxygen, and carbon dioxide levels.

In only a few minutes all the lines were gathered up to an IV pole with multiple infusions running, the two blood cultures had been drawn, and Emma was carried away toward a bank of elevators.

Julie had had time only for one last caress and a soft word before she was sent back to the waiting room. *I need to talk to her parents.*

***

"Lachlan, this is Charlie Baker in the ER. I've got a patient for you, coming up to fifth floor ICU. Name is Emily Robinson, she's a twenty-one-year-old white female in DKA with an infected left ankle as the precipitating event. The ankle abrasion was acquired yesterday morning, after which early this morning she ill-advisedly swam in the ocean. No other pertinent past medical history. Temperature 30.1, pulse 125, blood pressure 108 over 56 with an arterial line in her left radial artery, respiratory rate 35. Restless, distractible, not combative. The left ankle is red, swollen, and hot, for about a fifteen-centimeter stretch, with some crepitance suspicious for subcutaneous gas, several hemorrhagic bullae interspersed in this abrasion. Oddly, no lymphangitic streaks. No nodes behind the knee or in the groin."

"Charlie, has she ever been in DKA before?" asked Dr. Lachlan Rawlence in his deep baritone, gripping his phone with his left shoulder as he typed in a note on another patient, as medical folks obligatorily have to multitask. It was another night on call.

"Not since her original diagnosis about four years ago. Okay, I've got some labs for you. White count seventeen thousand, with fifty-five percent polys and fifteen percent bands, looks like it might be sepsis. We already sent off a couple of blood cultures, as well as samples from the wound. Hemoglobin is 13.5, so at least she's not anemic—"

"Though she might be a bit hemoconcentrated if she's really dry."

"Yeah, I'll grant you that. Platelets normal, PT and PTT normal, so at least she's not at any unusual risk for bleeding. Initial blood sugar 482. She vomited a couple of times in the car on the way here, so it's no surprise her potassium is low, at 3.1, so as soon as she proves she has some urine output, you'll want to add some to the infusion. Her barcarb is also down at sixteen. Blood gases are pH 7.1 with oxygen ninety, carbon dioxide twenty-two."

"Charlie, this is a young, physically active, healthy woman except for her diabetes. This DKA sounds eminently manageable and not of long duration. But I can tell the wound must be what's really bothering you, right?"

"Absolutely. I'd consider gas gangrene, or sepsis, or vibriosis."

"Not *Vibrio parahemolyticus*, but *Vibrio vulnificus*, right, I get it," Dr. Rawlence commented.

"You could consider treating with ampicillin/sulbactam, or instead piperacillin/tazobactam if you find out *Vibrio* is the problem."

"I can see they're wheeling somebody into an ICU room as we speak—"

"Lachlan, let me add one more thing. I'd get a surgical consult right away. The bad news is she may need an amputation if she has, as I suspect, necrotizing fasciitis, down through the fascia into the muscle. The good news is if you catch this in time it might end up being a below-the-knee procedure instead of above the knee."

"I'll call the surgical resident as soon as I have a chance to look her over, Charlie."

"They won't be happy about operating, if indicated, until you get her ketoacidosis under some degree of control. And they'll want a type and cross for a couple of units of packed red cells if she goes to the OR."

"I'm bettin' you sent off a couple of extra tubes just for that reason."

"We're trying to run a full-service shop here, Lachlan. Let me know how this turns out."

"This will likely all play out in the next couple of hours, one way or another. Hope her limb is still salvageable."

TWENTY-SIX

Soothsayer

Nothing in the world can one imagine beforehand, not the least thing, everything is made up of so many unique particulars that cannot be foreseen. —Nostradamus

After there is great trouble among mankind, a greater one is prepared. The great mover of the universe will renew time, rain, blood, thirst, famine, steel weapons and disease. In the heavens, a fire seen. —Nostradamus

The chief resident, clad as usual in her long white coat and a severe expression, looked up from her notes on the lectern, and the crowd immediately quieted. "Okay, folks, time's a-wasting," Stacey Armstrong declared.

"We're in for a real treat this morning, some wide-ranging analysis of three serious infectious diseases that we've seen in this med center in recent months and their implications for public health. Instead of starting with a single case presentation as we usually do in these grand rounds, think of this as more of a survey course, the showcase of a medley of pertinent afflictions." She gestured to her left with an arm fully extended.

"I know most of you are already acquainted with Abbey London, a specialist in this area with a focus on invasive tropical and subtropical disorders that will be increasingly problematic in the coming years, and who readily acknowledges her chief preoccupation is with vector-borne diseases."

Abbey wore her hair in a russet ponytail, as she often did on days spent at the hospital. She strode briskly up to the front of the room with her lapel microphone already clipped on.

Can't stand being stuck behind a lectern when I feel the need to stretch my legs.

"Several of the cases on which I've recently consulted are truly enthralling. While they are all infectious diseases, they range widely from parasitic to viral to bacterial categories. Why don't we start with one transmitted by anopheline mosquitoes.

"By the way, don't hesitate to raise your hand for a question, comment or challenge at any time," she said, as she turned to print on the whiteboard:

Malaria

"It is only appropriate as Americans that we focus first on this classic parasitic disease, as there is a long history of malaria in the United States, dating back to when we were a group of British colonies, the site where the capital was eventually going to be established was still largely swampland, and the mosquitoes were no less irritating then than they are nowadays. Several months ago, in this hospital, we had a case of so-called 'airport malaria,' cared for by a medical student named Madelyn Pennyfarthing if I remember correctly."

I thought I saw her arriving here, but can't see her now.

"The malarial species turned out to be *Plasmodium vivax*, which is the dominant species in most countries outside of sub-Saharan Africa. The World Health Organization reported that in 2022 there were an estimated 249 million cases and 608,000 deaths in eighty-five countries from the combined five species of this protozoan parasite.[48] The WHO African Region is home to about ninety-five percent of the cases and deaths, with children under five accounting for about four-fifths of fatalities.

"Additionally, pregnant women, travelers with no history of prior exposure, and HIV-infected and other immunosuppressed individuals are all at accentuated risk of serious disease.

"Let's start with its convoluted life-cycle beginning in the mosquito. From med school you should all be familiar with the mind-boggling sequence of stages for this curious parasite," she said, as she turned for a moment to aim her laser at the slide projected behind her, "beginning when the microscopic gametocyte form is ingested by a female mosquito seeking a blood meal, without which she cannot reproduce. The human red blood cells rupture in the mosquito gut to release male and female malarial gametes, or sex cells. Over the next seven to ten days paired gametes fuse to form zygotes—comparable to the first stage of human pregnancy—which elongate and push out through the insect's gut like tiny spears. These then mature into 'oocysts,' which in turn grow and rupture, releasing 'sporozoites,' also in the shape of tiny needles. The big picture is that the parasite DNA is replicated by sexual reproduction of gametes just as it is in our mammalian cells.

"The sporozoites migrate through the mosquito's body and enter into the insect salivary glands, ready to be injected into the next unwary host. Mosquito saliva helps numb the human skin and prevent coagulation of the blood as it's being sucked up. As perfect a vehicle for transmitting infection as one can imagine, you gotta give it credit.

"As if this were not complicated enough, recall the stages of the parasitic cycle in us humans. The sporozoites enter our bloodstream and are carried to the liver, and first infect the liver cells. An individual malarial 'schizont' stage grows inside a liver cell, then ruptures, suddenly releasing thousands of individual merozoites back into our bloodstream. The bloodthirsty little merozoites infect more red blood cells and consume almost all the packaged hemoglobin, next forming what is called a 'ring stage.' Under the microscope this actually looks like a signet ring—hence the name."

She turned again to aim her pointer at the slide. "It's always exciting to see these under the microscope, after setting up thin and thick smears and using Giemsa stain."

"Are thick and thin smears still considered to be the gold standard?" asked a student.

"Absolutely—in clinical medicine—especially in less developed countries. There are of course other more sophisticated techniques used in research, as half the cases are missed using only traditional microscopy.

"Next up is a trophozoite stage, progressing to the other form of schizont—inside a red blood cell instead of a liver cell—but again eruption releases merozoites to infect again the bloodstream. Pesky little critters, aren't they?

"As you can imagine, when either type of schizont ruptures, our immune system is confronted anew with the invading horde of muscular merozoites, and the resultant immune attack against the Pac-Man-like invaders causes the cycle of shaking chills, high fever, and lassitude. Added to this is the progressive anemia from destroyed red cells. If there are enough cycles of recurrent releases, or especially if the parasite gets into the human nervous system, then this can be fatal."

"Why can't the immune system fight this off?" another student asked.

"In most of the stages and intervals inside a human host, the parasites are protected either inside liver cells or inside red blood cells. But when they're released as merozoites the numbers are those of a marauding horde, like Genghis Khan and his horsemen suddenly rising up over a hillside. But with ongoing or recurrent infection, some progressively potent immunity develops. The two core interventions against the vector itself are insecticide-treated nets, or ITNs, and indoor residual spraying, or IRS. As you might guess, evolutionary pressure is selecting for mosquitoes which bite early before people go to bed."

"What about experimental vaccine work?" asked Stacey.

"Since 2021, WHO has recommended a choice between two vaccines to be used for kids living in regions of Africa with the bulk of *P. falciparum* transmission, which fortunately has not reared its ugly head in this country."

"So, no indication for vaccine in the US," Stacey followed up, arching one eyebrow impressively.

"No, at least not at this point."

"What drugs should be used?" asked another faculty member.

"Artemisinin-based combination therapy meds are the most effective for *P. falciparum* infection. Chloroquine is recommended for treatment of *P. vivax* infection in those geographic areas where it's still effective. Primaquine should be added to infection with *P. vivax* and *P. ovale* parasites to prevent relapses erupting out of the liver. Artemether and lumefantrine are a couple of the most recent drugs added to our armamentarium.

"The CDC has a travel medicine website accessible to both medical providers and tourists, which contains advice about which prophylactic or preventive drugs should be prescribed to travelers while they are in malaria-endemic areas. Finally, countries that have achieved at least three consecutive years with zero indigenous cases may apply for WHO certification of malaria elimination. Notably, the US would not now qualify for this recognition, as several cases unrelated to travel have been reported in Florida and Texas.'

"If there are no other questions, let's move on." Abbey paused to scan the audience, then turned to draft another heading:

Dengue Fever

"Okay, next let's discuss a virus. This new slide is a picture of an *Aedes* group mosquito such as *Aedes aegypti*, the most common vector harboring dengue fever viruses. While there are early descriptions consistent with dengue outbreaks as far back as 1779, it was not until the early twentieth century that science had advanced to the point that the culprit virus could be identified. While cases are frequently asymptomatic, those with symptoms usually fall ill four to ten days after the mosquito bite. These symptoms include an abrupt fever as high as 106 degrees, swollen lymph nodes with variable rash, headache and pain behind the eyes, abdominal pain with vomiting, topped off with joint and muscle aches. The evocative nickname is 'breakbone fever' for the deep achiness in joints, as patients really do feel this 'bone-deep.'

"Recovery usually ensues in two to seven days, except in those with severe dengue, which can involve low platelets and therefore bleeding— both internally and externally—leakage of blood plasma out through the walls of capillaries resulting in low blood pressure and shock . . . which, if not managed, can be fatal. Fluid can collect outside the lungs as pleural effusion, or in the abdominal cavity as ascites surrounding the intestines. With shock the patient may experience difficulty breathing, fatigue, and irritability or restlessness.

"This is a tropical and subtropical disease, which means half the world's population is at risk, and with the changing climate I suspect soon enough the majority of people will find themselves in peril. There are four strains of the virus, which can be identified by blood tests for antibodies or by direct virologic testing.

"One of the great ironies of this disorder is that while infection with one strain of the virus may generate lifelong protection—*only* against that particular strain—thereafter reinfection with any other of the four sero-types of the virus even years after the first may be more severe and result in shock and even death."

"How do you predict or prevent that outcome?" Stacey asked.

Abbey nodded and paced away from the lectern for a moment. "Pre-vention is the touchstone of course, everything we just discussed with malaria, aside from the obvious point that the mosquito vectors are dis-similar. So different, in fact, that *Aedes* group mosquitoes break a couple of stereotypes by being more likely urban than rural and biting in the day-time instead of the nighttime. Logically, it helps to use DEET-based insect repellents on skin and clothing, alternatively, permethrin-sprayed exterior apparel."

She could see some people frowning at the mention of DEET.

"If you are counseling a patient about travel to an area with endemic dengue, explain how staying in well-screened and air-conditioned areas would be to their huge advantage.

"Second, maintain a high degree of clinical suspicion about any patient with a flu-like illness, especially if there is a travel history, and I don't just mean to a foreign country. At this point, travel to Florida, Puerto Rico, and Hawaii, and soon other states, will be considered perilous endeavors.

"Third, always bear in mind that unlike a malady like malaria or coro-navirus, which results in some degree of acquired immunity, an experience with dengue may paradoxically put your patient in heightened jeopardy down the line."

Andrew Wyatt raised his hand for just a moment before speaking up. "Just to clarify, if an individual is infected a second or third time with the same serotype of dengue, there should be stronger immunity built up, just as with vaccination. But what about actual vaccines?"

She pursed her lips for a fraction of a second. "Glad you brought that up. Clearly a candidate vaccine would need to protect against all four strains simultaneously. In 2024 there was an outbreak of dengue fever in Brazil, described by Stephanie Nolen in *The New York Times* as 'staggering in its scale—a million cases in Brazil in a matter of weeks, a huge spike in Argentina, a state of emergency declared in Peru and now another in Puerto Rico.'[49] Nolen went on to say the 'mosquitoes that spread dengue thrive in densely populated cities with weak infrastructure, and in warmer and wetter environments—the type of habitat that is expanding quickly with climate change.'

"The Pan American Health Organization stated in March of that year the Americas had already experienced 3.5 million cases and over a thousand deaths, far ahead of any previous year.[50]

"The vaccine story as described in the *Times* article correctly laid out the state of the art.[51] One of the preexisting vaccines is a pricey two-shot regimen. The other is indicated only for individuals who have had a prior experience with the virus. The new candidate vaccine, as the journalist reports in her article, was 'created by scientists at the National Institutes of Health in the United States and licensed for development by the Instituto Butantan, a huge public research institute in São Paulo.'

"Butantan has a good track record with production of most of the immunizations in Brazil, and importantly has the capacity to craft tens of millions of this new combination agent."

She stopped for a moment and frowned.

"Alas, this vaccine will be produced only for Brazil. Fortunately, 'the multinational drug company Merck & Co., which also licensed the NIH technology, is developing a related vaccine which will be sold to the rest of the world; the efficacy of that vaccine has not yet been tested in a late-stage clinical trial.' But I've seen some preliminary data, not yet peer-reviewed and published, and the results look promising. And not just for the

Americas; the mosquitoes and viruses have spread in tandem to places like Croatia, California, Italy, and other regions with no prior involvement."

Abbey shifted her gaze around the room. "So, if no further comments, let's move on to *Vibrio* infection, specifically *Vibrio vulnificus*, associated with brackish or salty water." She turned to scribble on the whiteboard:

Vibriosis

"Finally, a bacterial entity to finish up with. *Vibrio vulnificus* stains as a gram-negative, curved, rod-shaped pathogenic microorganism. It swims around with a single flagellum at one pole. It is a relative of *V. cholera*, the causative agent of cholera, and is present in coastal areas in the United States, from the whole stretch of the Gulf of Mexico up as far as Maine.[52] Clearly, as the world warms, this range may extend even farther poleward. At least one strain of the organism is bioluminescent. It protects itself from being engulfed by a human phagocytic cell with an antiphagocytic capsule of polysaccharide surrounding it like a peanut shell. One curiosity is that infection tends to be more serious in patients with higher blood iron levels, as might be seen in the disorder of hemochromatosis.

"There are three types of infection with this extremely virulent organism. The first is acute gastroenteritis associated with eating raw or undercooked oysters. Second is a necrotizing wound infection in injured skin exposed to contaminated marine water, even with puncture wounds by sea life such as stingrays. Third is invasive sepsis, either from the gut or a wound as the portal of entry. This bloodstream infection is more common in immunocompromised patients, especially those with liver disease."

"Why liver disease?" a med student asked.

Her answer was that the liver has phagocytic cells called reticuloendothelial cells lining the portal blood vessels of the liver, which helps screen out invaders breaking out of the intestines.

"Our current patient is a twenty-one-year-old white female who presented in diabetic ketoacidosis with a leg wound that was appropriately bandaged but then, only hours after her soccer injury, immersed in the ocean. That same day she developed fatigue, dizziness, nausea, vomiting, and progressive pain in her left ankle, just in front of her lateral malleolus. Her initial blood sugar was 482, and her arterial pH was 7.1. The ER and admitting residents were appropriately alert and concerned about the possibility of *Vibrio* infection, and swabs and cultures eventually proved out this organism.

"I'm glad to say the surgical consult was accomplished less than an hour after admission, after which she was taken directly to the OR. The initial debridement during that surgery showed extensive devitalized muscle tissue to within fifteen centimeters of the lower patella, and the attending surgeon concurred with the residents that immediate amputation was in her best interest. They opted for a below-the-knee procedure with an option of reoperation above the knee if she deteriorated.

"Fortunately, her surgical site showed no signs of infection, although her DKA initially proved difficult to bring under control. She is now post-op day number nine, was successfully weaned off the ventilator after three days, her ketoacidosis has resolved, blood cultures remained negative, she has been tapered down to a single antibiotic, her acute oliguric kidney failure is improving slowly as her urine output increases, and she never developed acute respiratory distress syndrome. It would not have been unexpected had she developed ARDS in this clinical context. Her youth and athleticism may be partly responsible for this successful outcome, but I believe the admitting medical and surgical teams coordinated extremely well in this case. I see there are several residents here who were involved in her care. Good job, all of you."

She turned to look at Stacey, who gave her only a curt nod, so Abbey turned back to face the group of med students and residents.

"Just a few final comments. All three diseases tackled today were originally purely enzootic, but at some point, each made the successful jump to humans. Unlike influenza viruses, not one of the three has shown any great propensity to transfer human to human, aside from transfusion of blood products or transplantation of tissue and organs. But never forget the potential is there."

She tugged at an ear, wondering whether or not to bring up another concern, then decided it was justified.

"Finally, it is not enough to just research, teach, and practice competent medicine. Additionally, each and every one of you has a responsibility to engage with and educate the public, in both small and large venues, in schools and houses of worship and conferences. Initiate outreach, don't just wait for an invitation. Health care workers need to regain the respect that they deservedly held before the Covid epidemic. So, so much depends on this, perhaps for our very survival from the next great pandemic disease."[53]

There was brief applause, then all the sounds and flurries of activity and conversation as almost everybody headed off to address their remaining work for the day and night to come.

Stacey offered only a brief, curt thanks as she departed, but several med students had final questions for Abbey.

TWENTY-SEVEN

Code Name Schoolmarm

Space for the sunflower, bright with yellow glow, to court the sky. —Caroline Gilman

There are two kinds of light—the glow that illuminates, and the glare that obscures.
—James Thurber

Catarina sat in the parlor with a shawl around her shoulders, sipping a cup of tea. "My husband used to call me Cat, as did most of the rest of my family. My students called me Mrs. Noether."

Jake admired the way she held herself, straight-backed in her chair, her white hair tucked into a bun. "But your full name is Catarina Noether, hope I'm pronouncing those names correctly." He was atypically having a cup of tea, surprising himself, perhaps in response to the stormy weather outside.

The rain was relentless. Earlier there had been pounding hail.

"Before you ask, yes, I do have a cat, an old tabby named Schrödinger. I suspect you know the significance of that name."

"Well, so the mystery is finally resolved, your particular cat is alive, if that's what you mean." They smiled at each other.

Mina was rocking Hopie to sleep in her arms, and Jake could tell she was fascinated by this particular guest. "I'm sorry, Jake, but why would you say that?"

It was Catarina who answered first. "Back in 1935, in the early days of quantum mechanics, physicist Erwin Schrödinger came up with a thought experiment about quantum superposition in a discussion with Albert Einstein. He said to consider a hypothetical cat which simultaneously could be considered both alive and dead, so long as it was unobserved in a closed box, with a flask of poison that would be smashed by a hammer linked to a radiation detector and a source of alpha particles."

"Why would anybody do that though?" Mina persisted.

"Don't worry, dearie, this is all just purely speculative, a conjecture of physics. No cat was injured in this case. I'm quite sure Erwin had no idea how many stories and jests and cartoons would be inspired by this poor creature over the years." She set her cup down.

"Would you like some more tea?" Jake asked.

"Yes, please." Jake picked it up and headed into the kitchen right across the hallway.

"How old is your cat?" Mina inquired.

"He's twelve now, a very mature rascal. But he stays in the house and is not allowed to harass birds. Probably a bit too slow for that now anyway.

"And you, Mina, besides working as a nanny, what else do you do?"

"I'm attending two schools remotely, a community college back in Vermont and also the US Nanny Institute. I'm completing a whole bucketload of online classes."

"Very excellent to hear this. I have always been a great believer in education."

Jake returned the teacup to the side table for Catarina. "It is starting to hail again, I saw it on the lawn from the kitchen window, bigger chunks this time." He looked her straight in the face and knew he wore a quizzical look. "Ma'am, you have a set of unusual names, how did that happen?"

"My mother was Portuguese and my father Russian. I was their third child and first girl after two boys, and my mother wanted a name to remind her of her beloved Iberian Peninsula."

"Where were you in school and what did you teach?"

"My four years in school were at Bryn Mawr, Pennsylvania of course, and afterward I began teaching physics and English in a high school in Harrisburg."

"Ah, yes, the town made famous—or infamous—by the meltdown at Three Mile Island. So, you were there at the time, were you? What year was that again?"

"March of 1979, beginning at four in the morning, though unhappily the town was not notified until hours later. Mina, it was a LOCA, a 'loss of coolant accident,' which ultimately resulted in the release of radioactive gases, including radioiodine, which can cause cancers of the thyroid. It was a real blow to and a permanent stain on the nuclear industry, which would like to simply erase it from history now."

"I'm sure they'd prefer to gaslight it," Jake said, with a slight sneer. "Even though it was rated as a level five on the seven-point International Nuclear Event Scale, which I think is the level called something like an 'Accident with Wider Consequences.'"

"I'm old enough to actually remember that old film, *Gaslight*, which came out near the end of World War II. That's where the expression gets its name. The TMI meltdown certainly crystallized antinuclear outrage in the general public. You may remember in the 1970s when we occupied the Seabrook nuclear power plant site in New Hampshire."

Jake's eyebrows moved up, more on the right. "You say 'we' because you were involved in that action?"

She smiled merrily through her wrinkles. "My husband Joseph was not entirely happy with me about that. But I was a member of the Clamshell Alliance back in the day. Seabrook never got its second reactor partly because of our ongoing opposition to the whole idea. It remains controversial of course. I lost my Joseph three years ago. He thought I was a saucy old lady and I thought him cantankerous, but we lasted fifty-four years together." Her granny dress fell well below the knees, a calico design of some sort.

"Do you have any children, Catarina?" asked Mina.

"I do, Mina, a son Brody and a daughter Celeste. Brody has a son and daughter, Celeste had twins but still has one of each."

"Bet her hands are full," Mina said, and Catarina nodded.

"Are you still active in antinuclear work?" Jake asked.

"I don't travel as much, even with Seabrook to focus on. But a small group of us in Harrisburg have set up an all-ladies book club that we call the Nuke Knockers Alliance. Not in any serious way."

Jake could swear he saw a secret smile.

"We mainly write letters to the editor of *The Patriot-News* and the Dauphin *Daily Voice*. As a book club, we actually read more poetry than anything, and I even write an occasional poem I share with the ladies. Time and again we may discuss an antinuclear book, sometimes even climate fiction."

"So, what brings you this way?"

"I was waiting for you to ask, I think. I'm not really as humble a person as I make out to be. I am still a member of the Clamshell Alliance, which has been arguing that it's time for a 'no nukes' comeback.[54] They like to use me as a secret weapon sometimes, because I am old enough to play the doddering fool. Goes back to my acting days in college. What the Alliance said, was that with 'Biden and Harris sinking billions into nuclear energy, we should reunite to spark a new wave of resistance.'"

"Even worse have been Trump and his cronies following down the same tortuous path," he added.

She nodded. "I agree with that sentiment, so I'm here because tomorrow morning I'm going to present a statement to the House Committee on Energy and Commerce."

"Wow, you're going to be talking to one of the congressional committees?" Mina sounded incredulous, but Jake just tapped his fingertips on the arm of his chair in excitement.

"Jake, you probably already know that the Nuclear Regulatory Commission every six months provides a report on the status of its licensing and regulatory activities—but we feel we need to balance their input to Congress with ours. So, I've been delegated to testify for the Alliance. And for my book club."

Outside the hail hadn't let up, and the rain was loud enough that they had to speak up a little.

"Cat, I appreciate the gravity of what you're trying to do. You must know what you're up against though. In 2023 at the Dubai COP conference more than twenty countries pledged to triple global nuclear energy generation by 2050—serious backsliding if you ask me. Countries like France of course, but also Japan and the UK as well as the US. Even Biden's climate envoy John Kerry claimed that science has proven you can't get to net-zero 2050 without some nuclear, which I found extremely disappointing."[55] His lips tightened into a narrow, straight line.

Cat raised her hands as if in horror. "What I do know is that prior climate meetings paid little attention to nuclear, because of its fantastical costs and from controversies surrounding safety, trafficking by undesirables in stolen nuclear materials, poorly proposed management of the radioactive waste materials, and so forth."

"Not to mention attractive targets in conventional war," Mina almost whispered.

Catarina and Jake looked at her. *A surprise, but what a pleasant surprise*, he thought.

"Why did opinions shift toward nuclear? In just one year?" Mina asked.

Jake scratched his nose. "Maybe part of it stemmed from the United Arab Emirates—the UAE. At that time it was on the verge of completing the Middle East's second nuclear station, which now provides a quarter of its electricity. In an area of the world with a lot of geopolitical threats, it creates a vulnerability much like the Zaporizhzhia reactors in Ukraine, still periodically getting shelled or cut off from outside power.

"And there has been intense lobbying by nuclear industries in many of the developed countries, especially the heavyweights like the US," Jake finished.

Mina nodded and whispered, "Hopie is sound asleep now, so I'm going to put her down."

Jake stood up to stroke his daughter's back and kiss the top of her head without waking her. Mina headed down the hallway.

"Are you going to talk about the Vogtle reactors?" he asked.

"I am, because Energy Secretary Jennifer Granholm is scheduled to give testimony immediately following me, after she visited the newly operational reactors numbers three and four in June of 2024 and parroted the line about the global necessity to triple the number of nuclear facilities.[56] But the average customer supplied by the two new reactors is paying an extra four hundred twenty dollars a year, about thirty-five dollars a month."

"I bet she won't talk about customer costs, so you'd better."

"The two combined reactors were initially projected to cost fourteen billion dollars, but arrived seven years late and some twenty-one billion dollars over budget. And while everyone keeps calling nuclear power carbon-free, in the whole nuclear supply chain there are releases of greenhouse gases, especially from the enrichment step. Moreover, the small modular reactors have never been proven commercially viable, unless they get a tidal wave of government subsidies."

Jake sighed. "After some seventy years of subsidies, federal and state."

"It should be easy for me to present our case. Jake, you remember the failed nuclear renaissance of the late 2000s sputtered out after the dreadful Fukushima disaster and *preposterous* cost overruns with reactor projects, bless their hearts. Then the second time they tried to stake a claim to a renaissance, what really happened is that nuclear went backward last year. A fella named Jim Green explained what happened. 'There were five reactor startups in 2023 matched by five permanent closures. But nuclear power slipped down the hill by 1.7 gigawatts of capacity. And there were only six reactor construction starts that year, five of them in China.'"[57]

By this time, she had put her glasses on and pulled out two pages of carefully and legibly handwritten notes and was peering at them. "And the IAEA, you know Mina"—who had returned—"the International Atomic Energy Agency projects out ten reactor closures and a loss of ten gigawatts per year from 2018 all the way to 2050." She shook her head in what Jake figured must be mock sorrow, just like that of the walrus in *Through the Looking-Glass*.

"And Mr. Green said the number of operable power reactors ranged from 407 to 413—depending on your definition of operability—well down from the 2002 peak of 438. And nuclear power's share of global electricity is down to a forty-year low, at only 9.2 percent. Jake, you probably don't remember that nuclear power peaked at 17.5 percent in 1996, because you were just a young tyke then—if you were even born." She looked at him over her glasses with a glint in her eye, and he had to shake his head.

Catarina continued. "SMRs are small modular reactors, which have gotten a lot of press, but nowhere did they have any construction starts or startups of power last year. Mr. Green said the 'biggest SMR news in 2023 was NuScale Power's decision to abandon its flagship project in Idaho despite having secured astronomical subsidies amounting to around four billion dollars from the US government.'"

She pointed a finger at Jake. "I'm living in retirement with very limited income, so at least my tax dollars are not supporting this boondoggle, and that's just what I'm going to say tomorrow. X-energy, another previously promising SMR company, announced it was canceling plans to go public and was forced to lay off about a hundred workers. Now what will become of them I wonder?

"And back in early 2022, a company called Oklo reported its first license application was summarily rejected by the NRC even before the agency had commenced a technical review of its novel Aurora reactor design. I'm going to tell those congresspeople that company should change its name to OhNo."

Jake heard the most delightful chuckle from her and had to laugh himself.

"Mr. Green goes on to say that 'meanwhile, forthcoming new cost estimates from TerraPower and XEnergy as part of the Department of Energy's Advanced Reactor Deployment Program are likely to reveal substantially higher cost estimates for the deployment of those new reactor technologies as well.'"

Jake smiled at her beautiful articulation. *She's going to give them a lesson tomorrow they'll never forget.*

"I saved the best part for the very last. When nuclear power was losing 1.7 gigawatts of capacity in 2023, in that same year global renewable capacity *additions* amounted to a record 507 gigawatts, almost five percent higher than in 2022. And that year was the twenty-second year in a row that renewable capacity additions set a new record."

"That's a string any professional sports team would be envious of," Jake said, with a wide smile.

She lifted her chin again. "The International Energy Agency said it, so you may take that to the bank. And my final point to them is going to be that the IEA expects renewables to reach forty-two percent of electrical capacity by 2028 due to a projected 3,700 gigawatts coming into play over the next five years."

Catarina peered at Jake with a sly smile. "They won't know what hit them."

"They'll just think you're a little old lady school teacher when you start, but I bet they'll be mumbling to themselves and yanking to loosen their ties by the time you finish. I sure wish I could be there tomorrow, but I've got to be at the university pretty much all day.

"You know there's a question I'm not allowed to ask you, ma'am, or any woman for that matter."

"I do appreciate that, Jake, and so I will simply tell you I'm eighty-eight." There was a long, comfortable pause as they each sipped some more tea.

"I may just have them write on the blackboard one hundred times."

"What would you have them compose?" Jake opened his eyes widely and leaned forward.

"Our daddies told us not to be such pissants."

***

It wasn't much later in the conversation that Abbey burst through the door. "*Jesús, María, y José. Mierda*—" Just then she crossed past the doorway to the parlor and stopped short. "Oh, I am so sorry, I didn't think we had anybody here." She couldn't suppress the fire in her eyes.

Jake started up quickly, then calmed himself. He took another deep breath. "What's the matter, honey?"

"Some idiot skidded in all the hail on the street and ran into my rear bumper. I spent the last forty-five minutes dealing with exchanging insurance information and talking to the police. They had so many accidents it seemed like it took them forever to get there."

"But you're not hurt."

"No, but—"

"Well then, let me introduce you to Catarina Noether. You may remember that she has a two-night reservation with us. And there is going to be another couple coming in after they've had dinner in town."

Abbey stepped into the room. "I'm so sorry . . . I didn't see another car out there, so it didn't occur to me we had a visitor."

"That's completely understandable, Abbey. I had one of those new-fangled Uber drivers drop me off from the train station."

"And right now I'm really hoping you don't speak Spanish—"

"*Solamente un poquito, señora. Pero no me importa, seriamente.*"

"Okay, now I am really embarrassed."

Jake could see Abbey wasn't ready to do any smiling yet. "Honey, why don't you go check in on Hope and Mina. I just heard Hopie wake up a bit ago, and Mina went to check her diaper or something." He gave her a quick hug. "While you're doing that, I'm going to go out and check on the damage."

Catarina smiled with tenderness. "This is the kind of thing you'll look back on and laugh about in future years. Just not today, not yet."

TWENTY-EIGHT

Conspiracy Theories

Don't squat with your spurs on. —A plainsman

Never pee on an electric fence. —A plainsman

Elliot used his bandana to wipe his face, then complained, "Gonna be another scorcher." The sun was barely above the horizon, but soon even the lizards would be scurrying for shelter. There were a few clouds far to the east, though the descending rain was cheated from even reaching the parched plain.

The wind was just now picking up a bit, barely enough to move a flag, not enough to cool off the sweat soaking their shirts.

Matt drank from his canteen, a long draught. "Yeah, another day hot as—"

Buck couldn't work up enough moisture to spit. "What the double-barreled, buggered, blooming, holy bastard, horse-fucked, headless mule, sonuvabitching, moronic son of a whore . . . goddamn hell it's hot."

Elliot slowly raised his eyes to look at him. "Buck . . . you been practicing your blasphemy again? Pretty impressive, but I gotta say . . . still needs work."

Matt just shook his head. "We're most of the way through June, boys, and I understand y'all need to blow off a little steam once in a while. But we need to stay steady here. Often the anticipation . . . it's worse than the actual fighting. And Buck, the heat is part of the reason we're out here so early in the day. No chance for onlookers like the last time we were here."

Elliot took his hat off for a second and stretched his arms toward heaven. "Look at the upside, Buck. No flash flood this time, no dust storm, and nobody's caught on to our plan. Most of all, no federal agents nosing around the town."

"Ground's already hot enough for mirages," Matt observed, but he didn't even smile as he took a few panting breaths. "Remember back to what happened to Phoenix in 2023. They had something like thirty days in a row where it hit at least 110 damn degrees. They beat that in 2024 when they had 113 days in a row where it hit at least a hundred. So just enjoy the fact we all have jobs where we work in the shade most of the time. Just not out here, not today.

"This is the practice closest to what we're going to be actually doing. July 4th is coming up in a couple of weeks. And we leave town in one more week. We need to concentrate on stocking enough provisions in our trucks. Hauling a fair amount of water as well, though that's easy 'nuff to fill up along the way. Each of us bringing enough cash that we won't need credit cards. But right now, we've got to practice shooting in a seated position. We've got our scopes zeroed in, we're getting used to the extra weight of our suppressors, but our accuracy is dropping off. And in theory this should be more accurate than standing position, not less. And we can't shoot prone, you know that for a fact."

"How about we rig up a rest for the back of the trucks, just at the right level for sighting on target," Elliot offered. "A simple bar across the back. Inside the shell."

"That's up to each of you. But it would hafta be one you could install after you clamber inside the back of the truck. Not a bad idea, Elliot, but you gotta be able to take it down real fast after you're done shooting and need to skedaddle out of there. And meaning no disrespect, Buck, but we're not all the same height, so it'd have to be custom fit. Remember the risk if you try to shoot inside a box, you have no choice but to use full protection for your ears and eyes. No two ways about it. We got to run silent, run deep once we take off running. But not deaf."

Buck bit off a chew. "These targets, when we hit them, will they spark or catch fire? We want some fireworks, right?"

"Not certain about that, don't wanna go online and search for videos on how to do this or that or what it looks like. Even on the dark web best stay off every kind of radar we can. Ain't asking for any kind of advice from nobody." *Is it time to let them in on the surprise? Nah, not yet.*

They all gazed out at the distant targets. Seemed pretty small without using the scopes. Wooden fruit boxes set on end, weighted down with a few rocks on the bottom, with several paper targets set in a triangular formation higher up. The bullets were punching through, splintering the thin wood without tipping them over. They put their earmuffs back on and sat down again.

The shots rang out in a steady staccato, with tendrils of smoke hanging in the air.

Three men in a row planning to make a statement to force people to sit up and take notice. Not just plinking bottles and cans. No siree, Bob.

But I gotta tell them the real plan before we leave town.

TWENTY-NINE

Hodgepodge Concoction

Everything we hear is an opinion, not a fact. Everything we see is a perspective, not the truth.
—Marcus Aurelius

If it is not right do not do it; if it is not true do not say it. —Marcus Aurelius

The coffee maker hissed to a gradual stop, just about the time Brian walked through Jake's office door. "Did you hear or smell that coffee, Bri, or am I just too damn predictable?"

Maybe that's why Abbey always says I've always had a fine grasp of the obvious.

"It's two thirty, Jake, which is usually when you make the last pot of the day. But yes, buddy, I could smell it all the way down the hall from the graduate student lounge." He poured himself a cup, reaching down into the small fridge to get some oat milk or whatever other concoction he was using these days. Opened the carton, sniffed it, nodded to himself, and poured in a generous splash.

"If you wouldn't mind, could you pour me a cup also?" Jake requested.

"Want milk in yours?"

"Yes, my poor man's latte as usual. But only if there is enough actual cow's milk in there."

"Why are you reading the newspaper?"

"I brought it from home. It has been sitting on my desk there for weeks, and I wanted to extract an article with some information on the grid." His feet were up on the desk.

"Don't you usually do that online?" Brian chided.

"Every once in a while, I like the feel of the newsprint, you know, the smell of the printer's ink."

"You're reading the Old Gray Lady, you know. Might smell of antique perfume, or maybe mothballs," Brian said.

"Very funny. But I prefer to think of her as the paper of record. This *New York Times* article that stuck in my mind was an essay by Peter Fairley from April of 2024.[58] Apparently, he's been writing about power technology and policy for a couple of decades. His argument is that some parts of infrastructure are just too damn important to be targeted in warfare. He said, and I quote, that in March of 2024, 'Russia knocked out half of Ukraine's power supply.' He said that 'missiles and kamikaze drones had mostly [previously] targeted . . . substations . . . [b]ut this time they hit the plants themselves, severely damaging and destroying hydroelectric and fossil fuel stations—all of which are difficult to repair or replace.'"

"And there have been a ton of reports about the risks for not just Zaporizhzhya but other nukes in Ukraine," Brian said, scowling. "People die without power, especially come winter. Clear case of crimes against humanity, if you ask me." He put his feet up on a chair and sighed.

"Think what happens when the grid goes down, Bri. Sudden pervasive darkness except for flashlights and those rare installations with backup power. Water treatment and pumping and sewage treatment stop in their tracks. Food spoils in fridges and freezers. Electrified vehicles, including school and other buses, can't get recharged. Clothes washing must be accomplished by hand. Drying happens only on racks and clotheslines. Computers, printers, Wi-Fi, and the internet fail. Phones get used only until their batteries peter out. Medical devices like ventilators and anesthesia machines cannot work. Sterilizers are worthless. Operating rooms don't usually feature windows for backup lighting—and even if they did, that would only work in the daytime. No imaging is possible, not even simple X-rays, much less CT and MR equipment. Pathologists may not be able to use microscopes, or incubators for bacterial specimens. The list goes on and on." Jake's fingers tapped restlessly on the desk.

"Major bummer, Jake. So, what should we do about this?"

"Fairley says power grids are 'still legitimate military targets, according to both international law and our own military rule book.' But even before Russia's most damaging assaults, the International Criminal Court in The Hague concluded that the country's pummeling of Ukraine's power system had already crossed the line and issued arrest warrants for a pair of senior Russian commanders, Adm. Viktor Nikolay . . . evich Sokolov and Lt. Gen. Sergei Ivanovich Kobylash, whose units are accused of launching the missiles. Supposedly, this was a first."

"How was that a first?" asked Brian, and he got up for more coffee.

"A forceful precedent, the world's first prosecution of combatants for attacking electrical infrastructure. Fairley recommends the world community define levels of protection for power grids. Think of generators like hydroelectric dams and nuclear plants. And hospitals and other medical facilities for sure. Perhaps codifying this into the Geneva Accords or similar policy documents. Laws in the Geneva Conventions define power grids as 'civilian objects,' to be protected in warfare.

"The problem is militaries can make use of exceptions to justify almost any strike, arguing the anticipated gains . . . outweigh the projected civilian suffering."

Brian had picked up the paper to scan the article. "But it says here Germany struck Britain's grid with zeppelins in World War I. And in 1991 the US took out Baghdad's power in the Persian Gulf War. As recently as 1999 NATO jets bombed power plants in Serbia. I suspect this could be a much longer list."

Jake had Brian hand him back the paper. "There is a guy named Gregory Noone, a judge advocate in the US Navy, who is quoted here, as saying the 'military took great pride . . . that they turned off all the lights in Baghdad in the first Gulf War . . .' but by the time of the second conflict about a dozen years later, 'we realized that wasn't such a good idea.' And here: 'Putin may never face consequences for plunging Ukraine into darkness, but now that General and Admiral may never leave Russia, for fear of being picked up outside its borders to face trial.'

"I love this last line: 'Prosecutors who pursue war criminals can keep hunting for decades.' Ain't that the truth. Hunt those dogs down."

Brian responded, "Somehow this reminds me of a quote from Halla Tomasdottir in 2021 when she became Iceland's new president, and I paraphrase, Use your voice, vote and wallet for climate action."

"What you're saying is we need to add international political action to that short list?" Jake asked.

"Yeah, tell me about it. But here's an idea that's actually working for Ukraine. They have discovered that wind farms are a lot harder to knock out than central generators like hydroelectric dams, or substations. This is from another article in the *Times*, by Maria Varenikova."[59]

"Pretty name that. Sounds Ukrainian in fact. I even like your accent."

"Kinda rolls off the tongue. What's funny is that she may be an expert on Ukraine, but she made the beginner mistake of calling wind turbines"—he grimaced—"windmills."

"What you're saying is that she's an expert on what may be her native country, but not particularly sophisticated on wind power. So, big deal."

"Yeah, that's what I'm getting at." Jake took another sip of coffee, breathing in the warm, sweet aroma and enjoying the taste on the back of his tongue. "She talks about the new Tyligul . . . ska wind farm in the southern Mykolaiv region, sited only a few dozen miles from Russian artillery but paradoxically more resilient to obliteration. It's ironic that the need to construct turbines many hundreds of feet apart to better capture nonturbulent wind also makes them more difficult to destroy. Yes, they're out in the open—but unless hit in the center of mass, which is stationary, the blades are clearly a moving target. Varenikova states a wind farm can be temporarily disabled by striking a transformer, a substation, or a transmission line, but these are more amenable to repair. Long-term plan for . . . Tyligulska . . . is for eighty-five turbines producing up to five hundred megawatts of electricity."

Brian raised a finger. "You keep talking about how the Russians control the Zaporizhzhia power plant, ever since they invaded in 2022."

Jake nodded. "Which totals 5,700 megawatts, has been damaged repeatedly, and has stopped transmitting energy to the grid at this point. Hard to imagine them getting their own green energy transition going even after the conflict when reconstruction can get started—with the return of foreign investment—or so states the Center for Strategic and International Studies.[60]

"These crazy fuckers even started expanding their wind farm during the war. The turbines they are putting in place are from the Danish company Vestas. Problem was that they needed a crane that could lift a hundred tons. They found the last heavy-duty crane left in the country, modified it, and named it their 'little dragon.' Just like our Inn, right? Our own little dragon.

"Varenikova said the builders were working in wide-open fields about sixty miles from the front lines, 'hiding in a bunker when the air raid sirens sounded.' Now listen to this—truly extraordinary—they could watch the cruise missiles flying lower than the turbines, trying to evade radar detection by Ukrainian defenses."

"Tough little buggers, amazing when you think about it. I'd have been scared shitless," Brian said.

"Same here. Now, here's another article about how the risk of hurricane-associated power outages may become half again as common in some parts of the US, including Puerto Rico. These researchers at Pacific Northwest National Laboratory and the Electric Power Research Institute created an open-source, interactive map of projections for where future hurricanes may be affecting power supplies.[61] I checked it out, and there are a couple of obvious caveats. First, these projected power outages assume a static system without any attempt to harden grid components and other structures. Second, they state 'the future period modeled . . . represents the 2066–2100 timeframe under a high emissions scenario [SSP5-8.5] and there is still significant uncertainty as to how climate conditions will evolve.'"

"What you're saying, Jake, is that this study is extrapolated way into the second half of the century, uses the highest level of emissions of all the

IPCC scenarios, and assumes we don't get our act together in terms of tackling emissions—or rectifying the grid, right?"

"Yeah, but this is just scientists purposely being quite conservative. Still, if you look where we live, Arlington County in Virginia can expect up to 1.7 more loss-of-power events per decade. Definitely weighted in the wrong direction. The report notes the rise of climate-driven storms could see cities like Boston experience outages on the order of 70 percent more per decade. Miami could see a 119 percent increase."

"Okay, buddy, this is where you come in. Gotta get these grids ready, right?"

"Vegetation management comes first. With heavy rains, soils get saturated and tree canopies overweighted. Destabilized tall trees fall on power lines and landslides knock out electrical infrastructure. One thing that can help is undergrounding transmission where economically feasible, unless in areas subject to inundation or landslides. Greater interconnections between grids. More distributed and utility-scale battery backup. Strengthening power poles." He shook his head thoughtfully.

"And the Union of Concerned Scientists published a statement that 'sea level rise could expose more than 1,600 critical buildings and services to flooding twice a year, including more than 150 electrical substations.'"[62]

"You know what they say, Jake, don't give me problems, tell me solutions."

"Simple, stop burning fossil fuels and clearing forests."

"Little simplistic, don't you think?"

"Granted, but good messaging."

"Speaking of which, have you set your students out on their scavenger hunt yet?"

"They are deployed out on the savannah, with safari hats and cameras, going after big game. We shall see what they catch."

THIRTY

Full Disclosure

Genius has its limits. Stupidity knows no bounds. —A plainsman
Careful is a naked man climbing a barbed wire fence. —A plainsman

Elbows on the table at the Pearl Handle, quiet as a nun sneaking out of a rectory, Matt had the face of a man trying to sidle up next to a controversy without getting caught in the lie. He took another long, slow sip of his beer. The bill of his cap hung down low over his forehead.

Elliot looked at him with more of a squint than a frown. "You know we're ready and raring to go, so what's eating you? Spill it." He turned and lifted a finger to Caroline, who nodded to him.

Matt shook his head, stuck his tongue in his cheek. "We're following precautions and not writing anything down. I have to keep running the details through my mind to make sure we ain't missed anything."

"We've got the trucks stocked up with enough supplies we almost don't need to buy any groceries."

"I've got several jugs of water in my truck," Buck said quietly.

"We all do, Buck," Elliot said. "But I can't believe how much crap, how many cookies you packed in yours."

"I can't help it if I like Fig Newtons."

Caroline began to head to their table in the back, wearing a sleeveless blouse in the heat and faded jeans with a few holes for ventilation. The ceiling fans turned lazily, but the one closer to their table had a squeak.

"Do you all have can openers, in case you make the mistake of buying chili?" Matt asked.

"You guys planning to go camping somewhere?" asked Caroline.

Elliot leaned back in his chair. "We're thinking we might try our luck up along the San Marcos River."

"Aiming to catch some largemouth bass, are ya?"

"Or maybe some rock bass, you never know until you dip your rod in the water," Buck said, only raising one eyebrow slightly.

Caroline apparently decided to ignore the jibe. "Right, you outlaws, ready for some more beer?"

Matt said "Sure" and the other two nodded.

"What'd you get at the food truck?" she asked.

"Stopped at Estela's Enchiladas for some tamales and tacos."

"Appears to have been money well spent, looks like you just about polished them off. Must have been spicy enough for you three to be guz-zling so much beer this evening."

"Hot enough," agreed Matt. He had a toothpick on the right side of his mouth, rolling it around and back and forth.

"Okay, I'll be back in a jiffy." As she set off for the bar, Buck kept her in sight from the corner of his eye.

"We've done enough camping over the years, so I know you two packed enough toilet paper, aluminum foil, tents, and all the rest," Matt said.

"Burner phones all around, extra batteries for flashlights and head-lamps," he continued.

"Enough cash in your wallet for if problems crop up. Do not try and bring a spare credit card along." Matt looked at Buck until he saw him squirm.

"Don't look at me, I know the rules."

"We don't need all that much ammo, nothing that would look suspi-cious if a cop searches your truck. No patriot literature, ya hear me?

"We're all gassed up for tomorrow morning. I want us to stay within ten miles of each other, maintaining contact all the way. No speeding, Elliot will take the lead to make sure of that.

"We all have an empty milk carton, I hope you practiced using that while driving, just like real truckers do."

"Some rags and glass cleaner might be good to clean the windshields, to minimize time spent in gas stations," Elliot said, looking at the bottom of his beer mug. "And this is the last alcohol we get until this is all over."

Matt leaned forward and put his elbows on the table. "So, drink up boys, this is your last beer walking over here now, then I have one last thing I wanna discuss."

They listened to the squeak of the fan until Caroline had dropped off the beers and taken their empties back to the bar.

Matt looked at each of them. "The trucks look pretty clean. I will say you did a good job of scraping off the decals and bumper stickers that could have given us away.

"You know me as a good poker player, and in fact I've been holding some cards pretty close to my chest all these months."

Elliot tilted his head sideways and tugged at an ear. "What're you trying to say?"

"This has always been a bigger operation than you realized," Matt said, and he could see they both looked shocked.

"What the hell does that mean?" Buck asked in a hoarse whisper.

"There are more people involved in this Fourth of July action, it's been planned for a long time." The silence drifted away with the ceiling fan going *tick, tick*.

Elliot lifted his chin. "And you waited until now to let us in on this plan?"

"It's been on a need-to-know basis from the beginning."

"How many people know about this?" Elliot asked.

"I don't think anyone knows really. It's been a very decentralized push. But I can tell you that there will be cities hit all over the country. But I don't know or care to know how many."

"So, this is all in cities, no rural attacks?"

"Yeah, Elliot. We don't want to hurt people in small towns, those are our people."

"I like the idea of just hitting big cities," Buck said.

Elliot tilted his chair back again. "Lot of the states are in a big heat wave. There're wildfires not just in the West, but in the Carolinas, Minnesota, Wisconsin, Washington, Oregon, California—all over."

"Maximum impact has been the plan all along."

"Hot diggity damn dog, Matt, I like this. A lot." Buck smiled finally.

"Boys, time to settle up with Caroline. We need some sleep tonight. We're going to saddle up in the morning, not at the break of dawn, but not long thereafter. I want to get some serious mileage in tomorrow.

"Since we can take breaks in the shade at rest stops, we plan to do some of the traveling under a full moon with the coyotes."

It got quieter as they sipped their last beers thoughtfully.

THIRTY-ONE

Proliferation of Storage

The Tube or Sphere, that are rubb'd, do, in the Instant of Friction, attract the Electrical Fire, and therefore take it from the Thin rubbing; the same parts immediately, as the Friction upon them ceases, are disposed to give the fire they have received, to any Body that has less.
—*Benjamin Franklin*

We will make electricity so cheap that only the rich will burn candles. —*Thomas A. Edison*

Jake was sitting on the front of his desk, with one hand on the edge and the other tapping the front quietly. "Sam, since you're already talking, why don't you go first. Whaddya got for us?"

Sam stood up and came to the front, distributing his handout to rows on the left and right. Jake moved over to his wheeled swivel chair at the side and accepted one of the typed sheets as well. Sam looked around the room. "I'd like to start with a review article from 2023 about iron-air energy storage, referenced on this sheet. It's kind of ironic because this new Massachusetts-based US energy storage startup Form Energy ended up building their first facility in the iconic coal-producing state of . . . West Virginia.[63] They got serious federal support with a 290-million-dollar incentive package from the Inflation Reduction Act. As we all know, the Department of Energy has been keen on newer tech and extended duration storage modalities. Utilities have been accomplishing storage with grid-sized lithium-ion batteries, but their duration of backup on the whole has only been in the two- to four-hour range. The DOE is seeking ten hours or more for a grid saturated with wind and solar to help ensure stability and reliability."

"Tell us how this reversible rusting concept works," Jake said, as he stood up to inscribe on the board:

Iron-Air Battery

"Form Energy is counting on a scalable, modular system, each unit the length of a chest freezer. Each module is jam-packed with some fifty individual cells, interconnecting with iron and air electrodes. The non-flammable electrolyte is a lot like what you'd find in a AA battery. Charging up this new battery requires only applying an electrical current, which reformulates the rusted iron back into pristine metal. Appropriately they call this 'reversible rusting.' Discharging is accomplished by exposing the iron to a stream of air with an assist from an electrolyte and a membrane, with the flux of electricity in combination with atmospheric oxygen leaving behind only rusted-out iron.

"And then they turn this collection of rust back into iron."

Jake whistled. "How big can these batteries get?"

"The article states that 'hundreds of these enclosures are grouped together in modular megawatt-scale power blocks.' Get enough of them connected and a one-megawatt system takes up about half an acre, but higher density configurations could achieve more than three megawatts per acre."

"Game-changing if they could pump out three megawatts nonstop for a hundred hours," Jake said.

"This is not as simple as it sounds apparently. The article says 'the foundational technology has been around for about forty years before pathways to commercialization have emerged.' So, the new battery modules are grouped together in environmentally protected enclosures, says Form. 'Then hundreds of these enclosures are grouped together in modular megawatt-scale power blocks.'

"The article goes on to say 'that's a lot of cells and a lot of power blocks, and Form was meticulous about choosing a suitable site to manufacture them.' The attraction of West Virginia was based in part on a suitable unused brownfield, and the abandoned Weirton Steel plant on the Ohio River."

"Seems you are trying to imply access for transport by barge on that river," Veronica said.

"Not to mention rail and highway, and high-voltage electric power," threw in Mark.

"What else?" Jake asked of the whole class, raising both hands.

"I'm guessing a whole crowd of under- or unemployed guys who know how to work with metal," Veronica said, sounding excited.

"The state offered up a unique incentive package worth up to 290 million dollars in asset-based performance financing that sealed the deal." Sam said. "West Virginia Economic Development Secretary Mitch Carmichael was confident the new plant would bring in at least 750 new full-time jobs.

"Other states are lining up to receive these novel iron-air batteries. In June of 2024 Form 'announced that it is moving forward to deploy a fifteen-megawatt, 1,500-megawatt-hour iron-air battery for the Georgia Power branch of Southern Company,' which should begin operating in 2026.

"Next, in August, Form announced that it had received a 12-million-dollar grant from the New York State Energy Research and Development Authority to get its ten-megawatt, 1,000-megawatt-hour iron-air battery up and running also by 2026, making these two installations the only multiday energy storage systems in both states.

"Third and last, and actually the first mover, is California. The California Energy Commission chimed in with a 30-million-dollar commitment to Form for a five-megawatt, 500-megawatt-hour version of the iron-air battery, which will also be the first multiday energy storage project when it goes online a year earlier—around the end of 2025 in that state."

"Anything else?" Jake asked.

"Sure as both my grandmothers have corns, the article makes one final point: Form also has a sulfur-based flow battery in the works, with funding assistance from the Energy Department's ARPA-E office for high-risk, high-reward projects."

"Well done, Sam," Jake said, and the young man returned to his seat. "Who's next?"

Veronica raised her hand and stood up. "I've got an article about Finland, which is, as you know, a pretty cold place in the winter. And I also have a handout like you suggested last time that we bring, so here it is." She followed Sam's lead in distributing it as she marched forward.

She stood tall in front. "If you think iron makes for a strange battery, now imagine—sand. But not storing electricity but rather heat, which is an imperative for every Scandinavian country. Since today's class is all about a future perfect, this soapstone battery the article discussed was set to go online in 2025. But the geopolitical history here is important."[64]

Jake turned to the board, scribbling again:

Sand Thermal Battery

"This project was launched just as Russia cut off gas supplies in retaliation for Finland joining NATO. There had been a precursor rigged by the company Polar Night Energy in 2022, a single-megawatt design for a power station in Kankaanpää town. The concept they had was of using sand as an affordable way to store the plenitude of electricity available when solar and wind power were providing power to the grid. The article stated that 'grains of sand, it turns out, are surprisingly roomy when it comes to energy storage.'

"The new sand battery in Pornainen will be about ten times larger than the prior pilot plant. The process starts with resistive heating, in which 'friction,' or resistance, results from trying to pass electricity through any material that is not a conductor. The heated air is then circulated through a heat exchanger into a tall, super-insulated tower filled with low-grade sand. Low-grade it may be, but the magical part is it can be heated to around five hundred degrees Celsius and hold that heat for several days or even months.

"When the district heating system needs energy, the hot air from the tower warms water, which is distributed to homes, offices, and even an indoor swimming pool. A fellow named Markku Ylönen, chief technical officer for Polar Night Energy, was quoted as saying, 'The complex part happens on the computer; we need to know how the heat energy moves inside the storage, so that we know all the time how much is available and at what rate we can charge and discharge it.'

"The sand battery equates to almost a month's heat demand in summer, and nearly one week's demand in winter. They are proud to eliminate any need for oil and anticipate that their combustion of woodchips should plummet by sixty percent."

"What about the issue we've discussed previously, that global shortages of sand are already being recognized?" Jake asked.

"Initially the builders used construction sand so as to limit transport emissions, but they can use any sand-mimicking material with a 'high enough density, within certain thermodynamic parameters.' In Pornainen, Polar Night Energy found a sustainable material in crushed soapstone—a by-product of a Finnish company's manufacture of heat-retaining fireplaces. They always search for a thermal energy storage medium based on the customer's requirements. As the company stated, 'Examining and testing different materials is crucial for us to use materials that are suitable in terms of properties, cost-effectiveness, and promotion of [a] circular economy.'"

"Is this scalable? Is this only for temperate and polar regions?" Jake asked.

"The company claims they have the ambition to take its technology worldwide, build a hundred times larger, and deploy it around the world with lightning-like speed."

"Well, I guess that answers that. Good job, Veronica. So, Russell, looks like you get to bring in the anchor leg. Come on up." *I see he has on his Yankees T-shirt again. He must sleep in it.*

"I picked up on a report from the Australian Renewable Energy Agency, or ARENA, though I suspect its findings would transfer well to our grids. They explored how EVs can participate in Frequency Control Ancillary Services, or FCAS, markets to aid in stabilizing electric grids through Vehicle-to-Grid, or V2G, technology. All the figures I'm going to be discussing are in Australian dollars, or A$, which when I last checked one A$ converts to sixty-six cents in US dollars or USD, so bear that in mind."[65]

Jake stood up again to print out:

Vehicle-to-Grid Support

Russell glanced down at his notes. "This represented the first time a fleet of vehicles had been used to supply ancillary frequency control services to the national electricity market. They decided a business case could be made in the context of fleet operators accelerating electrification of their commercial fleet. Their metrics include quantifying the potential economic value and assessing the user experience of the drivers and fleet operators. It's called vehicle to grid, or V2G."

Mark spoke up for the first time. "So, these cars or trucks were hooked up to chargers, level two chargers I assume?"

"Yeah, level two, in dedicated fifty-amp circuits, charging at about a 7.5-kilowatt power rating."

"But Russell, what if the vehicle battery starts at a low level of charge?"

"The software algorithm allowed them to access only the cars that had a relatively high level of charge."

Jake could see that Mark seemed satisfied with that answer, but as their professor he wanted to clarify something. "Very tight control of frequency is required to keep the grid coherent, which would be at sixty hertz in this country but presumably fifty hertz in Australia."

"That's right, Jake, but usually only small amounts of charge were subtracted from the car batteries and regardless, often replaced pretty quickly. In fact, the total energy exported from EVs was only about one percent of total charging energy, highlighting how the trial vehicles were rarely called upon to provide FCAS services. They set up fifty-one Nissan vehicles with bidirectional Wallbox Quasar chargers via CHAdeMO ports. The electronic request came from a FCAS controller that modulated and managed the charge/discharge sessions of the EV through ethernet communication."

"How did they end up using so little of their charge?" Jake asked.

"Because the contingency FCAS consisted of eight really short scenarios, high and low scenarios for one, six, sixty, and three hundred second markets."

"So, five minutes max. What do the lower and higher markets stand for, amount of discharge?" Jake asked.

"No, no, you've gotta understand that if there is too much generation, too much electricity supply, then the frequency goes up, whereas if generation is lagging, then frequency starts to drop. Both require immediate attention to unexpected frequency fluctuations as a means of ensuring that the grid remains within its safe operating range, otherwise electronic equipment can go haywire or even get damaged."

Jake began to understand his point. "What you're saying is that a fully charged battery would only be able to provide the electrons to raise the frequency back up to target level, while below a certain cutoff state of charge, the car could only participate in taking electrons back in in order to adjust the frequency down."

Jake mused, "What's the bottom line here, what's this worth to the grid?"

"Their main economic evaluation involved the sixty second market, and if I understand their logic, an average electric vehicle could bring home about two thousand dollars a year, and the report claims the contingency FCAS market is unlikely to have a significant impact on driver experience or EV battery degradation."

Jake shook his head. "But this is an experimental trial in a totally different grid with the parameter of a different frequency, and you'd have to drop that cost number by one-third to compare to US dollars. But I'm impressed that the ancillary service is worth a lot to a grid operator. We should all bear that in mind.

"Okay, Russell, interesting case. So, in terms of energy storage, we've discussed an iron-air battery, a sand battery, and finally a Vehicle-to-Grid strategy that may serve to provide support services as an increasingly competent backup for the grid.

"But you'll all remember that other task we were planning to discuss today. As per instruction, you all chose different electrical substations to visit, photograph, and assess for vulnerability to some sort of kinetic attack, like the historical event we discussed at length a couple of months ago. I know you got this all done, because you all sent me your pictures.

With only a little bit of prodding. Your protocol was to take long-range pictures, mid-range photos, and close-up—and be prepared to discuss.

"We've had some nice weather this June, therefore good for photography, though professionals know it's better either early morning or early evening." By this time Jake had powered up the flat-screen monitor and booted up the computer to run the slides. "Okay, I've got these labeled by name and location. Warren, that's your three photos up first, what can you tell us about them?"

Warren was a short, alert fellow with a red goatee to match his hair. He explained that his chosen substation was very suburban, surrounded nearly entirely by houses, though the homes might have arrived later. "There was an impressive high fence with a lot of warning signs about high voltage and stuff. No way a kid could chase after a loose ball in there. There were several streetlights on two sides, so it never sat in darkness. Given its location, probably not particularly at high risk."

"Okay, here's the next one, these photos are yours, Sam."

Sam also remained seated. "A bit more open space around this one, as it sits in the back of an elementary school playground and a parking lot for the school. My long-range photo includes a pickup truck and camper that got in the way a bit. Hmm, Idaho plates, which seemed curious. Maybe some out-of-state visitor."

Jake gripped the edge of his chair, then stood up suddenly. "I knew there was something that struck me as strange when I reviewed these before. It's been haunting me. Wait, Sam, let's pan through these quickly to check one point.

"Next one's David's, but there's no truck in the pictures." David replied in the negative when asked if he had seen anything suspicious. "Okay, Veronica, that's right, I did see a pickup but didn't think about it before. And there it is—Idaho plates again—what are the odds, right?"

More pictures went up, everyone looking for a truck. But nothing more seemed out of place.

"Okay, guys, class dismissed. You know what to study for the final exam next week. I would in particular have you review chapter fifteen on

'Energy Sources and Alternatives,' as well as chapter seventeen on 'Electrical Theory.'

"Okay, I've gotta go talk to someone." He closed his laptop and walked quickly and purposefully from the room, not caring if he left some of the wondering what was going on.

***

Jake held the encrypted phone to his ear as he sat in his office back home after he booted up the laptop.

"This is Emmanuelle, Jake. My secretary just told me you called about something you said was important."

"I've never called you on this phone before."

"So, may I assume this is something you do think is urgent?"

"I was just finishing up a class this morning, after giving all of them an assignment a couple of weeks ago. Each of them was told to go out to an electrical substation somewhere in the DC area and take pictures."

"What were they told to look for?" Her voice sounded calm and intent.

"Just to take photographs from a variety of distances and angles, and get a sense of the vulnerability of the substation to kinetic attack. We had discussed the history of such a strike in a class about a month ago." He paused, tapping his fingers on the desk.

"Something must have stood out for you. What was it?"

"I just sent you an email, with the attached photos my students assembled. In two of the sites a picture included a pickup truck with a camper shell."

"Okay, give me a second, let me pull that up. While I'm doing that, tell me what it was that struck you as unexpected."

"There were only two substations where there was a truck, and both of them had Idaho plates. Idaho—these people were pretty far from home."

There was a pause. "That does sound a little too unlikely to be purely coincidental. Now give me another minute and let me have someone run these plates, while you continue with your story."

"In both cases you saw how the trucks were facing away from the sub-station but lined up with it. There was apparently nobody in the truck unless they were inside the camper. But nobody checked."

"What time of day were these photos taken?"

"I don't know for any of these." Another interval of silence.

Emmanuelle spoke slowly. "This is July 2nd. That's important because the police and the FBI and other parts of the federal bureaucracy are aware that terror attacks are often timed to coincide with holidays and other major events . . . Okay, hold for a moment while I take this other call."

Jake was nervously shuffling papers on his wooden desk for what seemed forever but was probably more like a minute and a half, then she was back.

"I can't tell you what we've found, but it supports the idea that you may have come up with information useful to us."

"Are you going to search for these trucks, Emmanuelle, can you tell me that much?"

"Jake, we appreciate your report and we'll handle this from here."

"Do you need to talk with my students?"

"I don't think so, but we'll let you know if that seems appropriate. I'm proceeding with this partly because of your track record of tipping us off about the cyberattack against Peach Bottom last year.

"You may say hi from me to Abbey and Hope, but for now I would ask that you not share any other part of this discussion with anyone, not even Abbey. Are we clear on this, Jake?"

"Yes, but—"

There was a curt goodbye, then just a click letting him know their discussion was over.

He thought for a moment, his fingers still tense, then decided to go warm up some oatmeal with raisins and have a snack. Classic comfort food.

THIRTY-TWO

Rift Valley

It is certainly within the domain of science to determine when the earth was first fitted to receive life, and in what form the earliest life began. To trace that life in its manifold changes through past ages to the present is a more difficult task, but one from which modern science does not shrink. —Othniel Charles Marsh

To spread healthy ideas among even the lowest classes of people, to remove men from the influence of prejudice and passion, to make reason the arbiter and supreme guide of public opinion; that is the essential goal of the sciences; that is how science will contribute to the advancement of civilization, and that is what deserves protection of governments who want to insure the stability of their power. —Georges Cuvier

Abbey looked around the room. "Thank you, Stacey, for that introduction again. Now we have an opportunity to discuss a novel virus, one new to North America so far as we know. Rift Valley Fever, or RVF, virus is a member of the *Phlebovirus* genus, first identified in 1931 during an investigation into an epidemic in sheep on a farm in the Rift Valley of Kenya, explaining the origin of the name.[66] The Rift Valley is more famous for the groundbreaking paleoanthropological work accomplished there." There were a few smiles, but no laughter.

Damn, I didn't mean that as a pun.

"*Homo habilis* was the earliest hominin species unearthed there, followed by others such as the australopithecines and *Homo erectus*. Finally, *Homo sapiens* emerged about 300,000 years ago.

"Evolution has proceeded apace not just with our hominin ancestors, but also with all the infectious diseases that have co-evolved with us, including many of the great viruses such as smallpox, influenza, and poliomyelitis.

"I'm sure most if not all of you have heard about this fascinating patient, admitted approximately a month ago. Rift Valley Fever is a zoonotic viral infection which primarily affects animals but also has the capacity to infect people.

"The World Health Organization states the majority of these infections result from direct contact with the blood or organs of infected animals, though the same outcome has been observed occasionally from the bites of infected *Aedes* or *Culex* mosquitoes, or rarely from biting flies. There have been no documented reports of human-to-human transmission. While as yet we lack a human vaccine, there is work in this space. Our hopeful model is evidence that a sustained program of animal vaccination can stop outbreaks in domestic animals like sheep and goats.

"This virus crashes livestock populations, causing abortions and deaths. Other outbreaks have been reported in sub-Saharan Africa. Next up was an explosive eruption in Egypt, introduced by the trade of infected livestock along the whole reach of the Nile. Also, in 1977, a major epidemic in Kenya, Somalia, and Tanzania following El Niño-inspired widespread flooding with proliferation of the requisite mosquitoes.

"An out-of-Africa migration materialized at the turn of the century in the year 2000, as infected animals reached Saudi Arabia and Yemen, raising concern that the disease could extend to other parts of Asia and Europe."

Abbey hesitated momentarily. "Obviously, sadly, now it has reached North America.

"Basically, human infections result 'through the handling of animal tissue during slaughtering or butchering, assisting with animal births, conducting veterinary procedures, or from the disposal of carcasses or fetuses.'

"One could imagine that certain occupational groups would be at higher risk, such as herders, farmers, butchers, and veterinarians. In these groups transmission can occur from a laceration with a contaminated needle or sharp instrument, contact with abrasions, or even aerosol during animal slaughter. There has never been a reported urban outbreak, so think of this as mainly an infection in the boondocks.

"Contrariwise, no transmission has been documented in health care workers using standard infection control precautions, which should be reassuring to us all—"

Stacey broke in. "Perhaps not completely reassuring, Abbey, as medical personnel have occasion to suffer contaminated needlestick injuries, as you know full well from personal experience."

"As I know *all* too well; I am an author on some of the reports of my own needlestick exposure to Crimean-Congo virus—we all know that story."

Can't believe she brought that up.

She turned back to the center. "The incubation period in humans is relatively short, from two to six days. Many remain asymptomatic, but those who do succumb to the mild form of RVF report sudden flu-like fever, muscle and joint pain, and headache. Sounds a lot like dengue or flu, right? Some folks develop a stiff neck, sensitivity to light, loss of appetite or vomiting, raising a question of meningitis. All these symptoms usually resolve over four to seven days, coincident with the appearance of antibodies to RVF and disappearance of detectable virus in the blood. But there are three serious complications seen in select patients."

What in the world was she thinking to bring that up? Abbey thought as she posted up:

Ocular RVF

"In the ocular form of this infection, seen in two percent or less, the usual milder symptoms are accompanied by lesions in the back of the eye. The WHO states the retinal manifestations begin typically one to three weeks after onset, though this was on the shorter side in our patient, a thirty-seven-year-old white male goat farmer from Virginia who presented with a history of having taken care of a doe—a female goat—who miscarried premature stillborn twins. His visual symptoms had onset only five days after onset of illness, but progressed on to complete blindness—fortunately only on the left side. He's been under regular ophthalmologic surveillance and last I heard has normal vision and benign retinal exam on the right. The disease will typically resolve without lasting effects within ten to a dozen weeks, but if the macular or central retina is involved, half of patients will suffer permanent loss of vision. Death is rare in this group, and I would judge this individual is lucky he still has good vision on the contralateral side."

"What's being done to deal with the epidemiologic situation in Virginia?" a resident asked.

"We're working with the public health authorities of course, with the lead coming from the Animal Contact Outbreak Surveillance System at the CDC. The point man in Virginia is the veterinarian, Benjamin Harris, who took care of the patient's goats. As a trusted local voice, he has been vigorously reaching out to the veterinarians in his area as well as to the general public. He and I have developed a good working relationship."

"Do you think the disease arrived with mosquitoes then? Not imported animals? And if so, what about mosquito abatement?"

"All the states, all the counties on the Eastern Seaboard are gearing up for surveillance, really countrywide we are on the lookout, and as I understand it, mosquito control is part of the plan. My bias is that it would be a reasonable measure to immediately, sharply restrict transport of livestock across state lines until we see how this outbreak plays out. Virginia is rolling out serologic sampling of herds in the whole state to get an immediate map of this infection. The obvious corollary is fast-tracking of the licensing of the vaccine in the United States so that we can get started on ring vaccination around involved areas, thus protecting farmers and butchers as well as domestic ruminants.

"With this case as an example, in theory it should be feasible to get the public behind this effort, comparable to what has been done for avian influenza, aside from the obvious point that there is already a livestock vaccine for RVF." Abbey glanced up at the clock at the back of the room.

"We have two more types of severe infection to discuss, so let's move along at this point."

One more time, she pivoted to scribble on the whiteboard:

Meningoencephalitic RVF

"The onset of meningeal and brain infection is delayed usually one to four weeks, occasionally as late as two months after early lower-grade symptoms. The features are intense headache, memory deficits, hallucinations, delirium, vertigo, seizures, and then lethargy slipping into coma. The fatality rate is low, but residual neurologic deficit is common and may be severe. This syndrome occurs in less than one percent of patients."

Once more, she printed:

Hemorrhagic Icteric RVF

"Half the people who develop this form of disease evidence bleeding problems only two to four days after onset of illness, heralded actually by fulminant liver involvement manifesting as bright yellow skin and eyes from escalating jaundice. Associated hemorrhage is discharged from almost any orifice, such as vomiting blood, the nose or gums, bloody or dark melenic stools, purpuric skin lesions, and leaking of blood from blood-draw sites. Death usually occurs three to six days after symptom onset, but in survivors, virus may be detected for up to ten days. As with meningoencephalitis, this syndrome occurs in under one percent of patients."

A hand was raised in back. "What's the word on human vaccines?"

Abbey lifted her chin and turned to write as she replied.

Vaccination

"Good question, with a qualified answer. WHO tells us that both modified live attenuated virus and inactivated virus vaccines have been developed for veterinary use. The live attenuated vaccine only requires a single dose for long-term immunity, but the vaccine may result in spontaneous abortion if given to pregnant animals. Sort of the same situation with the rubella vaccine for humans, which is deferred until after delivery. But the inactivated vaccine for ruminants requires multiple doses and is not, I repeat not, contraindicated in animal pregnancy.

"As far as humans go, there are no currently licensed RVF vaccines, period."[67]

"The WHO also reports that in Africa, Saudi Arabia, and Yemen, outbreaks are closely associated with periods of above-average rainfall, which can be monitored and measured by satellite imaging. Additionally, in East Africa a resurgence of disease is closely associated with the wet, warm phase of the El Niño-Southern Oscillation, or ENSO phenomenon."

She put up one last subheading:

Epidemiology and Pandemics

"A couple of last thoughts, then we should wrap up this discussion. Today I've described the four categories of mosquito-borne Rift Valley Fever. Human-to-human spread is essentially not part of the picture for this malady." She strolled to the center of the room.

"I've always found the history of medicine compelling. Take, as an example, smallpox, called antiquity's most feared disease, the only disorder eradicated from the planet, aside from a pair of labs some decades ago—and perhaps frozen in permafrost in some part of the Northern Hemisphere. Donald Henderson's paper in the journal *Vaccine* described a 'decade-long World Health Organization campaign which began despite skepticism and doubt and succeeded despite a never-ending array of obstacles occasioned by floods, civil war, famine, and bureaucratic inertia.'

"His review paper reports that during the '20th century alone, an estimated 300 million people died of the disease . . . and that in the last hundred years of its existence smallpox killed at least half a billion people.'

"I suspect there are faculty members in this room who bear a nickel-sized scar from smallpox vaccine on a shoulder. Clearly these are sobering numbers."

A hand was raised in the back of the room by Dr. McDavid, who had thick glasses and snowy hair. "I have two of those scars, the second one was for travel in Central America as a young man."

What a wonderful pathologist. "But you never saw a case of this disease, just as most doctors have never seen a case of poliomyelitis."

"No, not a case, but I reviewed slides from historic tissue specimens when I was in residency at Albert Einstein."

Abbey nodded. "None of us ever wants to see another case of the disease caused by the most serious of the poxviridae, technically the variola, or smallpox, virus. The reason I brought up this deadly example is the ever-present pandemic potential of emerging pathogens. Consider H5N1 avian influenza and mpox and Ebola virus and Zika virus and Lassa fever and more." She rested for a moment to take a breath and consider how to wrap up.

"Nipah virus can be transmitted from animals or contaminated foods or directly from other people. There is no vaccine available for either humans or animals. The clinical fatality rate ranges between forty to seventy-five percent." Abbey stopped for a moment, hands on hips.

"All of these are infections that keep epidemiologists up at night."

As before, she paused, pursing her lips. "A hypothetical disease X theoretically could be stalking us as one of the thousands of bat viruses known to exist. What would we do if we had to confront a new disease which kills half its victims? To say the least, it would constitute an immediate public health emergency of international concern or simply called a PHEIC. But in early 2024 the World Health Assembly held in Geneva failed to come up with an agreement attempting to, quote, 'correct the inequities in access to vaccines and treatments between wealthier nations and poorer ones that became glaringly apparent during the Covid pandemic,' as described by Apoorva Mandavilli in *The New York Times*. She also stated that 'among the biggest bones of contention in the draft treaty [was] a section called Pathogen Access and Benefits Sharing, under which countries would be required to swiftly share genetic sequences and samples of emerging threats.'"

Abbey shook her head, thinking, *Only absolute idiots would oppose this.* "Low-income countries, most prominently in Africa, were also asking the pharmaceutical companies to share information and equipment that would allow local companies to manufacture future treatments and vaccines at lower cost." She took a moment to sigh.

"So, time to skedaddle. I know you all have patients to take care of. And nurses to support, since we are understaffed. So—let's get to it."

THIRTY-THREE

Weaponized Heat Wave

Let your plans be dark and impenetrable as night, and when you move, fall like a thunderbolt. —Sun Tzu

In the midst of chaos, there is also opportunity. —Sun Tzu

Mina arrived in a rush, face flushed, with a death grip on a newspaper in her left hand. "Here, Jake, read this story on the front page, down at the bottom, it's about an attack in DC, the kind of thing I know you worry about—I just heard Hope so let me go get her."

Jake quickly dried off his hands from washing dishes and threw the dish towel on the counter. He picked up the newspaper and flipped it over to read below the fold. The headline was in large type: *ATTACKER SHOOTS UP AN ELECTRICAL SUBSTATION ON THE FOURTH OF JULY.* He walked into the parlor, dropped into his easy chair, and pulled his glasses out of his shirt pocket.

Damn, they pulled it off.

The destruction was up in the northwest corner of DC, alleged perpetrator escaped but was being sought . . . Attempted attacks at two other sites foiled by authorities . . . One individual wounded in firefight and was in George Washington University Medical Center, undergoing surgery . . . Authorities had not released the identities of the suspects.

The story went on: The attacks were apparently scheduled so as to overlap with fireworks . . . and apparently coordinated with attacks in a number of cities . . . There were no civilian injuries locally, but two tac squad members suffered gunshot injuries when confronting the individual now undergoing surgery . . . Both were evaluated in the emergency room and released.

Mina came back with Hope on her hip, bouncing her up and down. "So, Jake, what does this all mean?"

"Lady, on some level this comes as no surprise. We know there have been over a thousand attacks against the grid in the last few decades. But this one takes the cake for being spread out all over, with simultaneous attacks at the same time across the country. What with time zones and all, after dark here but up to three hours earlier on the West Coast, so broad daylight out there. Give me a chance to read the next story—*COUNTRY-WIDE ATTACKS ON ELECTRICAL INFRASTRUCTURE IN EIGHTEEN CITIES*. Authorities have arrested dozens, predominantly in large coastal cities, but many more being sought."

Wow, they hit Baltimore, still recovering from the cargo ship that hit the Key Bridge.

"New Orleans, with a couple of hospitals on backup diesels. Houston, a couple of areas of the city without power during this heat wave." *Jesus Christ Almighty.*

He whispered to himself, "Don't these assholes remember 2023, when extreme heat led to 120,000 emergency room visits and k-killed eleven thousand people?" He gritted his teeth in frustration, while Mina frowned.

"In fact, I just finished this *Guardian* article by a guy named Delaney Nolan, who said something like, 'Heat triggers respiratory distress, acute heart attacks and strokes, disrupted sleep and impaired cognition—in other words, heat makes it hard to breathe, hard to sleep, hard to think.'[68] And a study in 2023 projected a two-day blackout in Phoenix during a heat wave could kill more than twelve thousand people—what climate experts might call a 'Heat Katrina,' a mass casualty event.

"Hey, Mina, if you've got a minute, could you look up the temperature in New Orleans right now?" She said she'd get right on it, and moved to set up Hope on a blanket on the floor in the parlor.

She called out to him: "Right now the temperature in New Orleans is 101 degrees, but the forecast today is a high of 105. I don't see a heat index, but we all know New Orleans is humid, right?"

"Mississippi River Valley, so in July, yeah, it's gotta be humid. And full of mosquitoes. Even with working air conditioners the heat is rough on people, especially when it doesn't drop below ninety at night—or worse yet—goes on for several days or more.

"I'm gonna call Abbey and see if she knows anything about the guy there." He held the phone to his ear as he listened to the ring at the other end.

"Jake, my dear, what's up?"

"I'm reading about the attack on the grid last night. Suppose we should have listened to the news, but we were both so tired. I read in the paper that one of the idiots who carried out this stunt last night was in the OR—"

"Let me stop you right there—there is some scuttlebutt going around, obviously this is a big deal. But I'm not able to share information about a patient with you."

She sounds uncertain. "Honey, let me ask you this way. This is not your patient, right?"

Abbey paused. "You know my specialty is infectious disease."

"And you haven't even laid eyes on him?"

"No." Another hesitation.

"I'm not asking you for any identifying information, right, like his name or where he's from?"

A deep sigh.

"And you know all this information is going to be in the next iteration of the news cycle, certainly by tomorrow, lady."

"Stop, okay, I get you. No, in no way is this my patient, which does not lessen my requirement to not talk about him. Clearly, he is going to have full national attention focused on him.

"There was some sort of firefight with a guy in a truck. He received two bullet wounds in his right lower extremity, striking from his mid-thigh down to his knee. Bet that opened both the femoral artery in front and the deep femoral artery in back. Another hit was in his right side, damaging the intestines and sending shrapnel through to the spleen on the other side. Therefore . . . he was exsanguinating by the time they got him out of the camper and into the ambulance."

"Did he survive, wait, obviously, I guess he did?"

"There is a great trauma team here as you know. They had to open up his abdomen and repair his small and large intestines, then resect what remained of his spleen. He's lucky they missed his spinal cord or he'd be paraplegic. The right lower extremity could not be repaired so the amputation was above the knee. Received a lot of blood products, plasma, the works. He's in the surgical ICU and still on a ventilator. No word on his prognosis but it should be clarified by tomorrow. Of course, if he develops sepsis, they might want me to weigh in, but really, they don't need my expertise here."

"I think Emmanuelle has taught me some of her interrogation techniques. I think you just told me more than you wanted to." *Probably should avoid this snark.*

"Well, you certainly have done a good job on establishing a relationship with the person being interrogated . . ."

She's letting that hang, but I'm not sure where to go with that. "Now you're going to tell me I can't share this story with anyone else."

"You are so right, not Mina or anybody."

"Sure, I get that . . . but I thought I'd call Brian and see if he wanted to come over to discuss all the implications for the grid." He waited for a prolonged and pregnant moment.

He listened to her breathy silence, then she spoke. "Actually, you're asking permission to share this story with Brian. Aren't you the artful dodger here."

Jake was quick with his response. "I'd just give him the short version. With your permission of course."

"Damn, I'd hate to negotiate buying a car from you. Okay, look, I gotta go, work to do. I'll see you round about dinnertime."

"Bye, love."

"Bye."

Click.

"Brian, whaddya doing? You've seen the news I assume."

"Natch, exactly what you and I discussed before, the bastards. Homeland Security and the FBI are going to be testifying to congressional committees on this one. And the president is going to take flack as well. I bet the White House will have a press conference by this evening."

"Wondered if you wanted to drop by this afternoon and discuss this debacle. Maybe around two or three?"

"Sounds good. I'll bring a six-pack."

"I'm going to jump on the computer and check some of my contacts to get a handle on what sorts of grid failures resulted and what kinds of responses worked. See ya soon."

***

"I was listening to the radio on the way over," Brian said. "Unbelievable reports coming in. Since this was obviously a widespread conspiracy, how the hell did the authorities let this happen? Oklahoma City got hit by that truck bombing, when was that?"

"1995, I think. Or 1996, I forget. Now this . . . same pattern. On the message boards it sounds like three or four substations were hit, several by rifle fire, one by a couple of Molotov cocktails, not really clear yet. Only one or two of the sites were put out of commission, so no widespread outages. There was a study by some mathematicians I looked at about how networked systems with enough interconnections between nodes can almost always create identifiable circular patterns that can bypass attempted disruptions. The people planning these attacks weren't sophisticated enough to understand this," Jake said.

"Or, maybe the political impact was the plan from the beginning. Actually knocking out power was a secondary concern."

"Bri, you got a point there. So maybe they'll call this a limited success. But they probably had higher expectations." Jake got up to pace, rubbing his face. "What are the commonalities here? Look at this list: Juneau in Alaska, Salem in Oregon, Boise in Idaho."

"First thing that comes to mind is that most of these are state capitals. Thus conceived of as political targets."

"But they also trend toward smaller cities, making it more feasible to take down the local distribution network. Flagstaff, but not Phoenix. Tallahassee, not Miami. Austin, not Houston." Jake turned to pace back the opposite way.

"Not near large military bases, which are more likely to be resilient and feature hardened systems with backup power," Brian said, doodling on scrap paper, making lists, drawing diagrams.

"I gotta say Boise is a really obvious target, what with Idaho's wasp nests of anti-government sentiment and lots of weapons." Jake sat down again, then immediately got up to grab one of the beers Brian had brought over. "Want one of these?" he called from the kitchen. "Sure is hot today."

"Yeah, I do. By that argument, Lansing in Michigan fits these selection criteria, whoever did this. Also, Arkansas, with Little Rock the target," Brian practically growled.

Jake brought him his beer, then sat and leaned back in his chair. "So—only one city per state so far. And about half the states. Still—a large conspiracy to have slipped under the radar."

"Homegrown or foreign-influenced?" Brian asked, rolling his shoulders back and taking a deep draught.

"I don't know if this is good news or bad, but I suspect purebred domestic terrorism from the far right. With foreign connections, I like to think somebody would more likely have stumbled onto this plot."

"Atlanta doesn't fit our criteria. A state capital, but a really big city."

"Which may explain why they failed to induce a lasting blackout. Three substations, all taken down, but power rerouted within an hour.

"But note attacks were not limited to blue states," Jake said, rubbing his chin. "Helena in Montana is not exactly a center of progressive political thought."

"But it is a state capital again," Brian said. They were both quiet for a bit.

"From the standpoint of grid resiliency, we came out pretty well. The political fallout though will reverberate for a long time. Fortunately, no grid control centers were targeted. None of the large, well-nigh irreplaceable transformers for big-time generators like nukes or coal plants or gas plants were in their crosshairs."

Brian sat up. "Another argument I guess for undergrounding large high-voltage and feeder distribution lines, protecting them from storms and easy attacks like what happened today."

"How do we even know these attacks are all done? Could there be other parts of this? We don't know—I mean, you and I don't know, but there is someone I could contact for some information later. She's probably pretty busy right now. I'll give her a jingle after a while." *I'm willing to bet my eyeteeth Emmanuelle is presently dressing down some people.*

He listened to the news on NPR as he finished the dishes after Brian left. *Leftover lasagna tonight. And a salad. I've got some dip and crackers to start with.*

THIRTY-FOUR

Adjudication and Revelation

The weight of this sad time we must obey, speak what we feel, not what we ought to say.
—William Shakespeare

And the great dragon was thrown down, that ancient serpent, who is called the devil and Satan, the deceiver of the whole world . . . he was thrown down to the earth, and his angels were thrown down with him. —Book of Revelation, Christian Bible (ESV)

Brian sneezed in the middle of his sentence. "—damn allergies acting up again.[69] Rachel's not as bad off. Really got going after our bike ride yesterday." The two of them were sharing the couch in the parlor. The ceiling fan eased the stifling heat somewhat.

Abbey frowned at him, arching her eyebrows impressively. "Brian, you know Hope is picking up language right now. How many times do I have to tell you to watch your mouth when you're here?" They glared at each other mock seriously until Brian conceded the staring contest and apologized, first to Abbey, then again more gently to Hope on Rachel's lap next to him, who seemed oblivious anyway.

She's gotta learn it someday, but Abbey's right, Jake thought.

"Brian," Abbey said, "remember we're right at the verge of August, not really yet ragweed and mold time of the year. Also, the oak, birch, and pine trees are pretty much done releasing pollen. But the grasses are aiming little itchy darts at the inside of your nose and throat, maybe especially that—dagnabbit—Kentucky bluegrass."

"I'm no racehorse, Abbey, except maybe when I'm on a bike." He sneezed again. And one more time for good measure.

Jake recalled his friend had let him know that he was already on anti-histamines and nasal steroids. "So . . . guys, I mentioned to Brian that there was someone I wanted you two to meet. She was a guest at the Inn last year, and we got to know her pretty well. Bri, you told Rachel something about her, right?"

But Rachel spoke up first. "He made it sound a bit mysterious, but I have ways of wheedling information out of him, as you can only imagine. So, I know she works for the government, and that she may have some information to share. Or want some information from us, it wasn't really clear." She bounced Hopie on her lap, listening to her coo and babble, and took a moment to match her smiley face. Then she switched the little rapscallion to her other knee, because she was hot even through her diaper.

Jake knit his eyebrows almost together. "I'm gonna confess here and now that I let slip to her that I had mentioned something to Brian a few months ago . . . and Abbey and I had promised her—in writing mind you—we wouldn't tell a soul, except maybe Anne and Colby when they came for a visit. And she's not one to forgive little indiscretions."

"Whaddya tell her a few months ago, Jake?" Rachel inquired.

"Probably better to let her lay this all out."

Abbey added, "They're bringing their daughter with them."

"And how old is she?" Rachel queried.

"Somewhere around two and a half, I think, maybe almost three," Abbey said, pulling out the neck of her T-shirt and blowing down it.

Jake tapped his fingers on the arm of his chair. "If I forgot to mention to you before, the evolving climate insight here supports a longer allergy season. More heat, more carbon dioxide. Plants love it—though only up to a point for both factors—so they cast off more pollen. Thus, the allergy season starts about three weeks earlier than it did in 1990 and lasts a week longer at the end. And a fifth of children have seasonal allergies and about a quarter of adults."

Abbey pulled at her lower lip. "So, sad to say, 'wheezier and sneezier for more of the year.' Jake showed me this article by Lisa Jarvis, but I've been following the technical discussion in medical journals for a couple of years now. The long and the short of this is that everyone has an 'individual pollen threshold, above which the immune system is triggered and allergy symptoms appear.' And it's my understanding that anticipation is best of all, so people should start antihistamines a week or two before their individual season starts.

"If symptoms are intolerable, they can consider seeing an immunologist about possible allergy shots. And it's always sensible to shower after being outside, throw your clothes in the wash, and think about getting an air purifier. Which is also a good way to deal with wildfire smoke exposure during fire season. Most cities have pollen monitoring stations, which I learned from Jarvis are 'often run and funded by volunteers with the National Allergy Bureau.'"

"There's gotta be an app for that," Rachel said, and Abbey nodded.

"Years ago, cities decided to plant mainly male trees of species that had more or less two genders, because people didn't appreciate the mess left by the females."

Brian sat up straighter. "You should see our bathroom if you wanna see what kind of mess can be left by women," he said, but then thought better of it and avoided looking at Rachel, probably in an effort to not break out in a guffaw.

Abbey finally finished. "But male flowers can put out prodigious amounts of pollen, so they're messy, too, Brian, and we all know about the mess men can leave all over their . . . the place if they get too eager." A brief silence followed and Brian's jaw went slack.

The doorbell rang.

Jake sprung up. *Saved by the bell, even though clearly, she wasn't talking about me.*

"Ben, Emmanuelle, Margaux, how're you all doing?"

Jake wasn't sure he saw a subtly sardonic smile on Ben's face.

"Fine, Jake," Ben said, "just fine."

Jake did a slight bow to Margaux, who seemed a lot less hesitant than the last time he'd seen her. "And you, young lady, how are you doing this fine day?"

"I'm . . . good . . . two years," she responded, holding up two fingers.

Emmanuelle corrected gently, "Three months short of being three."

"She doesn't seem as shy as when I first met her."

"That was half a year ago at least," Ben said.

"Well, come on in, let me introduce you to our friends Brian and Rachel," Jake said, as they walked down the short hall to the parlor.

Rachel still had Hopie on her lap, but Brian stood up to shake hands with them both. Introductions were made all around.

Margaux stared with fascination at Hope, perhaps attracted by her gurgling and pudgy handwaving.

Emmanuelle gazed for the first time at the other two people she presumably had already investigated. "I've been looking forward to meeting you two, friends of Jake and Abbey. There are a couple of stories I'd like to discuss, but first I suspect you know I need to have you both sign non-disclosure agreements, NDAs, as Jake no doubt mentioned."

She glanced over at him, adding, "Apparently he forgot that old adage about loose lips sinking ships." Her tone was mild but her stare unblinking and her forehead subtly crinkled. Ben just smiled.

Jake shifted uneasily in his chair and suddenly decided his nose needed scratching.

Emmanuelle pulled out the forms from her briefcase and handed them over, while Rachel handed off the infant to Abbey.

Jake understood Emmanuelle relied on people's intrinsic inquisitiveness to get them to sign. *I bet she realizes knowing Abbey and I have already been through this is instrumental.*

Nevertheless, Brian and Rachel sure took their time reading through the documents.

Emmanuelle cleared her throat. "Realize that these NDAs have teeth in them, with risks including imprisonment should you be so unwise to let slip any information that I'm about to share with you to the wrong parties. That includes talking to the press.

"So . . . Brian . . . you will get your sheepskin this year but plan to stay in Washington, and you have applications into several places requiring a degree in mechanical engineering. I also understand you are interested in a civil service position with Architect of the Capitol, which would give you responsibility over the systems supporting the Library of Congress and other critical national infrastructure."

Brian looked up from the document in surprise. "Did Jake tell you all that?"

"No." She paused. "He told me only about your character and academic credentials. And also, no, you have not been under direct surveillance."

"But you have other methods of obtaining information," Rachel said calmly.

Emmanuelle only nodded. "Rachel, you are also finishing up a degree, in international studies and population biology, as well as having a special interest in coast guards and naval affairs. I find that fascinating.

"We also know you are contemplating an application to the Department of State, to its Bureau of Intelligence and Research. I'm sure you're aware of the quality of their work, including a couple of historic calls contrary to those of much-better known intelligence shops such as the National Security Agency. This in spite of the relatively diminutive size of the Bureau. Some five hundred people at present."

"I am," replied Rachel, still sounding serene.

"Would you therefore consider yourself a contrarian as well?"

Brian laughed. "Yeah, if the shoe fits . . ." Rachel didn't take her eyes off of Emmanuelle, only making a slight, dismissive shrug of her shoulders. Brian finished up and signed his form before Rachel. He seemed matter of fact about it, but Rachel took a last deep breath before signing and handing over the paperwork.

Margaux slipped off her father's lap and walked right over to touch Abbey's baby. "So, this young girl is about two years older than our kid," Abbey said, reaching over to touch the youngster's blond locks.

Emmanuelle reached into her purse and got out a sippy cup for her daughter. "First of all, Jake, I'm sure you're aware of how your information facilitated our interdiction of two of the three people who tried to attack electrical substations in DC. Since we knew the exact locations and surmised that they planned their attack on the Fourth of July, we had officers in place well in advance of their belligerent barrage."

"Who coordinated that response, if I may ask?" said Jake.

"The FBI coupled with police tac squad officers.

"Our efforts to locate them before they showed up were unavailing, but once they arrived, their tactical decision to shoot from inside camper shells left them blind on three sides. With all the noise from fireworks— some of that distraction their own work—the older brother was swiftly subdued and disarmed before firing a single shot. It came down quickly enough that there's no evidence he had time to communicate with his confederates."

She came to a standstill and looked at each in turn. "The younger brother was a different story altogether. An officer approached from the left side of the camper; a flash-bang grenade was tossed inside. But apparently its effect was muted since he was wearing ear and eye protection. When the first tac officer came around into view, he found the suspect had pulled a revolver and got off several shots, striking center of mass, knocking him down. Fortunately, the bulletproof vest saved him. The assailant then lunged forward and was able to shoot another officer, with more grievous injuries. Counterfire from the team, mainly through the metal wall of the shell, immediately incapacitated the suspect."

"Must have been like the way Bonnie and Clyde were taken down," said Brian.

"No, not necessarily intending to kill, but he was seriously wounded." She turned to face Abbey and raised her face.

"Abbey, I understand you have some insights and information that may be pertinent here. That's part of the reason I wanted to come over today."

There was a longer halt. "I feel that I can speak here since I was in no way involved in his medical care, never laid eyes on him in fact. I don't even know his name yet, though of course soon that should become public knowledge. But it was common knowledge throughout the hospital that a suspected attacker had been brought in by the police. I've thought about this, and I don't think it would be breaking the principle of confidentiality if I tell you what the rumors were. Reportedly, he did have three critical gunshot wounds, one to the abdomen and two to the right lower extremity. The first bullet entered below the tenth rib and traversed the abdomen, penetrating both the small and large intestines, luckily missing the vertebral column and thus spinal cord but lacerating the spleen badly. These were the findings at surgery as he underwent an open laparotomy by the trauma team, with end-to-end reanastomosis—a reconnection of his first part of the upper small intestine, the duodenum, to the middle part of the jejunum, the second part.

"The large intestine on the right was penetrated through and through, so a section of colon was resected with a temporary colostomy created in the right upper quadrant of his belly. The spleen was badly fragmented, so the bleeding splenic blood vessels were tied off by suture-ligature. You should know that if the spleen is damaged this way, it turns out a lot of the small fragments will reimplant in the peritoneum, grow, and actually over time reestablish spleen function back to normal as a filter of the blood. This is called splenosis and is actually well understood physiologically.

"The two bullets to the right lower extremity struck the distal thigh and knee. The blood loss here was also quite serious and the rest of the lower extremity was not deemed salvageable, so he concurrently underwent an above-the-knee amputation by the orthopedic members of the trauma team.

"I understand he is still on a ventilator in the ICU, and we can safely assume he received many units of blood replacement, packed red blood cells and platelets for sure."

"I guess our daughter is going to grow up having to get used to hearing these sorts of stories," Jake commented, after an interval.

Emmanuelle looked at Ben, then resumed her dissertation. "We now know there were three marksmen in this team. The third member was ex-military, and he successfully struck his selected substation. Fortunately, with the information we obtained from the older brother, we were able to intercept him as he was heading toward northern Michigan for a safe house, apparently planning an escape into Canada. He is in custody in that state now but will be extradited back to DC."

"There are enough redundancies in the DC grid that I happen to know there was no significant interruption of power at all," Jake said.

Emmanuelle nodded. "There were no injuries from his attack aside from the two tac squad officers, one more serious than the other, unlike a lot of sites around the states. You've seen the newspaper stories I'm sure, with power outages in a number of state capitals, shootouts with local police leaving five dead and at least twenty wounded, half of them still hospitalized. The prolonged outages in some of the Midwestern and Southern states have been deemed responsible for suspected heat-related deaths, but it will take longer to collect and corroborate all these datapoints."

Rachel stirred, rubbing her eyes. "Would it be fair to say this was not comparable to 9/11 in terms of mortality, but equally as appalling in terms of a blow to civil society?"

Emmanuelle sighed. "Since it was already a fraught time, I might almost agree with you on that point."

Margaux continued to try and get Hope to respond, and finally succeeded in eliciting a tiny smile.

"Seeing these two kids together gives me confidence that the nation will survive, will grow, and will return to a time of comity, which we all need so desperately," Abbey said in almost a whisper.

Brian looked at Rachel, communicating with only his eyes.

"Well, Brian and I have something to say that may help give all of you a reason to stay optimistic about the future."

Jake's eyes lit up, and he sensed what might be about to come.

"Yep," she said, "seems like everyone around is having babies, and we didn't want to get left out of the party."

Abbey shrieked, handed the baby to Jake, and ran over to give her a hug.

Hope springs eternal, thought Jake, now with a broad smile.

The Long Goodbye

I didn't have the guts to become an artist, I had the ignorance. —*Jack Sorenson*

It is not early morning at this time of closing up shop, but rather early evening. On a curious note, this summer, for the third year in a row, we have observed multiple praying mantises, which our grandsons love; they are learning to pick them up carefully and set them on their forearms to walk around. So, for the last two summers we had bountiful numbers, but for the twenty-seven years before then, nary a one. Thus, we shall hope to see more next year.

On a more somber note, this is also a day with wildfire smoke in the air, mainly from British Columbia to the north, but also a component from east of the Cascades, which I can see out my office window. A low level of particulates, not enough to wear a mask, but a harbinger of hard times. We have had such smoky days every year since 2018, and I realistically anticipate that we will experience this every year from this point on. Ironically, just this morning a friend was telling me of the beautiful sunset he had seen over the ocean last evening—obviously this is an insufficient consolation. We must not normalize and simply accept this, but rather use this as motivation to fight like hell for the living, as Mother Jones enjoined us to do.

There is nowhere on Earth where climate devastation can be escaped. One should not run, and cannot hide, but each and every one of us must join in this fight against the climate dragon.

Acknowledgments

When you arise in the morning, give thanks for the morning light, for your life and strength. Give thanks for your food, and the joy of living. If you see no reason for giving thanks, the fault lies with yourself. — Chief Tecumseh

The earth provides us with everything we need to survive and thrive. It's important to remember to give thanks for all the resources it offers us. —Chief Seattle

Village Book in Bellingham, Washington, has been an invaluable supporter of a multitude of writers over many years, including the last five years that I have been learning the craft and trade of scrivening, and I owe them immense gratitude.

Also critical in my education has been the Village Fiction group in the alphabetical order of Lee A. Brown, Eliza Chien, Nathan Dodge, Luke Kuiroz, Kari Lisa Johnson, Morgan Jones, Marie MacWhyte, George Murray, Kim Owen, Delaney Peterson, Gail Pinto, Joseph Riddle, Christy Rommel, Kathy Smith, Patti Thomas, and Andrew Vinyard.

The estimable graphic artist Bob Paltrow receives credit for the cover of all three books of this trilogy of dragons. As a disclaimer, aside from an online thesaurus, no artificial intelligence was involved in the researching, writing, or editing of this work. However, the cover design by my competent, independent graphic designer Mr. Paltrow was created with assistance from the AI imaging application Monet.

Finally, I note the District of Columbia shares borders with Maryland and Virginia, and connects with lands along the Anacostia and Potomac Rivers. As such, I recognize the historic presence and influence, dating back at least four thousand years, of the Piscataway, Pamunkey, Nentego

(Nanicoke), Mattaponi, Chickahominy, Monacan, and Powhatan Native Americans.

In parallel fashion, the area around present-day central Texas was inhabited by Indigenous peoples for over fifteen thousand years, including the Comanches, Caddo, Cherokee, Coahuiltecan, Lipan Apache, Karankawa, Tonkawa, and Wichita tribes, who spoke numerous languages, adopted multiple beliefs and creation stories, and all lived off this land differently. For all these tribes and nations, I formally acknowledge their sovereignty and stewardship as Indigenous peoples who have an enduring relationship with these traditional territories.

Notes

1. Gabbatt, Adam. "Experts Warn of Increased Risk of US Terror Attacks by Rightwing 'Lone Wolf' Actors." *The Guardian*, May 28, 2023. https://www.theguardian.com/world/2023/may/28/lone-wolf-far-right-terror-attack-warning.

2. Baker, David. "FBI: Attack on PG&E South Bay Substation Wasn't Terrorism." SFGATE, September 11, 2014. https://www.sfgate.com/business/article/FBI-Attack-on-PG-amp-E-substation-in-13-wasn-t-5746785.php.

3. "Why the Battle for Supremacy in Asia Begins with China's Coast Guard." *The Reporter*. https://the-reporter.org/archives/9761.

4. Ibid.

5. Carver, Jayme Lozano. "Texas High Plains Walloped by Dust Storms Fed by Drought, High Winds." *The Texas Tribune*, February 6, 2024. https://www.texastribune.org/2023/02/24/texas-lubbock-dust-storms-drought-haboob/.

6. Mora, Camilo, Tristan McKenzie, and Isabella M. Gaw, et al. "Over Half of Known Human Pathogenic Diseases Can Be Aggravated by Climate Change." *Nature Climate Change*. https://doi.org/10.1038/s41558-022-01426-1.

7. Plumer, Brad. "A Bottleneck on the Grid Threatens Clean Energy. New Rules Aim to Help." *The New York Times*, July 27, 2023. https://www.nytimes.com/2023/07/27/climate/electric-grid-ferc-bottleneck.html.

8. "Kauai." Wikimedia Foundation. Last modified: January 8, 2025. https://en.wikipedia.org/wiki/Kauai.

9. Spector, Julian. "Kauai Became a Clean Energy Leader. Its Secret? A Publicly Owned Grid." Canary Media, November 7, 2023. https://www.canarymedia.com/articles/clean-energy/kauai-is-a-clean-energy-leader-its-secret-a-publicly-owned-grid.

10. Cocke, Sophie. "Kauai Utility Blazes Ahead on Renewable Energy." *Honolulu Civil Beat*, October 12, 2012. https://www.civilbeat.org/2012/10/17359-kauai-utility-blazes-ahead-on-renewable-energy/.

11. "Powering on with Grid-Forming Inverters." Energy.Gov. https://www.energy.gov/eere/solar/articles/powering-grid-forming-inverters.

12. Energy and Policy Institute. "Utility Carbon Targets Reflect Decarbonization Slowdown." October 7, 2024. https://energyandpolicy.org/utility-carbon-targets/.

13. "Unveiling the Historic Plantation Mills of Kauai." Kauanoe O Koloa, October 4, 2023. https://kauanoekauai.com/kauai-mills/.

14. "AES Corporation." Wikimedia Foundation. Last modified December 1, 2024. https://en.wikipedia.org/wiki/AES_Corporation.

15. Lovins, Amory B. "Energy Strategy: The Road Not Taken?" *Foreign Affairs*, January 30, 2023. https://www.foreignaffairs.com/articles/united-states/1976-10-01/energy -strategy-road-not-taken.

16. Behr, Peter. "Grid Monitor Warns of Blackout Risks as Coal Plants Retire." E&E News by POLITICO, December 19, 2023. https://www.eenews.net/articles/grid -monitor-warns-of-blackout-risks-as-coal-plants-retire/.

17. ACCC InfoCore® System. CTC Global, November 13, 2024. https://ctcglobal .com/accc-infocore-system/.

18. Shirasaki, and Yasuda. "12 - Membrane Reactor For Hydrogen Production from Natural Gas at the Tokyo Gas Company: A Case Study." Science Direct. https://www.sciencedirect.com/science/article/abs/pii/B9780857094155500123.

19. Alderman, Liz. "It Could Be a Vast Source of Clean Energy, Buried Deep Underground." *The New York Times*, December 4, 2023. https://www.nytimes.com/2023 /12/04/business/energy-environment/clean-energy-hydrogen.html.

20. "The Potential for Geologic Hydrogen for Next-Generation Energy." US Geological Survey. April 13, 2023. https://www.usgs.gov/news/featured-story/potential -geologic-hydrogen-next-generation-energy.

21. "Free-Piston Linear Generator." Wikimedia Foundation. Last modified April 4, 2023. https://en.wikipedia.org/wiki/Free-piston_linear_generator.

22. Zhou, Yingcong, Aimilios Sofianopoulos, Benjamin Lawler, and Sotirios Mamalis. "Advanced Combustion Free-Piston Engines: A Comprehensive Review." *International Journal of Engine Research*. https://doi.org/10.1177/1468087418800612.

23. Agrawal, Nina. "Spring Allergy Season Is Getting Worse. Here's What to Know." *The New York Times*, March 25, 2024. https://www.nytimes.com/2024/03/25/well /live/spring-allergy-symptoms.html.

24. Einhorn, Catrin. "The Widest-Ever Global Coral Crisis Will Hit Within Weeks, Scientists Say." *The New York Times*. April 15, 2024. https://www.nytimes.com/2024 /04/15/climate/coral-reefs-bleaching.html.

25. Cornwall, Warren. "Deadly Marine 'Cold Spells' Could Become More Frequent with Climate Change, Scientists Warn." *Science*, April 15, 2024. https://www.science.org /content/article/deadly-marine-cold-spells-could-become-more-frequent-climate -change-scientists-warn.

26. "Drill Bit (Well)." Wikimedia Foundation. Last modified October 17, 2023. https://en.wikipedia.org/wiki/Drill_bit_(well).

27. Tabuchi, Hiroko. "Air-Conditioning Use Will Surge in a Warming World, U.N. Warns." *The New York Times*, December 23, 2023. https://www.nytimes.com/2023 /12/05/climate/air-conditioning-electricity.html.

28. Guardian, Hannah Ellis-Petersen. "'A Matter of Survival': India's Unstoppable Need for Air Conditioners." Grist, December 18, 2023. https://grist.org/extreme-heat/a-matter-of-survival-indias-unstoppable-need-for-air-conditioners/.

29. Wilson, Eric Dean. *After Cooling: On Freon, Global Warming, and the Terrible Cost of Comfort.* Simon and Schuster, 2022.

30. McKibben, Bill. "The U.N. Announces the Hottest Year." *The New Yorker*, December 12, 2023. https://www.newyorker.com/culture/2023-in-review/the-un-announces-the-hottest-year.

31. Wallace-Wells, David. "What No One at COP28 Wanted to Say Out Loud: Prepare for 1.5 Degrees." *The New York Times*, December 5, 2023. https://www.nytimes.com/2023/12/16/opinion/cop28-climate-change-renewable-energy.html.

32. Chen, Susan, and Francine Lacqua. "Bill Gates Says Chances of Meeting 2C Warming Goal Fading Fast." Bloomberg. December 3, 2023. https://www.bloomberg.com/news/articles/2023-12-03/cop28-bill-gates-says-world-probably-won-t-meet-2c-climate-warming-goal.

33. Einhorn, Catrin. "The Widest-Ever Global Coral Crisis Will Hit Within Weeks, Scientists Say." *The New York Times*, May 21, 2024. https://www.nytimes.com/2024/04/15/climate/coral-reefs-bleaching.html.

34. Yoder, Kate. "How to Describe 2023 in Two Words? Global Boiling." Grist, December 17, 2024. https://grist.org/words-of-the-year/grist-2023-words-year-language-global-boiling-aqi/.

35. "Topic: Geothermal Energy in the U.S." Statista. December 18, 2023. https://www.statista.com/topics/2692/geothermal/#topicOverview.

36. Ricks, Wilson, Jack Norbeck, and Jesse Jenkins. "The Value of In-Reservoir Energy Storage for Flexible Dispatch of Geothermal Power." *Applied Energy* 313: 118807. https://doi.org/10.1016/j.apenergy.2022.118807.

37. Thomas, Michael. "Harnessing the Heat Beneath Our Feet: Geothermal's Past and Future." *Canary Media*, December 14, 2023. https://www.canarymedia.com/articles/geothermal/harnessing-the-heat-beneath-our-feet-geothermals-past-and-future.

38. Fourqurean, Robert, and Sagatom Saha. "Geothermal: Policies to Help America Lead." Third Way, April 18, 2023. https://www.thirdway.org/memo/geothermal-policies-to-help-america-lead.

39. Anderson, L.V. "The Best Coffee for the Planet Might Not Be Coffee at All." Grist, July 30, 2024. https://grist.org/food/beanless-coffee-sustainable-alternative-climate/.

40. NorthernWonder. n.d. "Coffee Free Coffee Filter Blend Caffeinated." https://northern-wonder.com/products/filter-blend-caffeinated-1.

41. Anderson, L.V. 2024. "The Best Coffee for the Planet Might Not Be Coffee At All." Grist. July 30, 2024. https://grist.org/food/beanless-coffee-sustainable-alternative-climate/.

42. Goldfarb, Ben. *Eager: The Surprising, Secret Life of Beavers and Why They Matter.* Chelsea Green Publishing, 2018. 27.

43. Ibid., 26.

44. Ibid., 143.

45. Waterman, Jon. "My 500-Mile Journey Across Alaska's Thawing Arctic." *The New York Times,* December 14, 2024. https://www.nytimes.com/2024/12/15/opinion/alaska-salmon-climate-change.html.

46. Goldfarb. *Eager: The Surprising, Secret Life of Beavers*, 168.

47. Ibibd., 173.

48. "Malaria." World Health Organization, December 11, 2024. https://www.who.int/news-room/fact-sheets/detail/malaria.

49. Nolen, Stephanie. "The Push for a Better Dengue Vaccine Grows More Urgent." *The New York Times,* April 12, 2024. https://www.nytimes.com/2024/04/11/health/dengue-vaccine-brazil.html.

50. "PAHO Calls for Collective Action in Response to Record Increase in Dengue Cases in the Americas." Pan American Health Organization and World Health Organization, March 28, 2024. https://www.paho.org/en/news/28-3-2024-paho-calls-collective-action-response-record-increase-dengue-cases-americas.

51. Nolen, Stephanie. "The Push for a Better Dengue VaccineGrows More Urgent." *The New York Times,* April 11, 2024. https://www.nytimes.com/2024/04/11/health/dengue-vaccine-brazil.html.

52. "Vibrio Vulnificus." Wikimedia Foundation. Last modified November 30, 2024. https://en.wikipedia.org/wiki/Vibrio_vulnificus.

53. Mandavilli, Apoorva. "Countries Fail to Agree on Treaty to Prepare the World for the Next Pandemic." *The New York Times,* May 24, 2024. https://www.nytimes.com/2024/05/24/health/pandemic-treaty-vaccines.html.

54. Alpert, Arnie. "45 Years After Three Mile Island, We Need a 'No Nukes' Comeback." *Waging Nonviolence*, March 25, 2024. https://wagingnonviolence.org/2024/03/three-mile-island-45th-anniversary-no-nukes-comeback-clamshell-alliance/.

55. "At COP28, Countries Launch Declaration to Triple Nuclear Energy Capacity by 2050, Recognizing the Key Role of Nuclear Energy in Reaching Net Zero." Energy.gov. https://www.energy.gov/articles/cop28-countries-launch-declaration-triple-nuclear-energy-capacity-2050-recognizing-key.

56. Dickherber, Audrey. "As Energy Chief Touts Vogtle's Bright Future, Some See a Darker Side." WRDW–TV, June 3, 2024. https://www.wrdw.com/2024/06/03/energy-chief-touts-vogtles-bright-future-some-see-darker-side/.

57. Green, Jim. "Nuclear Goes Backwards, Again, as Wind and Solar Enjoy Another Year of Record Growth." RenewEconomy, January 24, 2024. https://reneweconomy.com.au/nuclear-goes-backwards-again-as-wind-and-solar-enjoy-another-year-of-record-growth/#google_vignette.

58. Fairley, Peter. "There Is a Part of Modern Life That Is So Essential Armies Should Never Attack It Again." *The New York Times,* April 15, 2024. https://www.nytimes.com/2024/04/15/opinion/ukraine-russia-power-grid.html.

59. Varenikova, Maria. "Ukraine Sees New Virtue in Wind Power: It's Harder to Destroy." *The New York Times,* May 29, 2023. https://www.nytimes.com/2023/05/29/world/europe/ukraine-russia-wind-power.html.

60. Cahill, Ben, and Allegra Dawes. "Developing Renewable Energy in Ukraine." Center for Strategic & International Studies, December 19, 2022. https://www.csis.org/analysis/developing-renewable-energy-ukraine.

61. Gaffney, Austyn. "How Future Hurricanes Could Stress Power Grids of U.S. Cities." *The New York Times*, July 8, 2024. https://www.nytimes.com/2024/07/05/climate/hurricanes-power-outages.html.

62. "Projected Changes in Hurricane-Induced Power Outages in a Future Climate." Climate Readi Resilience and Adaptation Initiative. https://interactive.epri.com/readi-storymap/p/1.

63. Casey, Tina. "Coal State Sells Coal-Killing Iron-Air Energy Storage to Other States." CleanTechnica, December 25, 2023. https://cleantechnica.com/2023/12/24/coal-state-exports-iron-air-energy-storage/.

64. Limb, Lottie. "'A Very Finnish Thing': Big Sand Battery to Store Wind and Solar Energy Using Crushed Soapstone." *Euronews*, March 11, 2024. https://www.euronews.com/green/2024/03/10/sand-batteries-could-be-key-breakthrough-in-storing-solar-and-wind-energy-year-round.

65. Energeia. "Insights From the Realising Electric Vehicle-to-Grid Services Project – Final Report." https://arena.gov.au/assets/2024/02/ARENA-Vehicle-to-Grid-Insights-Final-Report.pdf.

66. "Rift Valley Fever." World Health Organization, December 20, 2024. https://www.who.int/news-room/fact-sheets/detail/rift-valley-fever.

67. Alkan, Cigdem, Eduardo Jurado-Cobena, and Tetsuro Ikegami. "Advancements in Rift Valley Fever Vaccines: A Historical Overview and Prospects for Next Generation Candidates." *Npj Vaccines* 8, https://doi.org/10.1038/s41541-023-00769-w.

68. Nolan, Delaney. "'It's Unbearable': In Ever-Hotter US Cities, Air Conditioning Is No Longer Enough." *The Guardian*, June 13, 2024. https://www.theguardian.com/us-news/article/2024/jun/11/air-conditioning-protect-extreme-heat.

69. Jarvis, Lisa. "You're Not Imagining It. Your Allergies Are Getting Worse." Bloomberg, April 18, 2024. https://www.bloomberg.com/opinion/articles/2024-04-18/seasonal-allergies-are-getting-worse-because-of-global-warming.

About the Author

Photo by Cheryl Crooks Photography

Born in Minnesota, I grew up in Missouri, then at eighteen realized my California dream with undergraduate years at Stanford, including two years on the tennis team. After med school back in my home state, I completed a residency at UC San Francisco, during which I gave my first public lecture, a talk on nuclear power. Two weeks later I started teaching full time in a UC Davis-affiliated family medicine residency, with much of my practice focused on obstetrics but also HIV care starting in early 1983. I taught full time for sixteen years, with my main academic appointment at the public university, but coming full circle, a community faculty appointment at Stanford Med Center as well, since I taught a number of their PA students.

I lost my heart in San Francisco, and my wife became a certified nurse-midwife, and between the two of us, we delivered thousands of babies and had three of our own, all graduated, married, and two of them with a couple of sons apiece. We moved up to Bellingham almost thirty years ago, and are now both retired. Over the last dozen years, I have continued to lecture widely, including several seminar series at Western Washington University, plus many other venues, including a couple of out-of-state conferences. But I no longer teach medicine, rather about the climate system, energy systems, epidemiology, and the electric grid, and this set of fourteen or so lectures form the basis for many of the chapters in all three books.

Our biggest climate-related trip was in Europe in 2015, which included biking in Berlin, Copenhagen, and Oslo, then a two-week cruise from Svalbard to Greenland and Iceland. We accomplished hiking, kayaking, and a true polar plunge well north of the Arctic Circle while in Greenland. Additionally, we explored some of the eastern Canadian maritime islands in 2023. We attended a geothermal conference in El Salvador on our calendar in the last month of 2024. Puerto Rico, after a Covid delay, will be a destination in 2025.

www.ingramcontent.com/pod-product-compliance
Lightning Source LLC
LaVergne TN
LVHW010533240625
814502LV00007B/23